MW01138645

Special Means

Andrew Ceroni

outskirts press

Outskirts Press, Inc.
http://www.outskirtspress.com

ISBN: 978-1-9772-2576-4

PRINTED IN THE UNITED STATES OF AMERICA

Also by Andrew Ceroni

THE RED SHORE
SNOW MEN
MERIDIAN

For my father, Andrew,
The leader of the band,
Always and forever

The truth is incontrovertible. Malice may attack it, ignorance may deride it, but in the end, there it is.

Winston Churchill

CHAPTER 1

Denver, Colorado
Early December

Harvey and Emma Goodman stood at the counter in Ben's Burgers waiting for their food tray, oblivious to the glowering stares of three young men seated at a nearby table. Two of the young gangsters in the Santana Hood street gang, Gerardo and Carlos, crinkled their faces in malevolent smiles, stalking the old couple with their eyes. The third, Vinnie, grimaced.

Well into their eighties, Harvey and Emma had grown weary of feeling the need to always be on guard. Always alert for danger. There seemed to be an abundance of danger these days. It lurked everywhere. Harvey had been mugged twice in the last three years, each time within a few blocks of their home. The robberies had resulted in minor injuries, a punch in the face, a shove slamming him to the sidewalk. In each instance, the few dollars he'd had in his pocket were really no big loss. Still, the trauma of the muggings was hard to shake.

The young female server slapped the food tray down on the counter in front of Harvey. He leaned over to grab it and caught her expressionless stare. He noticed a tattoo with three different-colored human skulls running down the pearl white skin of her neck from behind her right ear to beneath the collar of her blouse. She smirked at his stare, her lifeless eyes locked onto his. He shook his head and looked away, assuming she was probably stupid too, like the whole damn generation. He stuffed the thick fold of bills back into his rear pocket.

Emma reached out for the change. The server dumped the coins all at once into Emma's hands. Nickels, dimes and pennies skittered through her narrow fingers, sprinkling down to the tile floor and rolling off in all directions. It caught the attention of several patrons seated nearby, but not a soul stooped to help.

Emma bent to her knees, almost losing the wool cap stretched loose about her gray hair. Her eyes followed the sudden comedy of the coins spinning down the aisle, under tables, and clinking to a stop at the glass doors. Not missing the spiteful smile creasing the server's lips, Harvey's angry scowl turned from her to Emma.

"Emma Jean, let it go, honey. It's just a few cents. Let it go."

Flustered, she shoved herself to her feet, realizing it was hopeless. Kids scrambled across the floor. They scooped up the coins and ran off through the fast food restaurant giggling, not looking back.

"Dammit," Emma muttered.

Harvey began to search out a table, Emma trailing behind. A rigid frown washed across her face, frustrated that her skeletal, arthritic fingers couldn't grasp the coins trickling through them.

The two of them were bundled up like two old elves struggling to prepare for yet another holiday season. Emma wore a loose, red wool cap that had a white snowball knitted on top, red sweatshirt, black pants and a gray wool coat that had seen better times. Harvey had donned a faded red flannel shirt, blue jeans, and a slightly tattered blue parka. His disheveled silver hair concealed a slender bald spot.

The food at Ben's wasn't all that bad, just nothing to write home about. The deep fryer's oily odor of fish, chicken, and fries hung in the air like shantytown smog. But then, the food wasn't really the attraction. It was the price. Cheap. Dirt cheap.

The old couple began munching their burgers and fries. An occasional smile. Hands reaching out to touch. It was enough for them. Harvey and Emma had settled into a comfortable companionship. The press of the wad of cash in a rear pocket had Harvey squirming in the hard seat. He'd never embraced the lure of credit cards, so shopping excursions like this one meant he dealt with a big lump of cash in his pocket.

With stores brimming with Christmas goodies, the Goodmans were determined to save every penny possible to buy gifts for the grandkids out east in Virginia. They'd skipped their annual Thanksgiving turkey feast a week ago at a favorite buffet restaurant, and caught the free church dinner instead. The pair harbored no thoughts of martyrdom–this was just a simple sacrifice allowing them to make yet another Christmas special for the grandkids.

Emma rubbed her hands together. The dull pain persisted. Degenerative arthritis in her knuckles often brought bursts of excruciating agony, but the disease took a far greater toll in her hips. The constant ache occasionally overwhelmed her spirit, painting her face a sullen sheet of gray.

"I'll be okay, Harvey," Emma's eyes misted.

"All right. Thanks, honey," Harvey said, his brow wrinkled.

"You know, it just gets me down sometimes, but I'm okay," she creased her face with a smile and reached out, gently patting his forearm.

Outside the burger joint, jagged shards of icicles jutted down like shark's teeth from frozen gutters. The roof creaked under a heavy burden of snow. A mid-December storm had blown through the Rockies two days earlier and iced Denver with an arctic blast. Temperatures plummeted thirty degrees. The night sky had cleared, but appeared frozen and dark as black ice. While the storm had since moved east to Kansas and Nebraska, temps still remained glacial in Denver, Colorado.

Beyond Denver's posh downtown environs, on the east-side mean streets near Ben's Burgers, subwoofers' deep beat of drug-infused Rap music reverberated down the streets and avenues. Ben's Burgers was as deep inside Denver's black gang territory as one could get. The owner, old Ben Holzfeld, didn't plan it that way, it was just how things evolved over time.

West of the I-25 corridor, Hispanic Gangs thrived on their own brand of gang banging. Business was good all over for the street gangs in Denver. They were making a good living out of it, that is, if one believed killing was good, and dying was living.

"Check it out. Shit, this gonna be easy," Gerardo Ventana grinned as he eyed Harvey. He nudged Carlos, a broad-shouldered member of the Santana Hood Gang. "Sweet. This is so sweet."

Carlos nodded in agreement, sipping his cola. Gerardo's dark eyes glittered, his smile stretching. Twenty-six years old and well known to the Denver Police with a long rap sheet of numerous offenses, Gerardo conveyed a presence. Distinctions in his appearance were a long ponytail hanging over the collar of his black leather jacket and his eyes. Gerardo had eyes resembling two menacing, coal black holes sucking in light like a void in space. He knew this well and employed it to his advantage.

"Vinnie, gimme a roll," he said, turning to the third member of the group sitting across the table from him, his coarse voice mumbling.

"Sure," Vinnie nodded, pulling out the smokes.

Gerardo snatched the cigarette, sticking it between puckered lips.

Vinnie leaned across the table, cautious to speak in a low voice. "Gerardo, we gotta be careful here on the East Side. Shit, I got bad vibes about this, man. Any Crips or Bloods walkin' in here would be bad news. And, those two over there…the old people. Why them? That old lady reminds me of my grandma," he said, nodding in the direction of Emma and Harvey.

Gerardo stiffened in his seat. He didn't like even the slightest, inadvertent challenge to his authority. His eyes drilled into Vinnie.

"Fuck them. Listen up. We gonna do them 'cause that old white bastard's got a huge stack of bills on him. And, because I told you we gonna do them. What the fuck is wrong with you tonight, Vinnie? This ain't like you, man," Gerardo said, his eyes glaring.

"Si, Sorry," Vinnie's eyes fell in embarrassment.

Gerardo shifted abruptly to his left, distracted by movement. He eyed Emma as she rose from her seat. Harvey, his lanky figure stooping, reached down to pick up the tray.

"Party time. Let's do it."

Gerardo stuffed his right hand in his pocket and gripped the pistol. The three gangsters slid along the bench seats, and rose to their feet in unison. They turned together toward the exit doors, trailing behind the departing old couple, and entering the frigid Denver night.

Harvey held the door as Emma stepped out into the bracing, wintry air. Swirls of frost had begun to spiral across the windshields in the parking lot of Ben's Burgers, including an unmarked police sedan parked under a leafless oak.

The blue Dodge Charger belonged to the Denver Police Gang Squad. Tonight was another random surveillance…a weekly routine, but this week, this night, and this hour, the random surveillance just happened to be at Ben's Burgers. Inside the police cruiser, Detective Lieutenant Steve Dutton, Gang Squad Chief, rolled his eyes at his deputy, Detective Sergeant Rob Hudson.

"It wasn't all that long ago when this part of the city was nice. Safe. It looks like hell now. And, it's spreading like some damn disease all over the east and west sides of the city. Bloods, Crips, Black Gangster Disciples, Folk Nation…this is all their turf now," Dutton said.

Pale light from parking lot lamps danced on Hudson's eyes. He pivoted his head about to face Dutton.

"I'm with you on that. Disease is right. But I'm saying, I've got the cure, if somebody would only let me put it in action. Black gangs, the Latins, the Asians, MS-13, all of them… those who don't wanna abide by the new rules and play nice, we bury the sonsofbitches. I'd sweep their collective asses off the streets and into the graveyards."

"You think that's the way it should be? Just go out and kill them? Come on, that's frustration talking, not justice. That'd end up being worse than it is now," Dutton frowned.

"Worse than it is now? Hell, I don't see how. Lieutenant, we ain't exactly stemming the tide here. We don't even put a dent in it. You know that. Victims don't have rights anymore. No, I say we go on the offensive and stick it right back in their faces," Hudson's black face took on a tinge of blue in the darkness.

Both men abruptly turned their attention to the windshield as their headsets crackled. It was Detective Chaz Montoya. He and Will Bolles sat in a second unmarked sedan on the opposite side of the parking lot.

"Lieutenant, do you see him? He's walking right toward you!" Montoya blurted out.

"What?" Dutton perked up.

His eyes widening, Hudson leaned toward the windshield. He sat up in his seat and stuck a bony finger toward the windshield. "Pay dirt! That's Gerardo Ventana! Ventana! What the hell's a Santana Hood gangster doing over here in the middle of black gang territory?"

Dutton peered out the window, his eyes scrutinizing the sinewy figure leading the pack of three gangsters. He raised his headset mike. "Okay, good catch. Go ahead and check your weapons, gentlemen."

"Lieutenant, okay if I go inside to the counter? I think I can get behind them pretty quick from there." It was Montoya.

"Sure, good idea. Easy, though. Bolles, back him up," Dutton ordered. At Dutton's command, Montoya slid off the seat, exiting the car in the west lot.

"Got it," Bolles replied, climbing out of the passenger side. His right hand unsnapped the retainer on his hip holster as he watched Montoya enter the front doors of the burger joint. Once inside, Montoya swerved, snaking around the tables toward the opposite side doors. He paused at the glass, watching the gang members walking away.

"This looks bad, Lieutenant. There's an old couple walking toward a Chevy. The gangbangers are making a beeline for them."

"Dammit. All right, guys, time to go earn our paycheck. Let's move!" Dutton said.

Dutton yanked the Beretta 92fs pistol from its holster, jerked back the slide and chambered a round into the breech. He released the safety. Hudson reached under his jacket, gripping the butt of his Glock 22. There was another loud metallic *clank*.

The two detectives stepped out into the frigid air, doors thudding into their jams behind them. Dutton raised his mike. "Bolles, call the dispatcher for back-up. I want at least one cruiser, two if they're available…and pronto! Then come over here, we might need you."

"Roger," Bolles adjusted his own mike to make the call.

Gerardo, Carlos, and Vinnie strutted across the lot, hands in their jackets, heading directly for Emma. Harvey stood by the driver-side door, fumbling with his key chain.

Dutton's eyes swept over his detectives, man to man. His left arm raised and swept through the air. "Flank 'em. Hudson, don't move too fast. Hold back."

Dutton and Hudson spread apart as they crossed the parking lot. Jackets open, the gold badges clipped to their belts glimmered in the floodlights. Montoya stepped from the glass side doors of the burger joint and approached the gangsters from the rear.

"Police! Put your hands in the air! Hands up! Now!" Dutton barked, his pistol drawn and already in a two-hand grip.

Hudson and Montoya drew their weapons on Dutton's lead. Bolles sprinted through the playground area, drawing up alongside Montoya. His panting breath clouded in the freezing air.

The three gangsters abruptly spun around, facing off against the detectives. They stared down the barrels of four drawn pistols.

"What you racist white boys want?" Ventana snapped back defiantly, his eyes narrowing to black slits.

Emma stood frozen at the passenger door, now only a few steps behind the gangsters. She turned toward the shouting voices, a look of confusion spreading across her face.

Abruptly, Ventana slipped behind Emma. His left arm shot around her neck in a chokehold as his right hand drew his S&W M&P .40 caliber pistol from under his jacket. He shoved the barrel against her temple. She shrieked in terror. Ventana sneered at Dutton and Hudson.

"Stop it! Dammit, take your hands off her, you bastards!" Harvey shouted. He stood on the other side of the Chevy, his mouth agape. Looking suddenly as though he was trying to catch his breath. An expression of stark horror splashed across his face, which was now turning abruptly gray, ghost-like. His eyes appeared sunken, like two black raisins stuffed in a white clay skull. He glanced to Emma and then to the detectives, his voice unsteady.

"You police? Do something, dammit! Please, don't let them hurt her!" Harvey said, muttering in a weak voice. He leaned forward, his hands pressing against the side window.

Carlos and Vinnie drew their pistols, squaring off against the four detectives. Like cornered wolves, they inched backward to their alpha leader.

"Okay, pigs, come on! You want some? Come over here and I'll blow this old lady's brains all over this parking lot!" Ventana shouted.

"Gerardo, put down the gun and you won't get hurt!" Dutton stepped forward, slowly lowering his Beretta. Hudson followed suit.

"Know what? You fucking cops go to hell!" Ventana cocked his head to the right. The night air filled with the sound of sirens wailing in the distance. Police vehicles were racing down Colorado Boulevard in route to the burger house at 3rd and Josephine Street, the screeching of their sirens growing steadily louder.

Ventana turned back to Dutton, "You want my pistol? It's right here, asshole. Come get it!" He cocked the hammer.

"No, Gerardo...don't!" Hudson pleaded.

"Emma, honey? You okay?" Harvey shuffled feebly to the corner of the Chevy's hood. He leaned over, his knees quivering, his voice frailer. The keys slipped from his hands, jangling against the bumper, then to the ground.

"Stay where you are, asshole!" Carlos swung the weapon to him. "I'll blow you in half too! You and your old bitch!"

"Harvey...please!" Emma wailed. Her red wool cap tumbled to the pavement.

"Em...ma?" Teetering back and forth, Harvey struggled to steady himself. He stared down into his reflection rippling across the Chevy's hood.

All heads turned to the street. The first blue and white cruiser barreled into the entrance sliding sideways, its tires grinding as the brakes slammed. The cruiser shuddered to a halt. The cruiser's roof lights flashed upward against the ragged, leafless arms of trees reaching out to the deadly drama below. The parking lot took on the surreal look of a midnight nightmare.

Carlos instantly broke ranks. He rushed straight for the blue and white, his right arm thrust out in front of him. Blast after blast erupted from the pistol's barrel, rounds thudding into the hood and windshield. The patrol officer flung open the driver's door, and tossed himself to the pavement behind the cruiser.

"Halt!" Bolles bellowed. "Drop the pistol!"

Instead, Carlos abruptly swung the pistol toward him.

Bolles didn't wait. Three blasts trumpeted in rapid succession from his Sig Sauer P226.

The bullets pounded into Carlos' chest and shoulder, jerking him violently sideways, and breaking his forward momentum. Bolles fired again. The fourth bullet blew a hole in the side of Carlos' head, exploding in a fusillade of blood from a gaping fissure now at the rear of his skull. He dropped down to the asphalt like a broken doll, what remained of his cranium cracking on the macadam. Brains and other gore squirted into pooled blood.

The patrolman pushed himself to his feet behind his cruiser. He reached in the open door, and angrily yanked the shotgun from its rack. A look of fierce resolve washed across his face. The officer rose and stomped past the front of the cruiser and across the lot, nodding to Bolles with a fleeting glance at Carlos' now lifeless form.

A second blue and white cruiser lurched into the entrance and pulled up behind the first.

Hudson turned to Ventana, stepping forward tentatively. "Is this what you want? Gerardo, you want to die here tonight? Put the gun down now and let the woman go."

"Robbie, easy," Dutton said, turning to Harvey, who was now sliding along the front of the Chevy.

Ventana snarled at Harvey. "I told you to stay where you were, asshole!" He pushed the barrel of the Colt deeper into Emma's temple. He swung fretfully back to Hudson.

"Em..." Harvey stopped in his tracks. His right hand grasped the flannel shirt on his chest, unexpectedly paralyzed by searing pain.

"Oh, my God..." Harvey slumped downward, struggling to brace himself, his arms shaking.

Ventana screeched at Hudson. "No, pig! Put the gun down? That ain't gonna happen!" He backed up further toward the Chevy's trunk.

The patrolman stomping into the mix caught everyone's attention as he chambered a twelve-gauge, three-inch magnum round of Double-00 buckshot. He marched ahead, straight to within a few feet of Vinnie, and leveled the barrel directly at the gangster's head.

"Drop it, son. I won't ask you again. Now," the patrolman demanded.

His eyes wide, Vinnie stared at the patrolman's index finger poised on the trigger. In terror, he gawked at the muzzle of the shotgun's barrel. The officer's emotionless eyes drilled into his own.

"Gerardo!" Vinnie yelled, "This is bad, man! We ain't got a chance!" He shoved his pistol downward, releasing his grip. As the pistol clattered to the pavement, he thrust his arms over his head.

"You chicken shit!" Ventana roared, recognizing the situation as suddenly hopeless.

"Fuck!" Ventana pushed away from the car and thrust Emma forward. She stumbled, falling to her knees, sobbing. He dropped the pistol and raised both arms above his head.

Heads turned as Harvey's tall skeletal frame fell sideways. His chest thumped against the bumper as he slid downward, his head coming to rest against a front tire.

Dutton, Hudson, and Montoya rushed forward. They spun Gerardo and Vinnie on their heels and slammed them into the side doors of the Chevy.

"Spread 'em!" Hudson shouted. Bolles cuffed Ventana's hands behind his back. Dutton handled Vinnie.

"Harvey! Harvey!" Emma cried out, now on bloodied

knees, her hands gripping the sides of her face. There was no answer. Bewildered, her eyes searched the parking lot. It spun around her. She rolled her eyes in a sudden dizziness. On the palms of her hands, she crawled toward the Chevy, spotting him sprawled against the wheel. Emma scurried over to Harvey's motionless form and pulled his head onto her lap. His eyes were closed.

"No! Help, somebody help me!" She bawled. Her voice echoed through the frigid night.

Emma's thin white hands stroked Harvey's head, her words slurring, fading to whimpers. Her eyes rose, scanning the December sky. Over the ragged edge of a cloud, a narrow slice of Cheshire cat moon grinned back at her in seeming delight.

"Robbie, come on!" Dutton shook his head frantically. They sprinted to the Chevy, squatting next to the old woman. Emma howled, rocking back and forth against the bumper, her eyes filled with tears. Harvey's head lay motionless in her lap.

"He's gone. My Harvey's gone. They've killed him," Emma moaned.

Dutton leaned forward and placed his fingers against the clammy white flesh of the man's neck.

"No pulse, Robbie," Dutton looked at Emma.

"Your name, ma'am? What's your name?" Dutton placed his hand on her shoulder.

"Emma Jean Goodman," She stared down at Harvey. "Can you help my husband?"

"Yes, Emma, we're going to help."

With a sweep of his hand, Dutton directed Hudson to the old woman. Robbie placed his arms gently around her. Dutton slowly pulled Harvey from her and laid him flat, methodically ripping off the suspenders and tearing open his shirt. Dutton pushed up the tee shirt and leaned over, listening for the thumping of a heartbeat. There was none.

"Bolles! Come over here, I need you!" Dutton shouted.

"Lieutenant, ambulances are on the way. They're at 1st and Speer. Be here in minutes," Bolles said.

"Take Mrs. Goodman to a cruiser. I don't want her close and seeing this."

"Robbie, give me a hand please. Come over here. Start working his heart. Let's do it."

Dutton cocked Harvey's head back. Pinching the nose, he pushed his mouth over Harvey's, and began blowing air into his lungs. He could feel them inflate. Hudson overlapped the palms of his hands on Harvey's chest. He pushed on the heart, up-and-down, thumping hard.

The two detectives lost their sense of time as they feverishly repeated their actions over and over again. There was the sudden wail of another set of sirens. The rescue vehicles were near.

Dutton sat up on his knees, wheezing. He glimpsed over his shoulder to the cruiser straddling the entrance to the parking lot. Emma sat in the back seat, struggling to see around Bolles. Their eyes touched. Her grim look sent Dutton's heart sinking in his chest. He returned to Harvey, but to no avail. No response. The old man's skin was growing cool.

A white-and-orange rescue vehicle's bright lights flashing and its engine roaring filled the parking lot. It rammed over the curb away from the cruisers, plowing down a row of hedges as it burst into the lot. Two white-suited med techs dashed toward them.

"I'm Johnson. Situation?" The first man asked, pulling Dutton from Harvey. He waved at Hudson to back off.

Leaning over, Johnson pressed a stethoscope against the old man's neck.

"Attempted armed robbery. The male over there is gone. Nothing you can do there," Dutton said.

Johnson nodded as he briefly glanced at Carlos' motionless, blood-spattered body. Looking like black ice, pools of blood had swelled around him.

"This old guy's the husband. He just suddenly fell down. Maybe a heart..." Dutton said.

"Right! Myocardial infarction. Tom, help me get his shoulders! You guys get his legs. Lift him up. Let's get him over to the van, onto the gurney. One, two, three...up we go!" Johnson exclaimed.

The two EMTs and the two detectives scrambled as fast as they could to the rear of the van, grunting with the weight of Harvey in their arms. Emma shoved Bolles aside and rose from the rear seat of the cruiser. She tossed the cup of water aside, stumbling forward, heading for the van. Bolles followed.

Montoya and three patrolmen pulled Gerardo and Carlos off the pavement. They guided the gangsters to a cruiser, and shoved them against the vehicle.

The two med techs backed the detectives out of the rear of the van. Johnson yanked on gloves, pulling up the two metallic pads from the defibrillator unit. He grabbed the handles. Tom adjusted the settings.

"Clear!" Johnson yelled.

Johnson slammed the two pads on Harvey's chest, sending huge impulses of voltage plunging into his body. The electrical shock raced through his heart, simulating impulses from the man's right atrium. His chest heaved off the table with a violent spasm of ventricular fibrillation. Harvey dropped back to the gurney. Nothing.

"Again!" Johnson barked. "Clear!"

A grotesque wrenching of Harvey's body repeated itself, but again nothing. A third time.

"Tom, we gotta roll! I'll call the ER, tell them to get prepped! Lieutenant, clear those vehicles, fast please! We're rolling!" Johnson snapped.

"You got it!" Dutton withdrew from the closing rear doors, motioning to Rob Hudson. Emma suddenly appeared at his side.

"Open those damn doors! I'm going with my husband!" Emma shrieked into the cold night air, her eyes red with tears. Dutton turned to Johnson in the open bay. The med tech nodded.

"Go ahead. Lift her up. You too, Lieutenant, I may need you. Let's go!"

The doors slammed shut. The rescue vehicle lurched forward, tires spinning, white smoke pluming into the air. They roared away over the curb, bursting out onto the street.

Hudson joined Montoya and Bolles watching the swirling lights disappear into darkness down Josephine Street. The van's siren wails seemed surreal, like a banshee come to foretell death.

CHAPTER 2

The next day's early morning sun strained to inch its way over the clouds, scattering the dawn with freckles of light. Mottled shadows from drifting clouds slipped slowly across the grass and patches of snow. It was seven o'clock. Twin Ford sedans sat nudged to the curb outside the Emergency Room, Detective Hudson in one with Montoya and Bolles in the other. Lieutenant Dutton had gone in the hospital by himself to check on the Goodmans.

"Dammit," Dutton muttered to himself minutes later as he ambled down the antiseptic-smelling corridor and approached the exit doors. The news he'd received was not what he wanted to hear. It was a lousy start to a gloomy morning. Harvey Goodman was dead. Emma was in a coma. The more troublesome news was that she'd worsened significantly during the night. The doctors had tried to sound hopeful, but said eventually that she could go either way.

As the three gang-unit officers noticed the lieutenant emerge from the hospital's glass doors, they slid off their seats and climbed out of their cars. Pausing for a moment, they glanced at each other and then walked toward their leader.

Dutton sucked in a gulp of cold air, stuffed his hands in his trench coat and stiffened in the wind whipping down the walkway. Seeing the detectives, he rubbed his forehead, scowling, and stopped, waiting for them. He kicked the toe of his shoe at the pavement.

"Lieutenant? Any status yet? Did the doctors tell you anything?" Hudson asked as he, Montoya, and Bolles gathered around Dutton.

"It's not good, guys. Harvey Goodman was dead on arrival–DOA. A massive heart attack. The docs said that even if he'd arrived earlier, there would have been nothing they could do. They couldn't help him."

"Shit," Hudson mumbled.

"Yeah, I know," Dutton said, glancing at Montoya and Bolles…the two slowly shook their heads as their spirits plummeted.

"Mrs. Goodman?"

"Emma…she went into shock after she arrived. They moved her up to the Cardiac ICU. They said she could go either way. They're hopeful, but that's all."

"Sonofabitch! What the hell did we accomplish?" Hudson's voice rose.

"Look, I understand. I do. The bottom-line here is we've got a manslaughter charge and a dead gangster. This was a tough one last night but you all did outstanding work. I'm proud of you, and I'm damn glad we're all together on this team!" Dutton exclaimed.

"Thanks, Lieutenant. You, too," Bolles spoke. "Sir, this is all over the news this morning…on the front page of the Denver Post, too."

"I expected that. Captain Lacey wants to see me this morning to go over the sequence of events last night. Oh, and what's the status on Gerardo and Vinnie?" Dutton said.

"They're in the detention center. They're booked on everything we could think of," Hudson answered.

"Again, good work, guys. All right, let's roll," Dutton said, pointing to Montoya and Bolles. "You two go get some coffee and something to eat. Hudson and I will be at the department with Captain Lacey."

"Got it, Lieutenant," Montoya said. He and Bolles ambled toward their sedan without another word between them.

Hudson jogged off to the waiting Ford and clambered behind the wheel. He reached over and shoved open the passenger door. Dutton shuffled his way to the cruiser, plopping into the seat with a sigh. He offered a weak wave as Bolles and Montoya made a U-turn, their tires screeching north toward Speer Boulevard.

Hudson abruptly swung the cruiser away from the curb and headed south. He glanced at Dutton. "You okay, sir?"

"Yeah. Rob, please know this…I am damn glad you were right with me every step of the way. Damn glad. Last night was a bitch. I hope that Emma pulls through, but I've got a bad feeling in my gut that…"

"Don't go there. It's in the Lord's hands."

"It is indeed. Thanks. Well, let's go see what Lacey has to say."

Indifferent to his reflection in the window glass, Dutton's mind fogged, his head collapsed against the seat back. His eyes stared blankly into the fabric of the ceiling.

Hudson looked over, but no words came. He gripped the wheel and pressed his foot on the gas.

CHAPTER 3

The White House
Two Weeks Later
Mid-December

Crumbles of the last snowfall drifted in icy, blustery winds. A few remaining dead leaves scattered across the lawn fronting Pennsylvania Avenue, most coming to rest beneath the line of bushes paralleling the steel fence. It was a frosty Friday evening with splotches of ice crystals flecking across the windows. Christmas trimmings adorning trees on the grounds rustled among the branches. Inside the Oval Office however, things were heating up.

Flustered, Attorney General Bill Cannon loosened his necktie, undoing the top button of his shirt. Moisture had gathered around his neck at the collar. His hands stroked the top of his head…not much hair left there to brush back. The air in the room seemed thick. Cannon grimaced at the tone of the discussion, now over a half hour long. He decided to break in.

"Mr. President, we've all seen the news stories about the gang incident with the old couple in Denver. It's gone viral. The media has painted it as bad as they could, and it's become a symbol for what's occurring in our cities. However, CNN, MSNBC, ABC, the Washington Post, the New York Times, hell, the entire left-leaning media are going way over the top on this. Fact is, we just don't have the resources available to go after all these bastards, if we wanted to. Not on a nationwide scale. They're everywhere in the big cities and well organized. There's just too many of them. Last night, George Blanton was once again making nasty remarks about you on CNN. He said it was despicable of you to allow this situation to continue. So now, it's not just your foreign policy he's attacking. At least, he wasn't wearing his uniform."

"Blanton? I don't know what's driving that man to do that in public! The fact remains that I'm his Commander-in-Chief! If anything or anybody is way over the top, he is. Uniform or not, that idiot is acting like he doesn't give a rat's ass if he loses his four stars. And, let me say that's not outside the realm of possibility," the President paused.

"I agree, sir." Bill replied.

"Now, to the matter at hand. I'm sorry, Bill, but I disagree with you on the news coverage. This time I think the media got it right. The death of that old fellow in Denver, Harvey Goodman–hell, that's only one example of what's raging across this nation. And Harvey's wife, Emma...damn, that poor gal died three days later lying in a hospital bed, probably of a hopelessly broken heart. But what about the young couple on vacation with their little girl in Miami...gunned down in a street battle that erupted from nowhere? And the six illegal MS-13 members who brutally stabbed a man to death in Maryland? Also, the two high school cheerleaders kidnapped after a football game, raped and murdered in Los Angeles? Those two twelve-year-old boys playing in their front yards in Chicago shot to death in a drive-by shooting? All this and the ambushing of police officers. I could go on and on. This crap is playing out every day somewhere in a city in our country. It's vicious and it's endemic," the President said.

"I agree with you again, Mr. President, but..."

The president cut him off. "Bill, the essence of our quandary in this is that we really don't have time for legislation. A bill that could solve this issue would take years, and it'd probably fail to get through both Houses of Congress. No, we need to somehow demonstrate to the American people that we recognize the seriousness of the problem and we're making progress in neutralizing it. Now, not five or six years down the road."

"Mr. President, state and local police..." Bill began.

"No. We've already seen that the locals can't handle it. It's too big, too pervasive. This is America–the land of the free and the home of the brave. Remember? Our fellow Americans in the cities don't feel free. Look, a couple decades ago, we eliminated the core of the Mafia in this country, and I think we can do it again with these violent street gangs. We've walled the southern border up now, closed. Finally. So now, we need to eliminate the gangbangers already inside the country. What's a workable solution? That's why I've asked us to gather here tonight. We need to put the kibosh on the gangs. Now, not later."

"Mr. President, there's a wheelbarrow full of other budget priorities and not enough resources. Especially in the international realm," Bill said.

Jack Barrett, Director of Central Intelligence, looked at his deputy, Pete Novak, then chimed in. "Bill does have a point, Mr. President. I have Pete Novak with me tonight–Pete's my Deputy for Operations. We're locked nose-to-nose in multiple engagements and in different theaters of operation–with Iran,

North Korea, Russia and China. Those things are more than just challenging."

"Hello, Pete. Welcome to The White House. I've heard a lot about the good work you and your folks do. So, thank you," the President said.

"Thank you, Mr. President. It's an honor to be here," Pete replied.

Vice President Vince Simmons interjected. "Mr. President, I agree with both Bill and Jack. Some senior people in the defense department are openly speaking against our policies in the international arena. They say that in trying to juggle all these threats, the risks of war have greatly increased. General Blanton's just the loudest."

The President turned to Vince. "Blanton again. That bastard's out of line and he knows it. The day will come when I will rip the stars off his uniform!"

"He's not the only one, sir," Vince said.

"All right. I agree with Jack, however, those are external threats. Abraham Lincoln once said that '*America will never be destroyed from the outside. If we falter and lose our freedoms, it will be because we destroyed ourselves.*' I agree with Abe. Self-destructing from within is a serious threat and I think an immediate one."

"North Korea, Iran and their missile developments..." Jack began to respond.

"Let's pause a minute and take a look at the reality of that. The fact is North Korea knows damn well that if she were to openly attack any U.S. assets or those of our allies, within 72 hours that country would cease to exist. And, I'm convinced that relations with Russia will work out if we stay involved with her in up-front, well-intended negotiations. Our Bolshevik, Soviet Commie-thinking Congress is wrong about Russia. That's not what Russia is anymore. Instead of helping her after the wall came down when she imploded, collapsing, we encircled her…we brought previous Warsaw Pact nations into our alliances and surrounded her. We raised Russia's paranoia once again. I'm convinced the relationship with Russia is fixable."

"I agree with you on that, sir," Jack said.

"Also, China? We're handling China very well, I think. On the economic battlefield. Mark my words, gentlemen, China will cave eventually. So, that leaves Iran. If we're forced to tangle with Iran militarily, she will be the ultimate loser! We have the air power to do it, and without putting a boot on the ground. I'm hoping the mullahs see the light."

"And General Blanton and his like?" Vince asked.

"I'll take care of Blanton. He's down at SOCOM in Florida, not here in Washington. I will deal with him. As I've already said, if Blanton keeps this up, I'll strip the uniform off that sonofabitch. He can run for office after that if he wants."

"Sir, have you had the opportunity to discuss Blanton with the Army Chief of Staff?" Vince asked.

"Yes, I've mentioned my displeasure to General Davidson regarding Blanton's derisive public outbursts. Davidson's agreed to talk with Blanton, but I don't expect too much to come from that. They're both West Pointers, only two years apart. However, if it turns out that I need to call Blanton on the rug in this office, read him the riot act, and threaten him with a court martial, I will do just that."

"Mr. President, the resources needed to support action against large gang organizations are scarce. And, there have been successes like taking down an MS-13 Gang in New York City for one," Bill said.

"New York City? That was one time. Once. From what

I've heard, that operation was exceedingly expensive and it addressed only the veritable tip of the iceberg. Bill, you give me an effective solution, a workable program that can be used to mitigate the gang problem in our cities, and I will find a way to get you the resources," the President said.

"From where, sir? There's no way..."

Jim Owens, Homeland Security Director, rose from his seat. He exclaimed, "You're wrong, Bill. I fully agree with the president. And, since we're all senior level officials sitting in this office and I've checked, all of us have at least Top Secret collateral clearances, I can tell you that we may indeed have a way to deal effectively with this."

"Jim, please enlighten us," FBI Director Bob Wilkes leaned forward in his easy chair.

"I know the FBI is responsible for the internal security of the United States. It's your mission. That is, until..."

"Until what?"

"Let me finish. Even though we all have high clearances, please understand I can only go so far with this. If the president determines that the security and stability of the nation are in serious jeopardy, and he states so publicly, then he could declare a national crisis–not a state of emergency like what has occurred previously for the southern border or for a hurricane slamming the east coast. A national crisis."

"What does that do for us?" Bill asked, his face wrinkled in a puzzling look.

"The answer to that question lies in Annex K to the charter of the Federal Emergency Management Agency...FEMA. That's the classified annex defining Presidential Authority for Special Means."

"FEMA? What classified annex? I'm not aware of any classified annex to FEMA's charter. Nor a *Special Means* authorization as you called it. What the hell is that? How...?" Bill replied.

"Seriously, Bill, do you really know anything at all about FEMA's charter?" Jim asked.

"No, I guess I don't."

"FEMA was created by Presidential Reorganization Plan No. 3 of 1978. Soon after, it was implemented by two Executive Orders on April 1, 1979, at which time the classified Annex K was added. To date, no president has felt the need to declare a national crisis and implement Annex K. However, I think the horrific situations our citizens are facing daily in our decaying cities may mean that now the time is right to do so."

"Go on, Jim," the President said.

"We are now, at this minute, involved in a national crisis, though we may not have declared it as such. What's happening to Americans' constitutional rights to life, liberty and the pursuit of happiness? I think the time couldn't be more appropriate, and the capability to deal with this damned problem already exists," Jim continued.

"Jim, like Bill, I'm interested in just what this classified Annex K states. Please continue," the President remarked.

"Mr. President, I brought a copy of the unclassified section of charter's annex with me just in case our discussion moved in this direction. This section is not classified, it's For Official Use Only–FOUO. I'll read the one paragraph:

ANNEX K: Authorization for SPECIAL MEANS–*'Should the internal security of the United States become immersed in crisis and determined to be under imminent threat of collapse, the President may, without the informed consent of Congress, authorize extraordinary measures, Special Means, to neutralize the threat, and restore stability and security to the nation.'*

That's it, sir. In essence, it's a highly classified, covert operations program. It's operational now and has been since FEMA was established. We have it. George Stiles, Director at FEMA, runs it. This can be a very powerful tool, if the president makes the decision to use it," Owens said.

"My goodness...without the informed consent of Congress? What specifically is the covert operations program that implements this, *Special Means* concept? Does it have a name?" The President asked.

"Yes sir. The unclassified nickname is STARDUST. George Stiles has told me that the program can go fully operational if and when you declare a national crisis, and then exercise your authority in Annex K," Owens said.

"STARDUST?" The President asked.

"The word is an acronym. Spelling it out for you in this forum however, Mr. President, would be a security issue. We shouldn't go there."

"Okay, how would it be employed?" The President responded.

"Mr. President, this program is highly classified and it's a Special Access Required–SAR program to boot. I'm certain not everyone in this room is on the access list. So, other than suggesting that consideration be given to selecting three cities to test the concept, I suggest that's as far as we should discuss it here. I can say without a doubt though, that this program is workable, it's immediately deployable, and it's extremely efficient, lethally so. I feel certain that if implemented, it would assure the removal of the hard-core nucleus of street gang activity in the chosen cities."

Bill rose to his feet. "Lethal, you say? I read that as murder! Are you proposing that we consider killing American citizens? Does George Stiles see it like that? I say no, we can't do it nor should we even consider such a thing!" He shouted.

Jack Barrett rose from his seat. "Mr. President, without any demonstrated involvement by foreign intelligence, the focus on this matter is completely domestic and beyond the mission of the CIA. Sir, I ask your permission for the Agency to bow out."

"I see your point. Please feel free to leave, Jack, and thanks for coming," The President stood.

Bob Wilkes stood as Barrett and Novak disappeared out the door. "Sir, I ask to be excused as well. This issue is not within the purview of the Bureau and I guess I don't really want to know where all of this is headed. It's a discussion I don't think the Bureau should be a party to. Please understand, Mr. President."

"Okay, Bob. All of us here have to admit that this is an extremely difficult situation the nation is facing. I believe the solution to this coast-to-coast nightmare may require firm action, and yes, perhaps even some measure of lethal action. Best wishes to you and your family. Have a Merry Christmas."

"Thank you, Mr. President," Bob said. His face reddened, he spun around toward the door.

Once outside, Jack glanced to Pete before climbing into the limousine waiting for them in the drive. "Pete, have you spoken to Dave McClure recently?"

"No, but I expect a call soon. He's in Berlin."

"Still chasing that same rabbit?"

"Yes. There's been lots of dead ends, but the search is edging nearer. I think they're close to an apprehension."

"Hope so. That damn mole is compromising Top Secret-Codeword information. We can't afford not to wrap him or her up as quickly as possible. Pete, whaddya say we stop somewhere and have a drink before we split for the night?"

"Sounds like a plan!" Novak smiled.

In the Oval Office, Bill Cannon stood, continuing to argue his case. "Mr. President, as bad as all this gang violence is, if I'm understanding correctly what this STARDUST program portends, and I believe that means killing American citizens, then for goodness sake, even discussing such a thing is horrific. I suggest..."

Jim Owens stomped to his feet. "Bill, really, American citizens? Please, spare me! We know that the cores of these organized gangs are, in fact, illegals. These killers are in this country illegally. They're vicious animals without a moral bone in their bodies and they're murdering law-abiding American citizens each and every day throughout this nation! American citizens? Horse shit!" His voice raised to a shout.

"Jim..." Bill started to reply.

"No! The President has clearly stated that we're very much up against it–that this problem has reached critical mass. So, are we going to be resolute about fixing it or are we not! We're not talking about killing American citizens! No, we're talking about exterminating vermin! Malicious, sadistic vermin!"

"Bill, and you say?" With a solemn look, Vince Simmons quizzed the Attorney General.

Bill's face blanched.

A sudden hush engulfed the room, the men scanning each other's faces in dead silence.

The President sank back into his chair and folded his hands on his desk. He stared briefly at the three men before him, then swiveled in his chair to reach behind him for the bottle of 18-year-old, single malt scotch. He leaned forward and set four old-fashioned crystal glasses on the edge of his desk.

"Gentlemen...please, come closer and have a seat."

Chapter 4

U.S. Embassy
Pariser Platz 2, Berlin
Mid-December

Dave McClure got a thumbs-up from the communications officer that the line had gone secure. He heard rings at the other end. It was a direct call to Headquarters CIA, Langley Center, in McLean, Virginia. The Duty Officer greeted him and immediately put the call through to Pete Novak, the DepOps.

"Pete Novak."

"Yes, Mr. Novak. I hope I didn't interrupt anything."

"Dave, that you? Hey, good to hear your voice. I know I keep telling you this, Dave, but please feel free to call me 'Pete'. You're what I refer to as a friendly insider on my staff. And nope, no problem. It's 9:00 a.m. and the staff meeting's over. Are you at the station?"

"Yes, I'm one door down from the station chief's office. Mr. Schiller just left for home. He said he'll probably come back after dinner. That's the daily working life of a station chief, I guess."

"Right. Station chiefs, the good ones that is, sleep very

little. At least that's what they'll tell you. What time is it in Berlin?"

"Ah, it's 4:00 p.m. here," McClure said, looking up at the wall clock.

"Okay, good. So, anything new yet on where we're going with this case? Are we any closer? This one's got the DCI's interest. You spoke with the German intelligence folks at the BND?"

"Yes, I did, this morning. The guys at the *Bundesnachrichtendienst* even took me out afterward to a local gasthaus, a great place for lunch. It was apparently a known German spook hangout. The food was awesome. I had a jägerschnitzel, spätzle, and a beer. Well, two beers. Superb. They're a good bunch. They said they'd closely examined the documents you had couriered over to them previously. They're pretty sure that from both the subject matter, the document markings, and the requirements for access to that level of material, the rabbit is most likely assigned down at USEUCOM in Vaihingen. Also, he or she is almost certainly a mid-to-senior officer or equivalent level Army civilian."

"Great. Good work."

"The BND said our source must be very good, have high credibility. Are they correct in their assessment?"

"Yes. In spades, actually. He's never blown a test. We turned him years ago when he was a case officer in Athens. The man he thought he was vetting for recruitment was ours. A dangle operation. We cornered Sergei, as I refer to him, in his auto out on a beach road in Glyfada. Of course, he protested and claimed diplomatic immunity. We moved him to a safe house and confronted him with the fact that everything he'd been sending to Moscow was controlled by us. And, that some of it had been altered."

"You rolled him over then and there?"

"No, it wasn't all that simple. There were other factors. If I recall, it turned out that Khrushchev had his parents killed. So, it wasn't really difficult to bring him over. He's remained in place and is now at a fairly high level...assigned at the Moscow headquarters working FSB matters. Fact is, we plan on extracting him soon. Maybe on one of his trips to Budapest–he's still active that way, too. The man's done a lot for us and he's at great risk. Anyway, that's how we got the documents and the lead on a deep cover mole who's hurting us so damn bad."

"Wow. Sounds like an extremely credible foreign asset. Thanks, Pete. Do you want me to head to EUCOM's Patch Barracks in Vaihingen? Nose around, get the lay of the land. I could fly to Stuttgart tonight or tomorrow morning."

"Ah no, I don't think so. Negative on that."

"May I ask why, especially now that we may have a good vector on this rabbit?"

"I don't think you should get too close, not yet. You're naked, no support. I'd rather assemble a good team to send over with full tech capabilities. They'll work out a plan for a surreptitious entry operation into the personnel center there, probably in the early morning hours. They can scan files and note any possible fits before they extricate themselves. If they find a good hit, we'll reshape the investigative plan accordingly, add a surveillance operation, other things. If it all continues to fit, looks credible–we'll move in for the apprehension. Dave, you've given us the next focus...so again, well done."

"Thanks. Should I come home?"

"No. I want you to fly down to Frankfurt. Rent a car at the flughafen and drive over to Wiesbaden. If I recall, it's direct route on autobahn 66. Check in with the BKA and see what their assessment is. They also received couriered copies of the documents in question from us."

"The *Bundeskriminalamt*? Okay, but since I've already talked with the BND and have their assessment, why go to the BKA?"

"Dave, it's sort'a like us and the NRO, the NSA, maybe even the FBI's Foreign Counterintelligence division. Sometimes one of us sees something that the rest of us miss. It's the same way with the BND and BKA. I'd like to ensure we validate this thing as best as we can. Make sense?"

"Yes, it does. Thanks. Is a flight out of here tomorrow morning okay?"

"Sure. I want to cover ourselves, be as certain as is possible, so when we decide to go active, we have the right target. I want to wrap this mole up soonest. Limit future damage. Damn, we've already had Top Secret SCI data compromised. I want this sonofabitch scooped up and his ass shoved behind bars for the rest of his life."

"I understand. I'm with you."

"Good. Get some sleep. Give me a brief recap call after you touch base with the BKA. Then, for now anyway, it's mission accomplished. Come on home. We'll try to keep you on this op–the investigative team and the surveillance team. I'm looking forward to seeing you."

"Got it. Take care, Pete."

"Goodnight, Dave. Check your six. Novak out."

Dave hung up the phone, rose from the chair, and stepped out into the hallway. Two young embassy secretaries walked past him and slowed their pace, their eyes scanning Dave from top to bottom, his trim fitness evident. Their focus paused on his curly brown hair and crystal blue eyes. They both smiled mischievously. He nodded, and smiled back.

They continued down the hallway, both taking a final glance over their shoulders.

His heart fluttered. Then, in a split second, his mind's eye saw Karen's auburn hair sweeping softly across her shoulders, her hazel eyes focused on his. Enticing. He shook his head.

Before heading down the stairs to the street, he glanced out the window to dark gray skies and a constant drizzle of rain. No snow yet, just an icy rain. It seemed as though one could pick almost any season of the year, and it would be gray and drizzling in Berlin.

It was obvious that he'd have to walk a few blocks in the weather to catch a taxi back to the Steigenberger Hotel. It was a good twenty-five blocks away just off the Kurfürstendamm. Then, he'd find a gasthaus for dinner. He looked up and down the street. By now, the protest marchers were soaked to the bone and breaking up. The liberal party, The Greens, *die Grünen,* was going one way, and the far-right party marchers, *Alternative für Deutschland,* the AfD, were going the other. The good news today was no violence had broken out.

Many here believed that Angela Merkel was hanging on to her Chancellorship by the skin of her chinny-chin-chin. Western intelligence agencies assessed Germany as teetering on the edge of serious confrontational, political turmoil. The straw breaking the camel's back was focused about the recent unfettered immigration of Muslims into Germany. There was a renewed sense of urgency for a need to return to a strengthened German pride and nationalism. Dave began sauntering past them, watching cautiously as the marchers turned in place and began leaving the street.

In any case, Dave was still going to have to walk a few city blocks to find an available taxi. He'd call later from the hotel and a book a flight to Frankfurt for the next morning. He swept his hair back from his forehead and wiped his hands over his eyes.

Karen McClure rested her elbows on the granite countertop in their two-story brick colonial on Pumphrey Drive in Fairfax, Virginia. She was near the double sink in the kitchen, her eyes peering over the windowsill into the backyard. Snow was everywhere, at least a good foot of the white stuff.

Late in the morning as it was, birds of all sorts were still scrambling among the feeders that she and Dave had strung up last autumn from the now barren and craggy arms of oak and elm trees. She had been thinking of lunch when the phone rang. Her hands cradled the phone. A smile spread across her face...it was Dave.

"Oh Dave, sweetie, how are you? I was hoping, praying you might call. I was beginning to get concerned."

"Karen, sweetheart, I love hearing your voice. I miss you so much. Honey, there's no need for worrying. No need, really. That's why a few years ago, I left this outfit to work for the Bureau instead. But I'm back with them again and there are going to be times, doll, when I have to go silent for several days or even weeks. Times when I can't risk calling you like this. Please accept that."

Karen knew she would still worry, but she'd be careful not to mention it again. "Okay. I understand. I'm sorry. I promise I'll put the brakes on the worry stuff. Can you tell me where you are now, is that possible? Will you be home for Christmas? Please, say yes."

"I'm at my hotel in Berlin. I'm flying over to Frankfurt tomorrow, but probably just for the one day. I should be free to fly out tomorrow evening or the morning after. So, yes sweetheart, it looks very much now like I will be home and soon."

"Great. Nothing dangerous, I hope?'

"Honeyyy..."

"Okay."

"And you? Are you finished with the issue down in North Carolina? The National Resources Division, they've let you come home?"

"Yep. That's over. The next assignment looks like it will be down in Fort Pierce, Florida. Something weird involving the Inland Waterway near Port St. Lucie, but I don't have to be down there until January 5th. That means we will have lots of good time together. I'm dying to see you, Dave. I'm desperate for a hug."

"I promise to take care of that pronto. I think we can manage a little more than a hug, then some," Dave chuckled.

"I'm waiting anxiously."

"What's that chatter in the background?"

"Oh, I'm sorry, it's the TV over the buffet table…I'll turn it down."

"Wait, what's on? What are you watching?"

"Cable news. CNN, NBC, MSNBC…they're all covering it."

"Covering what?"

"They're broadcasting from the Lisner Auditorium at George Washington University. General Blanton's a guest. That blowhard!"

"Is he in uniform?"

"Yes, this time he is. This is so wrong. Those four stars of his glittering on his shoulders and his fruit salad of ribbons covering his left chest top to bottom!"

"Speaking against the president's foreign policies again?"

"It looks like he's going to. They're feeding him the question. Here, I'll put the phone closer to the speaker."

"Thanks."

Karen walked to the buffet table and raised the phone toward the TV. General George S.

Blanton was seated in a chair on stage next to the news anchorwoman, Sharon Gilbert. The stage lights on Blanton's uniform made the four stars on his epaulets sparkle. The general cut an impressive figure. Gilbert looked down at her note pad and directed her next question to the general. The general paused for a moment, then looked directly at the cameras.

General George S. Blanton: *"Good question, Sharon, thank you. Most know how I feel about this, but I'll take the opportunity to say it again...the President's policies with Russia and China are not only badly misguided, but they're pushing America closer to the brink of war, and I can't rule out a devastating nuclear war. Throughout our history, the United States has always been a nation of peace and we've pursued peace at all times. We've only gone to war when we were attacked or threatened. Not so now, not with this hawk of a president we have. And we, as senior officers in the military, see the same intelligence reporting that the president does, and many of us pretty much agree that the current policies are not only misguided, but even decidedly dangerous."*

The audience on all three levels rose in their seats. A thunderous applause echoed throughout the theater. Both Gilbert and the general smiled, then nodded to the crowd.

Sharon Gilbert: *"And what would you say about North Korea, Iran?"*

General George S. Blanton: *"Thank you, again. North Korea's leadership is unstable and insecure. As such, they're near impossible to predict. We shouldn't push them to the razor's edge like we're doing now. In the dead of night or light of day, North Korea could* *go nuclear against our ally, Japan, and we couldn't stop it. As for Iran, the mullahs are an exceedingly dangerous bunch, yet we keep pushing them against the wall. The fact is, I fear Iran more than any other nation because they are totally unpredictable, and also because nuclear weapons are not only deliverable by missiles but can be sneaked into a nation in sealed containers. If we continue this course of action, then New York City, Chicago, Miami, and other major cities could be at risk of annihilation. Is it worth it? I think not. No, we need a change of course and now, not three years from now in the next election. Further, I think that..."*

Dave interrupted. "Damn. Sweetheart, I've heard enough."

"Yeah, me too."

"I don't know how that bastard gets away with it? It's really outrageous. And, in uniform?"

"Dave, I agree with you, but he seems to have a large bunch of supporters. The place is packed."

"Karen, I think that's even more of a concern. I don't think any man or woman in uniform should be allowed to speak out like this, especially a four-star general. One who's becoming more radical and yet garners more support every time he takes a podium."

"I agree. Scary actually."

"Yes, indeed. I'll be there in a day or two, honey. I promise. Take care and be safe. I love you...love you bunches."

"'Love you, too. Be careful."

Karen placed the phone back in its charging cradle. It had been only eight months now since their wedding, and her mind was crowded with visions of cuddling up in Dave's arms on the sofa, gazing at all the Christmas decorations. Listening to Dean Martin on the BOSE singing *Let It Snow, Let It Snow, Let It Snow*. She began to hum the tune, then sighed. She glanced out the window at the trees again. Knowing the bird feeders were getting low, Karen went to the front hall closet, donned her parka and stepped out into the garage where the seed was stored in sealed containers.

Sitting in his underwear on the edge of his bed at the Steigenberger Hotel and in the dim light of a nightstand lamp, Dave set the phone down. Blanton. What a brazen sonofabitch that man was. Someone, perhaps the Chairman of the Joint Chiefs, the Secretary of Defense or maybe even the President, should step up to zip that guy's lips shut.

Dave looked around the room. Fact was, he had to admit to growing tired of hotel after hotel even though as much a part of the job as it was, as it had to be. On a positive note, he also knew hotels were a helluva lot more comfortable than the relatively meager amenities of an average safe house. He picked up the glass of Red Breast Irish Whiskey he'd toted up to his room from the hotel's bar. He took a sip and eased himself back on the bed against the headboard.

His eyes drew a bleary, unfocused gaze at the opposite wall of the room where a framed lithograph of Berlin's *Brandenburger Tor* hung, the Brandenburg Gate. The 18th-century monument was the entry point to Unter den Linden, an avenue of linden trees that once led to the Prussians' Royal City Palace. The palace was ultimately demolished during WWII by allied bombing.

He closed his eyes, his thoughts wandering. Eight months ago, he and Karen made the decision to marry after the fiery, violent events of the operation in Bar Harbor, Maine. Their affections for each other rapidly evolved into a passionate love. Each of them had tragically lost a spouse, Karen's husband in Afghanistan and Dave's wife and son in a freak winter accident on Interstate 70 in the Colorado Rockies. The weighty ache of loss gradually receded and their love for each other opened a new vista on life.

As was promised, Pete Novak had made Karen an offer of employment at the Agency in the National Resources Division. She accepted his offer and left the NCIS. Dave went on to become a Section Chief in the Special Operations branch of the Clandestine Service. After Dave successfully sold his house in Colorado Springs, he and Karen bought a colonial residence on Pumphrey Drive off Commonwealth Boulevard in the northern Virginia suburb of Fairfax. Having been forced to face how very fragile life could be, the two of them cherished everything about each other. Once again, life was good.

Dave rose slightly, leaned on an elbow and took another sip of whiskey. A grin creased his face. In two days or so, he'd be on his way across the gray waters of the Atlantic. Home for Christmas. He set the glass back on the nightstand and edged himself down onto the pillow, still smiling. He clicked off the lamp.

CHAPTER 5

Denver, Colorado
Six months later
June

Captain Earl Wickman hunkered his tall, lanky body down behind a blue Ford Explorer parked against the curb across the street from the house. It was roughly 2:30 a.m. in the wee early morning hours in North-East Park Hill, one of East Denver's gang infested neighborhoods. Wickman, Chief of the Denver PD's SWAT Division, just a smidgeon under 6 feet 3″ and 210 pounds, peered over the hood to see light smoke still seeping out from the windows. The acrid smell saturated the street area.

Wickman scrunched his eyes, glancing first to his left and then right to see his twelve black-clad SWAT members lined up behind the line of parked vehicles. They watched him, waiting for his orders, and cradling M4A1 rifles and Remington shotguns in their arms, at the ready. Detective Lieutenant Steve Dutton was directly to his right, and behind Dutton huddled Detective Sergeant Rob Hudson, Chaz Montoya, and Will Bolles, all of them wearing tactical vests. They'd been in position now for about 20 minutes.

"Dead quiet," Wickman said.

"Yeah. Like the whole street has been evacuated," Dutton replied.

"Or, they've moved their families out of sight, squatting down in their basements. Probably a combination of both," Wickman paused, then muttered as he rose to his feet, his right hand slicing forward.

"All right, let's do it. Tactical formations," the captain said.

The team members mimicked his movement. Wickman drew his S&W .40 pistol. Wickman along with six SWAT members and Dutton's team moved forward around the vehicles and began crossing the street, pistols drawn, rifles and shotguns raised to their shoulders. His right hand sliced to the right again. The second team moved right focusing on the driveway alongside the house and then the back door.

The black sponge rubber soles of the teams' leather boots made no sound. Like a troupe of black cats zipping silently across the pavement, Wickman and his group tread over the curb and sidewalk, up the wooden front steps, across the porch and to the open front door. Pausing, they listened for any sounds inside. Nothing.

The captain entered first, sweeping the room with his pistol. The team followed closely behind. Bodies were everywhere. All were heavily tattooed on their torsos, neck, chest, back, arms. Tats of eagles over the letter 'M', black hands, Mexican grim reaper images, the acronym '*eMe*', and all arms had three dots-*mi vida loca,* 'my crazy life'. More than ten corpses lay strewn about in the living room alone, blood pooled in dark puddles across the flooring.

The team split up, three men breaking off to the left and down the hall to the utility room and bathroom. The other three started climbing the stairs to the second level.

"Basement?" Dutton asked.

"The team coming in the back will check that out, Steve. Houses on this street are all built in the same configuration–the door to the basement is just off the kitchen."

"God, it stinks like hell," Dutton said.

"Yeah, very distinctive. An iron-like, metallic smell of blood combined with an odor of gunpowder. It's similar to that you find at a much overused indoor shooting range."

Wickman, Dutton and the others began ambling around the room, eyeballing the dead bodies close-up. It was gruesome. Blood and other gore splattered everywhere across the walls and floor. An expletive was mumbled now and then. The SWAT members who had checked out the hallway rooms returned to join them.

"Captain, Lt. Dutton, come look at this," It was Chaz Montoya. He was standing near one corner of the room with six bodies.

"What do you have?" Dutton asked as he and Wickman walked over.

"It just struck me, sir. Every one of these dead men have been shot twice in the head. And, the two together lying out under the picture window...each of them is missing a leg and an arm. Blown right off. That one over there has his own internal organs and intestines lying next to him. His whole damn chest and abdomen has been blown out," Montoya pointed.

"Two taps in the head. That doesn't sound like the work of gang bangers, does it? I think there could have been pros involved in this," Wickman blurted out.

"Right. Sounds like professionals to me too. But what sense does that make? And, those gross wounds...that's not from firearms. Bullets alone didn't blow off those arms and legs, or rip out internal organs. Like you said, two taps to the head each? That's not my experience with gang shoot-outs. Look, there's more shell casings on the floor than Bayer has aspirin," Dutton exclaimed.

"Sergeant Suttman?" Wickman asked.

"Yes, Captain?"

"Take your guys and check out the bodies to see if all the dead had two bullet holes in the head. Also, if any more legs and arms were blown off. Guts blown out. Tell the other team to check those things as well."

"Yes, sir," Stuttman trotted away.

"Evidence is everywhere indicating weaponry with extremely high rates of fire. The door to the kitchen was almost sawed in half by one zip-stream of rounds."

"What could do that?" Dutton asked.

" An M249 SAW machine gun for one. But I don't see how gangs would get hold of those. They're a special operations item. Must be something else. Maybe the crime scene examiners and forensics will come up with an answer for that."

"Captain," Stuttman jogged back into the room.

"Yes?" Wickman asked.

"These gang-bangers were shot up bad. Some obviously died instantly from gunfire, but you're right, every one of them also had two taps in the head. Something else, too."

"What?"

"From the tats on their bodies, arms, neck, torso, back...it looks like all these dead guys are from one gang. This was one helluva lopsided gun battle. Unless...well, the attackers could have carried off their injured."

"Thanks. Yeah, that's weird, too."

Wickman, Dutton, Montoya, and Bolles walked down the hallway to take a gander at the carnage in the back rooms. It was pretty much the same situation. Minutes later, they returned to the living room, shaking their heads, with puzzled looks on their faces. All SWAT team members began to assemble in the living room.

"Still searching upstairs, Captain, but it looks clear," a black-clad SWAT member reported.

"You know, this whole damn place looks like some shot-out terrorist safe house or rebel stronghold, the kind I saw in Kabul, Damascus, maybe even Gaza. It's like a damn war zone. Except that it's not a war over an intended change in government. It's over turf, customers, needle and coke pipe houses. It's very much like the one we saw two weeks ago over in Englewood. Not quite as bad, but still similar in a lot of ways," Captain Wickman paused. He looked up at the ceiling and whiffed the air.

"Kabul? Ah, shit, I got it now."

"What?" Dutton asked.

"Now I know what the hell's been bothering me since we walked into this building! Dammit! I just couldn't put it together. Took a while to recognize it!"

"Yes?" Dutton exclaimed.

"Other than the smell of blood and a heavy odor of gunpowder, it's the fumes. The fumes." The captain glanced around at his men who began to sniff the air as well. Some turned their heads to him and nodded in agreement.

"Fumes?" Dutton asked.

"Yeah. I haven't smelled this odor since my days with the Army Rangers in Afghanistan. It's actually unmistakable."

"What...?"

"Composition C-4. Plastic explosive. The fumes. It's C-4. That's what blew off those arms and legs over there and blew that gang banger's insides out. There're probably more grisly wounds like this throughout this whole house. Whoever the attackers were, they had access to military spec explosives and they knew damn well how to use them."

"How the hell…? Gang-bangers?" Dutton was confused.

"I know. It doesn't make any sense, but I can't discount what I'm seeing and smelling either. It wasn't quite this bad at the Englewood house two weeks ago. I'll say this, though, if one of these street gangs has developed some surreptitious way, some inroad, to buy high-grade weaponry and explosives on the black market…well, this becomes a whole new ball game. And we, being the cops no less, could end up finding ourselves outgunned against these groups."

"There's gotta be some other explanation. We'll find it," Dutton said.

Stuttman approached Wickman. "Captain, Sergeant Ambrosi was clearing rooms upstairs and found one gang-banger still alive. The guy was hiding in a closet in one of the upstairs bedrooms. He was shot up pretty bad, but he had the strength to crawl in there and pull a bunch of clothes on top of him. The attackers missed him."

"Is he still alive?"

"No. He had really bad wounds, and a great loss of blood. He only lasted for a couple minutes. Tony said the guy kept repeating '*they said ritzi…back to rattin, rahtong,*' something like that. Tony wanted me to tell you what the guy was muttering."

"They?"

"Tony said it sounded like the guy meant that's what the attackers were saying. He might have been too out of it, though. He'd had lost a bunch of blood. He was dying. Like I said, he kicked off before we could move him, in just minutes. Captain, do you want me to call the crime scene team and forensics folks to come in and begin processing this place and all the bodies?"

"Yeah, go ahead. We've cleared it top to bottom. It's safe. Thanks. By the way, tell the forensics folks that Captain Wickman thinks some really strange shit went down in this house. Really strange. Ask them to examine all evidence as close as they can and tell me right away about anything unusual they find."

"Yes, sir."

"Captain, thanks for letting us tag along," Dutton said. Hudson, Montoya, and Bolles all nodded in agreement.

"Sure thing. We'll always make a point of working together on stuff like this, Steve."

"Thanks. And, please, let me know...keep me informed on whatever you find here."

"You can count on that," Wickman said. He stuck out his hand and Det. Lt. Dutton took it. The two men shook hands and turned around, heading for the front door and steps to the street.

CHAPTER 6

Old Town Alexandria
Northern Virginia

Senator Howard Sauter's navy pin stripe suit was rumpled from an early summer's stifling humidity in the Washington D.C. metro area. That, and what had been a tediously long day on Capitol Hill. Brushing disheveled hair off his forehead along with a few beads of sweat, he lumbered down King Street through a light drizzle. The droplets still lingered in the aftermath of an evening shower. He ignored the store fronts passing by on his left, just watched the sidewalk ahead. Streetlamps had flickered on an hour ago.

It was 8:00 p.m. on Thursday evening. At the last traffic light, Sauter trudged across North Union Street, his size 13 shoes leaving large tremors in the rain puddles as he splashed on through. Sauter's years as a lineman in college football at Yale had defined the size of his suits for years to come. He continued plodding down to the edge of Old Town's Potomac River harbor and marina.

The senator took a sharp left turn alongside the Torpedo Factory Art Center's walkway that lay adjacent to the river. The Chart House seafood restaurant was just ahead at the end of Cameron Street and to the right. Situated directly on the Potomac riverfront, the restaurant and its cuisine were rated excellent by all comers. The noise inside was boisterous, but in the back at the bar and along its adjoining riverside windows, things were usually somewhat more relaxed. That's where he'd asked Pete Novak to meet him.

Approaching the entrance to the Chart House at Number One Cameron Street, Sauter yanked open its shiny steel and glass front door, then wound his way around the reception counter and tables filled with chatting patrons. He headed for the area neighboring the bar's long counter. He noticed Novak seated at the last table on the row of tables to the left. Pete was wearing a white polo with a blue blazer and jeans.

Novak's face lit up. He rose from his chair, smiled, and extended his hand.

"Good to see you, Senator," Novak said.

"Same here. And, come on, Pete, why so formal… it's 'Howie', remember? After all, you're the Deputy for Operations at the Company!" Sauter said grinning as he pulled out a chair and squeezed his backside into it.

"Company? Now you sound like a spook yourself!" Novak laughed.

"Nah, I'm not cut out for your business, Pete. Never was. No, I'm a dyed-in-the-wool bureaucrat performing bureaucratic administrivia every day with 99 other bureaucrats in the Senate just like me!" Sauter heaved a laugh. "The way things are up on the Hill sure wouldn't be Plato's idea of a well-working *Republic*!" Sauter smirked.

A waiter appeared at the table's edge and looked to Sauter. "What's your pleasure, sir?"

"What are you having, Pete?"

"Red Breast Irish whiskey, twelve-year-old, single pot.

One of my guys, Dave McClure, probably my best guy, got me hooked on it."

"Well now, Red Breast Irish whiskey, that's top-notch stuff. This McClure fella does indeed know his Irish whiskey and you can tell him that came from Senator Sauter himself!" Sauter chuckled and looked up at the waiter, "Do you have Knob Creek bourbon?"

"Yes, sir, we do."

"I'll have two thumbs of that. Straight up, please."

"Yes, sir," the waiter turned on his heels and headed for the bar.

"So, Howie, how're things in Colorado? Your relationship with the governor still cozy…as golden as ever?" Novak sneered.

"Ah shit, there you go ruining my evening! Don't get me started on the governor. You know damn well how I feel about that peckerwood. Jeez," Sauter frowned.

In less than a minute, the waiter had trotted back with the senator's bourbon and placed it in front of him. The senator smiled and gave him a thumbs up. Sauter raised his glass and thrust it over towards Pete.

"To you and I, Pete, as well as to our Republican National Committee that's holding the constitutional fort together!" They grinned, clinked their glasses together, each taking a sip.

"Now, that was a toast! How about one more for the world's premier and most feared intelligence agency!" Sauter came right back. They clinked their glasses again.

"Not so loud about that, Howie," Novak grimaced and took a quick glance at the faces around the bar. No one seemed to notice.

"Oh, come on, Pete, this is Washington, D.C.," Sauter leaned forward. "Diplomats and bureaucrats like me with their hushed conversations are everywhere, both our side and on the side of those whose interests are inimical to ours! With all the embassies and consulates in this town, I'll bet that we have at least five intelligence officers from different nations in here, sitting among us at this very moment and discussing how to conquer the world."

"Okay, I admit you could be right about that...but, we still need to be cautious."

"Sure. Sorry then."

"So, how are things on the Senate Armed Services Committee?"

"Good actually, very good. We have a president who believes America needs a strong military. He's been very generous in that regard and forcefully so. Our armed forces have needed a president like this for quite some time. And you? How's Pete? The family?"

"Well enough, thanks. Next year, both our girls leave high school for college. I'm certainly happy for them, but it damn sure makes me feel old. And Sarah, I can't see how I could have deserved such a beautiful, caring woman like Sarah."

"You don't," Sauter snickered.

"What?"

"Sarah was a gift to you from God. And, that poor gal became strapped with a lifelong ministry to bring her sinner husband to the Lord. Yes, Sarah's task in life has been to bring you to Jesus!"

"Hey, I've been a good..."

"Yes, yes, yes, I know, you have. But goodness gracious, Pete, your sense of humor is badly in need of repair."

"Howie, there's not much to laugh about at Langley Center these days," Novak chuckled.

"I can certainly believe that. Pete, for over two decades

now, I've watched you being propelled up through the ranks at the Agency. It warms my heart to have witnessed it. You're a good man, and frankly, I suspect you're destined for even bigger and better things than being the DepOps at the Agency and the national underwriter of covert operations throughout this broken world. They hit the jackpot when they got you, Pete, old boy."

"Thanks. Don't make me blush. Back to you and the Senate. You wanted to meet here tonight and you said it was important. Howie, you're concerned. It's written all over you. I can see it."

"Fact is, I am concerned. More than just concerned, actually. I've noticed a significant anomaly budget-wise. Quite a large cabinet-level, interdepartmental transfer of money. What's more, I can't seem to get the access I need to take a good look at it. And dammit, I'm on the Senate Armed Services Committee, for goodness sake! Apparently, the transfer is classified. Access to the details is compartmented. I was hoping perhaps there might be a possibility, however remote, that you might have heard something...cabinet level small talk, rumors."

"Can't say that I have. Is that what's on your mind tonight?" Pete sipped his whiskey.

"Partly, but I'm not sure it's connected in any way to the second issue or that it's even a big concern. But, it's that...and gangs."

"Gangs? Street gangs–in Colorado? If that's the concern, why come to us? Why not the FBI? How could gangs within the U.S. borders affect the Agency?"

"I couldn't go to the FBI with this. The Bureau would make too big a deal of it, open an official investigation with news of it that would certainly end up leaked to media and into the public arena. I decided that, at this point anyway, it should remain close-hold."

"All right. Shoot."

"I'm specifically concerned with Denver. It's hard to get my hands on it exactly. I can't connect the dots. However, I do think that 'something is rotten in the state of Denmark' out there, and I'm not referring to *Hamlet* or Bill Shakespeare. Something's just...very off. I don't know where to go with it. I thought perhaps you could help."

"What are you referring to? What's off?"

The senator loosened his tie and took another sip of bourbon. He reached into his jacket pocket and pulled out a small plastic, zip-lock envelope.

"This," Sauter pushed the plastic envelope over to Novak.

"What is it? It's so small, tiny," Novak pulled out his reading glasses from inside the blazer. "Obviously electronic. What is it, Howie?"

"A miniature fuse. Extremely micro. Military grade, military specifications, low amperage and exceptionally fast acting. My staff researched it and I authorized them to speak discreetly with a few of their contacts in the Army. This miniature fuse activates an explosive detonator. It's not only controlled under the ITAR, but it's very highly classified. What's more, its design is primarily for use only in special operations."

"The ITAR?" Pete's eyebrows rose.

"International Traffic in Arms Regulations. The ITAR contains the U.S. Munitions List–those technologies and weaponry that have to be protected from foreign, bad actor nations. This tiny little piece of electronics is so highly classified and compartmented that it can't be shared...not even with many of our allies."

"The ITAR, right. That is interesting. What exactly is the issue with this micro fuse?"

"Detective Lieutenant Steve Dutton, chief of the Denver PD Gang Squad, gave it to me. His forensics examiners found it in a burned-out street gang house on Denver's east side that was riddled with bullet holes and lots of dead bodies...all of them gangbangers and Hispanic in ethnicity. Police forensics personnel didn't know what to make of it. So, Steve came to me with it. His Dad, Brad Dutton, is a retired U.S. Attorney who ran my last election campaign for me. Brad's a good man. His son, Steve, is just like his Dad."

"I see."

"Pete, there's no damn way that any gang member or really, any civilian, could or should be in possession of this fuse. Something's amiss here."

"I see. All right, you've got my attention. I'll have our tech folks examine it as well as the manufacturer to see if there's any known concerns."

"Thanks, Pete. Oh, and by the way, Senator Solomon Arends, he represents Pennsylvania and he likes to be called 'Solly', told me the chief of police in Philadelphia related to him in a phone call that some peculiar things were going on with street gangs there. Out of the ordinary, he said. Things they hadn't seen before. Mass shootings on a grand scale for one. Solly sits with me on the Armed Services Committee. I don't know what the police in Philadelphia are actually experiencing for him to make such a remark to me, or if there's any resemblance to what is happening in Denver, but I do find the coincidence interesting. Odd things going on in Denver for sure, and also a possibility in Philadelphia. It's perplexing."

"Howie, Senator Arends has definitely added to my interest. May I ask what specifics are with that other budget issue you mentioned that could remotely be of some connection, but may be improbably so?"

"Pete, you and I both know that some of the Defense Department's emerging black world technologies, Top-Secret, Special Access Programs, have been funded with money hidden in other departments' budgets. Like the development of the stealth fighter was, the F-117, for one example."

"Yes. It's a good technique, actually."

"Right. Well, one of my staffers who works in the legislative liaison business became aware recently that a considerable bundle of defense budget money has been skimmed, moderate cuts, from various weapon system programs and then moved internally, intradepartmental, over to the budget controlled by the Deputy Assistant Secretary of Defense for Low Intensity Conflict. It was basically peanut-butter-spread budget cuts against quite a few programs. No one program took a big enough cut to shout foul about it."

"Internal. A defense intradepartmental transfer?" Novak asked.

"Yeah, I know what you're thinking. Of course, an internal transfer wouldn't normally in and of itself be of any concern. But from what I understand, that same precise figure of funds was then transferred again into another completely different cabinet-level department. That's the part I don't figure. The Defense Department is now and has always been protective of its budgetary resources. This is highly unusual. It wasn't billions of dollars, but still, when aggregated, it's a lot of money. What's also bothering the hell out of me is that I can't get the access to the details. My request has been blocked and repeatedly so, and like I said, I'm on the damn Senate Armed Services Committee! I've been told that the transfer involved is highly classified, that it was not to a defense program, and therefore I don't have a need to know. That really pisses me off!"

"Interesting. Do you happen to know what department all the money went to?"

"Yes, it wasn't easy, but I have been able to ascertain that. Homeland Security. FEMA. Some program called the 'RTC'. Ever hear of it?"

"FEMA? Huh…and no, I haven't heard of anything named the RTC. Who runs FEMA now? Howie, do you know who's making this happen, the transfers? Who's pulling the strings and also has the authority to sign the paperwork?"

"George Stiles runs FEMA. I don't really know anything about Stiles though. But as to who's machinating all this… General George S. Blanton. Loudmouth Blanton. You know, in a lot of ways, Blanton reminds me of all the stories I'd read years ago about the way too outspoken George S. Patton, Jr. Patton was indeed one helluva combat leader, but President Truman had to finally take care of him to keep his mouth shut, especially regarding Stalin. Patton grew too public about his concerns."

"Truman had to finally…? Come on, that was an accident. A truck hit his staff car over in Europe. An accident."

"So, you say. However, it's not what I've been hearing about some new evidence recently being disclosed. Anyway, Blanton openly challenges the president on foreign policy and he does it often. What's more, the Army has just recently moved General Blanton from SOCOM down in Florida up to the Pentagon. He's assigned to the Army Secretariat now, and as such, he has his hands on budgetary issues. He's the one pulling the strings.

"I see."

"And get this, Leonard Hoerner, 'Larry' to those who

know him, Deputy Assistant Secretary of Defense for Low Intensity Conflict, and General George Blanton are West Point classmates. Close friends. Go figure. I don't like what I'm seeing and hearing even a little bit, but I just can't put the 'why' of all the pieces together in this puzzle."

"I see your concern here. Hmmm...shit."

"Double-shit, actually. A large bucket of funding is involved here, Pete, and General Blanton is manipulating the budget cuts and transfers. The bastard continually and publicly states that the President's foreign policies with Russia, China, North Korea, and Iran are greatly increasing our risk of war, major armed conflict. But this stuff...I just want to know why? Find out just what the hell is going on? It's keeping me awake at night."

"Howie, truth is, I don't care for General Blanton's antics either. He has absolutely no freaking business verbally attacking his Commander-in-Chief. Thanks, I'm with you on this. I'll take it to Jack Barrett tomorrow morning. Jack will decide if our tech guys should get a start on analyzing the fuse."

"Pete, thank you so much for listening. With your help, I do believe that one way or another, we can get to the bottom of all this. You know that quote from scripture that you spooks have carved in that marble wall in your lobby? I believe it's from John 8:32, "Then you will know the truth, and the truth shall set you free". Well, here's to you, me, and the never-ending battle for truth, justice, and the American way."

They raised their glasses, each smiling as they took a sip.

CHAPTER 7

Jack Barrett, Director of Central Intelligence, the DCI as he was known in the Intelligence Community, shifted uncomfortably in his leather chair. He winced slightly at the pain. Barrett had spent a great deal of time in his younger years riding horses with English tack and jumping cavaletti poles in many competitions in and around Chagrin Falls and Hunting Valley, Ohio.

Along with Jack's favorite youthful pastime came hundreds of hours of practice and with that, lots and lots of falls into the peat pits. Years later, he gained a painful awareness of his resulting spinal compression and developing degenerative disc disease. A bad back, a really bad back. He reached for his mug of coffee, all the while gazing at his deputy, Pete Novak.

"How're Dave and Karen McClure doing? Is she liking the new work?"

"As I think you know, Dave's been here at Langley for several months now. He left Europe right about Christmas. He's been doing some analysis work for us ever since. McClure's good, really good. And, Karen's fine. She's said she likes the core collection work, but she also says she's had two really strange assignments as well. Strange as to why we were involved in the first place. In January, she headed down to

Florida...something about the Inland Waterway, the Indian River. Truth is, it sounded like some *XFiles* episode."

"*XFiles*...ah, no, Pete, that would definitely be the FBI, not us," Barrett grinned. "Yes, I remember her trip there. What did that turn out to be exactly?"

"Ah, it turned out that it was some guy with a one-man submarine he'd constructed. He was spending nights trolling up and down the waterway with underwater lights on to scan the river bottom and photograph the nocturnal activities of manatees. Bizarre indeed. The local police and Coast Guard ended up handling it. With the Indian River having access to the open ocean, the guy needed a boating license that he didn't have," Novak chuckled. "Anyway, I'm glad that schedule-wise, being together again is working out well for them. I know they're not exactly newlyweds anymore, but, well..."

"I understand. Thanks for bringing me up to date on them. As for Florida, at the time, it sounded like we needed to send someone down there to take a cursory look and Karen drew the short straw. We wanted to be sure it wasn't something else. She did exactly what needed to be done. Now, switching subjects–can you tell me the latest on the Vaihingen investigation?"

"Yes. McClure said there were no hits. Nobody, military or Army civilian, ended up fitting what we already know about this mole. The BundesKriminalAmt had nothing new or useful to offer him either. Dave did say there's a chance the subject could be assigned at Headquarters USAEUR in Wiesbaden, that's U.S. Army Europe. Back in 2012, the Army moved everything from their longtime location in Heidelberg to the new Clay Kaserne in Wiesbaden. He said they did determine that some of the data markings employed at USAREUR are also identical with those used at USEUCOM in Vaihingen."

"That's interesting. Perhaps a good lead."

"So, after the necessary analysis of the files they'd scanned during several nights of risky nocturnal entry operations, the investigative team and their tech support moved to Wiesbaden to look at possibilities there. McClure's eager to rejoin them. He wants to, as he's said, 'catch this sonofabitch' and bring the espionage investigation to a successful conclusion…an apprehension followed by a trial for treason."

"I'm sure he is. Dave's a go-getter. I'm glad we have him back at the Agency. Good again, thanks. I like hearing that we're still engaged in the investigation, staying on it, and have another investigative vector to pursue. That blurry photo of the mole's brush contact with who is presumed his Russian case officer in Munich didn't give us anything definitive. Who knows what he passed; how much damage was delivered in that one singular brush alone?"

"What are your thoughts about the information from Senator Sauter?" Pete asked.

"As for what the Senator shared with you, the street gang issue, part of me is not convinced that this is something that we, the Agency, should be involved in. There's no foreign intelligence involvement so far that I can discern. I do seem to remember something like this being discussed at a nighttime meeting that you and I attended at the White House back in December. If I recall, we left early on in the evening…only sketchy details remain in my memory lobes, though. Hell, I may be getting too old for this job. Something tells me I'll be looking at retirement soon. Nevertheless, I'm not sure that meeting is directly related. The bottom-line then was I saw no need for our involvement."

"Okay."

"Hold on. On the other hand, though, I can't say the Senator's information doesn't bother me. It does. I certainly don't like the connection between General George Blanton and Deputy Assistant Secretary Larry Hoerner on the budget funds transfer either. That's more than a little troublesome. To top it off, according to Senator Sauter, there's ongoing intentional blocking of a senior senator on the Senate Armed Services Committee from gaining any information at all about the transfer. As for General Blanton, I don't know why the hell the Secretary of Army hasn't court-martialed that bastard yet for his disgraceful public statements about the president's foreign policies."

"I agree. Thanks, Pete. The device?"

"Right, the electronic fuse. I'm having our tech folks down in the lab take a look at it as well as the manufacturer. While we're at it, I'll initiate some discreet, low level inquiries regarding the general. I may also ask Mr. Deputy Assistant Secretary Larry Hoerner to come and pay me a visit here at Langley. I don't think Hoerner's ever been up here. Who knows? He may find the invitation intriguing. Oh, and I think I'll invite Jim Owens over at Homeland Security out to lunch too...tell him I just want to discuss a couple things. Get his opinion. Jim was at the same White House meeting back in December. My instinct also tells me that for due diligence, we should send someone out to have a chat with this Detective Lieutenant Steve Dutton in Denver. Dave McClure's my choice to go. Give Dave a little more time to spend with Karen, then have him fly out."

"Jack, Dave wants to go back to Europe. He's biting at the bit."

"Of course, he does. But you and I both know that Dave McClure has a surreal, almost uncanny ability to dive into something, mix things up a bit, and in the process, resolve them. Things that we end up wanting to be involved in anyway. For instance, the Iran–Russia nuclear ICBM warhead incident in the Wrangell-St. Elias Wilderness up in Alaska... that damn thing was a doozy. Our deep black *Meridian* system ended up being employed in that one. Then, what turned out to be a bloody Russian drone sub and Spetsnaz team operation up in Maine. Yeah, McClure has a sixth sense for such things. So, I'd really like to have him pursue the lead in Denver. Have him fly out there and talk to Detective Dutton. Nose around. If there's anything worthwhile to continue our pursuit in this, I'm convinced that Dave will find it. Agree?"

"Well, you certainly hit the nail on the head with Dave's ability to tumble into things, the details of which we end up wanting to have revealed anyway. As a matter of fact, I think it's quite possible Dave could end up more interested in the possibilities that this Denver mystery could ultimately offer."

"Great. Thanks, Pete. And you know, we're still planning on the usual July 4th picnic for the senior staff at my place. We'll expect you and Sarah."

"Count on that. Have a great day, Jack," Novak pushed himself up from the seat, leaned over and shook hands with Barrett who flinched at a back spasm as he rose from his seat.

Mid-morning on the following Wednesday, the phone rang at the McClures' two story brick residence on Pumphrey Drive in Fairfax, Virginia. Karen McClure picked it up in the kitchen.

"Hello?"

"Karen, Pete Novak. Is Dave around?"

"He's in the garage, Mr. Novak. I'll go get him for you."

Novak heard the phone click as it was laid on the granite countertop. Several minutes passed, then McClure picked up.

"Hi Pete."

"You and Karen enjoying the time together? You doing okay?"

"Oh yeah, immensely. Karen and I...well, it's wonderful being able to be together like this. Have no fear though, in my spare time, I'm picking out the stuff I need to pack for Europe."

"Dave, that's why I'm calling this morning. You're not going back to Europe. Jack Barrett's orders."

"What? Pete, I want to wrap this damn spy up. I have a feeling that we may be closer than ever to nailing him in Wiesbaden."

"The DCI knows that, but he has other things in mind for you. Jack Barrett hand-picked you for this new issue."

"Seriously, what could be more important than a spy whose identity we've not uncovered? A spy who has access to Top Secret-SCI information?"

"We're going to continue to work that. No doubt about it. The team is hot on it. As I said, the DCI himself picked you for this other operation, Dave. Your comrades and their tech support in Wiesbaden will be able to handle the leads for the espionage investigation. But you, you need to go to Denver. It's actually a compliment on your abilities. We'd like to have you fly out next Monday. Is Monday too soon for you, Dave?"

"To leave on an op, no. But..."

"Come in to Langley this coming Friday and see me. I'll spin you up on what we know so far about what's going on out west."

"Mr. Novak, Denver? What could possibly be going on in Denver, smack dab in the heartland of the nation, that the

Agency could be remotely interested in? This sounds sort of strange."

"Not over an open line. This Friday. My office. See you then. And please, give my best to Karen."

"All right, I got it. Sorry for my whining. See you in your office on Friday. Thanks for the call."

They both clicked off. McClure frowned, slapping the countertop with his right palm. "Denver? What the hell?"

CHAPTER 8

Route 72 East
Raton, New Mexico

Lester Hadley steered his white 2001 Ford F-150 through the wide turn of the exit ramp off I-25 onto East Cook Avenue. The pick-up's aged but powerful 5.4L V8 hummed through the curve. After several blocks, Cook Avenue transitioned into Route 72 East. He pushed back his weathered straw Stetson and leaned over the steering wheel to glance up through the windshield. Beads of sweat dotted his forehead. The truck had no AC.

The New Mexico afternoon sun was gleaming overhead. He could feel his face begin to heat up in the sunshine. He'd saved a few dollars buying the last replacement windshield without tinted glass. Every dollar spared now and then was a good thing for the 78-year old retiree. Lester settled back in his seat. His plaid shirt wasn't tucked in, but hung loose over his hips. Under the shirt on the right side of his belt was strapped a holster securing his S&W model 686, .357 Mountain Gun. He grinned…the day was going to be a gorgeous one.

He leaned slightly right and said to Baxter, the chocolate colored lab sitting next to him on the passenger seat. "Hey

Bax, we're gonna have fun on the trail today, boy!"

The eight-year old dog turned its head, yelped, acknowledging his master, and stuck his muzzle out the window once again to catch the air blowing past.

Lester slowed the pickup down to 45 mph as he drove east on the two lane road, now paralleled on both sides by rising knolls of ground running west to east. As he cruised on, houses became sparse, and only an occasional sight by roughly twenty minutes later. They soon passed the intersection with Route 526 on the left that led into Sugarite Canyon State Park.

Minutes passed. They approached a wide, short-grass meadow on the right side of the road that he, his wife Loretta, and Bax visited often. Tall stems of orange-red paintbrush adorned the edges of the grassy field. Today however, Loretta had scheduled a quilting class in town. The old gal did so love her quilts. Loretta had discovered that she could even sell them on weekends down in Santa Fe near the plaza. That added a nice boost to the discretionary spending money in their budget every month.

"Hey Bax, wanna chase the ball? Go get the ball, Bax! Go, boy!" Lester exclaimed, grinning.

He glanced over to see the dog bark in agreement. Eyes wide, Baxter suddenly leaped over the seat into the back of the crew cab to retrieve the lime green tennis ball. Lester slowed the pickup to a crawl and pulled over on the shoulder. He reached over and opened the passenger door. Bax leaped back into the front seat and jumped out, his paws hitting the gravel with the ball in his teeth.

Dog and master now on the grass together, Lester beckoned, "Come boy, give me the ball, Bax!"

The lab trotted over and dropped the tennis ball at Lester's feet. Bax spun around and dashed out into the field. He turned and sat, waiting for the toss. The ball soaring over his head, Bax exploded into a rapid sprint. As the ball descended, he leaped into the air and snatched it in his teeth before it struck the ground. The dog darted back to Lester, dropped the ball again, and tore back into the center of the field waiting for another throw.

For nearly a half hour, the ball was tossed high in the air just beyond the lab, who excitedly grabbed it in his mouth on each occasion. Bax again dropped the ball at Lester's feet, but then dropped belly down, front legs forward in a Sphinx-like position on the grass, panting.

"Had enough, eh, boy?" Lester said.

The lab glanced up at him, still panting. Lester smiled. It was clear that the pooch was bushed and sweaty-hot to boot.

"Let's go into Sugarite Canyon and give you a swim in that nice cool Lake Maloya! Eh, boy? Maybe walk over to the other side and see if there's any antelope there? You'd like chasing some pronghorns, wouldn't you?"

Bax let out a low squeal. The lab understood the word *pronghorn*. The two of them walked leisurely back to the truck. Lester opened the passenger door and Bax jumped in. Lester climbed in the driver's seat and started the engine. After a U-turn, they headed back to Route 526 where Lester swung a hard right and entered the park road into the canyon.

Cruising down the macadam, Lester looked up at the high, steep ridges flanking the road. There'd been a terrible fire in eastern Raton back in June 2011. It was a fire so severe that it closed the interstate highway down Raton Pass.

The ridgeline to the left of them had nothing but burnt-black, ghostly trunks of trees. However, the ridgeline to the right seemed to capture every shade of green. It was full, lush with long-needle, pinion pines and undergrowth thicker than a box of toothpicks. Everywhere, wildflowers poked their blossoms out into the sun…the yellows of Golden Banner and Wall Flowers as well as the pinks and lavenders of Penstemon. The canyon had acted as a fire break, keeping the fire from creeping further south to the other ridgeline. Lester suddenly jerked the wheel left to avoid two wild turkeys running across in front of him.

"Whoa!" He blurted out, pulling the pickup back into the right lane. Bax howled out the window at the sight of the turkeys.

"Jeez. That fire was a real doozy, Bax." Lester shook his head and looked over at Bax. The lab glanced back, his head cranked sideways, not understanding.

They passed the first and smaller of the two lakes in the park, Lake Alice, on the right. It was just a small strip of a lake, but still a lake, not a pond. Five minutes later, they rounded a wooded bend in the road and saw the beginning of Lake Maloya's shoreline, a much grander body of water. Lester nodded to the park ranger, the park pass resting on the top of his left dash, then drove past the gate and across the earthen dam.

"Park rangers," Lester said in a disdainful tone. Bax growled…this he also understood. His master considered park rangers an unnecessary pain in the ass–what with all their relatively worthless rules and regulations. So, Bax the lab agreed that park rangers were something of a lesser life form, most certainly deserving of a scornful growl.

Lester circled half of the lake road, then pulled off into a shady parking spot. He joined Bax at the passenger door. Lester had a leash in his hand. *All dogs must remain on a leash…* another worthless, pain-in-the-ass regulation of the park.

"Don't worry, boy. I'll take it off you when we cross the

road and get you in the water, okay?" Lester said. Bax yelped.

The two companions crossed the park road. Lester walked Bax over to a large bush on the shoreline. He knelt down and slipped the leash off the lab's neck.

"Go ahead, Bax. Go take a swim!"

The dog jumped into the cool waters and paddled around not far from the shoreline. If it's possible that dogs can smile, Bax was surely grinning. He glanced back at Lester who pointed out to the middle of the lake. Bax gleefully turned out more toward the center and continued paddling around in broad circles with obvious enjoyment. Lester sat down on the grass, the bush to his left providing a nice umbrella-like patch of cool shade. He watched the lab swimming around to his heart's delight, then leaned back, and closed his eyes.

In what seemed to be only a few minutes later, a very wet, cool tongue lapped at his cheek. Lester's eyes batted open. Bax had already shaken most of the lake water off him, but he was still damp. The lab crouched down next to his master.

"Hey there, Bax. Would you like to walk down to the end of the lake and find that old forest road? See if there's any pronghorns mingling around that you can go bolt after? It's been a while since we've done that. You'll dry off while we walk. By the way, that wet fur of yours stinks like hell, Bax. You're overdue for a scrub. So, when we get home, bath time."

The two of them rose to their feet and began an unhurried, leisurely stroll down the side of the lake. Trees and brush were continuous all along the roadside. They reached the dead end and the road's turn-around circle. Lester turned, looking up and down the road behind them.

"Huh?" There was no sign of the old strip of broken, crumbly macadam that marked the entrance to the forest road. He traced his steps back along the forested edge of the road.

Nothing. They walked along the edge of the forest. Finally, Lester saw it.

"I'll be damned. Look here. Somebody's removed the slabs of old macadam. What's more, some of these bushes look like they've been recently planted. It's just a narrow dirt two-track now and easy to miss, Bax. Hmm, that's a wonder, ain't it?" Lester entered the woods and began a slow walk up the two-track, Bax trailing him.

"Well, Bax, the macadam may be gone, but this dirt two-track looks like it still winds up to the ridge. Some deep tread-ed tires have been going up and down too. Big truck tires. Wonder what...? The road probably still goes up to and ends just south of Horse Mesa. Let's go take a look, boy. If you see a pronghorn, go on, just go ahead and take off after it. Don't worry about me," Lester chuckled.

Lester and the lab sauntered slowly up the steep trail in the cool shade of pines and leafy trees. Lester looked to his left and right. Everything else was as he remembered it–pinion pines, scrub oak, lots of undergrowth and all kinds of flowers. Apparently, it was just that the entrance to the old forest road off the lake's perimeter road that was now concealed, and appeared purposely so. He rubbed his forehead.

When they'd gone a little over two hundred fifty yards, the lab suddenly paused in place and began growling. He moved alongside Lester, facing uphill.

"What is it, Bax? What do you hear, boy?"

Lester leaned down, then straightened up. He too heard the snaps of twigs just up ahead and off to the right. Mountain lion? Bear?

The answer came abruptly. Two men dressed in camouflage clothing stepped out onto the two-track road. Both were toting M4 rifles, the barrels pointed downward. Baxter growled again, this time with his teeth showing.

The taller man on the left spoke, his voice abrupt. "Halt. Call off your dog, mister. You may not be aware, but this is a restricted area. Civilians aren't allowed up near the mesa anymore. Not for a while anyway. It's an exercise area now. We plan to open it up again, probably in October. So please, I'm asking you, turn back. Walk back down to the lake road."

"I didn't see any signs," Lester said.

The men drew closer to within twenty feet. Baxter lurched, but Lester caught the fur on the back of this neck and pulled him to his side.

"I asked you to call off your dog, mister. If he comes at us, you'll have a dead dog. Put him on that leash you've got folded over your belt or lose him. Please," The tall man spoke again and slightly raised the muzzle of his rifle.

Lester held the palm of his right hand out. "Hey! Bax, take it easy, boy! Heel, heel!" The lab stopped snarling, looking up Lester and sat at the command.

"Better. Okay, well, you're right. There are no signs posted due to the exercise nature of the facility. The leadership doesn't want signs. That's why we're posted out here...to caution folks and turn them around if they wander too far up the forest road. Again sir, please turn back. Have a great afternoon in the park."

"Facility? What facility?"

"Sir, that's not something I can discuss with you. I can't tell you that. It's classified. So look, I need for you to turn around now and go back down to the lake. I've asked you that twice already."

"Who the fuck do you think you're talking to, huh? This is all New Mexico state park land, and I've got an annual pass to all the park areas. Period. My dog and I are taking a short hike today to see if we can find some pronghorn antelope. He loves chasing them. That's all there is to it, nothing more. So, you two just move yourselves over back into the woods and get the hell out of our way!"

"Don't press it, mister. This is a U.S. Government restricted area and you have been duly advised. Now back off! Please!"

Both men took another two steps forward, closing the gap between them and Lester even more.

"U.S. Government, my ass! This is New Mexico Sugarite Canyon State Park! That means it's state park land. Fellas, I have to say that you two idiots look like some damn militia members, right wing nutcases. And, rude assholes at that!"

Lester had enough. He reached under his shirt for the .357 magnum. In his peripheral vision, his eyes caught a brief glimmer of light higher up in the forest to his right. Binoculars? Rifle scope? This was bullshit.

Lester rapidly unsnapped the retainer and drew the revolver from its holster. He leveled it at the tall man standing in front of him whose face immediately paled. The man gradually raised the barrel of his rifle, but extremely slow. No way did he ever expect a confrontation like this.

Lester didn't hear the shot due to the acoustic suppressor at the end of the rifle's muzzle, the rifle above them on the wooded ridgeline. He never heard nor felt the bullet that struck him in the right temple and blew his brains out.

CHAPTER 9

Langley Center, McLean
Northern Virginia

Pete Novak's secretary picked up her phone and punched her intercom.

"Yes, Barb?"

"Mr. Novak, Dave McClure is here for his ten o'clock appointment, sir."

"Send him in, Barb. Thanks."

"Yes, sir."

Novak reached across his enormous fortress of mahogany and grasped his mug of coffee. He had just begun taking a sip of the steaming java when McClure walked in the door. Pete looked up and grinned.

"Have a seat young man. 'Always a pleasure to see agent McClure!" Pete said still smiling and taking another sip.

Dave settled into a leather-bottomed chair, one of four positioned in front of the massive desk. His eyes focused straight ahead.

"Coffee?" Novak asked.

"No thanks. Already had mine."

"Okay. Dave, so, why Denver?"

"Exactly. Sir, I have a gut feeling that in Wiesbaden..."

"That's not possible. You can't go back to Germany now. You need to accept that. Jack Barrett has handpicked you for this task."

"Why me?"

"Because we're totally in the dark about the situation there. It's puzzling, and I'd venture to say even mysterious. The initial information came to us from a senior U.S. Senator, so there's indeed some credibility in the information, even though perplexing. And the DCI believes, as do I, that Dave McClure has this eerie ability to get into the meat of those kind of confounding situations and come up with the right answers. To wit...Alaska and Maine."

"Thanks for the compliment. What's the central issue?"

"Street gangs."

"Street Gangs? Gangs in Denver, in the continental United States? Why would Langley be concerned about domestic street gangs? Why not FBI, ATF, DEA, ICE ...those guys?"

"Yes, they are indeed operating inside our country, I agree about that, but I doubt they're domestic. Most especially the Hispanic gangs like MS-13 and a couple others. The way I understand things is that this is not so much the gangs themselves but how their weapons technology seems to have so rapidly advanced. From an evidentiary perspective anyway, that's how it looks. New weaponry, even military spec explosive devices. State of the art. Things that gangs should in no way have access to."

"I see."

"So, who's suddenly has a means to obtain such weapons technology and how? And, furthermore, who's actually doing the killing?"

Novak went on to explain what Senator Sauter had

described: The micro-electronic fuse, extremely high rate of fire in the weaponry, and all the dead being discovered with two shots in the head.

"Were all of these Hispanic?"

"Yes. And, all the dead were apparently from just one gang. The senator said things appear to be very lopsided in the confrontations, the shootings, and the killings. No evidence left from the assaulting gangs either, way too clean. That's also intriguing, although there could have been some wounded or dead that their comrades carried away. Lieutenant Steve Dutton, chief of the Denver PD Gang Squad, gave all that to the senator. There's also another senator, Senator Solomon Arends in Philadelphia, who mentioned that the police there are seeing similar things."

"I see. Definitely interesting."

"Dave, Detective Dutton will be expecting you. Call him first and he'll pick you up at the DIA airport. He's offered to do that and that spares you renting a car. I have no idea how this will play out at all, but try to focus on anything that sounds like 'RTC'. I don't really know what RTC means. It's a long shot. One of the wounded gang-bangers in the shot-out house uttered it before he died. Just be primed for it if you hear it mentioned."

"You think I should be armed?"

"No, I don't anticipate that kind of risk, not yet. Not at this point. If you pick up another lead that would vector us to someplace else, we'll talk about that then. You're just gathering info on this trip. Nose around. However, if at any time you feel you need back-up support, don't hesitate to contact us. In any case, Dave, it may just end up that we see no need for the Agency to be involved in this at all, that law enforcement will handle it. All right?"

"Sure."

"Oh, and on the way out, see Barb. You're going out to Denver documented as FBI, and there'll also be another, second set of identity documents and pocket trash identifying you as a special agent with Immigration & Customs Enforcement–ICE. She's got the badge and credentials to give you for both IDs. There's FBI business cards with your cell phone number. You'll have business cards for your ICE identity too, also your same cell number. We're giving you the second ID, the ICE credentials, because those agents are a great deal more common down in that neck of the woods. They're all over New Mexico, Arizona and Texas in great numbers. In the event that posing as FBI might come to appear too threatening in some situations, maybe make your presence too visible, you can always instead pose as an ICE agent."

"I can understand that. Thanks."

"You've been loaded in FBI personnel files as Special Agent Dave McClure and the Regional Field Office is aware of your travel. Same with ICE, except the regional office is Albuquerque. Your ICE credentials with your photo will show you're Barry O'Keefe. If any inquiries are made about you to either the Bureau or DHS, they'll call Langley immediately. However, if anybody, especially anybody in law enforcement questions you, tell them you're FBI. That's best. If they press it–then, you'll have the badge and credentials to prove it."

"Sounds good. Thanks for the cover documentation. Who knows, sometimes those things do come in handy. I'll get the flight booked, call this police lieutenant and then fly out there in the morning."

"Great, Dave. And look, thanks for understanding and going along with the reassignment. Let me know what you find out. If it's sensitive, call me from the FBI Regional office in

Denver. They'll have a secure phone. They're in north Denver on 36th Avenue. I understand it's a really nice building. They'll be primed to support you. Oh, and say hi to Karen for me."

"Will do."

Dave rose from his seat. He exited through the wooden doors and approached Barb, executive admin assistant's desk. She smiled, nodded, and opened her center drawer.

Karen looked at Dave, her eyebrows raised. She sat across from him at the oak kitchen table. Her hands gently twirled the glass of iced tea.

"Denver. Novak and Barrett want you to go to Denver. I agree with you. That's baffling…the Agency being interested in gangs in Denver? Strange. And, you're leaving me again. Tomorrow morning?"

"Yes. I'm flying out of Dulles. United Airlines."

"I'll miss you, honey. Again. Please be careful," Karen's eyes dropped to the table.

"Sweetheart, this is real low key. I won't even need to be armed for just some information gathering. There's nothing to worry about. You know, a lot of businessmen travel a whole helluva lot more than I do. You're headed out in a week or so yourself. Where'd you say you're going?"

"Oh, I know. I just hate to see you leave. And me, that's in two weeks. I'm flying down to El Paso and the border. ICE wants me to listen in on the interrogation of an MS-13 gang member. He was caught crossing with several others in a concealed compartment under the rig of an 18-wheeler. Dogs initially sniffed out some weapons and ammo. One thing led to another and ICE discovered the compartment. Anyway, they suspect the guy knows something that could have intelligence ramifications. They'd like us to hear what he has to say."

"That sounds interesting."

"It could be. ICE thinks it is. The guy apparently came up from El Salvador. He's a 'floater' who works with the leadership there, as well as with high level contacts in Honduras and Guatemala. They would like us to go listen in. It really boils down to what the MS-13 gang member actually offers up. Personally, I think it will be just an out and back. One day."

"For your sake, I hope so. El Paso is no garden spot," Dave said.

"Well, jeez, it's gotta be better than surveilling some nutcase who's photographing manatees underwater at night in the Inland Waterway near Port St. Lucie!" A giggle escaped her lips. Her smile lingered.

Dave laughed. "Yeah, you folks in National Resources do seem to get some doozies. UFOs might be next."

Karen leaned across the table, her lips puckered. "I love you so much."

"I love you back just as much. Bunches."

Dave joined her in a warm kiss. He rose from his seat, walked around the counter, and gently pulled her to him. They embraced. Karen rested her head against his chest.

CHAPTER 10

Interstate 225
East Denver, Colorado

His eyes fixed on Exit 10 for Colfax Avenue, Detective Lieutenant Steve Dutton pulled the turn signal lever and swung the black, unmarked Ford Explorer to the right lane on I-225. McClure leaned into his passenger side seatbelt in the exit ramp's turn. The Ford SUV had been waiting at the curb when Dave walked out of the baggage claim area at Denver's DIA airport. After throwing his singular bag in the back seat, they were now driving south on the interstate 225 in what seemed like just minutes.

"Colfax Avenue?"

"Yeah. Colfax runs pretty much all the way across town east to west. You'll get to see the changing flora and fauna as we go. You'll notice that in a couple minutes, after we pass the Veteran's Administration Eastern Colorado medical complex and the Anschutz medical campus, the areas get pretty funky. Welcome to Denver, Special Agent Dave McClure," Dutton chuckled.

McClure's eyes opened wide. To their right, the towering glass and steel buildings whisked by in the window. His eyes were glued to his side window, marveling at the huge and obviously modern complex of the VA and the University of Colorado Anschutz medical campus.

"Wow. I don't think I've ever seen a medical campus so huge and cutting-edge modern as this. Steve, Denver's lucky to have such healthcare facilities."

"We are. Hey, I forgot, where did you say they have you staying?"

"The Hilton on California Street. Know it?"

"That's right, yeah, nice place. You'll be just a short, two-block walk from the 16th Street Mall and all the restaurants, bistros, coffee shops on tree-lined pedestrian walkways. Take a stroll over there. I think you'll like it."

"Sounds nice. I'll take a look, but really, I came here primarily to talk to you. To see if you can provide any other info than what Senator Sauter gave Mr. Novak."

"I understand that."

"All right, tell you what, it was a long flight and it'll be about dinnertime in an hour or so. How about it, my treat? You probably know all the best restaurants to go to. You can start filling me in over dinner."

"Well now, that's a nice offer from an affluent federal agent to a city's underpaid public servant!" Dutton laughed, "You like Italian?"

"Affluent? Come on, not close. And yes, I do like Italian."

"Good, then we'll do Maggiano's tonight. Two blocks over, then two blocks south. I think you'll like the food."

"Sounds good. Go ahead and use the hotel valet parking and I'll put it on the room tab. I'll go register, throw the bag in the room, and we can start walking over. Oh, and I think you should know that I used to live in Colorado Springs. Truth is, though, I hardly ever found either the need or the time to drive up here and wander around in Denver."

"You used to live down in the Springs? Well, small world. Cool. All right, I'll wait for you in the lobby."

"It'll just take a couple minutes."

McClure sat back, gazing at the sights as Dutton cruised along Colfax Avenue. The detective looked to be in his mid-thirties, reddish brown hair and blue-green eyes. He probably has more than just a tad of Irish heritage in him, Dave thought.

Dutton swung a right turn onto Lincoln Street, then a couple blocks up to 18th Avenue. A short jaunt over to California Street and they were pulling into the entrance at the Hilton. The Ford Explorer was courteously snatched up by a young man in valet parking as McClure and Dutton climbed out, then proceeded through the glass doors.

McClure walked briskly to the registration desk, Dutton dropped into a lounge chair in the lobby and laid his head back. Not more than five minutes later, Dutton saw McClure exit from the bank of elevators. He perked.

"Off we go," The lieutenant said as they left the lobby, turned a corner and headed toward the 16th Street Mall. "The message I received said you were FBI. That right?" Dutton asked as they sauntered along.

"Yep, about five years now. How long have you been with the department?"

"Twelve years. This is my third year as a lieutenant."

"Congrats. That's quite an achievement. College?"

"Thanks. I got my B.A. in Criminal Justice from the University of Colorado. I'm working on my master's degree part-time."

"That's super. Do you think a graduate degree will set you up for a decent shot at promotion to Captain?"

"My mentors say it will. Takes about another five years to be considered though. And, that's also based on departures, retirements, and things like that."

"Well, good luck, Steve. Married?"

"Yes."

"Like it?"

"Oh, yeah. I got lucky. A great gal, gorgeous too. You?"

"Yes. Not quite a year together yet, but I'm very happy I found her."

The two men continued chatting as they approached and walked past the tables with Maggiano's reddish colored umbrellas on the sidewalk in front. Dutton pushed through the doors. Hanging ceiling lamps were everywhere, but the restaurant's interior wasn't lit too brightly nor too dim, just a pleasant ambiance. Classy red and white checkered table cloths adorned the tables.

A tall, slim young lady with brown eyes and jet black hair curling down to her shoulders greeted them and showed them to their table. She was graceful in her walk, wearing a simple black dress, stiletto heels, and a string of pearls at her neckline. Very chic. Dutton raised his eyebrows and smiled at Dave. McClure smiled back. The two men eased into their seats.

"Good choice. This looks like a really nice place, Steve," Dave said.

"Thanks. I suspect you'll like what the menu offers too."

Dave noticed the slight bulge under the left side of Steve's sport coat. Shoulder holster.

"May I ask, what's the holster?"

"Good eyes...now I know you're law enforcement. It's a DeSantis slant rig. It's got a Colt .45 Gold Cup sitting in it. I know, I know, but no, I'm not that old fashioned. The gun was a gift from my father, so I wear it occasionally."

"Hey, I think the Colt .45 is a good weapon. Great knock-down power. I have a Beretta 92fs myself. I like the large ejection port...I've never had a stovepipe jam. And, a high capacity mag. The rate of fire is terrific. For loads, I use Speer Gold Dot. Those DeSantis slant rigs, I like those too."

"Interesting, Dave. I have a 92fs myself. I guess it's not too amazing, but I also use the Speer Gold Dot ammo. I alternate between the two pistols. Today just happened to be the Colt."

A waiter approached tableside. "Gentlemen, to drink?"

"This is my treat, Steve. So, whatever you'd like," McClure said.

"Thanks again. I'm gonna have a glass of red wine, Merlot. The Tangley Oaks, Napa Valley, please. Red just seems to go with Italian."

The waiter nodded, smiling in a knowing manner. "You sir?" He asked Steve.

"I'll have the same. Thanks."

"When he comes back, Steve, what do you recommend?"

"Well, for me, without question it's the Veal Marsala. Excellent. I'll add a side house salad."

"Sounds good. Let's do it. So, Denver's street gangs?"

"Right."

Over dinner, Dutton filled McClure in on the gang situation and how the city's turf had been divided up by the gangs for narcotics and drugs as well as some prostitution business. Drugs were the money maker though. Other than the Hispanic and Black gangs, the Russians hadn't shown up in Denver yet, but some Albanians and Asian Triads had begun to appear in small numbers. Dave nodded and soaked it all up.

"Actually, what you've described sounds like the problems

that a lot of cities have, not that I'm sluffing it off. You have more than some, and less than others. Steve, what we'd been told was that it was more about what you were seeing as far as advanced weaponry, explosives, and tactics. Things you'd not seen before."

"That's right. I'm getting to that. So you're aware, there are some other differences here in Denver. For instance, in the gang world, Denver's called *The Hub*."

"The Hub?"

"Right. Word is, Denver's just got boneheads operating here, running things with no real smarts, no leadership. So, what's happening is that the street gangs in Denver are run essentially by the larger and far better organized gangs in both L.A. and Kansas City. I assume you might have some experience in working protective security operations, you know, details like motorcades?"

"I've been in a few, yes."

"Well, the big L.A. and Kansas City gangs operate the same way. Convoys come across Nevada, New Mexico and Kansas like a protective detail's vehicular movements. They have advance cars way in front of the main body on the lookout for any police presence. Lead cars, follow cars, and chase cars also. The car or cars holding the drugs or money are in the middle. It's remarkable, actually. And no doubt about it, you had best have superior firepower and shooters if you want to intercept one of those convoys.

"Jeez, I'd never heard of that."

"Right. Neither had we until a young New Mexico County Deputy Sheriff had the unfortunate circumstance of running into one. They shot that guy to pieces. It looked like full-auto weapons were involved. And what's more, law enforcement never did catch up with the convoy. They must have altered their routes after the confrontation."

"Go on."

"Well, I know that the tiny electronic thing your tech people determined was a micro fuse, a trigger for a detonator, was slightly damaged, but we'd never seen one of those before. Tomorrow morning, I can pick you up and take you over to the shot-out gang house where that electronic micro fuse came from. You'll see the damage from the high rate-of-fire weapons and the explosives that literally blew the gangbangers apart, arms, legs, torsos. There had to have been light or heavy machine guns with extremely high rates of fire. Captain Earl Wickman, Chief of our SWAT Operations, said that it could even have been something like an M249 SAW heavy machine gun. If that's the case, it scares the hell out of me. Oh, and by the way, each of the victims had two taps in the head. What does that tell you?"

"I see where all this is going. It tells me that what you've found isn't just about gangs. There's a real possibility that we're dealing with professionals. That's even more puzzling. This and everything else you're telling me does sound unreal. I see now what you think you might be facing. One last thing…were there any survivors?"

"No. Ah, wait, yeah, they found one on the second floor who had crawled into a closet. One of my guys, Gary Stuttman, told me. The victim was only alive for a few minutes. They couldn't help him fast enough medically."

"Did he say anything at all that might be of use to you?"

"The poor bastard had lost so damn much blood, whatever he was mumbling was most likely hallucination."

"What'd Gary say the guy was mumbling?"

"'*Ritzi, back to rattin, rahtong*'–something like that. It made no sense to any of us. Apparently, he'd heard one of the attackers say that."

Dave's eyes lit up. He remembered Dutton's last words in his office.

"I see. Steve, what do you think...is it possible that the victim was saying *RTC*?"

"RTC?" Dutton paused. "I really don't know. But I suppose that in his condition, he might have meant RTC. Why? What's the significance of RTC?"

"Truth is, I can't tell you because I'm not sure what it is myself. My senior supervisory agent told me to be alert for any references to it. Whaddya say we finish up this dinner and then have a cup of coffee?" Dave smiled.

"Sounds like a plan," Steve replied, smiling.

CHAPTER 11

The Willard Intercontinental
1401 Pennsylvania Avenue
Washington, D.C.

"My, my, aren't we the posh Washingtonians! Lunch at the Willard!" DHS Director Jim Owens declared with a grin as he approached Jack Barrett's table. Barrett rose in his seat and stepped to the table's side to shake Owens' hand.

"Good to see you, Jim. Thanks very much for coming," Barrett said.

"Seriously, lunch at the Willard? Jack, I would never refuse an invitation like this? Your ticket, right?" Owens said, still chuckling.

"Indeed, sir. The premier intelligence agency on the face of the planet that we call earth is picking up the tab for this. But, hell, you're also the very much praised Director of Homeland Security, so I would suggest that this is a typical example of a Washington power lunch!" Barrett retorted.

"Much praised? By whom, may I ask?"

"Oh, give me a minute. I'll think of someone, Jim," They both laughed.

A stone's throw from the White House, the Willard Hotel,

now known as the Willard Intercontinental, was a traditional Washington D.C. landmark for decades. Its dining room, chandeliers and all, has been for years and still remains unceasingly hyped in the District's small world of 5-star restaurants. If one wanted to optimize his chances of being noticed in Washington, the Willard was one of the two places to do it. The Old Ebbitt Grill, one block over on 15th Street, was the other.

A waiter in a white shirt and black bowtie approached tableside. "Anything to drink, gentlemen?'

"Just ice water for me. I'm headed back to my desk at the office. You, Jim?" Barrett said.

"The same please. Ice water."

"So, where's your security, Jack?"

"Behind you. Four armed men seated one table over and behind us. Please, Jim, I have to caution you…no fast moves or you might very well suffer perforations in that nice steel gray suit of yours by eight or more rounds before you can say 'CIA'."

Owens laughed. "Thanks for the warning. I have slow metabolism and I'm a slow eater as well, so no problem regarding any fast moves."

"Then, enchanté, Monsieur Owens," Barrett said, amused.

"I also assume that your armored, bullet-proof Yukon Denali, the black Batmobile, is outside somewhere too, right?"

"It is. And if you don't know already, the DCI has an elevator right in his office that takes him along with his security detail down to his Yukon. From there we enter the parking garage and exit. I like that, actually. It's a nice perk," Barrett grinned. Owen's eyebrows raised.

The waiter appeared again, placing the glasses filled with ice waters before the two men. "Have you gentlemen decided on something for lunch?" He asked.

Owens spoke first. "Yes, I'll have the combination…a cup of lobster bisque and a small Caesar salad. Ask the kitchen to put a dash of sherry in the potage please." He looked over at Barrett. "Okay, just a little cheating. I love a smidgeon of sherry in my lobster bisque. It won't affect my judgement in any meetings this afternoon," Owens said, chuckling.

Barrett smiled and looked up at the waiter. "Oh, *potage*, you say…so, Monsieur Owens speaks French as well. I'll have the shrimp scampi and baked potato. And ah, no sherry anywhere, please," He winked at the waiter.

"Thank you. I'll get to it," the waiter said smiling, and turned for the kitchen.

When the waiter was several tables away, Owens looked over at Barrett. "My French isn't what it used to be, but I could still get by on a trip to Paris. So, tell me, why the lunch, Jack? What do you need?"

"Jim, about six months ago, you, I, and other senior level bureaucrats were called to a meeting with the president at the White House. The subject was street gangs," Barrett said.

"Yes, I remember. And?"

"The Attorney General, Bill Cannon, was very much against a program that you were advocating, whatever the hell it was. The program was anchored somewhere in FEMA. That I do remember. I also think there was something mentioned about three test cities, something like that. To me, it was clearly a domestic issue occurring within our borders and it sounded like some sort of government-sponsored armed action was being considered. There was no indication of foreign intelligence involvement, so I eventually asked the president to be excused. Frankly, I saw no need for the Agency's involvement. Jim, do you know whatever became of it? Did we move forward on a solution? Before I left, you were all leaning toward a solution you were saying already existed. That's about all I remember, though."

"I have to ask, why the interest now, Jack, six months later?"

"I've been queried by a senator on the Armed Services Committee about things that could be related."

"Senator Howard Sauter?" Owens interrupted.

"Yes. Howie met with Pete Novak, my deputy for operations."

"I know Pete very well. Good man. Jack, truly, I don't want to sound high-handed, but the senator is off-base. This is not a defense matter."

"I understand that. Sauter related to Pete Novak that there were some cuts to several defense programs, a peanut-butter spread of cuts, as he described it. More importantly, Howie said the money was transferred from Defense to DHS."

"All right, that's true. The funds transferred first, though, to the Deputy Assistant Secretary of Defense for Low Intensity Conflict, Leonard Hoerner's office, and then to us. Jack, all of that shift in budget funding was approved by the president himself. The president is cognizant of those actions and personally approved the budget transfer."

"Well, can you tell me…what is this program that the money funded? This…RTC?"

"RTC? Where'd you get that, Jack?"

"Sauter."

Owens frowned. "All right. The answer is that it's highly classified and also a special access required, compartmented program–SCI. I really can't discuss any details with Senator Sauter or with you, Jack."

"Hmm, as I'm certain you recall, the CIA in fact wrote the

book on classification and special access required, SAR programs, Jim. You know, the Director of Central Intelligence Directives–the DCIDs? In that vein then, what is it that you can't tell me, and why are you reluctant to do so?"

Owens paled, his brow wrinkling. "Jack, this sounds like you're putting me on a witness stand. Fact is, you, Jack Barrett, are not on the special access list. And I, Jim Owens, can't change that. If you're determined to discover details about this program, and I have to say I can't imagine why you would be, then I suggest you meet with the president himself."

"That's it?"

"Yes. It has to be. I signed a Non-Disclosure Agreement, an NDA, regarding this and I don't have the authority to release information to you regarding details of the program."

"I see. You know, this is the first time that I can recall as the DCI that I've been denied access to any fucking national program, defense, DHS, or otherwise. And, that alone bugs the shit out of me. Pardon my French, Director Owens, but that's how it feels."

"Jack, please, I don't want..."

The waiter appeared next to the table and set plates in front of Owens and Barrett. Owens lifted his fork. Barrett did not.

"I think I've lost my appetite," Barrett muttered.

Owens set his fork on the plate. "Jack, I don't want to see our friendship destroyed over this," he paused. "Okay, there are maybe some things that I think I can honestly tell you that don't specifically address the program itself. I..."

"You said honestly?"

"Yes."

"Well, Jim, they say honesty is indeed the best policy.

However, it's also true that liars prosper."

Owens' ears reddened. "That was uncalled for. You know damn well it was."

Barrett blinked. "You're right, it was. I'm sorry, I'm just... well, getting pretty damn pissed about all this. But I don't want to lose my friendship with Jim Owens either."

"Thanks. Look, just like you, I as the DHS Director have a lot of irons in the fire at any given time. Fact is, I'm not all that involved in this program, not anymore, not since it went operational. Larry Hoerner and George Stiles, my FEMA Director, pretty much run the operation. In fact, Stiles meets regularly with the President and brings him up to speed with status reports. Fact is, based on results they're seeing, the president has gone so far as to authorize expanding the program. The three test cities you mentioned will eventually grow to a total of twenty-five or so, and will grow quickly."

"Wow. Jim, that has to involve a tremendous amount of resources. But, if you're well-funded, that takes care of that. All right, I see. I am really behind the power curve on this. And, Hoerner? Why the hell is Hoerner still involved? His play in this should have stopped with the funding transfer."

"Larry has an extensive special operations background, so he's in an advisory capacity to Stiles. As is Blanton."

"Wait, did you say Blanton? General George Blanton? Seriously, tell me how Blanton got involved in this? He was reassigned from SOCOM to the Army Secretariat in the Pentagon."

"That's right, and he is assigned there and he acts in that capacity. But General Blanton's experience running SOCOM gives him more wide-ranging experience in that business than anyone else in the Army or, for that matter, anywhere in the government. I think that includes your folks. He's *the* expert in the Washington intelligence community. So, he was made an advisor to the program."

"Okay. Who appointed Blanton as an advisor to your program? Surely, it wasn't the president. I'm confident of that."

"No, it wasn't and I get your gist on that. Hoerner and Blanton, well, they sort of appointed themselves. They offered Stiles their services and George accepted."

"Appointed themselves? I see. Jim, thanks. So, this program is about utilizing special operations strategy and tactics against organized street gangs in cities across the nation. That's it in a nutshell."

"I didn't say that, and I can't go there. Please, can two old friends have lunch together? Can we do that?"

"Yes, we can," Jack reached across the table.

He and Owens shook hands and once again eyed their plates of food. Lunch was waiting for them.

"Good. Thanks, Jack," Jim Owens said, raising his fork.

CHAPTER 12

FBI Regional Field Office
Denver

Detective Dutton pulled his black Ford Explorer to the curb on East 36th Avenue. He looked over the glass and steel building and its thick white roof, then glanced at McClure.

"Wow. You feds really do have the budget money, I'll say that. That's a gorgeous facility," Dutton blurted.

"You're welcome. We're leasing it, Steve. We don't own the building. Hey, and thanks a lot for the walkthrough at the gang house this morning. What I saw pretty much reflected everything you related to me last night. It was an excellent validation though to actually go and see the damage."

"My pleasure. Dave, if all you're gonna do is make a phone call, then I'll wait out here for you, okay?"

"You sure?"

"Yeah, go ahead. It's a beautiful day."

"Thanks. It shouldn't take long," McClure turned and headed for the front doors.

The reception desk made a phone call for McClure and, in minutes, a sandy-haired young man in a blue suit and yellow tie appeared to meet him.

"Hi, Mr. McClure. I'm Sean Connolly. I'll take you upstairs. You can make your secure call from a room we have there. The elevator's over here."

McClure followed Connolly to the bank of elevators. In a minute, they stepped in. Connolly pressed the button for the second floor.

"Thank you. Are you an agent, Sean?"

"Yes, this is my second year here. I came to Denver right after graduating from the academy at Quantico. This has been it for me so far. I like it here but, well, we don't see too much action in Denver."

"It'll get better with every assignment, Sean. Don't worry about engaging in action. Eventually, you'll see more of that than you ever thought you would or even wanted to. For now, just focus on the basics."

"Thanks. It seems as though everybody tells me that."

"And, they're right," Dave paused. "So, where're you from originally?"

"The Hudson Valley, Poughkeepsie."

"Pretty there?"

"Very. I miss it a lot. I do like the mountains and the forests out here. I hike often. But I find I still miss the cool, deep green forests of Dutchess County."

"College?"

"Columbia University."

"Great school. Expensive."

"Yeah, I'm still paying for it," Connolly chortled.

"Well, ask your Special Agent-in-Charge here to lobby FBI headquarters for your next assignment to be a posting at the New York Regional Field Office, the NYO. He can do that for you. You'll only be an hour's drive or so from Poughkeepsie. And, you'll see a helluva lot more action in the Big Apple than you will here."

"That does sound cool. Thanks. The room is over here to the right, Mr. McClure," Sean replied as the elevator doors opened.

Connolly punched some numbers into the keypad and unlocked the door. As they entered, the door closed behind them with a solid *thunk*. Dave saw the logbook on a table on the left and signed in. Sean pointed to a door in the wall on the right.

"It's in there, sir. All ready to go. Just close the door behind you, pick up the phone, and the comm officer will connect you."

"Thanks. I think it'll be pretty quick. Will you be waiting for me?"

"Yes, sir. I'll be right out here."

"Thanks, Sean." McClure opened the second door and closed it behind him.

Dave spoke briefly with the communications officer and gave him the number. In seconds, he heard the phone ring. He heard a recording advising him that the line was now secure.

"Novak."

"Pete, this is Dave McClure. I'm calling from a secure phone at the FBI Regional Field Office in Denver. Amazing."

"Good to hear from you, Dave. What's amazing?"

"That here in an FBI field office I have to go into a SCIF and use a secure phone when all you have to do at Langley is pick up the phone."

"That's what encasing this whole building in a metal-glass alloy cube gets you. Run a low voltage current through it and not one single electron escapes. No emanations whatsoever. One of the perks when you work with the premier intelligence agency in the world, as I admit I've said a thousand times. How're you doing?"

"Fine, sir. Thanks. Detective Lieutenant Steve Dutton drove me up here. He's waiting outside in the car. Super guy, really. I like him."

"That's good to hear. I'll thank the Bureau for their support. So, what, if anything, have you learned?"

McClure went on to explain what Dutton had related to him over dinner the previous evening, everything about the shot-up gang house, a street gang's obvious use of full auto weaponry and sophisticated explosives. And, about Denver being known as "The Hub" in the gang world. He mentioned that all of the damage was validated in their walk-through of the house this morning.

"Good work, as usual. Did you hear anything at all about RTC?"

"Possibly. It could be a stretch though. Steve said that when they entered the still-smoking gang house in the early morning hours, one of the SWAT guys found a fatally wounded gang member in a closet on the second floor. The man lived only a few more minutes after they found him. He'd lost a tremendous amount of blood. He was mumbling words that sounded like '*ritzi, back to rattin, rahtong*', like that. They said it gave them the impression the guy was actually talking about what he'd heard the attackers say. I asked Steve if he thought it was at all possible that the guy could have been muttering 'RTC'. He said yes, it was possible, but he was really unsure. With all the loss of blood, the dying man could have just been saying something nonsensical."

"I see. Well, it's something. It might be validation...I don't know yet."

"What would you like me to do next?" McClure asked.

"I had a lunch meeting yesterday that was somewhat

fruitful. I have another meeting this afternoon that could be even more so. That's yet to be seen, though. For right now, I guess you should stay in the area. I'd hate to bring you back and then find out we have to send you somewhere out that way again soon. Why don't you rent a car and drive down to Colorado Springs? Visit some of your old haunts. I'll let you know if I learn anything else in the next day or so. There's an FBI Resident Agency, an RA, in Colorado Springs. If we need to get anything to you, we can do it there. Okay?"

"I don't know, Pete, I sort of wanted to leave the Springs and the memories there behind me."

"I understand. Then go sightsee. Drive out to Black Hawk, Vail, Aspen."

"Vail sounds nice. It's fairly close…out on I-70. I think I'll do that."

"Good. Dave, I'll stay in touch with you and let you know where we think you should go next and what the task is."

"Thanks, Pete. Then Vail, Colorado, it is. Take care."

"You too. Novak out."

After Dave signed out of the secure area, he and Connolly went back down to the lobby. Dave thanked him, wished him luck, and left the building. He walked to the black SUV and slid into the passenger seat. Dutton looked over.

"Where to?"

"Back to the Hilton, please. I have new marching orders. I'll be checking out of here tomorrow morning. Steve, thanks for everything. I really do appreciate all you've shared with me. I hope that maybe we can meet again someday, maybe even work together."

"Me too, Dave."

They swung away from the building. Dutton managed a U-turn and they headed south back to the hotel.

CHAPTER 13

Langley Center
McLean, Virginia

Jack Barrett stood at a corner window in his office, peering out over the green woods to Tysons Corner and McLean. By this hour, shoppers would be in full force at the Tysons Galleria. Upscale lunches, cocktails, and shopping at designer stores...Nieman Marcus, Saks Fifth Avenue, Saint Laurent, Coach, Gucci–all the biggies. His head turned as the intercom rang. He ambled back to his desk.

"Barrett."

"Mr. Barrett, this is Brad Felsenthal in the main lobby. Secretary Leonard Hoerner has arrived and he's checked in. Is it okay to bring him up now?"

"Brad, yes, bring him up. But since Secretary Hoerner's never been here at Langley, give the ten-minute tour on the way. You know, lobby wall memorials, glass cases, etc."

"Will do. Up in ten. Thanks, sir."

Barrett walked over to the door and grabbed his suit coat from off the hook on the back side. Navy pin stripe today. Gold necktie. Very corporate. He eased back into the chair at his desk and pushed the intercom button.

"Barb?"

"Yes, sir?"

"Do we have any iced tea out there?"

"Yes, and freshly made."

"Great. If you will, please be ready to bring a glass in for both Mr. Hoerner and myself. He's on the way up."

Minutes passed. Barrett glanced at the letter on his desk from FBI Director Bob Wilkes about some foreign counterintelligence issue. He needed to draft a reply to that…maybe later this afternoon. Soon, the door to Barrett's office edged open. Barb peeked in.

"Sir, Secretary Hoerner's here. Shall I bring him in?"

"Yes, please."

Larry Hoerner stepped inside and approached the desk, all lanky six feet two of him. He had a full head of black hair combed back with a smidgeon of gray peeking out on the sides. Hoerner was decked out in a black suit and a crisp white shirt. A shiny, checkered black and white tie topped off the look. Hoerner appeared more like a pit boss stepping out of a back room in a Las Vegas casino than a deputy assistant defense secretary at the Pentagon.

"Secretary Hoerner, it's good to see you. Thanks for coming. I was about to have a glass of freshly made iced tea. Might you be interested?" Barrett walked around his desk to shake Hoerner's hand.

"Oh, that sounds delicious. Yes, I am. Thanks," Hoerner seated himself and Barrett stepped back to his chair and eased into it. He picked up the phone and pressed intercom.

"Hi, Barb. Could you please bring in two glasses of that iced tea you just made?"

"Coming," Barb replied.

Barb was in and out of Novak's office in seconds. She

placed one glass on the short table next to Hoerner and the other in Barrett's hands.

"Larry, if I may call you that, what do you think of the building?"

"Larry's fine. Then, Jack, it's fantastic. You are very lucky to have such ultramodern, impressive facilities."

"Thanks. However, just about everything you see here fits into the functional aspects of the campus. There are no frills. But we do like the place. How's business?"

"Rolling along as always. Some days quite frenetic, others on a more even rhythm. By the way, thanks for the invitation. I've never had the opportunity to see CIA headquarters up close like this before. In a way, your whole campus is mind boggling. I passed a large dome-shaped building. What is that?"

"In fact, we do call that *The Dome*. It's sort of a theater-auditorium. We hold award ceremonies there, high end presentations, things like that."

"Again, impressive," Hoerner reached over to take a sip of his iced tea. "So, what's up? To what do I owe this honor of visiting the numero uno intelligence agency on this whole wide planet?"

"Hah! Now you sound like one of us! Larry, that is, by the way, how we see ourselves," Barrett said, pausing and gathering his thoughts. He decided that, yes, he'd go for the long shot. There was nothing to lose, was there?

"So, to answer your question, I had lunch at the Willard with Jim Owens today and I asked him about some things that I've grown curious about. In essence, Jim said you were the man to query."

"The Willard? Nice. What's the subject?"

Barrett went for it. A direct vector. "This RTC program.

Ritzi. Rahtong. The program that received the budgetary funds transfer in a spread of cuts from various defense programs. The original three so-called test cities now expanding to twenty-five. The program that you and General Blanton are advisors to. What can you tell me about those things, Larry?"

Hoerner's face abruptly paled to a fearful shade of ashen white. His left hand suddenly trembled as he reached to set the iced tea glass back on the table. He cupped his hands in this lap. Barrett didn't miss the sudden shift in body language. The room seemed unexpectedly draped in silence. Hoerner glared at Barrett. His hands moved from his lap to wrap around the ends of the arm rests, gripping them.

"Well, what can you give me, Larry?"

"How the hell…? Where'd you get this stuff…? The RTC in Raton? Did Jim Owens tell you that? Jack, look, the bottom-line is you're not on the SAR program access list. Period. I don't want to appear rude, but this is neither a defense nor an intelligence issue. It's not in your bailiwick. You more than anyone else are fully aware of how SAR programs operate. The bottom-line is that you have no need to know."

"Larry, whoa, ease up. As a matter of fact, that's what Jim Owens told me. He didn't give me any information. I heard some chatter on the Hill about it. It did involve a transfer of defense money though, right?"

"You heard it on the Hill? Senator Howard Sauter, perhaps? That transfer of funds was authorized by the President himself, including the program's expansion that you're referring to. And, other than the initial transfer of budget money itself, there is no further Defense Department involvement. None."

"Well, you're involved, right? You're in the Defense Department."

"I see. My role in this is only as an advisor. Like General

George Blanton. We're in advisory capacities only. That's based on our experience in special operations. And that's only if program personnel decide they require our services. So far, the answer to that has been no, they haven't. Right now, we're just occasional observers."

"Okay."

"Jack, really, if that's what this invitation for a visit was about, I'm going to have to disappoint you. I can't discuss any of it. The subject's too restricted. But I do have to say that it incenses me, it angers me, to hear that you already have gathered information that you're in no way cleared to possess. That's not proper at all."

"How angry does it make you, Larry?"

Hoerner stiffened in his chair. His knuckles crunched on the arms, turning white.

"Don't push. Don't push your luck on this, Jack. This isn't something for you or the bunch of spooks you employ. I'm officially advising you to stay out of it. No more prying. Enough," Hoerner growled.

Hoerner started to rise from his chair. He immediately paused in place as without warning, Barrett stood, concealing the sudden ache in his back, and leaned as far over his desk as was possible.

"You know, Larry, that's quite unfriendly of you. Threatening the Director of Central Intelligence. Now, you get this–I'm officially advising you not even to think about going there. If you say defense and intelligence aren't involved and this program, whatever the hell it is, has the president's approval, I'll buy that. Can you at least tell me who briefs the president and keeps him informed? And, how frequently that's accomplished?"

Hoerner pushed his chair back and stood. "As I've already

warned you, Mr. Barrett, this is none of your fucking business. Stay the hell out of it."

Barrett smirked. He leaned forward even further, now only a few feet from Hoerner's face.

"So, the RTC. It's near Raton, New Mexico," Barrett said.

Hoerner blinked as Barrett's voice inched up in volume from deep in his chest. Barrett snarled loudly at close range.

"Honorable Leonard Hoerner, Deputy Assistant Secretary of Defense, I suggest you listen up now and you can count on this in spades: if you ever come within even a razor's edge of threatening me again, or if I discover that you stepped just one damn centimeter over the line of the law in this program, I promise you that I will use all the resources at my disposal, all my power, to see your boney white ass in an orange prison jumpsuit! That is, out in the bright sun busting fucking rocks! Do you understand that, you peckerwood? Well, do you?"

His ears appearing like the reddest beets, Hoerner swiveled about, walked quickly to the door and, heaving it open, stormed from Barrett's office.

Jack Barrett dropped back in his seat, wincing at the pain in his back. He pressed the intercom.

"Barb, you out there? Everything okay?"

"Yes, sir. My, what happened? Secretary Hoerner just blew by me. I got up and watched until I saw him stomp over to the elevators."

"Don't worry about it, Barb. Say, do you have some Motrin? I'm all out. My back's killing me."

"Yes, sir, I'll bring you two right away."

"Bring three."

Barrett leaned slightly forward to his keyboard and struck a key. The monitor fired up. After entering his password, he brought up a search engine. He began typing the word.

"So, Raton…not *Rahtong*," he whispered to himself.

There it was–Raton, New Mexico. The little map next to the descriptive information showed it was less than ten miles from the New Mexico–Colorado border. Topographically hilly, somewhat mountainous. Immediately off I-25 and near the bottom of Raton Pass.

"Hmm…Raton," Barrett smiled.

Still fuming while winding down residential streets, Hoerner eventually made his way over to Wisconsin Avenue in his silver ultra-sleek Mercedes S 500 sedan. He took a right turn, heading north toward Chevy Chase, Bethesda and the I-495 Beltway. That would be the fastest, easiest route. He stretched his neck left then right and switched on the air conditioning, trying his best to chill out.

"Dammit. Barrett, you asshole," He grumbled quietly to himself, settling into his leather seat back. His hands eased their viselike grip on the steering wheel.

"Dare to threaten him, eh? I'll…"

Hoerner's muttering ceased at the ring of his cell phone. As he accelerated up the entrance ramp to merge onto 495, he reached over to the console and pushed the button to answer.

"Secretary Hoerner," he answered.

"What in hell's name were you doing up at the Agency, Leonard? You've got to know that nothing good can come of that!"

"Who is…?"

"Jack Barrett and Pete Novak are fucking spooks and they can't be trusted. No way. Damn, you know better! Shit! Neither of them has been authorized access to the program. They have no need to know whatsoever, DCI, DepOps or not!

You're supposed to know better, dammit!"

"What the hell? I'm being followed? Are you having me followed, Blanton? Who gave you that authority? You are grossly out-of-line!" Hoerner angrily scrunched his eyes at highway lanes ahead, merging left into the center lane."

"You should expect it, you jackass. Don't give me that out-of-line bullshit. We watch your back for your own safety. Now, what did you tell them?"

"Don't you talk to me like that, you sonofabitch. I'm a Deputy Assistant Secretary of Defense! If I say the word, I can have your ass..."

"You, Mr. Deputy Assistant Secretary, can't say shit and you can't do anything to anybody! You're way, way too damn low on the totem pole and what's more, you're too implicated. Now, listen up, dumb ass. This program is highly classified and restricted. Answer my question, what'd you tell them?"

"I told Barrett nothing! Nothing! I told him he wasn't cleared for access!"

"You told him nothing? For an hour, the two of you meet at Langley and you want me to believe that you told him nothing? I seriously doubt that. Come on, you're holding back. I thought you were smarter than this, Leonard. You're a West Pointer and now you're acting like you have shit for brains! You should never have been at Langley in the first place!"

"Blanton, I'm not holding back anything and, frankly, I've had enough of your..."

Blanton's phone clicked off.

First Barrett, now Blanton. Hoerner's knuckles turned white again as he gripped the steering wheel. Panic raced through his brain. Barrett apparently knows...he knows about the RTC and Raton, and he knows Blanton and I are involved. He said Owens didn't tell him all that. So, where...?

Damn. And, Jack Barrett's no less than the Director of Central Intelligence, the DCI. He has tremendous power and a great deal of influence with the president.

Hoerner fought against the panic chomping at his guts. He needed a drink. Maybe two. Shit, maybe three or four. And, he needed to think. He had to give this whole damn thing some serious thought. Heading south through Virginia, he maneuvered the Mercedes over into the exit lane, taking Exit 54B for Braddock Road. He would head west on Braddock to Brion's Grille at the University Mall across from the George Mason campus. They had a nice lounge. He would think and drink.

Chapter 14

Marriott Mountain Resort
Vail, Colorado

His socks and shoes lying next to the suitcase, McClure lay on the bed, sipping ice water and wiggling his toes at the cool breeze coming through the open sliding door. His fourth floor room at the Marriott Resort in Vail was just high enough to catch the pine-scented breezes flowing down from the mountains. Lots of sunshine as well.

While there were certainly more high-end restaurants in Vail, he knew he would be heading to an old favorite for dinner, Pepi Gramshammer's Gasthof restaurant. Pepi had come from Austria many years ago, started the very first ski school at Vail, and then founded the tavern-restaurant that bears his name. The jägerschnitzel and homemade spätzle noodles at Pepi's were to die for. Washed down by a Pils pale lager, it would make a perfect dinner. He could almost taste it, and he felt a pang of guilt enjoying such a pleasure without Karen nudged up next to him. He picked up his cell phone and dialed their number in Fairfax, Virginia.

"Hello?"

"Hi Sweetheart."

"Dave, oh honey, I was hoping so much that you'd call! I miss you so much. It's quiet here without you. Are you still in Colorado?"

"Yes, but not Denver...Vail. Pete told me to hold in Colorado for a day or two. He had a couple of one-on-one meetings coming up that he hoped might shed some light on this case. So, I came up to Vail. And sweetie, I do wish you were here with me. Vail and the mountains are gorgeous."

"Vail? Oh, now you're making me jealous. I wish you were here with me. Really though, I'm glad you can finally get a bit of rest and chill out some. Have any idea at all where you're going next?"

"No, I don't. Not a clue. I may not be able to tell you anyway if I have to go somewhat covert. I know you understand that. It may be a few days before I can call you again. Say, what about El Paso? You haven't been down there yet, have you?"

"It was cancelled. Apparently, somebody somehow was able to stick a shiv in the MS-13 gang member's neck. Jabbed it in several times. He bled to death."

"Damn. Sounds gruesome. Did ICE give you any idea what they wanted you to hear?"

"Yes, just tidbits though. The guy was coming up to check with the gangs in several U.S. cities to hear the details about reports of a cluster of deadly attacks. Attacks on their gang houses have apparently by men dressed in black with tactical gear. Apparently, they don't think it was police, not SWAT. The attacks were always being carried out at night, in early morning hours. That was about it."

"That does sound interesting." McClure paused in thought. "Do you have any new assignments?"

"Not yet. I've been just sitting here all by my lonesome

waiting for you to call. And, you did! Thank you. I love you bunches."

"Boy, you sure can make me feel sad. Honey, this is the life we chose. Even when you were NCIS."

"I know, and I really do understand, hon. Bad comment… forgive me. You can spank me when you get back."

"I'll look forward to that. Sounds sexy!" Dave laughed.

"Yes, it sort of does. Don't spank too hard though," Karen giggled.

"Sweetheart, if I can call, I will. Please, just bear with me."

"I will. I love you, honey," Karen said, almost in a whisper.

"I love you back. Bye for now, sweetie. Sleep tight."

"Bye, darling." They hung up.

Jack Barrett was ready to slip on his jacket and call it a day. A long day. Like all his days seemed lately. He had just signed the letter he owed back to Bob Wilkes at the Bureau when Barb peeked in through the edge of his office door.

"Mr. Barrett, Pete Novak's here. He said he needs to see you…just briefly."

"Sure, let him in, Barb."

"Hi Boss," Novak walked through the door, strode over toward the desk, and plopped in a chair.

"What's up, Pete?"

"It's probably just anecdotal at this point, but I'd thought I'd pass it on to you. I got a call about twenty minutes ago from Senator Sauter. Howie."

"Yes?"

"Two things. First, he said that Senator Sarah MacKenzie, ah, she's from Missouri, told him that the police in St. Louis are grossly confused trying to figure out what's going on with the street gangs there. Not unlike a gang war, but far worse. Same damn things that have happened in Denver and Philadelphia. Gang houses completely torn apart by heavy automatic gunfire. Explosives too."

"Damn. Denver, Philadelphia, and now St. Louis. Three cities. Cities not with huge, overwhelming gang problems, but still, serious issues. What in the Lord's name is going on in this country?"

"Right. Where do we go from here?"

"Maybe if we can find out what the hell 'RTC' and its connection to Raton means, maybe we'll lock in on it. So far, however, I have several people telling me the president has signed off on it. He approved it, whatever it is. And, if the president has both authorized it and is being kept fully informed on it, then what would be our justification for messing with it? This is becoming a kind of 'damned if we do', 'damned if we don't' situation. What was the second thing that Sauter told you?"

"Oh, he sounded almost apologetic about this part. He said that street gang crime statistics, not inter-gang violence, but gang related crimes against citizens in the drug business and prostitution in Denver have dropped off just over 41 percent in the last four months. At the same time, inter-gang violence increased during that same period...it rose something like 44 percent."

"Go on."

"The senator said he didn't give a rat's ass about that though, to just '*let them all go kill themselves*'. Sauter said he gave Senator Solomon Arends a call and Arends told him the police in Philadelphia are seeing a dramatic drop in gang related crimes against citizens as well. He said that whatever this thing is that's taking place in those cities is actually having some definite, positive impact."

"You know, it sounds like the after-effects we all saw in New York City years ago from those vigilante killings, as grisly as they were. Street crime fell off the map for a year."

"Yeah, it does, doesn't it? That never crossed my mind."

"Anything else from Sauter?"

"Not really. Again, though, he sounded almost contrite. Like he was sorry he'd involved us and asked us for assistance."

"Okay, and?'

"Yeah. So, I asked the senator if he felt we should back off on this. He said no, the issues were still there. He said a lot of people, even though they're criminal gang members, hundreds or more by now probably, are being slaughtered. It could be some new, very well organized and very well-armed, brand of vigilante group. Perhaps ex-military people. Or it's something else. He said it didn't really matter. It looked like massacre-type tactics and that's not supposed to be who we are in America. And that in spite of the precipitous drop in crime rates."

"Howie's right. I agree with him on that."

"So, Jack, we're staying on it?"

"Yes. That is, until the president himself tells me to back off. By the way, where's McClure?"

"Okay, thanks. Dave's in Colorado waiting for further orders."

"Well, with this RTC's probable connection to Raton, New Mexico, I think I'd like to send him down there. Low key. Do some collection."

"Sounds reasonable. Jack, do you think we need to get him armed up at this point?"

"Yes. In the unlikely event of a worst case situation arising, go ahead and send his pistol, mags, ammo, one of our multi-spectral camouflage suits, and a pair of night vision goggles out to him. Maybe think about including some other things, you know, binoculars, Maglite, stuff like that. Never know, he may have to do some stalking in the forest out there at night. Just in case."

"Thanks, Jack."

"Now if you don't mind, I'd like to head home for dinner. And a drink," Barrett smiled.

"Me too, as a matter of fact. I'll call Dave tonight."

"Great."

CHAPTER 15

Vail, Colorado

McClure strode along, enjoying the fresh mountain air, and just now crossing the bridge on Willow Bridge Road. He turned left onto Gore Creek Drive, a block or so away from Gramshammer's Gasthof. His cell phone rang.

"Hello," McClure said. He paused and moved to the side of the road as groups of people walked on by.

"Dave, Pete Novak."

"Hi, Pete. Orders?"

"Yes. Where are you now?"

"Vail. The Marriott Mountain Resort. It's in Lionshead, a stone's throw from the Eagle Bahn Gondola."

"Good. Dave, the Bureau FCI guys in Denver will be bringing a package to you. It will include some things for you to gear up as well as instructions on where to go."

"Pete, can you give me any idea at all where I'll be headed?'

"Well, I can tell you you'll be heading south on the interstate. It will take you right there. The best hotel is a Best Western Plus. Not bad. We'll make the reservations for you on a new VISA card we're issuing you for three nights from tonight. There's a Denny's across the road. I don't want to say more on an open line. Unfortunately, the package I'm sending out will take about another day to get out there, so go ahead and continue to enjoy yourself."

"Thanks, Pete. I really do appreciate all the support."

"You're welcome. It's what we do for our own. Dave, not to sound overdone, but I want to emphasize this is still about information gathering. That's it. Talk to the locals, the police, anybody in town who might be aware of any unusual activity? Follow your gut. See what you might be able to develop."

"Okay."

"Nevertheless, if by some chance a worst case situation arises, you'll be prepared with what I'm sending out. I don't expect things to get dicey, not at this point. And I sure as hell don't want to have to make any more hospital visits, okay? This isn't Alaska…or Maine," Novak chuckled.

"Jeez, Pete, you are so demanding. What you're saying is you don't want me to hurt anyone?" Dave grinned.

"That's right, or be injured yourself."

"Pete, the package. They'll bring it right to the Marriott?"

"Yes. They won't leave it for you at the desk. They'll give you a call in advance on your cell and personally hand it off to you."

"I understand. Be prepared, as you always say."

"That's right."

"Am I empowered?"

"Yes. Dave, understand this, despite all the cautionary stuff I've just related to you, Dave McClure is always empowered. That's the bottom-line. Always. And, not just for using harsh language!" Novak laughed.

"Thank you, Pete."

"We'll be waiting to hear from you. Take your time. Godspeed and check your six. Novak out."

Chapter 16

Old Town
Alexandria, Virginia

Pale light from streetlamps washed the road in a dim glow. He moved his neck to one side, then the other to shake off the wooziness. The first things he thought he heard were footsteps. Footsteps running. Running away from where he was, fading. He felt a cool breeze snake across his face. Motion. He was moving. He was sitting on a leather seat, going downward, maybe downhill. He sensed it. But, downhill to where? He could feel bumps beneath him. Road bumps? Where the hell was he?

The man's vision was blurred. He was disoriented, groggy. It was dark ahead, but there was a flickering of lights on each side as he moved past them. Streetlamps. Why couldn't he focus? Was he drunk? No, that couldn't be–he was the lightest of drinkers. All he could remember was being at Brion's Grille in Fairfax, when was that? Recent? Nothing more.

The breeze had picked up. Air was now whistling to his left and right. From where? He struggled to open his eyes and keep them open. His hands rubbed his face. He rubbed again, hard. He slapped his face with both hands. Wake up, dammit!

His hands reached forward in the dark void. There was a circular thing in front of him…a steering wheel. He grabbed it. He yanked it, jerking it side to side. It wouldn't budge. It was frozen, locked in place! A car. He's in a car? His car? Still woozy, he could make out a window next to his left shoulder. It was cracked open. That's where the wafting air was coming from.

He reached even more forward to where the dashboard should be, recognizing the position of things. Yes, he was in his own car, the Mercedes! His hands slid along the dash. There were no keys in the ignition! What? He suddenly realized there was no sound from the engine.

What time was it? Raising his arm, he looked at his watch, but in his muddled, blurry vision he couldn't recognize the numbers on the luminescent dial. The force of the air gusting in from the window had increased. He was going faster. And, straight downhill.

He jammed his right foot fiercely down on the brakes. Nothing. No screeching of brakes grabbing the pavement. His hands punched the horn on the wheel repeatedly. Nothing. No sound. Nothing!

The lights on both sides were now flashing past him rapidly. He squinted his eyes…he could almost see out the windshield. The street before him appeared as though it was approaching an end! What the hell? He jerked the door handles. Locked! He tried to unbuckle the seatbelt, but his fingers and hands had hardly any strength at all. For seconds, he struggled with the buckle. It wouldn't give.

What the hell is happening? The sedan was going fast. Way too fast. He turned his head to the slightly cracked window and pressed his lips to the open crack.

"Help! Somebody, please help me! Help me!" He screamed.

"Help me, I'm locked in my car!" He shrieked as loud as he could until his lungs felt like bursting.

His eyes began to focus. Finally. Yes, the street was ending ahead! The sedan had to be doing over 50 mph now!

"Help me…!" He sobbed, tears gathering in his eyes.

The sedan rammed into the curb at the end of the street, jolted over it and went airborne. His head hit against the ceiling. The steering wheel was still locked. The brakes were frozen. He jerked at the doors, but still…nothing!

The sedan dashed between two slender trees and sprinted across a grassy area. Ahead, he saw the backs of what looked like two benches. The Mercedes hit the bench on the left, crunching it, lifting the car's frame at the front bumper. The sedan slid a bit sideways, but the Mercedes charged forward.

There were two metal railings along a waterfront sidewalk–maybe they'll stop me. His eyes bulged in horror as the sedan smashed through both railings, flinging twisted pieces of tubular steel over the roof, some banging along the car doors. An icy, strangling fear gripped him. He was going over!

The Mercedes soared over the wall, the front of the car dipping lower as the rear lifted. The sedan flipped onto its roof as it struck the water's surface. A thunderous splash like an explosion followed, filling his ears. The car settled briefly on the surface, rolling about upside down, small waves forming and rushing away from the vehicle.

He was upside down! In the crash, his shoulder and torso had slipped through what was now a large, gaping hole in the sling of the seatbelt. Maybe, just maybe? He struggled to pull his legs through the belt across his lap. It only tightened further!

Water was rushing in, wetting his hair. A frosty chill of

river water crawled across the top of his head. The Mercedes began to sink, descending into the depths of the dark, murky water. Climbing its way down his forehead, the surface of the water in the sedan unexpectedly surged into his nostrils. He gasped, a burbling hiss emanating from his throat. He reached up and pinched his nose, stemming the flow of water. He screamed.

"Help me!" He screeched at the top of his lungs.

He struggled to pull his body up from the ceiling toward what was now the overhead floor of the sedan. No use. The steadily rising water reached his chin, streaming into his mouth, and gushing down his throat. His eyes bulged from his head in absolute terror.

Seconds passed. Slowly, a soothing darkness, a black void, enveloped him.

Jack Barrett was startled awake at his colonial home in Potomac, Maryland. The phone was ringing. He rose from the pillow, leaned on his elbow, glancing at his alarm clock. He squinted at the glowing luminescence. It was 3:45 a.m. His head wobbled as he reached out to grab the phone on the nightstand.

"Hello?" He managed in a drowsy voice.

"Jack, Pete Novak. I'm sorry for the late night call."

"Late night? Pete, it's a quarter to four in the morning. Something's happened? What? The duty officer hasn't called me."

"Yes, I know. This is not about one of ours."

"A death? Who?"

"I just got a call from Spence Wells, our National Resources Division chief here in the District."

"Yes?"

"One of his agents was notified by Alexandria police. He said there's been what so far looks like a bad accident in Old Town. On King Street. And, there was a fatality."

"Go on?"

"A guy in an upper floor apartment of a nearby building was up and getting something from his refrigerator. He heard a booming crash from down on King Street and then a large splash."

"A car went in the river?"

"Yes. Jack, they just pulled Larry Hoerner's dead body out of the Potomac."

CHAPTER 17

Fairhill, North Philadelphia Pennsylvania

Clad in black tactical clothing, the man leaned against a porch railing, an assault rifle slung over his shoulder. The muzzle was pointed downward to the wood flooring. Fatigued, he pushed the stretch cap up from his forehead, where it wrinkled against the straps of the night vision goggles. He took a deep breath of the cool early morning air. It was 3:30 a.m. The night was about over. The op had been a cakewalk this time. They caught the bastards completely by surprise, dead asleep. Now…they were all just dead.

Glancing up and down the street, he squinted at his watch. The avenue was quiet as a county morgue. His eyebrows rose as he alerted to motion at the end of the street. He stiffened in place.

Bright red, white and blue lights flashed from the roof, a vehicle was turning the corner. It was employing a silent approach, no siren, rushing up the street toward the house. The man bolted from the porch, scurried through the living room, leaping over two bullet-riddled bodies. He raced into the smoky kitchen.

"Manzetti! Where's Major Manzetti?" The man blurted out.

A man in black seated at a table in the kitchen nook looked up as he spoke. "Over here, Johnson. I'm patching up Jankowski's arm–one of these assholes apparently woke up and stuck him with a knife. I need to finish it up before we take off. What's up?"

"Cops, Major! A police car just turned the corner–he's got his lights flashing. They're coming up the street fast! Somebody must've called it in!" Johnson said.

"Shit!"

The major leaped from his seat, grabbing his assault rifle as he rose. He motioned for Jankowski to stay put.

"Jankowski, just keep pressure on the gauze!" Manzetti exclaimed.

Manzetti, Johnson and two other black-clad figures sprinted through the house and vaulted out the front door.

The blue and white police cruiser screeched into the curb, rocking on its shocks, the driver door already flung open. The uniformed driver jumped onto the sidewalk carrying a pump shotgun in his right hand. Another officer hurdled from the passenger side and sprang around the hood.

Manzetti and the other three raised their rifles. Manzetti fired immediately with no hesitation. The rest followed his lead, firing full auto. A hail of shots exploded from the sound suppressed barrels. A staccato of clicking sounds filled the air. Rounds thudded into the side of the patrol car and the officers' bodies. The two officers hadn't yet raised their weapons. Tremors shook throughout their bodies as dozens of rounds struck them from their heads to their gun belts and below.

Both officers slammed backward against the cruiser, their heads jerking violently back and forth. They slumped slowly to the sidewalk. Blood seeped down their faces and chests, pooling near the curb.

"Harper! Kean! Get the team out now! Two taps in the head on all the targets! Go! We're gone! Now!"

"Paul, what the hell? We just killed two cops. Not gang bangers…white hats, good guys! What the hell are…?"

Manzetti turned toward him, a fierce, angry look washed across his face. He stomped forward face-to-face with Johnson.

"That's right, Johnson. And you know the fucking rules, dammit…no witnesses! No witnesses, period! Nobody! It was unfortunate. But we…ah shit, it doesn't matter. Get your ass in the Yukon! We're outta here!"

Six black-clothed men, tactical gear and rifles piled into the dark blue Yukon, doors slamming. Manzetti looked over his shoulder from the front seat and conducted a quick head count.

"We got everybody! Yes. Roll, Tom!" He barked. The vehicle lurched from the curb, rapidly accelerating down the opposite end of the street.

CHAPTER 18

Interstate 25
Colorado South to New Mexico

McClure pulled his head in from the driver-side window. A bright, radiating Colorado sun shimmered overhead, a gleaming orb in an empty sapphire sky. Intensely beautiful in its own way. The air blowing in from the windows of the white Volvo XC90 rental was turning more than a tad warm. The rental agency had two of them. Dave chose the XC90 Inscription T8 with a ferocious 400 HP engine. He had to admit he liked vehicles with powerful engines…you never know when you might need that extra horsepower, he thought. He hadn't switched on the AC yet. He was so close to the destination, he was hoping he might not have to.

His eyes gazed through the windshield, the dashed highway lines to his left and the straight line marking the shoulder to his right disappeared ahead into the distance, seemingly never ending. His thoughts wandered. Images of Anne, the first woman he had ever loved, and Michael, the son he knew he would never forget, began to flutter across his mind from some dark, cobwebbed corner. His eyes grew misty.

It had been a freak accident in late autumn that snapped

his beloved wife's and son's lives short. They were driving back on I-70 from a soccer game in Grand Junction, Colorado. A micro blizzard materialized out of nowhere as they sometimes do in the Colorado Rockies–snowing, sleeting, skies rapidly darkening. The interstate highway through the mountains was icing, and growing so slick that an 18-wheeler couldn't hold the road on a curve. It blasted through the median and smashed into the 4Runner. Anne and Michael didn't have a chance. It took them both.

Dave had been in Cleveland running leads on a domestic terrorism investigation when the call came from Langley's operations center. He remembered the phone falling from his shaking hands. He remembered jerking out a trashcan from under the desk and then vomiting his guts into it.

It wasn't long after the funeral when the dead nights, dead days, dead weeks and months came. Until the operation in Alaska. The savage battle for survival he'd fought there had somehow helped him to begin letting go. He began to leave behind the horror of losing Anne and Michael. The ferocity of the clash in the arctic wilderness helped him to refocus.

Nearly two years later, he met Karen in Bar Harbor, Maine, just before he returned to the Agency. They'd each suffered a tragic loss, Karen having lost her husband in Afghanistan, and together, what was a simple attraction turned into a fervent love for both of them. It was something neither had any real hopes of ever happening again. Even though he loved Karen and their new life together, Dave would never, could never, forget Anne and Michael. His nightmarish dreams were long gone now, but cherished memories of them still resided in him. Their smiling faces appeared to him so vividly that he knew in his soul his love for them would never leave him. He shook his head and stared out to the road ahead.

He glanced at the clock on the dash. It had been nearly six hours of driving from Vail, although truthfully, it wasn't all that monotonous. An occasional thing or two of interest appeared along the way that he was seeing for the first time. He'd just driven past Trinidad, Colorado. The New Mexico border was just ahead and then, less than ten miles after that, the small township of Raton. Dave smiled in relief.

The FBI had delivered the package from Novak as promised. It contained his Beretta, three mags, and two 50-round boxes of Speer Gold Dot 9mm +P jacketed hollow-point ammo, his favorite. The package also included a light Kevlar vest, a set of Nikon binoculars, a thick metal-gripped SOG knife, a Taser, a small Maglite and a new VISA card. Dave was surprised only by the Taser…well, he decided, there may be a use for it.

To Dave's surprise, they also included a Kevlar-lined multi-spectral camouflage suit with a pair of night vision goggles, just like the ones he'd used in Maine. The suit has refraction capability–it bent light in both the visible and infrared, thermal spectrums. It cooled and concealed body heat. No one could actually *see* the wearer, not at all, that is, unless the wearer moved, and even then, they could only see movement. A remarkable piece of technology.

Dave's face creased in smile as he saw a highway sign rapidly approaching reading: '*Welcome to New Mexico, Land of Enchantment.*' The next sign immediately after it indicated Raton was only seven miles ahead. Not two hundred yards behind the sign and pulled over snug on the shoulder were two black sedans with orange lettering across the trunk and along the sides...New Mexico State Patrol. It was a good spot for a speed trap. Dave smiled as he cruised past them.

Exit 451 was coming up, Clayton Road. He'd turn right,

then west. The Best Western would be on his left and Denny's on his right. He swung the Volvo around the exit ramp. No traffic coming his way, so Dave turned right on Clayton and moved into the left lane. There it was. It appeared a bit more stylish than the Best Westerns he'd seen in the past. It flaunted a chic concave, translucent roof over the entrance. Nice.

He walked through the double glass doors, his suitcase in tow. It was a large lobby. The stone-faced reception desk was straight ahead. He paused as he walked through, passing a magnificent wood carving of a Native American Indian wearing an eagle suit on his shoulders. It caught his attention. Some fifteen feet high, the statue was carved, varnished and polished handsomely. A magnificent piece of sculpture.

"May I help you?" The receptionist asked politely, her eyes devilishly scanning his physique from head to waist. She smiled, standing across the counter from him. Dave guessed about 5′ 6″…blond, blue eyes, attractive.

"Thanks. Dave McClure. I have reservations."

As she tapped away on the keyboard, he glanced to his right. A hallway and sign were prominent for Mulligan's, the hotel restaurant.

"Yes, Mr. McClure, you have four nights reserved, a King bed room. It's on our second floor."

"How's your restaurant, Mulligan's, Miss, uh?"

"I'm Sherilynn. Sherilynn Kosko. I like to go by 'Sheryl' though. Seriously, Mulligan's is the best you'll find in Raton and that's not an advertising pitch. It really is. I recommend the fish & chips…it's my favorite. It has a nice bar too. By the way, in case you didn't know, we have a breakfast buffet that's on the house. It comes with the room."

"Thanks, sounds great. You have an interesting name, Ms. Kosko. And that's a nice touch with the free buffet breakfast.

Sheryl, can you tell me, are they open for a late lunch or early dinner? I'm starved."

"Yes, they opened fifteen minutes ago at 4:00 p.m. They're open until 9:00."

"Great, thanks again."

Sheryl processed McClure's credit card and gave him his room sweep card. She smiled at him intermittently.

Dave thanked her and swiveled about, eyeing the restaurant once again. His stomach was grumbling. isHe hadn't stopped for lunch along the way. And, her name…where had he heard that before, Kosko? Armenian, Ukrainian, something like that. Definitely Eastern European.

Sheryl watched him as he walked away, smiling impishly. She picked up her cell phone and punched in a number.

Dave threw his suitcase on the bed, walked into the bathroom and washed his hands. He then splashed his face with cold water. Oh, that felt good! Ten minutes later, he walked into Mulligan's, chose a seat and was immediately approached by a waiter. Good, fast service. He ordered the fish and chips that Sheryl had recommended and a Heineken to take off him the tedium of the long drive.

As he munched his dinner and worked his way through a second bottle of beer, he concluded it was too late to go anywhere, even the Police Department. Instead, he'd take a shower, maybe come back down for a drink at the bar, and then hit the sheets for the night.

First thing tomorrow, grab the breakfast buffet, and ask the front desk how to find the local police station. At that point, he'll finally get to do some work.

CHAPTER 19

Raton
New Mexico

Sheryl was right, breakfast was free and not half bad, either. A pleasant surprise. Dave wolfed down scrambled eggs, bacon, wheat toast and two cups of coffee. Even though it was free, he left a couple of bucks on the table for the wait staff. With his keys in hand, he went out to the lobby and front desk. Sheryl was there again and she grinned as he approached.

"Hi Sheryl!"

"Good morning, Mr. McClure. You remembered my name. Thank you!"

"And, you mine. I'm good with names and faces."

"I bet. I saw that your reservations were made through a U.S. Government issued business card…a high-end VISA. It didn't show exactly what agency though. Spooky."

"Nah, nothing like that. I'm with the Justice Department. I'm a research analyst working on immigration policy from a law enforcement perspective. I came here to talk to some law enforcement officers and ICE agents. And, I do a whole bunch of other administrative stuff."

"Administrative? If you say so, but I doubt that. You look as fit as James Bond, maybe even Jason Bourne," She giggled.

"Which Bond? He smirked. "No, no, really. You have me pegged completely wrong. I just work out," Dave laughed.

"Well then, good for you on working out. It seems so many men these days don't even try."

"Sheryl, can you tell me where I can find your police department?"

"For administrative stuff, huh?" Sheryl smirked. "Somehow, I don't think so."

"Yes, it really is. Like I said, I have to talk with some law enforcement folks, I just need some information."

"Well, that's what spies and counter-spies do, right? Collect information," She grinned.

"Not in the least. Believe me."

"Okay, just kidding. Go left out of our parking lot onto Clayton. Then turn right, north on 2nd Street. It's up a ways. Turn left at Savage Avenue. It's on your right…the police are in the Municipal Building."

"Specibo, Sheryl!"

"What's that, specibo?

"It means 'thank you."

"What language?"

"Russian. Maybe I should have said *aufwiedersehen* or *aurevoir*."

"Those I know…I've heard them before. German and French. You speak several languages, Dave?"

"No, just a few conversational phrases for when I travel. That's the extent of it."

"You've been to Russia?"

"Oh, no. I just thought maybe your name, Kosko, was a derivative of Armenian, Ukrainian, maybe Russian."

"I don't think so. My great grandfather was Polish. He came over in the early 1900s. I wouldn't know that word you used. Anyway, good luck, Dave," she said.

McClure gave her a big smile, turned and walked to the front doors.

Her eyes followed him until he disappeared into the parking lot. Sheryl's cell phone was once again in her hand.

Dave drove the white Volvo north up 2nd Street and at what seemed to be near the edge of the town, he turned left on Savage Avenue. The Raton Municipal Building at number 224 Savage Avenue was a one story, white building. Black lettering across the front wall read: '*Police / Communications / Informatio_*' with the 'n' at the end missing. The building was in obvious need of some repairs.

The entrance to the police department was at the left end of the building. Dave walked through the exterior door, then another. What looked to be a woman in her forties or so approached him.

"Hi, can I help you?"

"Yes, I'm Dave McClure, FBI." He flashed his badge and credentials case. "Can I talk to one of your officers? I just need some information. It won't take long."

"Actually, they're all out on patrol. The chief's on vacation. The only one here besides me right now is Lou Carmello. Lou's our dispatcher."

"That'll probably work, if he can spare a minute or two."

"Let me go get him. I'll watch the phones and radio for a while as you two talk."

"Thanks very much," Dave said. A dispatcher? That might actually be better. He sees all law enforcement calls in Raton.

Lou Carmello walked out and joined him in the hallway. He looked fifty-ish, balding and about five foot eight.

"Mr. McClure. You're FBI? May I see your credentials, please."

"Sure," Dave once again flashed his credential case.

"Thanks. What do you need? By the way, I'm Lou...Lou Carmello," he said. Lou stuck out his hand and Dave grasped it.

"Pleased to meet you, Lou. Well, we're dealing with very general information. We've heard that there's been some unusual activity down here."

"Like what, exactly?"

"I guess it could be anything from large groups of men coming through town. Men who look like military folks would–short haircuts, well built, you know, and quite a few of them at that."

"That's an odd question, really, and I have to say the answer is 'no'. We have the usual bar fights, domestic abuse calls, an occasional knifing or a weapon discharge, but that's about it. Nothing outside the norm lately."

"Okay. I wish I could be more specific, but..."

"Say, I forgot. We did have a death case recently. Weird one, actually. A local man, retired. I think the sheriff's office is still calling it a homicide, but as far as I know, they don't have any suspects or good leads yet. I heard the old guy was shot in the head with a high powered rifle round."

"Where'd they find him? Not that I know much about Raton. What direction?"

"West on Route 555. Way, way out. That road eventually narrows down to nothing and finally ends. From what I think one of the deputies told me, the man was lying next to his truck, an old Ford F-150."

"Huh, interesting. One of the deputies? Lou, the police department didn't have jurisdiction?"

"No, Dave, we're a small town with a small department. The Colfax County Sheriff's office has that case. They're far better manned. Bigger budget, a lot bigger."

"Lou, thanks very much for taking the time to chat. I was headed to the sheriff's office anyway. How do I get there?"

"You just need to go back to 2nd Street and follow it all the way south. It's the Colfax County Judicial Center. A real nice facility. They're at 1413 South 2nd Street. It'll be on your left. There are signs. You can't miss it, really."

"Mr. Carmello, thank you very much. Have a great day," Dave said, sticking out his hand and Lou took it.

"You too. Anything for the Feds!" He laughed.

McClure sat in the front seat of the Volvo, jingling his keys. So, the Sheriff's office was all the way south on 2nd Street? That's past Clayton Road. It would be a short jaunt to the Denny's across from the hotel. A burger and fries sounded excellent. So, he took the left turn on Clayton to the restaurant.

The Denny's in Raton was the smallest Denny's restaurant he could ever remember visiting, but the lunch was more than decent. He washed lunch down with a coke. Satisfying. After paying a very reasonable tab and leaving a nice tip, he headed back to the Volvo.

CHAPTER 20

Along the way south on 2nd Street, McClure passed a myriad of small, dated-looking storefronts and the much larger Super Save Discount Foods grocery store. He might stop at the grocery store tomorrow for an apple or two and a pear. As he eventually neared what appeared to be the ending of 2nd Street, a large sign announced the Judicial Center and Sheriff's Office. He glanced to his left, then swung the Volvo into the parking lot.

The Colfax County Leon Karelitz Judicial Center was a modern looking, attractive building with a black granite exterior, white roof, and block lettering in silver across the front. The center was so striking a facility that it seemed a bit out of place in the relatively gnarled, timeworn town of Raton.

He pushed through what looked like recently polished outer glass and steel doors and then another interior door for the sheriff's office. Walking down the hallway, a counter with a glass enclosed reception desk loomed to his right. Just ahead, a hefty young man in uniform turned a corner on the right and approached him.

"Help you, sir?" He asked.

"I'd like to speak with the sheriff if that's possible. I'm SA McClure, FBI," Dave flashed his badge and credentials.

"Sheriff Wells is in his office this morning. If you'll tell me what this is about, maybe I can help you. The sheriff really values his free time. "

"And you are?"

"Deputy Lance Garvey. Pleased to meet you, Agent McClure," Garvey offered and they shook hands.

"Lance, thanks, however what I want to discuss is really only for the sheriff's ears, that is, if he can spare a few minutes."

"I see. Okay, please wait here and I'll go check," Deputy Garvey turned and stepped back around the corner from whence he came. He returned quickly.

"Mr. McClure, Sheriff Wells said to bring you right in."

"Thanks, Lance."

The two of them turned the corner and walked down a short hallway. Deputy Garvey leading, they walked into a spacious office. The office sported good-looking, light oak paneling with clusters of certificates and award plaques sprinkled across it. The sheriff was at his desk. He nodded to the deputy who departed and closed the door behind him. Sheriff Wells' four shiny silver stars adorning his collar sparkled as he rose from his seat. He extended his hand to McClure.

As Sheriff Wells approached, it was immediately obvious to Dave that Wells had not let the management end of law enforcement go to his head. The sheriff was fit and trim. His brown hair was peppered with gray specks on the sides and his piercing brown eyes were wrinkled at the corners with crow's feet. Wells looked as though he was in his mid-fifties, yet in excellent condition with a light bronze tan on his face and arms from the New Mexico sun. A model of a western lawman. A genuine smile creased the sheriff's face.

"Well now, I can't remember the last time an FBI agent walked in my office to pay me a visit! So, welcome to Colfax

County! Have a seat please, ah, Mr. McClure is it?" Wells said as Dave seated himself once again.

"Yes, Sheriff, Dave McClure."

"Okay, Dave, you can call me Frank, Frank Wells. Where you from?"

"The Denver Regional Field Office."

"I see. Well, Denver is closer than Albuquerque, so I can see the logic of you driving down here. What's up? What brings the Bureau to the rural township of Raton?"

"To tell you the truth, Frank, it's quite sketchy. The Bureau's interest comes from some information a Senator passed on to our headquarters in Washington. It was about Denver. After one lead led to another, the investigative trail took me down here. We're looking for information concerning any unusual events in the adjacent areas, people, large groups of men, events that may seem out of the ordinary."

The sheriff scratched his head. "That's certainly sketchy. I'd say even vague. Dave, to be honest, nothing really comes to mind. Raton is a small town and Colfax County hardly ever sees anything as you put it, out of the ordinary, enough to be notable anyway. Other than people passing through on the interstate, maybe staying overnight at a hotel, we just don't get any actual tourists."

"I understand that–it makes sense. This morning, I stopped by the police department up on Savage Avenue. The officers were all out on patrol, the chief on vacation, so I spoke with the dispatcher, Lou Carmello."

"I know Lou very well. He and I go fishing together occasionally. Did Lou tell you something that piqued your interest?"

"Possibly. I'm not sure if it could be related to what we may be interested in, but Lou said there was an older man killed recently, maybe a week or so ago. He added that he thought it was weird. The man was apparently shot in the head with a high powered rifle. His body was found by his pickup truck far out west on Route 555."

"Right. Damn, that slipped my mind. Lester Hadley...in his eighties and a nice fella. The caliber was .308 Winchester. The round entered his left temple at a downward angle, so the shooter was above him, perhaps on a ridgeline. Worst case would be the killer standing directly over him with the rifle, but I doubt that as there was no tattooing present on the skin around the wound. No powder burns. Colfax County has jurisdiction, but I have to say we have no damn leads whatsoever to follow up on. Whoever did it beat feet out of there and cleaned up after themselves as they left. And, I have to say that the circumstances were surely a little weird though, like Lou mentioned to you."

"How so?"

"Fact is, we found Hadley's body out to the west on Route 555 near Deer Canyon just past Canadian River. It's not a through road-it eventually ends. What makes the case more perplexing than it would be is that the old guy didn't die where we found him."

"What?"

"Some lividity was already present, not much, but it had begun. As I'm sure you know, post mortem lividity begins about two hours after death. It wasn't immediately obvious, no staining of the derma that we noted at the scene, but the county coroner found it in his examination. Also, you'd expect a bullet that pierces the cranium and plows into the brain like that would leave a large splattering of blood and brain matter. Nothing at all like that was present near the corpse. Whoever was involved in the killing of Lester Hadley, also moved his body."

"Moved the body? I wonder...why would a killer would take the extra time as well as the added risk of exposure to do that?"

"That question plagued our minds as well. Strange indeed. Maybe it was a poacher who shot Lester accidently and panicked. Hunting season doesn't begin here until late fall. So then, he ends up fleeing the scene?"

"But again, why move the body?"

"Exactly. Either way, it's a homicide. Oh, and we never did find the dog. It just, well, ole Bax disappeared."

"Dog?"

"Yeah, a dark brown Labrador Retriever named *Baxter*. When we interviewed Lester's wife, Loretta, she said he'd left the house with *Bax*, as they call the pooch, in his 2001 Ford F-150 Lariat. It was early afternoon. And, Mrs. Hadley also told us that Lester and Bax always went out east, never west. When I went over to her house to inform her, damn that's always hard to do, it was heartbreaking."

"I can imagine."

"The poor gal went nearly hysterical when we told her. Wailing, crying...jeez. Wet my eyes really good. Those two had been married for over 60 years. We brought Loretta over to the clinic here, it passes for a hospital, to have her checked and maybe give her something to calm her. They did just that. Fact is, I've been looking in on her now and then...you know, make sure she's okay."

"That's good of you, Frank. I'm sure she appreciates that somebody cares. I'm curious, why did they always go east, not west."

"Antelope. Pronghorn antelope. Loretta said that Bax loved finding them and chasing them through the hilly forest. There's hardly any antelope at all out to the west of town, but bunches of them roam to the east. That's why."

"I assume you searched both areas, east and west?"

"You know...just a minute, Dave," The sheriff picked up his phone and pressed the intercom button.

"Yes, sheriff?"

"Nancy, is Carruthers in now?"

"Yes, sir."

"Have Rich come to my office, please," Sheriff Wells hung up.

"Dave, Deputy Rich Carruthers is sort of the only detective with hands on expertise that we have here. He's fairly new to the department, but he does have enough of the skill sets we were looking for. Rich is also our liaison to the park service. He asked for that additional duty, so I gave it to him. He handled the search of the areas involved and came up with nothing useful. No clues to follow up on."

"Thanks, Frank."

The door eased open and a man appeared in a deputy's uniform. He had short, sandy hair in a military type haircut, and he was large, maybe six feet three inches, perhaps 240 pounds or so. He looked extremely fit."

"Sheriff?"

"Rich, this is Special Agent Dave McClure, FBI. He and I were just discussing Lester Hadley's death. You handled the searches, right."

"Yes, sheriff. We conducted detailed searches but didn't find anything that would be evidentiary at all. Nothing whatsoever," Carruthers said.

"Rich, the areas to the east that have pronghorn antelope. What are the roads one takes to go out in that area? I might want to take a look myself. Just drive around, take a gander at the area," McClure offered.

"The roads most usually traveled are routes 72 and 87. However, there's nothing out there to search for. We combed that area for two days straight, and meticulously so. It would be a waste of time, Mr. McClure," Carruthers replied.

"I've got some extra time. I just thought I'd..."

"I just told you there's nothing there for you to..." Carruthers interrupted.

"Rich. Easy," Sheriff Wells broke in.

"Sorry, Sheriff. I apologize, Mr. McClure. It was an extremely difficult case. And then, to come up with nothing?" Carruthers eyed McClure, assessing him.

"Thanks. That's okay, Rich. I understand. I didn't mean to challenge the effectiveness of your search procedures. I guess I'll pass on that trip out there."

"All right. Thanks, Rich. Oh, you working that domestic abuse case from last night?" Wells asked.

"Yes, sir. The wife is here now making out a statement."

"Super. Thanks."

Carruthers took a last glimpse at McClure, abruptly turned, and left the office.

"Dave, that was a bit odd, sorry. I'll talk to him later. Rich doesn't normally get that touchy."

"That's okay. At one time or another, that can happen to any of us when an investigation goes in the toilet. You said Rich was fairly new here?"

"Yep, about four months now. He came down here kind-a right out of the blue. He's from Montana. Said he was tired of the bitter cold winters and he liked small towns like ours. We were looking for someone with some investigative experience. Rich applied, and well, he's working out fine. Thanks for your understanding."

"Thanks to you for sharing that info. Frank, do you mind

if I speak with Loretta Hadley…just briefly?"

"No, not really. We've already talked with her at length. She's much better now…but I could see she's still struggling. To her credit, she's also finding some ways to deal with the loss of her husband. They were a very religious pair. I'm sure she's prayed to the Lord for peace. Loretta lives over on 4th Street, just south of Legion Drive. I forget the house number. It's across from Legion Park, the ball field. It's a two story house, porch on the second floor, and light blue with dark blue trim. It's not hard to spot."

"Thanks, Frank. Well, I guess that's about it."

"You know what, I'll give her a call and tell her that you'll be coming. That way, she won't be startled or concerned."

"That would be great, Frank. Thanks."

"Oh, Dave, and Loretta's a quilter. She's gone often on afternoons to quilting classes with a bunch of other, mostly older gals. She drives a 2007 gold Buick Lucerne. She parks it out front at the curb. If you see that car there, Loretta should be in."

"That's a lot of good info. Thanks again. Frank, it was a pleasure meeting you and chatting."

"Same here, Dave. We locals love the feds," Wells rolled his eyes and smirked. They both laughed.

McClure sat in the Volvo crumpled up against the tan leather driver's seat. He glanced out the windshield at the nearly empty parking lot. Sheriff Frank Wells was a super guy, a pro. Rich Carruthers? He hadn't made his mind up yet about him. He was touchy…either about the investigation itself that perhaps was faltering or the areas they had searched. Maybe too much so. Wells did say that wasn't Carruthers' normal disposition. Was it because this homicide investigation had gone south on him? Or something else? Dave wondered about that.

The time on the dashboard clock read 3:25 p.m. In another hour, dinner time would be upon him. It would be better to visit Loretta Hadley in the morning. He stuck the key in the ignition, and the engine fired. McClure drove the Volvo back north on 2nd Street. A thumb or two of 12-year-old Red Breast Irish Whisky with two ice cubes sounded nice.

CHAPTER 21

Thursday morning. McClure once again took advantage of the Best Western's free buffet breakfast, only this time it was waffles with maple syrup, sausage links, and a mug of hot coffee. Again, not bad. After eating, Dave walked out through the lobby to the parking lot. Sheryl wasn't at the reception desk. Probably her day off. Minutes later, driving west on Clayton Road, he swung the Volvo to the right shoulder and into the Conoco Station. Time to fill the tank.

After filling up, Dave took a right turn, north, on 2nd Street. Legion Drive was nearly as far north as Savage Avenue and the police department, but after he'd driven just a tad more than a few blocks north, he saw the street on his left. He turned down Legion Drive. The park and ball field were to his immediate left.

The next intersection was 4th Street. He turned left, south, and cruised slowly down the street. After passing a few houses, he saw the gold Buick Lucerne on the right-side curb. There was the Hadley's house, just as Sheriff Wells had described it…light blue with dark blue trim and a porch jutting out on the second floor. He pulled in behind the Buick.

McClure walked up the steps to the front door. He faced a screen door…the wooden interior door was open. It probably gets pretty damn hot here, especially with no air conditioning, he thought. He rang the bell. Again.

"Is that you, Sheriff?" asked a female voice. He could hear footsteps drawing near.

"No, Mrs. Hadley. I'm Dave McClure, FBI. Sheriff Wells said he'd give you…"

"Yes, he called me. What is it you want, Mr. McClure? I've told the deputies everything I know," Loretta Hadley walked up to the other side of the screen door. She looked concerned.

"I promise it will be just a short chat, Mrs. Hadley. To confirm a couple things. It won't take but a few minutes."

"Oh, all right. Come on in," She sighed and reached up to take a hook off the inside of the door.

"Thank you so much," Dave said as he brushed past her. He paused.

"Let's you and I walk over here to the parlor. I'll take the couch and you pick out an easy chair," Loretta said, her brow easing.

As she sank onto the couch cushions, Dave eased into a chair. It was very comfortable… probably so after years and years of use. The parlor, something that most people now refer to as the living room or even the family room, looked like a film set off the old black-and-white Mayberry RFD TV reruns he'd occasionally stumbled across while browsing through the channels. It was Aunt Bee's house with Andy and Barney Fife seated on the couch and Opie telling them about his run-in with a bully at school.

It was more than that to Dave though. As he scanned the room...wallpaper, furniture, framed photos of what were probably family members hanging from hooks on the walls, memories rushed over him. Déja vu. Loretta's parlor brought him back to years and years ago. For a fleeting moment, he could imagine he was ten years old and just stepping through the door to his grandparents' home in Chardon, out in Geauga County, Ohio. Dave's eyes were unfocused, instead he was now seeing images of Grandpa John and Grandma Millie race across his mind's eye.

"Mr. McClure?"

"Yes, I'm sorry," Dave jerked away from the daydream. "Mrs. Hadley, first..."

"You may call me Loretta, young man. You're Dave, I presume."

"Yes, ma'am. I mean, Loretta. Please know that I am so sorry for the loss of your husband," Dave said.

Loretta wore a thin, cotton print dress with a tiny flowers motif. Not unlike the wall paper, Dave mused. Her gray hair was gathered in a bun on the back of her head. It was her facial appearance that startled him. She looked gaunt, her eye sockets dark and sunken, probably from too little sleep these last nights.

"Thank you. I'm glad the FBI is interested, Dave. Make no mistake, I want whoever killed my Lester hanging in a noose. I want that man or men dead."

"Rest assured, the sheriff, the police, the FBI, we are all determined to bring Mr. Hadley's killer to justice. We will find him."

"That's good to hear. But...justice? You just find him, that's all. Then I want him dead. You must understand, Lester and I spent over 60 years together. We loved each other dearly. My husband never harmed anyone in his life. He did always wear that .357, but I can tell you he never used it or even threatened to use it against anyone."

"Loretta, your husband was armed? A .357 magnum? The sheriff didn't mention that?"

"Probably because they didn't find it. The holster neither.

They told me that. A Smith and Wesson model 686 stainless revolver. Lester said it had *Mountain Gun* etched across its 4" barrel. He kept it loaded with Federal Premium semi-jacketed, Hydra Shok rounds. Lester must have told me all that a million times. He said those rounds were 'nasty ammo' that would send any bandito threatening him to meet Jesus in a heartbeat."

"My goodness. I believe it would indeed. And, the sheriff's deputies never found the gun or the holster?"

"Nope. That's what they said. I loved that old man. Lester was the only man I ever loved."

Loretta's eyes were growing misty. She glanced downward, her hands folded in her lap, fingers interlocked.

"Loretta, I am so sorry for you."

"I do believe you're sincere in saying that, Dave. So, thank you very much," She glanced over at him, their eyes meeting.

"May I ask how old your husband was?"

"Eighty-six. He was the spring chicken in our relationship. I'm eighty-nine, so I was the older woman," She chuckled, wiping her eyes with her hands.

"The sheriff said they also never found Baxter, the Labrador retriever."

"That's right. Let me tell you, those two, man and dog, were inseparable. If Lester went outside and approached his pick-up without calling Bax, you were gonna hear a lot of barking. The two of them left that afternoon and had to have driven east like they always did. I'm sure of that. Sometimes, I went with them, but I had a quilting class that day. So, off they went, just the two of them, together. It was the last time I saw them. I feel confident that Bax is dead too. If someone acted like they were going after Lester, they would have to go through Bax first. It was that kind of relationship."

"I see. Did they tell you exactly where they found Lester and his truck?"

"Not precisely, they just said out west on Route 555. Let me tell you, that there's bullshit. Lester and Bax always went east, out Route 72, not west. Like I said, I sometimes went with them. We took the same routes every time. Always. We went into Sugarite Canyon a lot. Past Lake Alice and then to Lake Maloya, the big lake. We would drive around Lake Maloya to the end of the road, park the truck, and let Bax take a short swim."

"Lake Maloya?"

"Yes, if you drive out there, and you're on the park road, you just keep driving…the road stops at the far side of Lake Maloya. It's hard to see because of all the low brush, but one time Lester showed me that near the end of the park road, that is, if you look hard enough, there's a two-track dirt road going uphill through the forest. Again, it's hard to see, but it's there. The two-track continues all the way up to near Horse Mesa. That's where Lester would let Bax take off on his own. Bax would almost always spot some prong horn antelope and sprint after them. It was fun for us to sit and just watch."

"Good info, thanks. Did they ever use Route 87 going east at all?"

"No, it's much too big a road. Lots of residences, buildings and such. No, it was Route 72 every time, smaller and prettier scenery."

"Loretta, I think that's all I really needed to have you confirm for me. Thanks for telling me about the revolver that Lester always wore. That's interesting indeed. Thank you so very much and again, I am sorry for your loss. I promise to add you to my nightly prayers."

"That is awful sweet of you, Dave. Just meeting you like this, I think you're gonna make some gal happy when you marry."

"I am married."

"Well then, she's a lucky girl is all I can say. Please, I want you to understand this so you don't leave here feeling too bad for me. When you reach the age of Lester and I, well, you both know you love each other and will never leave each other's side. You also know that sooner or later, one of you is going to leave to join the Lord. That's the way life is. And, it could happen with no warning. We knew that and accepted it. I just wish Lester hadn't passed on the way he did, such an unnecessary, violent death. I hope he didn't feel pain. He was too good a man for that," She sniffled.

"I understand, sincerely."

"So, what I want now more than anything else is for you law enforcement professionals to find Lester's killer. Find that bastard and then let justice take him to his own meeting with Jesus. Pardon my language, please. Other than that, Dave, I'm glad you visited with me and do know that I wish...I wish you and your wife the best in life. Now go on, get outta here before I get teary."

Loretta half-smiled. She was near tears. She rose to her feet, her hands were trembling.

Dave rose from his chair. He walked over to Loretta. The old woman collapsed into his arms. She laid her head on his chest and sobbed. Dave caressed the back of her neck and gently patted her back. The grief overwhelming Loretta had risen to where it couldn't be contained. She cried for what seemed several minutes.

Loretta looked up at Dave. Their eyes met.

"My goodness, that's the first time...I've had the chance..."

She paused. "God bless you, Dave McClure. Now go on, get to work."

Her arms loosened from around his back. Dave gently released her.

"Yes, ma'am. Please, take care, Loretta," McClure blinked.

"You too. Be safe."

Dave turned to the door, looked back over his shoulder and smiled. He walked out on the porch. His eyes were wet.

Loretta Hadley stood alone in her parlor, her arms down by her side, staring at the now empty doorway. She reached up to wipe the tears trickling down her cheeks. She slowly shook her head. Loretta had a feeling she would never see that young man again.

CHAPTER 22

Langley Center
McLean, Virginia

Pete Novak fidgeted in the leather easy chair waiting for Jack Barrett to walk back to his desk from refilling his coffee cup. Pete brushed his rustled hair back from his forehead. His eyes wandered, flitting across all the framed memorabilia on the walls, photos and plaques he'd seen a thousand times before.

"You sure, Pete? No coffee?" Jack asked.

"No thanks, Jack. I'll pass. I've had my limit of caffeine… ah, wait, no, I think I will take you up on the offer."

Jack poured another mug with coffee and handed it over to Pete, now smiling.

"I guess in this business you really can't have too much coffee."

"I agree. Did you happen to see Blanton on TV last night? He was being interviewed by CNN on the seven o'clock news."

"No, I guess I missed that. He's one loud-mouthed bastard. Did he say anything new?"

"He said we need a change in Washington before we find

ourselves engulfed in a major world war. And, we need that change soon."

"I think the man's dangerous," Pete said.

"I don't know about that, but, yeah, he's definitely a pain in the ass. I don't think many people take him at all seriously."

"Perhaps," Pete raised his mug and took a sip.

"Heard back from McClure yet?" Barrett approached his desk, a mug of coffee in hand.

"No. He's in my thoughts, though. He's got a burner phone. He should be checking in soon."

"He will. What else is on your mind other than Dave McClure? Something is. I see you're twitching around in that chair a bit. If my mother were here, she would say 'you've got ants in your pants!'" Barrett chortled. "Come on, what is it?"

"I guess we've known each other too long, Jack. You've got me figured out pretty well."

"Believe me, I've had to work on that a lot. I only try to look inside someone I care about. I want to know if they're being up front with me or not, when they're concerned about something or just loving the day's sunshine. You're one of them. Most others…hell, I don't have the time or inclination. Come on, what's up?"

"A lot."

"Let me have it. What's number one on Pete Novak's hit parade today?"

"Larry Hoerner's death."

"Suicide?"

"I doubt it, Jack. Alexandria police found he had twice the alcohol limit for a DUI in his blood…sixteen percent."

"You don't think he could have boozed himself up first?"

"To drown himself in the Potomac? No. An emphatic no. Hoerner wasn't really even a drinker. Oh, he'd have a glass of wine with dinner now and then, but that was it. His wife said she couldn't understand it. Larry was happy in his job. They were happily married, no problems, nothing there. And, he was never a womanizer."

"Pete, when Hoerner and I met in my office, I pissed him off pretty good. I got very direct with him and then he got nasty with me in return. So, I got even further in his face and told him what I'd do to him if I found out he was even one centimeter over the line with the law on this RTC stuff. Maybe I made a bad mistake with that...I underestimated his fortitude. Maybe got him beyond just angry, stressed, depressed, hell, I don't know."

"Jack, I don't think that played at all. No. There's no need to even question yourself about that. You responded to his innuendo. I think it's far more likely that Hoerner was grabbed, alcohol poured down his throat until he was nonfunctional, maybe even unconscious. Oh, and get this–the door locks weren't working. A shiny new Mercedes S 500 and the door locks froze up? The wheels were locked so that the sedan was aimed straight between two young, narrow-trunk trees at the end of King Street. No, I'm not buying it. The keys weren't even in the ignition, but they did find the keys in the car."

"Pete, the electrical system, the battery...they could have shorted out when the car hit the water."

"Okay, I'll admit that's possible, but I think it's a long shot. In my estimation, Hoerner was murdered, assassinated. That's what I think, it's what I believe."

"And, the motivation?"

"It has to be somehow connected with this RTC program. The damn thing must be somehow way off the beacon. Wrongful. It's the only thing I can think of."

"I'm not accusing anyone, Pete, but have you checked on

General Blanton's whereabouts near the time of Hoerner's death? Just a wild ass guess on my part."

"Actually, that was one of the first things I thought of. And no, Blanton was gone, out of town. He'd flown to Taos, New Mexico. George Stiles went with him."

"George Stiles? Director of FEMA? He flew to Taos too, this time of year?"

"Taos has the closest airport to Raton that handles large jets."

Barrett paused in thought. "Raton. You think that's it?"

"I do. I suspect Blanton is doing a helluva lot more than just acting an advisor to this program. And George Stiles traveling with him…I don't like that either. Not at all. Dave McClure's in Raton."

"Right. Excuse me just a minute, Pete," Barrett pressed his intercom button.

"Yes, sir?"

"Barb, please get hold of Phil Reese down in Research and Analysis. Tell him I want a full bio report on General George S. Blanton. Tell Phil I want everything, residences, assignment history, warts and all. I would appreciate it a great deal if he can get it to me by one o'clock. If he can manage it."

"Yes, sir. I'll call him as soon as we disconnect."

"Well, that sounds like I've got your attention?" Novak said.

"You do. I want to find out just who George Blanton is, birthmarks and all. Pete, back to where we were. If you're guessing correctly, then damn, there he goes again. McClure. I told you. Our covert operations' agent Dave McClure always pops up where something ain't quite right. And the next thing we know, that something turns out to be pretty damn significant. Jeez, I do hope you're wrong on Raton, but it sounds credible."

"Me too, Jack. This is unlike Alaska and Maine, though... this time, we're the ones who sent him down to Raton. I'm waiting. I hope to hear from him soon."

"I'm sure you will. All right, then let's wait until McClure calls and tells you what he's come up with, if anything. Before we pass on the subject, is the Alexandria police department making any progress at all investigating Hoerner's death? Have you heard anything about that? And then, what's number two on your mind?"

"The Hoerner homicide investigation is floundering. Captain Dan Grayson tells me that they have no suspects at all. They did determine Hoerner was at Brion's Grille out in Fairfax earlier in the evening and had a few drinks, but that took them nowhere. And, his work was so highly classified that they can't look there either. He said that lacking any new leads, the case will most likely go dormant in a week or two. Now, Philadelphia. Two cops, patrolmen, shot to death very early this morning."

"Go on."

"A citizen up in north Philly phoned in a '9-1-1' early this morning, very early. The guy called about what looked to be a burning house, smoke coming out the windows. It was up in Fairhill, a bad neighborhood. It's one of Philly's worst...street gangs, daily shootings, high crime rate. One cruiser with two patrolmen responded. They executed a silent approach–lights, but no siren. They reported that the house they were moving in on did have some smoke coming out the windows."

"Okay."

"Jack, the reports I received this morning state that it looks like as soon the officers exited the cruiser at the curb, they were immediately gunned down, riddled with bullets.

They were ripped apart from head to waist, just like the gang bangers lying dead all over inside the house. No one reported hearing gunfire, so it's pretty certain that acoustic-suppressed weapons were involved. Initial forensic reports say full-auto weaponry had to have been used. The initial 911 call reported that two loud booms were heard first. That's what brought the citizen to his bedroom window in a house across the street. He then saw smoke. So, that could mean flash-bangs were used."

"Victims?"

"Eighteen dead gang-bangers. A mess. Almost all their weapons were cold, unfired. Every single one of them took two rounds in the head. The attack must have grabbed them totally by surprise. But now there's also two dead cops who were shot to death on the sidewalk. They were in uniform… no way they could have been mistaken for anything but cops."

"And?" Jack asked.

"I haven't heard from Senator Sauter yet, but I'm sure I will. Nor have I heard any statements on the news from Senator Solomon Arends of Pennsylvania. When Sauter and I met, he said Arends had told him the police in Philly were seeing some of the same sorts of things that Denver was. A dramatic change in tactics as well as weaponry."

"I fully understand your concern. I agree with you, no mistake about that. So far though, from what you've said and what I've learned myself, all it tells me is that I have to conclude this is all still primarily a law enforcement matter. I don't see a legitimate justification for Agency involvement."

"I know. But now we have two dead police officers shot to death with automatic gunfire from suppressed weapons. I think this now adds a new dimension. Why kill responding cops? Those officers were murdered because their quick response was unexpected and whoever shot up the gang house didn't want witnesses. So, they murdered the cops too. I don't think this involves vigilantes. What group do we know of that is so sophisticated? I think it's something else. And, it doesn't make me feel good to say that."

"Again, I agree with you. So, you did indeed have a lot on your mind this morning. That's for sure. All this stuff explains why you looked a little unsettled when you came in my office."

Barrett pushed up from his seat, flinching somewhat from the effort. He walked to the eastern corner window and gazed out to where the Potomac River dwindled down to just a rocky stream. He glanced over his shoulder to Novak.

"This RTC program…why the hell so mysterious? Police officers shot to death in Philadelphia. And, my deputy for operations believes this adds a new dimension? Well, yes, I think it does. Further, our own Dave McClure is in Raton. Now you and I must ask ourselves, what's the truth in all this? Just what the hell is going on?" Jack Barrett said, slowly pivoting back to the window.

CHAPTER 23

Raton
New Mexico

Dave McClure mumbled to himself as he turned the Volvo south on 2nd Street. *'What a jewel of an old gal. For a minute there, I thought I was hugging Grandma Millie.'* Raton might be a small town, but it has some good-hearted people. No doubt about it, Loretta Hadley is one of them. The sheriff is a great guy too. Dave managed a smile.

After Dave passed Clayton Road, he spotted the large, one-story Super Save Discount Foods on his left. He steered the Volvo into the turn lane and pulled into the parking lot. After finding a close-in parking place, he walked through the double doors, moving directly toward the produce section.

He was instantly surprised and quite impressed. Everything in that end of the store looked truly fresh, sparkly clean–apples, pears, oranges, grapes. It was going to be hard for him to choose. He wandered around the displays of apples, finally selecting two McIntosh apples and a Bartlett pear. He would chill them up nicely in the hotel room's small fridge.

"Finding everything okay, sir?" A male voice came from

behind him. Dave turned. A tall, lean man in an apron stood by the grapefruit and oranges display.

"Yes, thanks. You know, everything looks so good here... it's hard to pick."

"We work pretty hard to make that the case, sir. Anything I can help you with?" The man said.

"Well, it does make me curious. Don't get me wrong, but Raton really isn't all that big. And yet, you look to have almost as many employees walking around here and stocking things as you do customers. Sales are going that good for you?"

"I suppose it does seem that way, I guess. Sales are okay, but it all really boils down to the new contract we have. By the way, I'm the manager of the produce department. Have been for twenty years!" He laughed.

The produce manager certainly was a lanky fellow. He looked to be every bit of six feet five inches. In his day, he was most likely a team star playing at center on his high school basketball team.

"And I'm just a new customer. Pleased to meet you."

"Same here. Anyway, we had to bring on some more people to meet the contractual requirements. I understand it's a six-month contract...a doozy, pretty big for a business like ours. It was awarded to us last April and as far as I know, it runs through to September 30th. That's the end of the federal government fiscal year. I don't have a feeling yet as to whether it'll be renewed or not."

"A federal contract? Here, in Raton?"

"Yep, that's what I've been told. I don't often get involved in the contract end of things, but then I've been working here for nearly 25 years and I've seen almost all aspects of the business. The trucks drive in here late every Thursday evening to get loaded. And, today's Thursday, so we're buzzing...

making sure we have everything ready."

"Trucks?"

"Yeah, big 2½ ton trucks. Olive green, like Army trucks. There's usually about six of them and I expect that many will be here tonight. They drive in every Thursday right at closing time–that's 8:30 p.m. for us. There's hardly any customers still in the store by that time, so we can concentrate on loading them up."

"Every Thursday? What do they buy?"

"The contract calls for all sorts of food stuff. We load refrigerated containers of varied types of meat as well as crates of fresh vegetables, canned goods, eggs, bread, biscuits, some dry goods, things like that. It takes us nearly two hours to get everything loaded, and then they're off again."

"Six of them...every Thursday. That much food for a week? It must be feeding a lot of people. Do you have any idea where they take all that stuff every week?"

"Nope, and I don't pry either. As far as I know, it could be a Christian youth camp. It'd have to be a big one though. We just load 'em up and they take off. That's it. But I can say I've known our store manager, Bob Miller, for a lot of years. He and I are Raton natives. Bob told me that the over-arching contract apparently does the same thing at a couple of other distribution centers. That's what Bob called them, distribution centers."

"Really? Any idea where those are?"

"They're all on the east coast somewhere. Bob said all those contractual requirements for those sites are almost the same in our contract that he's seen copies of."

"That's pretty interesting. I guess it's great for the store and your employees. A robust federal contract for six months. So, the trucks will be coming by tonight?"

"That's right. They'll be pulling up to the loading dock over here by 8:30 p.m. sharp. That's a contractual requirement too. And right now, we already have everything pretty much set up, ready to load."

"Well, thanks for chatting. I can't wait to bite into one of these cold, crisp apples. Guess I'll head for the registers. Take care now."

"Bye. Come back and visit us again soon," the manager grinned. He turned and walked toward a young man stocking a new batch of tomatoes. Dave walked up to one of the registers with his two apples and a pear.

'I will indeed be back soon, like a little before 8:30 p.m. tonight,' he whispered as he approached the end of a register's short line of customers.

CHAPTER 24

McClure reached for the cup resting in the console holder and took another sip of coffee. It was still warm. Earlier, after dinner, Dave found himself searching for another cup of coffee to take along with him. The Best Western nighttime receptionist, a young guy named Don, steered McClure to the Chevron station just down the street on Clayton Road, not far from the I-25 overpass.

It was now 8:20 p.m. The Volvo sat parked at the far north end of the parking lot of Super Save Discount Foods–in shadows, engine and lights off. McClure had rolled both front side windows down to allow a slight breeze to carry in some cool night air.

He sat slumped in the front seat, still tasting the steak from Mulligan's. It had been grilled perfectly, juicy. An easy listening channel on the radio was thrumming a golden oldie through the speakers, Paul Mauriat's '*Love Is Blue.*' With that music playing, it wasn't hard to get lost in thought. Relaxing.

Tonight, Dave decided to wear his blue blazer with a white tee shirt underneath. That better enabled him to wear the slant-rig shoulder holster for the Beretta. Two more mags sat snug in the pouches under his right arm.

During the late afternoon, he'd gone over in his mind tonight's upcoming events and had an idea on how to approach it. He decided to carry his ICE badge and credentials along with the Maglite to make his actions appear logical. He also tucked his FBI credentials into the blazer's interior coat pocket. Dave stuck his head out the window and inhaled a lungful of the crisp evening air.

He glanced over to the exit doors. It was a few minutes before closing time, and the last of the night's customers were beginning to leave Super Save Discount Foods. He took another sip of coffee. The few cars left in the parking lot were now pulling out of the lot and onto 2nd Street. Dave's eyes caught the movement from a quick glimpse in the rear view mirror. He straightened in his seat. A long line of headlights on large vehicles was coming south on 2nd Street in the left lane. Right on time. He smiled.

McClure watched as six bulky 2½ ton trucks swung left through the green turn signal and drove into the parking lot. As the store's large loading doors opened with a grinding sound, the trucks pulled up in line at the south end of the building, Men pulling flat carts loaded with crates bristled from the building, and other men who had been sitting in the back of the trucks now lowered their rear gates. Dave watched with interest. He'd give them another fifteen minutes or so.

At ten minutes to nine, he exited the Volvo, soundlessly securing the door behind him. He reached down with his right hand and pushed the shiny brass ICE badge clipped to the side of his belt up to the front where it was easily noticed. Lights on the parking lot's poles slowly flickered off. Walking through the now dimly lit parking lot, he noticed the banks of interior store lights also begin to shut down.

Dave walked to the farthest vehicle at the rear of the line of trucks, ignoring the ongoing loading operation. He flicked his Maglite on, and started pacing slowly alongside the last truck, bending over to examine the undercarriage. Completing that truck's alleged inspection, he moved on to the next truck in line. He didn't think it would take long for someone to show up and inquire about his presence. He was correct.

A man carrying a clipboard marched toward him from somewhere up near the front of the line. The man looked to be in his early thirties and was wearing jeans and a black polo shirt. He appeared about five feet ten inches or so and had a closely cropped, short haircut. McClure acted as though he was ignoring the man's approach, instead continuing to move along to the third truck in line, scrutinizing the underside. The man stopped roughly ten feet away.

"Hey you, mister, may I ask what you think you're doing here?" The man blurted out.

McClure rose in place, his face as stern as he could muster. "Excuse me, whoever you are! You said 'hey you', did you? I'll tell you what, *mister*, you go ahead and feel free to add a 'sir' to that question. Then, maybe I'll answer it. My name, if you're interested, is Special Agent Barry O'Keefe, Immigration and Customs Enforcement, ICE." He pushed the flap of his blazer back to expose the badge on his belt.

The man was taken aback. His eye brows twitched as he blinked. "I see. Sorry, I didn't know..."

McClure interrupted. "So, to answer your question, and like I've already mentioned–whoever you are, this is a routine but official process. I'm conducting a search for illegal aliens as authorized by federal statutes as well as my badge and credentials. How does that work for you, that is, whoever you are?"

"I'm Darrell Chilton. If I came across as rude, I apologize."

"Okay, Darrell, better. Thanks for that."

"Mr. O'Keefe, I can assure you, there are no illegal aliens

associated with these trucks. None at all. These trucks haven't been anywhere near the southern border in the last six months or even south of Santa Fe for that matter."

McClure decided to put his idea in play. "Well, I...oh, wait, are you and these trucks with the RTC? If so..."

The man's face paled instantly. "Ah, may I ask, just how would you know anything about the RTC?"

"Darrell, I'm Immigration and Customs Enforcement, ICE–we fall under DHS. And, if you're assigned to the RTC program, then you're DHS also. Everyone down here with ICE has had a classified briefing, and we were asked to give you and your folks a wide berth. I suppose I should've asked that to begin with. If that's the case, well, there's no need for me to continue to search."

Chilton paused in thought. "I guess that makes sense. Then, Barry, I'm pleased to meet you, if I may call you Barry," Chilton's demeanor loosened up noticeably.

"Sure. I am curious though. What do you do for the program, Darrell? I see you're carrying a clipboard. Are you checking the loading to ensure what's being included is what needs to be?"

"Actually, yes, that's correct. I'm Captain Chilton. I'm active duty and I've been detailed from the Army to provide logistics assistance to the program. My background and training are in contracts and I have logistics experience as well."

"I see. Do you also cover the three centers on the East Coast? The...uh, distribution centers. Back east, we, ICE, watch out for those too. You know, we run some interference for them when deemed necessary, stuff like that. I forget where our briefer from Washington, D.C. said they were?"

"Richmond, Herndon, and Baltimore. And no, I'm only concerned with Raton and the training site here."

"Herndon, Virginia? That's right near Dulles International Airport. I know that area well. I've had some conferences I had to attend out in Herndon. It's very convenient with the airport being right nearby."

"Well, Barry, all three of our three distribution centers are at or near major airports...Richmond International, Dulles International, and Baltimore-Washington International, BWI. As a matter of fact, they're flying me out to the East Coast next week. I'll be taking a look at all three centers–an inspection, make sure everything's as it should be. I understand a major deployment is coming up. Sometime around the first week in September. Leadership wants me to make sure everything is ready. Some kind of exercise. I'm not sure."

"Thanks. Now I remember from the briefing. Your DHS contract is basically all there is for the RTC here and all the other three sites? Just the government contract. That has to be quite a complex task for you. You said you didn't know what this major deployment is for?"

"Well, what you just said isn't really the case. There is, or rather was, another contract for all the required construction. A lot of construction. That was accomplished by VA&S Construction Company. They handled everything to do with that part of the contract."

"VA&S Construction?"

"Yes. VA&S is headquartered up in Colorado Springs. They had all the heavy equipment and I have to say I was impressed with their work. They were very capable."

"Okay."

"I didn't deal with that contract itself though. I don't know what federal agency was paying VA&S for their construction on the site. In any case, all of the construction required with us and the other three centers was completed, oh, roughly two and a half months ago. So now, basically, we're it. We account for all the remaining logistical support. Oh, and I really don't know anything about the deployment. I've just heard talk."

"Thanks for all that. Much appreciated. I was just curious," McClure said. The logic of the RTC acronym suddenly dawned on him.

"Darrell, where exactly is the Raton Training Center located? I assume it's not too far from here, from town?"

"Well that, Barry..." Chilton hesitated, his head turning right and left to see if anyone was nearby, his face swiftly turning a watery white. A look of fear seemed to creep over him.

He continued. "Sorry, Barry, I hope you don't get angry with me, but even though you're ICE and you support us, I can't release info regarding the actual location. We've all been briefed, continually lectured, that the location itself is highly classified. So, I can't go there. I'm up for promotion to major in a year and...well, a security violation like that would kill it."

"That's okay. Forget it. Darrell, I'm pleased to have made your acquaintance. Have a great trip next week and please accept my best wishes for promotion to major. Special Agent O'Keefe will now get the hell out of your way, so you can finish things up. Search completed," McClure laughed as he spoke, and Chilton chuckled with him.

"Barry, thanks very much. I do need to get back to it. You take care now and watch your back."

"Indeed, Darrell, you as well. Say, here's one of my business cards. If you need anything, anything at all, or even if you just want to chat with somebody, feel free to give me a buzz," McClure said.

The two men smiled and shook hands. Chilton turned

and headed back to the front of the line of trucks. Dave swiveled about and walked back across the empty parking lot. He returned to the Volvo, settled in the driver's seat, flicked on the headlights and started the engine. He crossed the empty parking lot to the exit.

He turned the Volvo right onto 2nd Street, heading north. The line of six bulky trucks had initially come from the north, so he assumed that would be how they'd depart. After driving two blocks, and completely out of view of the parking lot of Super Save Discount Foods, Dave turned right into a small strip plaza of shops.

The store lights in the little strip plaza were out and the parking lot empty. It seemed Raton was one of those little towns that really did close down and roll up its sidewalks at eight-thirty. He drove to the north end of the strip of stores, turned the Volvo about and backed up along the beige cinder-block sidewall. Engine off, lights out.

He considered what he'd seen. Six trucks filled with food stuffs of all kinds, loaded up every week. That should feed a lot of people and feed them well. What exactly was the Raton Training Center, its program? Where exactly was it? Darrell Chilton, Captain Chilton, had been detailed from the U.S. Army. That was interesting in itself. McClure wondered how many more active duty personnel like him were at this training center.

Chilton couldn't and wouldn't tell Dave the exact location of the RTC. It was highly classified, yes, but Chilton appeared more than a bit fearful. Fearful of what exactly? Was it because of the classification itself, the security lectures they'd had? The potential loss of a promotion opportunity? If not about those things, then what?

McClure decided to wait quietly in the dark New Mexico

night, parked in shadow alongside the strip plaza for the convoy of six trucks to pass. Then, at a discreet distance, he'd tag along, maybe see where this truck convoy was headed. And so, if he was lucky, locate the RTC.

CHAPTER 25

McClure waited at the end of the strip mall for about forty minutes and saw the convoy pass by. As he had planned, he pulled out and followed. He would run at a discreet distance, hopefully, shadow them to their final destination, the RTC. McClure lingered back with the Volvo a considerable distance. They were all headed north on 2nd Street at an easy pace.

Dave could just see the taillights of the last truck. He made out the sketchy outline of what looked like two figures in the back by the crates. The right side blinkers on the trucks came on as they approached the right turn for Clayton Road. McClure slowed.

Dave's eyes abruptly scrunched as two excruciatingly bright, high-beam headlights reflected off his rearview mirror. A large SUV, something maybe the size of a GMC Yukon, approached rapidly from behind.

Dave instinctively accelerated, the Volvo XC90's 400 horsepower engine growling. Dave swung through the right turn onto Clayton Road. The mystery vehicle also swerved into the curve and stayed with him, drawing closer and nearly climbing up his rear bumper.

'And just how the hell did you miss that, McClure? Your observation skills? Very sloppy. Dammit,' Dave said to himself,

shaking his head.

Had the SUV been sitting somewhere on the other side of the parking lot, also watching? A countersurveillance op being run on the truck convoy? Shit. Perhaps it was sitting somewhere on 2nd Street and got very interested in him when he began following the convoy? He should've assumed worst case and pumped up his awareness level.

The trucks aligned in a straight row along the left lane. An old pick-up truck was in the right. The right shoulder was too narrow…that wouldn't work. The brilliant headlights behind him lit up the interior of the Volvo like a ballpark stadium on Saturday night. It was rapidly making another run at the rear bumper. Squinting his vision against the overwhelming bright light, he thought he could see at least four heads in the SUV, two in front, two in the rear.

McClure moved up to the road's double center line. Distant headlights were coming his way, although it was impossible to estimate their oncoming speed. Six trucks were lined up moving ahead of him. It was now or never.

Dave pressed the gas pedal to the floor and jerked the wheel left. The Volvo roared, exploding into the oncoming lane, its speed hastily escalating up to 60, 70 mph. He raced past the line of beefy 2½ ton trucks now to his right. The oncoming headlights were approaching fast.

He violently swerved the Volvo to the right, barely missing the grill of the lead truck. The truck's horn trumpeted a single long and loud blast. A Chevy Suburban's horn wailed in the night as it barreled past, barely missing him. Less than two seconds more would have been a disaster. He continued accelerating, the XC90's engine bellowing in protest.

McClure moved the Volvo left to take a look in his side-view mirror. He glanced down the line of trucks now trailing him. The large SUV had attempted to swing out and follow him, but jerked back, nearly colliding with the oncoming Suburban. It drew right back and then immediately leaned left again.

The Volvo approached 90 mph on Clayton Road, speed limit 45, but not a cop in sight. The I-25 overpass and its entrance ramp were just up ahead. Dave sprinted into the left turn lane and dashed up the ramp onto the interstate, heading north.

"Good girl," Dave patted the Volvo's dash, smiling.

He checked the rear-view again. The large SUV was entering the highway's merge lane from the ramp. These guys obviously wanted to get to know him better. He stomped the gas again and the XC90 snarled, thundering up the slow, steady climb of Raton Pass. He passed 80, then 90 miles an hour. He glanced at the mirror again...the SUV was growing closer. They must be flying.

Dave kept his foot floored on the gas. He'd seen a couple New Mexico state troopers on the way down the pass when he was coming into Raton. He suddenly wondered about that. The gas floored, the Volvo's speed mushroomed up past 100 mph, still increasing.

He could see the reflection of the dazzling headlights fading on the road surface of the curving interstate. They were still coming, but it appeared the big SUV had a hard time keeping pace on the uphill Raton Pass. The Volvo was steadily increasing the gap between them.

He wanted just a little more distance and, if luck would have it, just maybe...there it was, snuggled up against the right shoulder's low barrier fence. The vehicle's flashing roof lights alerted and came alive. Dave estimated he was passing the trooper's black-and-white Ford sedan at roughly 115 mph.

The cruiser pulled out, leaving a cloud of blue smoke, and accelerated rapidly up the inclining roadway, its red, white, and blue lights flashing intensely. Its siren screeched into the night air. Dave lost sight of the trooper's sedan on the curving road, but he knew the trooper wanted him…115 mph, a mere 40 miles over the speed limit? For sure, that trooper wanted whoever was driving the white Volvo.

Dave kept his foot on the gas. The interstate straightened a bit, just enough and the cruiser closed the gap. The trooper was on him. He pulled up behind the Volvo's rear bumper. Dave braked safely and pulled over to the right shoulder. The trooper, obviously pissed off, slammed his door in anger behind him and stomped toward the Volvo. Okay, 115 mph was a tad over the top. Dave lowered his driver side window as the trooper approached.

At that moment, a dark red GMC Yukon raced by them both, moving into the left lane as it passed. The trooper hopped quickly to his right. The Yukon had no other choice but to continue ahead, blowing by McClure and the state police sedan. Perfect.

As the Yukon raced past, Dave got a look, a fleeting glimpse, of the man in the front passenger seat. For a second, Dave thought he knew that face. But from where? The image flashed in from his memory. Yeah, he was sure that he'd seen that face in Sheriff Frank Wells' office. He was sure that the man he'd had just glimpsed was Deputy Sheriff Rich Carruthers, the Colfax County sheriff's liaison to the state park service.

Dave glanced immediately to his left. A furious, outraged New Mexico state trooper's face filled his driver side window. He looked to be in his mid-thirties, blue eyes. His state trooper hat covered his hair.

"Mister, that stunt you just pulled was in your face! In-your-face! Just where the hell…?"

"FBI, officer. Line of duty."

Dave purposely spoke in a dead pan voice while flashing his badge and credentials. He saw the trooper's nameplate, 'Delton'.

"What? You're FBI?"

"Look, Officer Delton, I'm sorry, but what you just did was what I was hoping you would do. That reddish Yukon that just blew past us was chasing me. I think there were four men inside. I was no match for them."

"Damn! Okay, Special Agent McClure, if I'm pronouncing that correctly, you were roaring. My radar clocked you at 117 mph. Jeez!"

"I know. If I could, I wanted desperately to get the attention of a New Mexico state trooper. If one was available."

"Well, you sure got that, all right. Can I help you? You want me to run them down and pull them over? Delay them?"

"No, no, let 'em go. But, thanks. You saved my butt."

"It's our pleasure…that is, the New Mexico State Police," The trooper said, breaking into a smile.

"Can I…would you let me cut across the median here to go back south?"

"Sure. But, pull out and go up about 100 yards. There's a dirt crossover there that we use fairly often."

"Thanks, Officer Delton. Really, thanks very much. You saved my ass," Dave extended his hand.

"Ben. Ben Delton. I'm pleased to help the FBI, even at 117 mph!" Delton laughed. McClure joined in.

The trooper stepped back. "Take care, SA McClure. And, check your six!" he said.

"Indeed. You too!"

The trooper waved as Dave swerved the Volvo off the shoulder, sped up to the median's dirt crossover just ahead and took it. Now heading back south, he accelerated up to the 75 mph speed limit and held the speed.

Minutes later, Dave steered the white Volvo into the well-lit entrance of the Best Western Plus hotel on Clayton Road. There was only so much time. Perhaps fifteen minutes before the men in that Yukon felt it was safe to turn back. Once up in the room, Dave tossed his clothes and dopp kit into the suitcase, snapped it shut, and headed back downstairs to the reception desk.

"Mr. McClure, leaving us? At night?"

"Yeah, I've got a small emergency back home in Denver. My son's headed to the emergency room to get some stitches on his left hand."

"My goodness. I'm sorry to hear that. Please come back and visit with us again soon," The clerk handed Dave the credit card receipt.

"I might just do that. Thanks. Take care."

"Bye. Drive safely."

McClure stepped through the double glass doors and into the parking lot. No more wasting time…he'd gas up once he was across the Colorado state border, probably at Trinidad. He fired the engine, and the Volvo XC90 growled as though it was once again hungry for speed. He headed out of the parking lot and east on Clayton Road.

Two hours and thirty-five minutes of driving later, after refueling in Trinidad, Dave steered the Volvo into the parking lot of the Marriott Hotel Colorado Springs. Initially, he'd taken the Circle Drive exit just south of the city, then spent fifteen minutes driving through the parking lot areas near the Cinemark Tinseltown theater complex to dry clean himself.

There was no surveillance, no tail.

The Marriott was situated in Rockrimmon, just off Tech Center Drive, a sprawling residential area northwest of Colorado Springs. He hoped the chances were good that the big hotel would have a room. It turned out that they did, a nice king-bed room on the 5th floor. He took it.

Dave pulled the dopp kit out of his suitcase and cleaned up in the bathroom, washing his hands, his face and brushing his teeth. He'd save a shower for the morning. He liked Marriott hotels, not too fancy but could almost always be trusted to be sparkly clean. This one didn't disappoint.

Dave looked at his watch as he slipped it from his wrist. It was well after midnight. He glanced to the beckoning king bed. It had been a long night and he could sure use the sleep. He'd drive over to visit the FBI RA office on Tejon Street first thing in the morning, call Langley and relate to Pete what he'd learned, including the late-night chase up the interstate.

He pitched his clothing onto a nearby easy chair and climbed in between the sheets. He closed his eyes. La-la land softly but urgently summoned him.

CHAPTER 26

McClure breezed through the door of Suite 600, 111 South Tejon Street, at roughly eight-thirty in the morning and was immediately greeted by a young female receptionist. It was the FBI Resident Agency, the *RA* for Colorado Springs. He'd found a two-hour parking slot just up the street near the intersection with Colorado Avenue.

After being issued a visitor's badge, a middle-aged agent wearing a steel gray suit escorted him past a maze of office doors to a room with the secure phone. The agent introduced himself as "Tom." Left alone in the room, Dave picked up the phone and spoke briefly with a communications officer. He heard ringing at the other end of the line.

"Langley Center. This line is unsecure. How may I help you?"

"Dave McClure for Peter Novak."

"Yes, sir. Hold a sec and I'll connect you directly," he said. There were several switching clicks.

"Novak."

"Pete, Dave McClure."

"Dave, good to hear from you! I was growing a bit anxious. Everything okay? I was hoping you'd call today. Where are you?"

"Yes, sir, all's fine. I'm at the FBI RA in Colorado Springs.

Are we secure?"

"Yes. The line's gone secure. You're in Colorado Springs? When did you leave Raton? Were you able to develop some information?"

"I got here after midnight last night. And yes, I have quite a bit for you."

"Great. Go ahead. Let's have it."

Dave began a complete rundown of events. He related everything from his visit with Sheriff Frank Wells and learning about the death of Lester Hadley, then conversing with Hadley's wife, Loretta, to the chance meeting with produce manager at Super Save Discount Foods, where he learned about the six month federal contract for food and dry goods. Finally, Dave covered his discussion with Darrell Chilton, U.S. Army Captain Chilton, alongside the truck convoy, and learning of a second, earlier contract with VA&S Construction Company and the existence of three other distribution centers on the East Coast.

After providing those details, Dave described the subsequent nighttime chase up I-25 through Raton Pass by a crimson colored Yukon, the SUV that McClure felt might have either been running a fixed-point countersurveillance of the trucks at the food market's parking lot or sitting concealed somewhere on 2nd Street. He ended his list of recalls with his belief that he had a glimpse of Deputy Sheriff Rich Carruthers, the Colfax County Sheriff's Office liaison officer to the park service, riding in the front passenger seat of the Yukon.

"Excellent collection work, Dave. Really. That's a good deal of information that we can now use to begin putting the puzzle pieces together. But hey, you missed picking up on a countersurveillance? Hmmm...could be it's time for some remedial training, eh? However, that ruse you pulled racing up

I-25 and engaging a state trooper was an outstanding tactic. Dave, splendid, rapid thinking on your part. I suppose that makes up a good bit for missing that Yukon."

"Thanks, Pete. My antennas weren't fully up, that's all. It won't happen again, I promise."

"All right. I'm very sorry to hear about the death of the old fella, Lester Hadley. A rifle shot in the head with a .308 Winchester round. And further, that lividity was beginning and thus made it clear to forensics that his body had been moved. Very unusual and also extremely suspicious. That does bother me. You also said Hadley had a dog that was nowhere near the body and they still haven't found?"

"Yes. His wife, Loretta, confirmed that. The dog was a chocolate-colored lab named Baxter. She said Lester and that dog were inseparable. So, that doesn't fit either. That Lab has to be out there somewhere, dead or otherwise," Dave said.

"Again, suspicious. Also potentially raises the risk posture, something we didn't expect. When you go back to Raton, which you will eventually, I want you armed up 24-7, okay?"

"Yes, indeed.

"Dave, do you have any feel, any idea, about what these three distribution centers near Richmond International, Dulles and BWI are? What they actually distribute?"

"No. The problem was that Chilton essentially had only so much time to talk. He was supervising the loading of six 2½ ton trucks. Once I was able to convince him that I was an ICE agent though, that we'd had a classified briefing about giving RTC operations a wide berth, and that we were both DHS, he did become fairly open."

"Again, young jedi, a superb piece of work on that aspect, Dave."

"Thanks, but what are your initial thoughts about these

eastern distribution centers?"

"Probably nothing. It's just that with those distributions centers near those particular major airports... well, I can visualize that they form an arc that sort of encircles Washington D.C.'s metro area, the national capital region, from the north, south, and west. And, the Atlantic Ocean is to the east. I find it interesting, that's all. Like I said, there's probably nothing there to examine further. I'll just make a mental note to myself. Chilton told you that VA&S Construction was located in Colorado Springs?"

"Yes. That contract's apparently expired quite some time ago though."

"No matter. The details could still be of some use. Ask the Bureau folks at the RA if they'll let you use a desktop computer to do some Internet research. See if you can determine where VA&S is located, that is, if they're even still in business. Then, pay them a visit. Use your FBI credentials and ask them about the construction contract they had, exactly what it was that they were building, and so forth. Lacking that, try to find out who the owner was or is, and see if you can run him down. If he's still in the Colorado Springs area, he may be willing to describe all that for you."

"Right. I'll get on that before I leave here, Pete."

"Dave, keep this to yourself, but I want you to know the results of some taskings I sent to the NRO for Raton. I asked them to move a spaceborne platform or two, ones that have the best spatial resolution, to take an imagery scan around the areas outside of the Raton Township."

"Pete, you tasked the National Reconnaissance Office? You once told me that the Agency has a land division and an air division. But jeez, no space division? No Obi-Wan Kenobi?" Dave chuckled.

"Don't be a wise ass, young jedi McClure. Fact is, there's no real need for redundancy in space-based imagery platforms. They're way too damn expensive anyway. We work quite often with the NRO. They have constellations of satellites in varying orbits that can read a license plate from 600 miles in space. So, I had them realign a couple of their birds to take a close look."

"And what did they see?"

"They identified some nocturnal activity, thermal image blips out to the east-northeast of Raton. What they said was weird was that the images appeared and then disappeared seconds later. The activity they were monitoring was at the far eastern end of...hold on, I have it here, ah, Sugarite Canyon. I agreed with them that the activity seemed more than a bit strange since it was occurring late at night in a non-residential area that's hilly and somewhat mountainous. I think we should take a closer look."

"How so?"

"Where are you staying, Dave?"

"At the Colorado Springs Marriott here in Rockrimmon. Not far from where I used to live."

"Good. Well, you've got VA&S Construction to run down. That may take a day or two. It will give us some time."

"Time for what? What are you thinking, Pete?"

"Do you remember Kevin O'Brien?"

"The Kevin from the Maine operation? The guy who was the tech lead in the Portland Field Office? Yes, I do."

"Excellent memory. I'm going to have the National Resources Division go ahead and secure us a place in Raton...a place somewhat remote, near the edge of town. And, with large enough space to expand if we need to send additional resources down there. I'll assign Kevin to come down to

Raton and support you."

"I liked O'Brien, but the guy's got a brutal, deadly sense of humor. I have to admit I wanted to kill him a couple times up in Maine. And, additional resources? What are you thinking there?"

"Yeah, I understand. Kevin's been chastised on occasion for being off-key at the wrong time with his humor. Nevertheless, he's one of our best."

"I would agree with that. He did know his business," Dave said.

"As for additional resources–that's a maybe. We'll see first where all this is going. If we do send some, they'd be from our Special Activities Division, the SAD. We might also include a few DARK RAPTOR pilots. That's to see if we can get really up close to whatever's out there in the east above Sugarite Canyon. Hopefully, we can determine just what those thermal blips are that the NRO identified."

"DARK RAPTOR?"

"Yes, that's the program nickname for BATS–Battlefield Assessment Tactical System. They're state-of-the-art drones with miniaturized GE turbofan engines and VTOL–Vertical Take-Off & Landing capability. The BATS are armed with both a 9mm gun and an EMP gun. Their original mission was for use as a battlefield reconnaissance and anti-personnel weapon system, primarily to eliminate enemy leadership on a battlefield. They're stealth enhanced and intended to be flown mainly at night, hence the BATS acronym."

"Is the term DARK RAPTOR classified?"

"No, like I said, just a nickname. Program nicknames are almost always unclassified. However, the term 'Battlefield Assessment Tactical System' is sensitive. It has a security sensitivity of *For Official Use Only*."

"Thanks. Pete, these are drones? You said pilots?"

"Yes, they can be flown manually with notebook computers by remote operators, pilots, or mission data can be uploaded and then flown solely by the drone's onboard computers. DARK RAPTOR or BATS as we prefer to call them, represent one extremely capable and lethal weapon system. However, we've discovered a thousand other uses for them."

"My goodness. Incredible, really."

"Dave, I'll also have a stealth unit shipped by air down there as well. It'll be a Subaru-like vehicle similar to the one that Kevin drove up in Maine. Do you remember?"

"By air?"

"Yes, we have that capability and use it fairly often, especially so in Europe. So, remember O'Brien's Stealth unit, the Subaru?"

"Yes, amazing technology. If I recall, little to no infrared, thermal signature. Engine exhaust is vented into a super-cooling system and then blown out beneath the middle of the undercarriage. Special alloy glass used on the windows along with composite, run-flat tires with no heat generation. Pretty much invisible to the visual light and thermal spectrums. Remarkable."

"Jeez, Dave, you do have one helluva memory. All of that's correct. I think you and Kevin may find good use for it down there. You already have the multi-spectral camouflage suit and night vision goggles. At least initially, I think you have everything you may need."

"Thanks, Pete."

"You're welcome. See what you can find out about VA&S Construction. Perhaps learn what federal agency was funding that particular contract and exactly what it was that they were constructing. If you do develop something you assess as some useful information, give me a call. Kevin and the Stealth unit will be there in a couple days. You can return your rental car at that time."

"The Marriott's okay for now?"

"Yes, I think so. You should be good there. We'll have a new place ready for you when it's time for you and Kevin to drive down to Raton. Oh, and when you do go back there, I think you should stay away from the Best Western hotel. Avoid it completely. Not even for lunch at their restaurant."

"Why's that, Pete? They have the best restaurant in all of Raton, and that's not saying much."

"It's an afterthought of mine. I admit it's sort of a conspiracy theory afterthought. From what you've told me about the Yukon chasing you up I-25 through Raton Pass, even though you saw the face for just an instant, well, if you're correct that you glimpsed that Deputy Sheriff Rich Carruthers riding in the front passenger seat, then we can pretty much count on him working for the RTC. He's running interference for them, covering their backs. So, extrapolate here. If that's the case, then it's very likely that they, the guys who chased you on the interstate, also have a paid source at the Best Western. Someone who reports to them about out-of-town visitors, especially those who stay more than one night.

"I understand. It does make me wonder."

"Wonder about what?"

"In retrospect, the desk clerk who first checked me into the hotel, Sheryl, Sherilynn Kosko. She did seem a tad overly inquisitive."

"Interesting name, Kosko."

"That's what I thought. She said her family always led her to believe it was Polish."

"Possibly. It very well might be. It could also be Ukrainian, maybe even Russian. Anyway, stay away from the Best Western. Kevin will be calling you on your cell in a day or two."

"Pete, once again, thanks for everything."

"Dave, you've done some damn good collection work down there. As I said, now we have to see if the pieces may fit into a puzzle…a puzzle in which the Agency can logically express a genuine national intelligence interest. Take care."

"You too. Bye, Pete," they each clicked off.

Dave walked out of the room and saw his escort, Tom, standing against the opposite wall.

"Long call," Tom said.

"Yeah, it was. I had to call Washington and I had a lot to relay. Say, Tom, do you have a computer, a sanitized desktop, that I could use for just a bit.

"Sure. Follow me," The man nodded.

CHAPTER 27

McClure was led down a long hallway at the end of which was a large, well-lit windowless room. He was given his choice of a seat at a long table partitioned for six desktop computers and phones with outside lines. Security training posters adorned two walls warning of phishing attacks and malware types as well as providing examples.

His escort said the computers in that room were primarily for use by occasional FBI and Justice Department visitors, and most usually during annual inspections. He was given a login user name and password and told to dial "9" for an outside line if he needed to make a call. Lastly, when he was finished, he could just come out to the large bay area and grab the escort agent again.

Dave was left alone in the room. The large, plain government-looking clock on the wall read that it was just a few minutes after ten o'clock. Settling into his chair, he logged on and immediately started a search for VA&S Construction Company in Colorado Springs.

Dave got an instant hit, a website for the company. The acronym "VA&S" apparently stood for *Vincent Armano & Sons*. He picked up the phone, pressed "9" for an outside line and dialed the two numbers listed on the website for the company. Separate recordings advised that both numbers had been disconnected. Interesting.

He left the website, next tapping in entries at a *White Pages* listing search for a Vincent Armano in Colorado Springs. Another instant hit, this one for a "Vince" Armano. Dave felt the probability was high that it was the same person.

Dave wrote the address and phone number for Armano's listed residence on a Post-It pad sheet, and then searched for the address and brought up a map. The street, Coyote Crest View, appeared to be in what looked like a very upscale residential area just north of Colorado Springs called *Flying Horse*. The map also indicated the residential development had a golf course, club house and spa. A realty company website showing MLS listings for the area revealed that homes were priced from a low of slightly over $500,000 up to $ two million plus. Vince Armano's home was not on the market, but was estimated at a value of $ 1.8 million. Upscale indeed.

He switched back to the map for Flying Horse community. There were two entrances, one off Highway 83 to the east and the other off North Gate Boulevard to the north which itself was an exit off I-25. He knew from living previously in Colorado Springs that North Gate Boulevard had been named after the north gate entrance into the U.S. Air Force Academy. It appeared as though Coyote Crest View in Flying Horse would be fairly easy to find.

First, Dave felt a break for an early lunch sounded reasonable. He remembered that Tejon Street was loaded with bistro-type eateries. He logged off the desktop, stepped outside the room and immediately saw Tom seated not far away. Once checked out at the desk, he thanked Tom for the assistance. When he queried Tom about places for lunch, Tom told him that he and several other agents really liked one across the street, *Colorado Craft*...great for soups, salads, and sandwiches.

Dave thanked Tom again, this time for the recommendation. That would be the place for lunch. He'd take a stroll up and down Tejon Street to reacquaint himself with its storefront offerings, catch lunch and then drive up to Flying Horse. He was anxious to see Armano's $ 1.8 million dollar home as the success of his construction business had obviously allowed him to do very well for himself.

Two hours later, after a BLT and a cup of corn chowder at the Colorado Craft eatery, McClure drove the white Volvo up I-25 to North Gate Boulevard and went east. After a few minutes, he swirled the XC90 through a right turn and into the Silverton Road entrance to Flying Horse. From there, it was just a short jaunt with another right onto Barossa Valley Road and Coyote Crest View was on the left.

The homes on the right side backed up against the golf course. He had to admit, they were stunning, gorgeous homes. Armano's was a couple houses down. It was exquisite...light beige stucco with a Spanish tile roof. Dave pulled into the long driveway.

The entrance sported two ornately carved wooden doors. He rang the bell. Twice. Footsteps were coming. The right-side wooden door opened a crack.

"Can I help you?" A woman's voice.

"Good afternoon. I'm here to speak with Vince Armano."

"Is he expecting you?"

"No, ma'am. I'm Special Agent Dave McClure, FBI," Dave pulled his badge and credentials from a pants pocket and held them up so she could see them.

"Oh, my...FBI. Is there a problem?"

"No, not at all. I just need to chat with Mr. Armano briefly about his company, VA&S Construction. It won't take long at all."

"You mean his former company."

"Former company? I guess I wasn't aware it had shut its doors."

"Well, come on in, ah, Agent McClure, is it? Vince is out back on the veranda conducting a wine tasting…a one-person wine tasting!" She giggled.

"Thank you very much. Are you Mrs. Armano?" Dave stepped across the threshold to follow her, closing the door behind him.

"I'm Jennifer Armano…Jenny to the FBI. Yes, I'm the better half, the wife," She laughed again. She was extremely attractive, long flowing red hair, green eyes, and wore a wispy, lavender colored two-piece pants suit.

McClure found himself winding through beautifully decorated rooms to the back of the house, finally past two sliding doors and onto the veranda. The flooring was Spanish tile, again, gorgeous. Rattan furniture with flowery cushions, easy chairs, two sofas and two cocktail tables were spread out both ways on the long, covered veranda. A large man, presumably Vince Armano, was stretched out on the sofa. He rose to a sitting position at the sight of McClure.

"Vince, honey, this is Special Agent Dave McClure. He's with the FBI and would like to talk with you."

"FBI? What the hell did I do now?" He chuckled and set his wine glass on the cocktail table in front of him.

"Go ahead, have a seat, Mr. McClure. I guess I'll leave you two," Jenny said, motioning to an easy chair and then turning back to the sliding doors.

"A glass of wine, Dave? It's a nice Merlot," Vince said.

"No thank you, really. Not on the job."

"I understand. I never did that myself when I was running my construction company and meeting with clients. So, how can I help Dave McClure and the FBI?" He reached for his glass and took a sip.

"Simple, sir. I have some questions about VA&S Construction so I can better understand your business."

"Well, first of all, I no longer own that company. I'm no longer involved with it in any real way," Vince said, setting his wine glass down.

"I see. Can you tell me what the contract with the RTC and Homeland Security involved? What your company was actually building for them?"

"No, I can't, sorry. I did receive a request for bids for a significant amount of construction work that would have begun almost immediately down in Raton, New Mexico. The contract also specified some work out on the east coast. Fact is, though, before I even had a chance to read the whole damn thing and begin pricing out a proposal, I received an offer to buy my company. And really, it was an offer I couldn't refuse."

"How so?"

"I was offered a tad more than thirty-five percent above the valuation of the company, its equipment and existing contracts. It was more than just a generous offer, the kind of offer you dream about, but never expect. I accepted. The contract for the buy-out specified that the buyers could continue to do business as Vincent Armano & Sons Construction Company, VA&S, for three years. I voiced no objections to that as my mind was envisioning a fantastic opportunity to retire in style. I'm 64 years old."

"My, my, 35% more than the valuation of your privately-owned company. Who were they, who was making such a generous offer?"

"J.J. Breeds Corporation, Manhattan, New York City. We

signed the contract right here on the veranda. My attorney, Frank Gianotta, was sitting where you are now."

"Wow. You did well, Mr. Armano. Congratulations. So, you really can't give me specifics about the construction down in Raton and the east coast?"

"No. Like I said, I'm not aware of any of the specific details, the contractual requirements. Look, Dave, so you don't take what you see here, this house, the furniture, in the wrong way–I was born in the Bronx. My father was a stone mason, a brick layer, and my mother did some part-time tailoring work at home. We weren't affluent, not by a long shot. My parents divorced when I was twenty and I moved out here. I got into construction, eventually formed my own company, and busted my ass my whole life. So, what you see here, this house, and everything in it, it's a dream come true."

"Thanks for the back story. Sincerely. Mr. Armano, the fact is, myself, I absolutely love it when I see an entrepreneur in this country build something of value and then find himself richly rewarded for his efforts. Ah, do you know if they kept some of your employees on the payroll?"

"Thank you for that, Dave. I know I ramble on about this stuff. Sometimes I catch myself and realize that, well, maybe I'm trying to defend why I'm living like I am now. That's all. I still have trouble believing all this." Vince swept his right arm from left to right, then continued. "As for the employees, my understanding was that all of them would be staying on their jobs. At least initially."

"Thanks. Well, that's the voice of a working man. Don't feel you have to defend it. Be proud of it. Now it's me who's rambling."

"Jeez, you're a nice guy, Dave. I wish there were more like you."

"Would you by any chance have the names of those people who came out to execute the contract for J.J. Breeds Corporation?"

"Sure, all that's in my study. I have their business cards and a photo of us too, celebrating the just-signed, completed contract. You can have it all. I have no need for that stuff any longer. My tax accountant already has all the information he needs."

"That would be fantastic. Thanks in advance."

"Follow me, Dave," Armano stood, and they walked back into the house.

McClure drove back south on the interstate to the Bijou exit for downtown Colorado Springs. Then a right turn south on Tejon Street to the FBI office. He saw a car just leaving a parking slot and he swung the Volvo into it. Two quarters jingled into the meter's coin slot. He walked the short distance to the entrance.

"You guys still open?" He asked the same young receptionist from the morning's visit.

"SA McClure, you're back again and so soon. Well now, it's three o'clock in the afternoon, and of course we're still open. The FBI isn't like the rest of the federal government!" She laughed.

"Is Tom still here? My escort this morning?"

"Yes, I'll call him. Have a seat," She motioned to a leather bench under a wall mirror.

Tom arrived in less than three minutes. He stepped through the door, walked over and extended his hand to McClure.

"Need some additional assistance?"

"I do. Tom, do you have a secure fax?"

"Yes. It's in the same room you were in this morning, It sits against the opposite wall. Can I operate it for you? It will go faster. We have a clunky secure fax machine. I won't look or try to remember what I see. I promise."

"No worries there. You're a trusted agent, Tom. Let's go."

Ten minutes later, with Dave watching, Tom had faxed the two business cards and the photo, all with a cover sheet to Pete Novak at Langley. Dave added some notes to the cover sheet regarding his meeting with Vince Armano to put the attachments in perspective. Afterward, Tom led Dave out to the lobby and Dave thanked him once again. He pushed the door open to the street and walked to the Volvo.

Dave sat in his Volvo at the curb and looked at the two business cards, George Mazur and Eric Baranek. The cards indicated the business address was in the Murray Hill, Midtown East section of Manhattan and that the men were both vice presidents representing J.J. Breeds Corporation at 27B West 24th Street, Suite 1406, New York, NY.

The photo showed four smiling men with arms wrapped around each other. There was a printed inscription written on the back of the photo in black ink that read: *February 3rd, Colorado Springs: Armano (far right), Gianotta (right), Mazur (left) and Baranek (far left).*

Dave smiled to himself. He'd stick the originals into a compartment of his locked suitcase. He was anxious to hear what Pete Novak and Jack Barrett would say about the business cards and photo.

Was there something of any use? He shook his head, wondering why a company like J.J. Breeds Corporation would pay over thirty-five percent more than VA&S Construction was essentially worth on paper. The actual timing of the purchase was quite interesting as well.

CHAPTER 28

Pumphrey Drive
Fairfax, Virginia

Karen McClure sat at the table in the kitchen nook, her hands in her lap, fidgeting. She had just put the phone back in its charger. The Walther PPK pistol lay on the table in front of her. It was loaded. The shoulder holster and the burner cell phone that Dave had given her for just such a situation as this were lying next to the pistol.

It was a few minutes after 6:00 p.m., and a couple minutes after the last call. She missed dinner. Her appetite vaporized. Dave told her, asked her, and begged her repeatedly never to try to call him when he was away on a mission. She understood the rationale behind that, but what the hell was she supposed to do now?

Karen knew that she had only one real option, one she'd never used before. She had to call Pete Novak. Given the time of day, would Novak even still be in his office? She decided that she had to give it a try. She picked up the burner cell phone and dialed Langley.

"Good evening, how may I help you?" A young male operations officer greeted her. After six o'clock in the evening, all calls coming in on the main public exchange number were routed to the operations center.

"I need to speak with Mr. Peter Novak if he's still in his office," Karen said.

"Ma'am, may I ask what this concerns?" The officer asked.

"I'm Karen McClure, National Resources Division. I'm also Dave McClure's wife. I consider this an emergency situation and I'm on a burner cell phone. Will you please connect me?"

"Yes, ma'am. Mr. Novak is still in his office. I'm connecting you. Please be aware this is not a secure line."

"Okay. Thank you."

After several rings, the line was opened. "Novak."

She recognized Pete's voice. "Mr. Novak, this is Karen McClure."

Pete instantly detected a tone of anxiety in her voice. "Karen, hi, good evening. Call me Pete, please. What's up?"

"Thanks, Pete. Well, I'm not sure. I don't know if I should be concerned or not, but if so, what I should do. As you know, Dave's away on a case. I felt calling you was my best and only option."

"That's okay. You made the right call, Karen. I'm with you. What's wrong? Forgive me, but it does sound like you're worked up, a little nervous?"

"I suppose I am. I'm sorry. I'm calling you on a burner phone that Dave gave me. This call should be safe. Pete, four times today, at precisely every half hour, beginning at four thirty late this afternoon, our phone, the home phone, rang. And, each time I've picked up the phone to answer, it immediately clicked it off. What do you think? Am I making a big deal out of nothing?"

Novak brow wrinkled. He paused in thought. Dave

McClure was now surely compromised. They, the black hats, whoever the hell "they" were, knew his name. If, and indeed that was a big "if", they had the ability as well as the resources, it was possible they might know by now that Dave's not really FBI. No, Novak didn't like it. They could have traced..."

"Karen, no, your senses are right where they should be. Do you have a weapon?"

"Thank you, I needed that. It's so good to be talking to someone. And yes, sir, I have a Walther PPK, .380 ACP. It's on the table in front of me–and loaded. My shoulder holster's lying next to it."

"Good. All right, no need to be nervous. Karen, let's continue on with you donning your agent's psychological hat. I want you to arm up. Right now, do it. Set the phone down, put the holster and pistol on now. Go ahead. I'll wait."

Karen gently set the phone on the table, slipped the shoulder holster on, shoved the pistol in, and snapped the retainer strap. She picked up the phone.

"Done."

"Good. I probably don't need to say this, Karen, but if by any chance you hear glass breaking, somebody breaking in, let them enter the house. Then, aim for center of mass and shoot them, just like out at the range in the tactical combat course. If you're close enough and they're not aware of your presence yet, aim for the head instead, shoot them in the head. No hesitation, don't think about it first, okay?"

"My goodness. Okay."

"Don't worry about it. If that happens, we'll clean it all up. Whatever you do, don't go outside the house in the dark alone. Stay inside. Ah, don't you have sliding doors off the kitchen that go into the back yard? I seem to remember from seeing the house when you were buying it that you do?"

"Yes. I'm near them right now. In the kitchen."

"Great. Karen, do you remember Tony Robertson? Tony was in Maine with you and Dave when you were NCIS. Tony led the special operations team I sent up there. Tony was the team lead for the assault on the Malset residence. You all participated in that. Do you remember him?"

"Yes, I do. Great guy. He was very confident in what he was doing. His presence took the edge off all of us. I liked him a lot."

"Great. Tony is one of the very best. Okay, as soon as you and I hang up, I want you to go through the house and close all the windows, blinds, curtains. Make sure all the doors are locked. Do that right after we hang up. Are we good so far?"

"Yes."

"Then, go upstairs to your bedroom and throw some things like clothes, cosmetics, into an overnight bag. Try to pack enough to last you for say, oh, three days or so at most."

"Pete, where…?"

"Not now, Karen. Please, listen. Pack those things right after you close all the windows and lock the doors. Then, sit down and take a deep breath. Have something to eat, force yourself to do that. Chicken noodle soup, maybe, that's benign enough. Next, at eight-thirty tonight, that will be at eight-thirty sharp, turn off all the lights in the house. All of them. Then, keeping your overnight bag by you, sit where you are now–in the kitchen, near the sliding doors."

"Understand."

"Immediately after you turn off all the lights at eight-thirty, a minute or so later, but no later than eight-thirty-five, you will hear five taps in succession on those sliding glass doors, one, two, three, four, five, like that. Not a fast rapping, but slow, steady."

"Okay?"

"Tony Robertson and his six-man special operations team will be in the back of your house, just outside the sliding doors. Look out the glass, verify that it's Tony, and then, let them in."

"How will they get into our backyard? We have homes and fences behind us."

"If I recall, you're a couple houses down from the intersection with Commonwealth Boulevard, right?"

"Yes."

"I'm thinking that Tony will probably choose a house on Commonwealth to come in alongside yours. He'll figure that out. Then, after they enter, you're going to leave the house with one of his men. It's totally safe. He'll lead you to a van or an SUV where you and a driver will drive up to Arlington. We have a safe house there near Wilson Boulevard and North George Mason Drive. I will be there to meet you when you arrive. Tony and the remaining five of his team are going to stay in your house. They'll be there as our official greeters. Get the gist?"

"You think this is that serious?"

"I think there's a good possibility that it could be, yes. There's actually a chance that this may have to do with what Dave is engaged in out west," Pete said.

Thoughts raced through Pete's mind. If it was connected to the goings-on in Raton, then kidnapping Karen could be an attempt to keep Dave silent on what he observes there. His brow wrinkled as a frown washed across his face. It had to be serious.

"Dave, is he okay? Forgive me, I'm with the company, but I'm also a somewhat worried wife," She paused. "Pete, boy, am I glad I called you."

"Dave is fine. He sent a fax today, but I haven't had a chance to look at it yet. And hey, I'm glad you called too. Karen, remember, take a deep breath, relax. Worst case, you're armed. Whoever's calling you, they won't expect that. That is, if they come before we arrive. I'll see you in a couple hours in Arlington. Everything's going to be okay. That is, except for the idiots who have been calling you and hanging up. Tony Robertson and his men will see to that."

"Remind me to give you a hug."

"I will indeed. Now, go close all your windows, blinds, curtains, and lock your doors. Then pack a small suitcase and come back down to the kitchen. Eat something. Soup. You've got two hours to kill."

"Bless you, Pete Novak. Thanks."

"Take care. See you in a bit. Novak out."

As soon as he hung up the line with Karen, Pete pressed the intercom and called Jack Barrett. Jack was also still in–that was life in the intelligence business. Things continually happened around the world on a 24-hour basis. Pete briefed him on Karen's call, what was happening, and what he was planning to do.

"Pete, right, Tony's the best choice. Do you have arrangements for a clean-up crew to be on stand-by?" Jack asked.

"I do."

"Then you're approved to press ahead. When you have Karen evacuated and safe, give me a call to let me know that. After that, I guess it'll be a waiting game."

"You're right about that, Jack. I agree in spades about Tony Robertson being our best team lead in the Special Activities Division. I've seen him in action and I wouldn't want to be the one who tries to fuck with him and his team."

"Gotcha on that. Keep me informed. I'm headed home. We'll talk later."

"Take care."

"You too. Barrett out."

CHAPTER 29

Seconds passed to minutes, minutes to hours. Karen sat at the kitchen table, her hands folded in her lap. She knew Pete Novak had best intentions, but an hour after eating, the Campbell's Chicken Noodle Soup wasn't sitting well in her stomach. The dead time, sitting and waiting, was putting her on a razor's edge again. She was still alone with nothing but darkness surrounding her.

She glanced at the luminescent, digital clock above the oven. It read 8:30 P.M. The interior of the house was now shrouded with a curtain of black shadows. Karen's eyes had adjusted quickly. She could make out everything in the kitchen. There was also a smidgeon of light seeping through the vertical blinds on the sliding doors. Pale light oozed from a sliver of moon hanging between clouds in an otherwise black sky.

Her ears perked. Karen turned toward the double sliding doors. There were five gentle taps in succession on the glass. She rose from her chair and stepped to the vertical blinds, one hand on her shoulder holster, the other pulling two blinds apart just a crack. She took a peek.

His face was close up against the glass and with a blue tinge in the watery light. Startled, Karen jerked backward a foot, stretched her neck to shake off the tension, and then opened the blind again. Tony Robertson. It was Tony. He gestured with a short, slow wave of his right hand and smiled. She could see several more very large, black clothed men standing close behind him.

Karen opened the blinds fully and unlocked the door. She slid the door open on its runner, then snapped open the lever on the screen door.

"Hi Karen. Remember me, Tony Robertson? Everything okay here so far?" Robertson spoke in a hushed whisper.

"Hi, Tony. Yes, I do remember you very well and all's fine. Come on in," Karen said, stepping aside.

The hulks of seven men carrying assault weaponry slung over their shoulders slipped through the opening. What looked to be night vision goggles were pushed up over the black stretch caps on their heads. Karen remembered that back in Maine, Dave had told her that Robertson's team were all real *ass kickers*, just as lethal, maybe even more so, than Navy SEALs. Seeing them up close like this, she had to agree that was probably gospel. They gathered between the table and the kitchen's center island. Karen closed the screen and sliding door. She locked them both.

"Karen, your basement, is it finished?" Robertson asked in the blackness of the kitchen.

"Yes, it is."

"How many rooms."

Karen paused, then murmured, "Five."

"Windows?"

"Two on each side of the house. They're set down in window wells. They slide open horizontally and oh, all have screen windows too."

"Are the window wells covered, you know, with metal grates or Lexan plate covers?"

"No. Dave and I were going to try to get them installed this year."

"Any sump pumps or other obstructions in the wells?"

"No. There's just pea gravel at the bottoms."

"Okay, thanks," Tony swiveled about to face his group.

"Sam, Bill, you go down and cover the basement. Maintain a close watch on those windows. Andy, you take the upstairs. Wander around a bit and between the rooms, but I doubt anybody's going to be scaling brick walls tonight. George, Don and I will take the main floor," Tony turned back to Karen.

"Karen, this is Doug Lang. Doug is going to take you out the back of your house in the way we just came in. The Agency will eventually reimburse your neighbors for the cut links in their fence," He chuckled, then continued.

"You and Doug will be going to a Chevy Tahoe that's waiting for you. Then it will be a short drive up to Arlington. Pete Novak said to tell you that he'll be meeting you there. Is all that okay with you?"

Karen stepped forward to Tony. She wrapped her hands around his neck, stood up on her toes and kissed him. His eyes blinked. If he was blushing, you couldn't see it in the darkness.

Doug opened the sliding doors, the screen, and the two of them stepped through into the backyard, Doug leading. Tony slid the doors closed and locked them.

"Okay, let's take our positions, guys. I'm going to take a wild ass guess that show time will be about eleven o'clock, perhaps a little later. Familiarize yourselves with the layout of the rooms and furniture. Know where the obstacles are that could pose barriers to your movement. Make sure your assault rifles are on full auto. Mr. Novak didn't specify we needed any witnesses, so that's our rule of engagement tonight. Bravo team is dispersed in their vehicles along Commonwealth Boulevard. If there is a driver, they've got that covered and will take him. Let's go."

The men raised their rifles in a silent salute, then dispersed into the darkness. Two men, George and Don, moved up closer to Robertson. Nodding to them, Tony turned on his head microphone.

"Chuck, Bravo team, Robertson here."

"Yes, sir, this is Chuck."

"You and your six are in three vehicles?"

"Yes. Three vehicles."

"When the time arrives, I'll call you. Do a lights-out, high-speed rush at the vehicle at our curb. Box it in. Whatever type of vehicle it ends up being, do your maneuver close, bumper on bumper, metal on metal. I don't know if there will be a driver, but if there is, he won't expect it. If it does turn out that you see one, then I want everybody out with their gun sights on the driver. Immediately. Take him alive, if you can do so safely. We good?"

"Yes, sir. Got it."

"Great. Later. Robertson out."

Robertson's eyes scanned the team. "They think they're coming after just one woman, Karen McClure. Karen's husband is one of us, and in operations. The key here is whoever shows up here won't expect our presence. So, at first, there'll be some shock, maybe they'll mess their pants. We're not going to waste that advantage. I expect no more than three, maybe four, coming inside. This is a come-to-Jesus welcome party. That's our mission."

Robertson paused and pointed to George. "George, take the front hall and living room. Don, living room and family room. I'll take the dining room and the kitchen. Best guess is they'll attempt an entry downstairs through a basement window. If that happens, Don, I'll signal you to go down and join Sam and Bill. If it ends up being a diversion, don't worry about it. George and I will stop their asses up here. Now, we wait. Let's go find someplace comfortable."

Tony found himself suddenly alone in the kitchen, the house dead quiet. He knew each one of his men was highly skilled. They were superb at their business and with any luck, this would go quickly. He backed away from the dim light of the sliding doors and up against the stove where he could also see into the dining room with its singular window. He checked his watch…two minutes after nine. So far, so good.

Minutes ticked away. Tony moved silently between the dining room and the kitchen as the first hour passed by.

At fifteen minutes after ten, a leaden gray Toyota Camry with four male occupants turned left off Braddock Road onto Sideburn Road and cruised south in unhurried fashion. It turned left again onto Commonwealth Boulevard, heading back to the east. Just after passing Roberts Road, the vehicle crawled to a near stop, pausing at the first junction with Pumphrey Drive.

"It's the next left. Go up one," The man in the right front seat said.

The Camry proceeded to the next intersection of the Pumphrey Drive loop. It turned left on the street. The driver turned off the headlights as the sedan crept forward along the line of houses. The sedan turned in against the curb, the engine keyed off.

All four windows slid slowly down into the doors. The men sat, listening. Minutes passed. The street was as silent as a county morgue at midnight. People in the entire Washington

DC Metro area were in bed, gathering what sleep they could before the early morning commute into the District began once again.

"Bauman. Jerry, after we're out, go down the street a bit and do a U-turn. Pull back here against the curb. We want to be out of here quickly. It shouldn't take long. I'm thinking five minutes or so, ten at the most," The man in the front seat murmured.

"Okay, John," Bauman said.

"Let's go."

The car doors were gently opened and even more quietly closed behind them as they exited. The three men in black clothing bent over, skulking up the lawn like alley cats, their boots leaving trails in the grass now wet with dew. They approached the side of the brick residence…the two window wells were directly ahead.

At a few minutes after ten-thirty, Robertson's ear phones clicked. "Tony, this is Sam. Bingo, they're here. You win the lotto on your guess. Downstairs, the rear, south-side window well. I have an eye on one of them…looks like he's using a diamond cutter on the window."

"Okay. Bill, join Sam, pronto. Don, go downstairs and join Sam. All team members, have your goggles on, safeties off, and rounds chambered. Gentlemen, show time. Let's go earn our paychecks."

Don, Bill, and Sam knelt in the hallway off the basement's rear, south room. They watched as the man in the window well jerked on the rubber cup to snap out the circle of glass he'd just cut. He reached in and up, and undid the window lock. He took out a spray can hooked on his belt and sprayed the sides of the window jam with some kind of lubricant, and soundlessly lifted the window. He climbed in the room. Two other men slipped down into the window well and into the room behind him.

Sam and the others eased back up in the hallway and around an intersecting wall. Sam whispered into his microphone.

"Tony, Sam, no diversion. Three of them are entering now."

"Good. Back up now. Take positions with crossing lines of fire at the doorway to the entrance room," Tony replied.

"Andy, George, down to the basement. Now. Fast and be super quiet about it. I'll join you there."

Two short minutes later, Tony peeked out and took a quick glimpse of the hallway, then jerked back behind the wall. The three men were cautiously stepping from the south room into the hallway. Their pistols were drawn, leading in front of them. No rifles. They also were wearing night vision goggles. They glanced behind them, then moved forward tentatively.

The lead intruder unexpectedly paused. He raised his arm. The two men behind him halted in step. As the lead man brought his pistol up to shoulder level, the others followed suit, slowly raising their pistols.

"Fire," Tony whispered, instantly going full auto with his Heckler & Koch light machine gun.

The rest of the team opened fire simultaneously. The men in the hallway were taken entirely by surprise. A blistering, muffled staccato of sound-suppressed gunfire filled the corridor. Dozens of rounds went bursting down the hall, jamming the entire, narrow passageway. Bullets crossed wall-to-wall and up-and-down, exploding into the chests and torsos of the intruders.

All three men were propelled swiftly backward from the sudden, concussive impacts of the scorching rate of fire. They stumbled sideways, slamming into the wall, and finally toppled, smashing down to the flooring. The black-clad men lay where they fell, torn apart, motionless. It was over. And in seven seconds.

Robertson lifted his finger off the trigger and raised his hand. "Cease fire. Remove your goggles." He pushed himself up, now standing by a corner of walls, reached over and flicked on the hall overhead light. Everyone's eyes squinted, blinking.

"Anybody hit?" Tony asked. He glanced around to each of the men, who shook their heads, scrunching their eyes in the sudden spray of bright light.

"Well done, you bad asses," Tony exclaimed, rubbing his own eyes.

"Sir, I don't think they got off even one shot," Sam muttered.

The men's eyes gradually adjusted. They stared down the hallway. Gobs of blood were splattered everywhere along the walls and ceilings. Pools of blood were amassing around the bodies on the floor.

"Jeez. My God," It was Bill, his face contorted in anguish at the sight before him.

"Easy now. Come on, you guys know you've all seen worse. Don, you and George start checking for IDs. I doubt you'll find anything, but check them out. Wear your gloves." Robertson swiveled in place and spoke into his microphone.

"Chuck, Bravo team!"

"Yes, sir, Chuck here."

"You're on. Take the vehicle and any occupants. Hit it!"

"Yes, sir! Let's roll! Slam that vehicle and block it. Then out fast, weapons at the ready. Go!" Chuck shouted into his microphone.

Chuck's three vehicles lurched away from their curbs, tires screeching as they made the turn onto Pumphrey Drive from

Commonwealth. They sprinted toward the sedan parked against a curb near the McClure house. The driver glanced through the windshield, his eyes bulging. He jammed the key into the ignition. Terror splashed across his face.

One of Bravo team's cars, a Charger, jammed against the vehicle's front bumper and another scraped along the street-side doors. The man paused, his eyes wide in horror, raising his hands in surrender. The men of Bravo team leaped from their vehicles, the muzzles of their rifles raised to their shoulders and focused on the driver.

Tony Robertson's team gathered in the kitchen, lights on. They took glasses out of the cupboard and went to the sink to get drinks of cold water. Robertson's earphones clicked.

"Tony, this is Chuck, Bravo team. We have the driver. Now?"

"Take him out to Manassas. The house. Cuff him, wrists and ankles, then put him in an interview room, no windows."

"Right. Will do. His vehicle's drivable. Drive that there too?"

"Yes. Put it in the garage and tell the guys there to go over it, inside and out. Also, run the plate, find registration paperwork if there is any. If no registration, they can run the VIN number down and see what turns up, where it was purchased and by whom, stuff like that. Maybe we'll get lucky and find the name of the last purchaser of record. Good work, Chuck. Tell your team that. Robertson out."

Tony immediately dialed another number. He heard the rings. It was a *hello phone*... there would be no specific person greeting him.

"Hello?"

"Tony Robertson here. Clean-up, please, 5200 Pumphrey Drive, Fairfax."

"Is the house empty?"

"It will be. We're leaving as I speak. Everything needing attention is in the basement." The line clicked off.

Robertson spun about, looking at each man. "Excellent work tonight, gentlemen, you bad asses. Tomorrow, 4:00 p.m., Green House Bistro on Chain Bridge Road, all beers are on me! Let's go."

The men grinning, they walked together through the front door of the house and out onto the walkway.

CHAPTER 30

Pete and Karen stood together on the concrete porch of the safe house, a redbrick townhouse unit. Doug stood on the walk. They arrived just minutes ago. Pete heard his cell phone ring. He jerked it out of its belt holder.

"Novak."

"Mr. Novak, Tony. Mission accomplished. Three men broke in through a basement window at ten-thirty. All three deceased. One's in custody, the driver, now being transported west to the house. A clean-up is imminent."

"Excellent. Thanks. See you in a few," They clicked off.

Novak placed one hand on Karen's shoulder just as he reached out to the door's lever. She turned to him.

"Karen, that was Tony Robertson who just called on the phone. It's over. You were exactly right to call me. Your senses were spot on. Good work, agent Karen McClure! So you know, I'm going to put a discreet twenty-four hour surveillance on your house for two days. Then, when you return, we'll have some agents drive by frequently, monitoring your house. I suspect that's it, though. You'll only have to spend two days here, three at the outside, and it's on the government. Whatever you need, don't hesitate to tell us. It's our pleasure," Pete said.

"Was it bad?"

"Karen, I don't want to relate all the details to you, but as I said, you were correct in calling. Some men did enter your house through a basement window. And, I feel certain it was an attempted kidnapping. They failed and we have one of them in custody. We'll most likely interview him in the morning."

"Mr. Pete Novak," Karen grinned.

"Yes?"

"Here's the hug I promised."

Karen wrapped her arms around Pete and laid her head gently against his chest. She squeezed. It was a big hug. If there was a light on the porch, she would have noticed his ears turning bright red. She gently let loose her arms and backed a step away.

"Wow. Hugged by a lovely young woman under a night sky filled with stars and a ghost of a moon! Goodness!" He said.

Pete turned to Doug who was still standing on the walk, not ten feet away. Doug smiled at the two of them embracing. Pete pointed his right index finger at him.

"Agent Lang, if one word of this gets to my wife, your next assignment will be to Abuja, Nigeria."

"Mr. Novak, sir, I saw nothing…I heard nothing…I know nothing," Doug said. They all broke out laughing.

"Doug, you and Karen go ahead inside and have some coffee and a bagel. It should be ready by now. Karen, by the way, we own this whole row of eight townhouses, so there's nothing to worry about. I'll join you shortly," Pete said.

"Thanks, Pete," Karen said.

Novak swiveled in place and took a few steps back down the walk. He lifted his cell phone again. Two rings and the line was picked up.

"Barrett."

"Jack, Pete. Karen's been evacuated. She's safe. We're at the safe house and about to have a cup of coffee."

"And?"

"Tony hasn't showed up here yet to give me all the gory details, but from his brief initial call, there were three men who entered the house at ten-thirty, a little earlier than we expected. They came in through a basement window and all had their weapons drawn. Tony's team wasted all of them–all three, gone. Chuck and his Bravo team got the driver. He surrendered. They're transporting him out to Manassas, the house. No casualties on our side."

"Outstanding. Good, now I can get some sleep. Pete, you get on home and get some sleep too."

"I will. I just want to get Karen settled in. Then I'm gone."

"All right, See you in the morning. Barrett out."

Pete Novak entered Barrett's office at 9:30 a.m. The morning staff meeting had been cancelled.

"'Morning, Pete. Have a seat. Were you finally able to get some sleep last night?"

"Yes, thanks. I came in at 8:30 this morning."

"That's late for you…but certainly understandable given the circumstances. Great job last night. Karen okay?"

"Yes, she is. I called the safe house on the way in. They were having breakfast. She had taken off her shoulder holster. I think she weathered that bit of psychological trauma fairly well. Tony said the same thing. She did all right, handled it well."

"That's a relief. I'm glad she called you. If we had lost her, I don't…damn, we have to find out who the hell these sonsofbitches are and why they feel they're authorized to do crap like this."

"Amen to that. Okay, first. Dave McClure sent in a secure fax. It had some information concerning VA&S Construction Company…two business cards and a photo taken at the signing of a buy-out. It turns out that VA&S was purchased, totally bought out, before the RTC program in Raton even kicked off. The contract stipulated that the buyer could continue to do business as VA&S for three years. Research & Analysis is going to check out the financial end of the buy-out–when it was finalized, purchase price, that sort of thing. Dave went ahead and met with the former owner, Vincent Armano of Vince Armano & Sons."

"Interesting. Who bought them?"

"J.J. Breeds Corporation. They're headquartered in New York City. Before I left my office to come up here, I forwarded a digital package via the secure pipe to Brent Atwood. He's the lead in our National Resources office at the office in Manhattan. I asked him to check out J.J. Breeds Corporation. I also asked Brent to see if, from the photos, he can locate the whereabouts of the two officers of J.J. Breeds who came out to sign the purchase paperwork, George Mazur and Eric Baranek."

"Well, you came in late but you jumped right into it. I'm really glad to have you as my right-hand, Pete."

"Thanks, Jack. I don't think I've ever worked for a better, more knowledgeable guy. But, ah, don't let that go to your head," Pete chuckled. "Now, second, the driver from last night's assault and attempted kidnapping."

"Right. You said he was transported to Manassas."

"That's correct. They called and told me this morning that they played the mixed audible recordings all night, very low but constant. That's the one with tapping sounds, distant calls of screech owls, dogs barking, a wolf's howl, crows cawing, and things like that. During the night, he moved over to a corner of the room, lying on the floor in an almost fetal position. He was uneasy, jerking, generally in and out of sleep."

"A little sleep deprivation. He'll be somewhat disoriented."

"I think so. Todd Jorgenson will go in the room at about 11:00 a.m. Would you like to drive out with me?"

"Jorgenson? That bear of an interrogator, I mean, interviewer? He's gotta be at least six foot five. Yeah, 'interviewer' is the politically correct term now. Sure, let's do that, see how things go. You drive, Pete."

With traffic, the drive to Manassas on I-66 took them almost an hour. Pete pulled his dark blue Lincoln Navigator to the curb in front of the house on Sherman Court. It was a two story, tan brick colonial situated near the cul-de-sac at the end of the street.

Barrett groaned as they approached the front door. It was August in Virginia now, the air exceedingly hot with ninety-seven percent humidity. Novak looked over, smiled and nodded in agreement. The door was pulled open for them.

"Mr. Barrett, Mr. Novak, good morning," Chuck Nagy greeted them, smiling.

"Superb work last night, Chuck. Your team did an outstanding job. Fast as hell and no casualties. Remarkable," Novak said, reaching his hand out. They shook hands.

"Ditto on that, Chuck. Good to see you," Barrett said.

"Thanks. We have him in a basement room...it's quite cool down there and we turned the humidifier way up. So, I think where we told him he was moved to is believable. It should work. Todd is just about ready to go in."

"Our view?" Barrett asked.

"Fiber optic cameras. Small holes near the top of all four walls."

"Great. Let's go, Chuck."

Minutes later, the three men stood in front of a 55" flat screen. It was divided into four images, one for each camera. The door opened slowly. Jorgenson bent over slightly as he walked through the door, locking it behind him. As he did so, the low sound of the mixed audible recordings ceased. Room lighting was moderate, not bright. A chair in the middle of the room was empty. The driver was curled up on the floor in a corner. He opened his eyes at the sound of Jorgenson's size thirteen footsteps.

"Good morning, whoever you are. Please come over here and sit in the chair so we can talk."

"Fuck off, asshole. How long have I been out? I can't remember. You drugged me, didn't you? And, where the hell am I?" The man sat up.

"Look, peckerwood, nobody drugged you. Truth is, though, you can have this easy or you can have it not easy. So, cut the foul language, come over here, and sit down. To answer your last question, you've been out over twelve hours. You were zonked. You're at GITMO. Ever heard of it?" Jorgenson said.

"GITMO? You shitheads flew me to Cuba? That's illegal! Release me, now! And, I want something to drink. It's freezing and humid as hell in here!"

"The air conditioning is for your benefit. It's well over a hundred and five degrees outside with nearly one hundred percent humidity. Would you prefer that? I can make that happen for you. So, yes, you're in the Guantanamo Bay detention camp. Our bringing you here is 'illegal,' you say? That's funny for someone who just participated in a breaking and entering of a residence, committed an attempted kidnapping of a female, and to top it off, attempted an assault on federal officers. You can't be serious. Oh, and something to drink? That comes later. Maybe."

"Fuck you."

"Such a nasty little doofus, you are. You know, cupcake, you really should be aware that we send some of the world's worst bad asses here. After just two days or so, they all end up crying like little babies. As I've already told you, you can have it easy or you can have it not easy. Your choice."

"Go to hell. I know my rights."

"Ah, yes, your rights, your Miranda, Fifth Amendment warnings. Well, if you insist. For the record then," Jorgenson pulled a card from his pants pocket and began to read from it.

"'Mr. Whoever the hell you are, I advise you that under the Fifth Amendment to the Constitution, you have the right to remain silent, that is, to say nothing at all. Anything you do say, any statement you make, oral or written can and will be used against you in a court of law. You have the right to an attorney. If you cannot afford an attorney, one will be appointed for you.' There now, those are the very basics. You've been read your rights. The problem for you is, you're at GITMO. I'll ask you again, have you heard of us?"

"Yeah, I know who you bastards are. You use waterboarding and torture to interrogate people. Where are the other three?"

"The other three? Oh, you're referring to your three colleagues in the multiple felony crimes that you yourself were involved in? Here's an easy question for you: Have you ever been over to Maryland's eastern shore, maybe to the village of St. Michaels?"

"What the hell? Yes, I've been there. So what?"

"Great. Then maybe you've been to *The Crab Claw* right on the Chesapeake? Awesome food and great views of the 50-foot sport fishermen boats and sail boats going in and out of the harbor. Really gorgeous."

"Okay, asshole, I've been there, and your point is?"

"I'm answering your question, scooter. Relax. Well, just south of St. Michaels, you know, as you drive down Route 50 toward the Blackwater National Wildlife Refuge, the woods there get pretty deep, very dense, lots of underbrush. Only a couple trails go in there. If you do go in and you trek way back into it, there's lots of snakes, mosquitos, and other bad stuff in there."

"What are you saying?"

"Like you, there were no identity documents on your partners in crime. So, we couldn't very well put them in a cemetery. That would be unfair to everybody else who paid to be buried there. No, all three of them are back there in that slime, in unmarked graves where they will never, ever be found. Fact is, they'll be deep in that swampy mud and dirt until the Second Coming."

"They're dead?" The driver's face turned white.

"Oh, come on, now, cupcake. We don't bury people alive. We're not animals…just determined patriots. Of course, they were dead."

"Shit."

"Indeed. So, your choice. You were examined when you were transported here. Some bruises and minor lacerations were found. Now that you're awake, they will clean all that up and treat it so you won't have any infections. It's quite routine for us. However, the process can be somewhat painful for you. I find that it's hard to watch actually," Jorgenson turned and stepped toward the door. He raised his cell phone.

"The subject has made his choice for pain management. Bring in the equipment, doctor and nurse, please."

"Wait a damned minute!" The driver yelled out.

The man struggled to rise to his knees, then stood and shuffled to the chair. He plopped into the seat, panting.

"Yes?"

"Look, I'm sorry for what I said, for what I called you! I didn't sign up for this shit! I'm only a driver!"

"And your training for that position was where?"

"They trained me in defensive driving out at the track in Chandler, Arizona. Please," The man's eyes had turned wet.

Jorgenson nodded. He raised his cell phone again.

"Ah, sorry, but that's a negative on the doctor and nurse, for the present anyway. It appears the gentleman has changed his mind," Jorgenson said. He walked to within three feet of the man in the chair and leaned over.

"First, your name is?" Jorgenson said firmly, with no emotion in his voice.

"Jerry Bauman…Jerome William Bauman. Look, I'll tell you anything you want to know. That is, whatever I do know, and believe me, that ain't much."

"Jerry, if you do cooperate fully, it will serve to mitigate the charges against you. So, tell me, who or what do you work for?"

"The program."

"What program?"

"DHS. FEMA. STARDUST."

"STARDUST? That's an intriguing nickname. What does it mean?"

"Please understand, this is only from what I've heard. The program name comes from an acronym: *__S__earch–__TA__rget–__R__econnaissance–__D__e__ST__roy*. STARDUST."

"All right. So, the last part...destroy? What exactly is this program intended to destroy?"

"We're given the targets. Target groups, personalities. I've heard guys talking, the ops team members themselves. They said the program gives them *sanction authority*, whatever that is. I thought sanctions were economic, like tariffs?" Jerry paused.

Standing at the large screen, listening and watching, Barrett and Novak looked at each other with a sudden uneasiness. They turned back to the screen.

Jerry continued. "The current structure of the plan though, you see, is primarily an anti-gang program, national-level. Clear the cities of the core, the worst of them. That's what I've heard. But then, I'm just a driver."

"Right, you said that before. Now, STARDUST is related to the RTC, Raton, and the three distribution centers on the east coast, right?"

"Yes, it is. You seem to already know a lot about it. We've been told that a lot of us are going to those centers on the east coast at the end of this week or just after. We weren't told why. An exercise, I think."

"The end of this week or the first week in September?"

"Yes."

"Going to those locations to do what?"

"I have no idea. Really, I don't. It's got to somehow be linked to anti-gang related operations."

"You know, Jerry, so far you're doing a whole lot better. I think we're off to a good start. Here, let me come around behind you. I'll see if we can take those handcuffs off," Jorgenson said, his face cracking a small smile up at one of the cameras as he stepped to the rear of the chair.

"Thanks," Jerry began rubbing his wrists.

"Before we start up again, you said you'd like something to drink. How about a sandwich?"

"Both, please."

"I'll be right back," Jorgenson said.

The driver looked up and began to scan the four walls. He wiped his eyes, glancing to the ceiling, and inhaled a deep breath. A sigh of relief emanated from his chest.

Barrett looked at Novak. "Damn."

"I agree."

They shook their heads slightly. Jorgenson was a true master. He was sometimes amazingly fast too. Like today.

What they'd just heard from the driver opened a million additional questions that they would want answers for. And soonest.

Novak turned to Chuck. "Chuck, do you know where the other three are? The dead ones from McClure's house," He asked.

"I believe the medical staff is taking fingerprints and dental X-rays, all for identification. Last, of course, will be the official autopsies."

"Thanks," Novak said.

With Chuck leading, the three of them turned and went back up the stairs.

CHAPTER 31

Colorado Springs, Colorado
Early August

McClure had just gulped down a gob of oatmeal in the Marriott's Ascent Restaurant when his cell phone rang. He reached for the coffee mug and guzzled just enough to wash it all down.

"Hello," Dave said.

"Dave, Kevin O'Brien. How're you doing?"

"I'm fine. Good to hear from you, Agent Kevin O'Brien, our own Portland tech lead extraordinaire!"

"You have a good memory."

"Where are you, Kevin?"

"I'm here in town–out at Peterson Air Force Base. I'm picking up the Subaru that they air-shipped out here. Are you still lodged over at the Marriott? If so, have you had a chance yet to turn in your rental car?"

"Yes, on both counts. I'm finishing breakfast right now in the hotel's restaurant. I dropped the Volvo off last night."

"Great. Dave, it might take me some time to get there. Go ahead and pack up. Check out. I'll meet you out front."

"We're leaving immediately?"

"Sure, why not? It's a good two and a half hour drive down there. We can chat on the way."

"That's true. Okay, Kevin. I'll be waiting."

"See you in a bit," Kevin clicked off.

McClure took the elevator back up, threw his suitcase on the bed and began tossing things in. He zipped it all up with the extras that Pete Novak had sent out. Ten minutes later and after checking out, he plopped into an easy chair in the lobby, sipping a glass of iced tea and watching people come and go.

O'Brien pulled up to the entrance a half hour later. Dave walked out and crammed his things into the back seat.

"Kemo sabe, Tonto say he very happy to see you again," Kevin leaned over and stuck out his hand. Dave climbed in the passenger side and shook hands.

"Kevin, please, no more Kemo sabe-Tonto stuff. This isn't Maine and Pete Novak said I have sanction authority on you this time."

"Hey, come on, up there in Maine, out in Tamarack Harbor, you were tighter than a hair in a biscuit. I was just trying to lighten you up. You had focused on that gal with the set of drones that were hovering so nicely!" Kevin chuckled.

Dave shook his head. "I remember. I pinged on the wrong vehicle, the gold Jeep Rubicon, and she was in it…that's history."

"Right. So, no humor?"

"Within reason. Come on, let's get outta here."

"We're off."

O'Brien grinned as he swerved from the entrance and dashed down the ramp to Tech Center Drive. They sat in silence until they had driven to just south of Colorado Springs on I-25. Kevin hadn't changed at all, but then, it was only a short time ago that they'd worked together on the operation in Maine. He was in his late forties, about five feet ten inches, thinning brown hair, but also muscular and obviously very fit. Kevin O'Brien was no desk jockey.

On the fairly open road, Kevin turned to Dave. "There's a burner phone in the center console, Dave. It's a new one. You can toss the old one you have. Rest assured though that any calls to the old number will be forwarded to this new phone. And, I need to brief you on something Pete Novak instructed me to. That's why the new phone. Afterward, you can use it to call."

"What is it?" Dave paused, his first thought was of Karen. "Karen, she's okay, isn't she?"

"Your heart's in the right place, pal. Yes, she's fine, but she might not have been if she hadn't acted so quickly. Karen's a smart gal. That's what I need to relate to you. Then you can call her. She's on a new burner phone too. Her number is keyed into yours."

"What happened?" A flash of alarm washed across Dave's face.

Kevin recounted the happenings at Dave and Karen's home in detail. He began with Karen's receipt of four phone calls late one afternoon that were spaced out every half hour with the caller hanging up as soon as she answered. Then, Karen's call to Pete Novak to express her concern and Tony Robertson's subsequent evacuation of Karen from their home to a safe house in Arlington. Finally, Tony's guys' ultimate lethal encounter with the would-be kidnappers. All were dead except the driver. Dave shook his head slowly back and forth in disbelief.

"Damn. Kevin, can I call her now?"

"Wait until we get a tad south of Pueblo and then I'll pull

over. Try to make it brief though, Dave. We've got quite a ways to go."

"Thanks," McClure leaned into the seat back, his brow furrowed with anxiety. Had his actions in Raton put his wife in danger?

Past Pueblo and with open fields appearing on both sides of the interstate, Kevin slowed the Subaru and pulled over onto the far right edge of the shoulder. With his new cell phone in hand, Dave climbed out of the vehicle. There were several rings before a pick-up.

"Hello?" It was Karen's voice.

"Karen, honey, this is Dave. Are you okay, sweetheart, I mean, really okay? I'm with Kevin O'Brien. Remember him from Maine? He told me what happened at the house."

"Kevin O'Brien? Yes, I remember him. I'm fine now, Dave, honest. I called Pete Novak as you've always told me to do. I didn't know if I was worried over nothing or what. But Pete jumped on it. He sent Tony Robertson with his team out to evacuate me and then stake out the house in case in the event it was a real threat."

"You're completely okay?"

"Yeah, I admit, I wasn't at first, but I am now. I'm at a safe house in Arlington. Dave, Pete didn't, wouldn't, tell me everything at first. I think he was trying to spare me from any additional stress, but I've learned about it all since then from the men who check in here on me every now and then. Three men did enter our house through a basement window about ten-thirty that night. They had their weapons already drawn. Robertson's team engaged them and killed all three. They captured the driver alive. Apparently, he's at some house the company has out in Manassas, has opened up, and is talking. Pete said he's fairly certain that I can go home in a day or two, and he's putting security on the house for a while. Pete Novak…Dave, that man acted so fast for me. He saved me from being kidnapped. He may have saved my life."

"Jeez, I feel so damn bad that I wasn't there to protect you. I'm sorry, Karen. I love you so much. I don't know what I'd do…"

"No point in going there, sweetheart. It didn't happen and it's not going to. I love you too. Whoever attempted this, well, you may be in danger yourself."

"We've got it under control. Kevin O'Brien's with me now."

"All right. So, don't worry, I'm fine now and I have great protection."

"Your protection should be me. I feel helpless."

"Don't do that. I was NCIS, remember? And now, I'm in National Resources Division at the company. I can handle it. You have work to do. Important work or they wouldn't have sent you. I'm fine. Really. Call me when you can, and I mean really have the time, can spare the time. It's me now who has to not worry about you. I love you."

"Okay, thanks. Love you. Be safe, honey," Dave clicked off. He walked to the Subaru and slumped into the passenger seat.

"Okay for now?" Kevin asked.

"Yeah, for now. Better now that I've talked with her. Tonto, kick that horse of yours, Scout, in the ass and let's ride into off into the New Mexico sunset," Dave grinned.

"You *are* better, Kemo sabe. That's good. By the way, I've got a satellite phone with me. It has a VPN secure pipe capability wired into it. So, whatever we find or maybe don't find, we can report immediately back to Langley and do so securely," Kevin said, smiling.

"That's super."

Kevin gunned the engine and pulled back onto the interstate. After five minutes or so of cruising down I-25, Dave turned once again to Kevin.

"Pete said not to go back to the hotel, so where are we headed?" Dave asked.

"Mr. Novak doesn't let any grass grow under his feet, that's for sure. Apparently, we have already secured a place, and from what he described to me, it's massive, more like a commercial facility than a residence. He said it was once used for assembly of cathode ray tubes or something like that on a 24-7 schedule. It's large, has a good-sized kitchen, multiple bathrooms and even showers. It can accommodate well up to 150 men. The folding beds, much better than cots, are supposed to have been already put in place. That also supports operators we'll need for the BATS–DARK RAPTOR, that is, if we have to bring them in. Have you been read in on that program?"

"Wow. That *was* fast. Yes, Pete gave me a brief overview on the BATS. It sounds like quite a system. Where's this facility?"

"It's in northwest Raton, out on the fringe a bit. You think you can guide us there?" Kevin said.

"Northwest Raton? I don't think it'll be a problem. I've been up that way. The police department's up that way."

"Pete mentioned that it's well past the police department. Moulton Avenue. Moulton's a road off of 2nd Street, and then to Hill Street."

"All right, that's good. That street, 2nd Street, is the main north-south thoroughfare in Raton. This shouldn't be hard. Do you want me to give you some background on things to the east, on Routes 72 and 526? That's where Pete said imagery platforms were picking up thermal blips at night out in the Sugarite Canyon area. An old gal here in Raton who lost her husband told me about a fairly hidden two-track road in the forest out there that ascends through the woods up to near a mesa, Horse Mesa."

"Lester Hadley's wife, Loretta?"

"So, you've already been briefed on Hadley's death. Excellent. Let's just go to the facility. Take the Route 72, Cook Avenue exit and go west. That eventually goes northwest and intersects 2nd Street. We'll take a right there and drive north until we see Moulton Avenue. It shouldn't be difficult."

"Super. Thanks, Dave."

"You're welcome. Do you think we should push it…you know, try for tonight?" McClure said.

"To go in the woods? Let's see how we feel after we've settled in, checked out building security, and had something to eat. Then, if you really think you're up for going in tonight, I'm game."

"Great. Then onward we ride, Tonto," Dave smiled.

"Indeed, sir," Kevin answered.

CHAPTER 32

After taking Cook Avenue off the interstate, then 2nd Street, Moulton Avenue, and a left onto Hill Street, they spotted the building on the right. Kevin was right...it was huge with a dirt and gravel mix parking lot surrounding it on all sides. Perfect for their needs. Kevin pulled the Subaru around to the back side of the building, out of sight. Dave noticed there was an entrance door on that side also.

Kevin climbed out, turned and walked away across the lot to the edge of the rear parking area. He approached a rusted and broken wheelbarrow that had a short pile of old, broken bricks lying next to it. There was nothing beyond that but woods. Dave went to the entrance door.

"Kevin, where're you going? The door's locked. How do we get in?" Dave asked.

"Right here. The key," Kevin said. He had dug down through three layers of bricks. He found the small plastic zip-lock bag. He held it up.

"I should have guessed," Dave said, shaking his head and smiling.

Once inside, they walked throughout the building, checking all doors and windows. Everything was locked up tight. The folding beds had already been set out and spread throughout the largest open room of the facility which had probably once been an assembly floor. The ceiling was painted black and had open piping and conduits of different sorts. The walls were painted white but had apparently dulled somewhat over the years. They each picked out a bed and threw their bags on them.

"Dave, you think you could eat lunch now? I know you said you had breakfast at the Marriott, but I'm famished."

"Sure. All I had was oatmeal. Raton is kind of thin for restaurants, Kevin. The Denny's out by the highway is okay for lunch. Their burgers are pretty good. It's on Clayton Road near the interstate."

"Let's do it."

Dave and Kevin both had burgers, fries, and cokes. There was little conversation, just chowing down to abate the hunger. In a little over an hour, they were back at the facility, and had begun unpacking their bags. Dave first laid the multispectral camouflage suit and night vision goggles on the bed. He pulled the Beretta, three mags, and two ammo boxes out of the suitcase and began loading the mags, then fitted the now-loaded Beretta into the DeSantis slant-rig shoulder holster.

Dave sat on the edge of the bed and watched Kevin unpack the satellite phone. The phone assembled, Kevin sat on his bed as well.

"Are you nervous?" Kevin asked.

"I suppose. A tad."

"That's good, actually. You still want to go in tonight?"

"Yeah, I think so. I feel good about it."

"Then we're on. Dave, remember that camouflage suit has a Kevlar lining in it. I screwed up back in Maine by not telling you that early on."

"No biggie. I found out fast enough anyway. That Russian's bullet hit me right directly in the chest. I should have been dead, but I wasn't. I had one helluva bruise though."

"Yeah, but it was a pretty bruise...sort of like a rainbow-purple, orange, and yellow!" Kevin laughed.

"It *was* a handsome bruise, wasn't it? I have to admit though, it was that damn suit and you getting me back to the hotel in Bar Harbor so fast that saved my life. You have a morose sense of humor, Kevin, but I have to say you're one good guy to have at your back when the heat is on. I'd have you on my team anytime, anywhere," Dave said.

"My pleasure to serve, Kemo sabe."

"What do you think we should do to kill time now?" Dave asked.

"Well, it's hot as hell outside and nice and cool in here. Why don't we just lay back and try to take a short nap. I'll gas up the Subaru later. And, ah, what can we do for dinner?"

"The Ice House on 2nd Street. I've driven past it several times. Everything's on 2nd Street. They have barbecue, ribs, salad...that should do."

"Great. We'll shoot for about six o'clock this evening. Let's get a little bag time now," Kevin said, stretching out on the folding bed.

"What time do you want to go into the canyon? Today's Friday, so there won't be any truck convoys coming to Super Save Discount Foods tonight...wherever it is that they come from."

"About eleven o'clock, maybe a little before. Things should be pretty quiet all over by then."

"Good idea," Dave took off his shoes and rolled over on his side. Kevin plopped his head in the middle of the pillow and closed his eyes. In minutes, they had both drifted off to a light sleep.

A little over three hours later, Kevin's eyes blinked slowly open. He raised his wrist and glanced at the watch. Five-thirty. Forcing himself to a sitting position, he rubbed his eyes and swiveled his feet over and onto the floor. The tile flooring over concrete was cool. The nap felt truly invigorating. He looked over at Dave and walked over to his bed. Kevin gently shook his shoulder.

"Hey, Kemo sabe, wake up."

One half-hour later, they were sitting on wooden chairs at a wooden table near a wood-paneled wall at the *Historic Ice House restaurant*. Above the top edge of the wood panels, the walls were painted red, decorated with rows of antique ice-block tongs, ice axes and picks. Definitely a back-home kind of restaurant…one fitting for Raton.

"Can we have a cold beer?" Kevin asked.

"Sure. Just one though."

They scanned the menu. Barbecue ribs seemed to be the highlight. They both ordered salads, ribs, mashed potatoes with gravy and, of course, for each an iced mug of beer. Their dinners were delivered promptly and five minutes later they were both well into munching at the meal.

"Say, Dave, this is really good. I'm glad we picked this place. The ribs are awesome. You know, the nap this afternoon and now a dinner like this…I am totally recovered. I've got the airplane off of me, and the drive down here as well."

"Great. And, I agree. Best ribs I've had in years. It's the sauce, the basting."

"Another beer?" Kevin asked.

"No, not a good idea."

"You're a meanie. I'm just driving, not going in like you."

"You, Mr. O'Brien, have to be on top of your game. Please, have an iced coffee instead."

"All right. Iced coffee. And, the rest of this evening?"

"Clean our weapons. Check out the camo suit. Is the Subaru topped off?"

"Yes. You saw me fill up. Why do you ask?"

"Well, I've been chased down here once before at high speed, so in case it happens again and we have to scoot up I-25, it would be with a full load of fuel. We would outrun them. We can't lead them back to the facility. Nothing's gonna happen like that tonight though. Like you said, it should be quiet."

"Agree."

The evening went fast. Dave cleaned the Beretta and checked all his gear while Kevin went out to ensure the stealth features of the Subaru were working as designed. Kevin then cleaned his own pistol, a Smith & Wesson .40 cal. They used the bathrooms and, afterward, washed up. The facility was really not too bad in its amenities at all.

The hours seemed to race by. Ten-thirty came quickly. Gathering up their gear, Dave and Kevin walked out to the Subaru, locking the door behind them. Each stuffed their things in the back.

"You think I should put the camo suit on now?" Dave asked.

"No, wait until we're just inside the canyon. I'll pull over and you can put the seat-back down like you did last time."

"Well, let's hit the road, Tonto. Drive south down to Sugarite Avenue–a left there takes us onto Cook Avenue and that becomes Route 72."

"Got it."

They both sat quietly, peering ahead through the windshield and checking the sides of the road for any suspicious parked vehicles. There was no traffic at all. The farther they went, there were fewer houses that still had interior lights on. Kevin and Dave relaxed in their seats. Once headed east out on Route 72, Kevin broke the silence.

"Not a sound, quiet as hell out here. How far to the intersection with Route 576?"

"A couple minutes ahead on your left. Take it slow as we enter...don't toss any gravel around."

"Right."

A sign for Route 576 appeared on the left. Right after it was a sign for Sugarite Canyon State Park. Kevin slowed the Subaru to a crawl and took the turn as soundlessly as possible onto the park road. He immediately lifted the lid to the center console and began turning on the myriad of stealth features, the cool headlights, vented exhaust and such. A second set of side windows with darkened glass rose gently up alongside the original glass, minimizing the escape of both light and heat.

He turned to Dave, smiled and slowly steered the wheels over to the road's edge. He shifted into park.

"Time to suit up, Kemo sabe. Remember, no one can see you in that suit unless you move. They can see the movement, but not you," Kevin said.

"I remember. Thanks. Don't worry."

Dave grabbed the camo suit from the back seat, pushed his seatback down and began slipping everything on except for the hood. Suited up, he pulled the seatback upright and glanced over at Kevin.

"Got everything? Goggles, pistol, knife, Taser?" Kevin asked.

"Got it all. I'm fully armed up."

Kevin gently eased the Subaru back onto the road. The

stealth vehicle slinked along like a whisper in a slight breeze, passing the relatively small Lake Alice on the right, and finally, the western end of Lake Maloya. The gate bar was down.

"Okay. I guess this is where we part, I'll be going back down 576 somewhere near the entrance. My cell's on speaker. Any issues at all, call me and I'll be here in a heartbeat," Kevin said.

"Thanks, Kevin."

They shook hands. Dave softly pushed his door open and eased it back into its jamb behind him. Once on the roadway, he pulled the hood up and over his head and then slid on the night vision goggles and tugged them down over his eyes. He checked his pistol, knife, and Taser. He saluted Kevin, turned and began ambling nimbly along the edge of the road on the sponge-rubber soles of his boots. He ducked under the gate pole.

Dave turned about in time to watch the Subaru return back down the road, but it had already disappeared. Even the tail lights were somehow shuttered. The Subaru was in total stealth operation now. It had turned around and headed back on Route 576. He smiled and began moving along the lake's perimeter road toward the dark, thick forest lying just ahead.

Dave followed the road as it curved around the lake, taking care to walk with silent, easy steps. He could make out that near the end of the lake road was a small, circular parking area. Vehicles could probably also turn around there. He moved to the furthermost edge of the road's shoulder, leaned over shrubbery and searched for the two-track pathway.

As Loretta Hadley had mentioned, it was hard to find. After gently pushing some scrub brush aside along the line of forest, he finally spotted it. He stepped into the woods and crouched to kneeling. Not moving, he listened, scanning the uphill path with his night vision. Nothing caught his attention. He rose to his feet and moved ahead.

Dave smelled it before he saw it. Smoke, cigarette smoke. There was a tiny beacon of light uphill on the right. He once again slipped down into a tight crouch, listening. A figure rose up from the shrubbery ahead. Then another. Two men with rifles slung over their shoulders. They said something to each other, then swiveled their attention downhill along the two track.

"Who's there?" One man said in a low voice.

Dave remained silent, balled up in a crouch. As he watched the two figures ahead, his right hand slipped onto the grip of his pistol. The men's heads were scanning left and right into the woods.

"Show yourself," The man said again.

The second man leaned over and spoke to the first. They shook their heads and gradually sank down behind the low brush. Dave waited where he was. Total stillness. Minutes passed. He could tell the men were still up on the right side of the path, but weren't moving. He heard low whispers. Whatever the two had heard, they'd apparently decided the slight noise was just some small critter in the woods, a rabbit, fox, something like that.

Sentries? In a state park? At this hour? Dave rose ever so slightly, watching the path ahead. It was quiet again. He swiveled about, bent over at the waist and began making his way downhill. He paused now and then to listen, but hearing nothing, he continued down to the perimeter road. He would have to go up into the high forest at some other point.

Treading his way down the road from the direction he had originally come, he stepped off a count of fifty yards, then turned back into the woods. He should be far enough away from the two sentries. He quietly tip-toed ahead in a crouch, occasionally brushing aside low shrubs. A sudden and gorgeous aroma like cologne filled his nostrils. Bending over to search where the scent was coming from, he touched what seemed to be soft petals.

Flowers. He bent lower. Raising his eyes, glancing right and left, he realized that he had stepped into a small meadow filled to its brim with blossoms. Even with night vision goggles, it was impossible to determine what kind of flowers were blooming all around him, but their fragrance was overwhelming. It was a glorious bouquet smack dab in the middle of alpine woods. Smelling flowers in the forest at night, in the darkness, was somehow surreal…it was something that one normally did in sunlight. However, what a pleasant surprise this forest had just offered him.

Dave stood up, smiling, and again began tramping uphill. Gradually, his feet told him the area was becoming more solid, stony. Flowers and rich earth had given way to some kind of sedimentary rock. A few steps further and he could see he was ascending what looked to be a solid rock floor.

With no warning, an abrupt, rotten stench assaulted his senses...an utterly disgusting stink. Whatever was just ahead of him reeked of the foulest odor he could imagine. He raised his head high to try to catch some clear air. Dave bent over, crouched low to the ground, and took the Maglite from a suit pocket. He thrust the Maglite low, flicked it on and pointed it at the rocky ground ahead.

The light caught the image about ten feet away of an animal and lying on its side along the rock floor. Dave cautiously approached. It looked to be the size of either a large coyote or a small wolf. As he grew even closer, he could see the animal's short-cropped fur–brownish fur. Perhaps a dog, yes, a brown

Labrador retriever. He didn't expect this. He was looking at the remains of Lester Hadley's chocolate lab, Baxter-*Bax*.

Fighting the stench of the decaying animal, Dave squatted on his knees and surveyed what was left of the dog's furry body. It was obvious there had been several days of assaults by insects and small predators. He noticed a dark crusting of what was probably blood around a hole in Bax's hind quarters. The dog had been shot.

Wounded by a high-powered rifle, Bax must have had just enough strength to dash away into the woods and finally, here to this spot, where Lester Hadley's chocolate lab allowed itself to lie down and die. So, this area in Sugarite Canyon had to have been where Lester Hadley had been killed, shot to death by a high-powered rifle round. Not out to the west on Route 555. His killers had moved his body. Patting the dog's neck, Dave shook his head in both anger and disgust.

He stood and walked by the creature, continuing up the face of rocky ground. As he ascended the incline, the air became increasingly cool and fresh. Just ahead, above him, he could tell where the shrub and tree line ended, where a clear black sky sprinkled with tiny orbs of light began. Apparently, he was only a short distance from the top. Dave instantly froze. He crouched again. A growling sound. Security watch dogs? He gripped his pistol once again.

Dave listened intensely. The growling was sporadic, in fact, not much like any growl he'd ever heard before. It was more like...snoring. Bent over, Dave climbed further up to the top of the hilly ground. Abruptly, he knelt on the hard rock floor.

He raised his head to take a peek. He could see the muzzle end of a rifle barrel pointing straight upward to the sky. Rising again to his feet, he could now see that a man at the top was prone, facing downhill. He was leaning against a rounded face of rock. Sleeping and snoring. Dave paused for a moment, then crept silently toward him. The man was motionless, sound asleep.

Dave stepped delicately around the man. He noted the scenery of the location and then, looking back occasionally at the still sleeping man, he proceeded across an area of flat ground. He heard voices ahead and the sputtering sound of engines, could be generators. He sunk down into a prone position and crawled further ahead on his belly.

He could see strips of light emanating from under a seam of… what? It was being raised and lowered as men entered and exited. He slowly crawled along the ground, paralleling the line of light, to a dark, quiet area. His face came up against a fabric of some sort. Camouflage netting?

Dave lifted the fabric and was startled to see that he was on a cliff-like edge of an excavated area. It was at least twenty-five feet to the bottom. The area was lit with cool, blue lighting. Not at all fond of relative heights, an admitted weakness of his, Dave backed up slightly.

Peering into the area below, he made out the profiles of large trucks, trucks like those that visited Super Save Discount Foods every Thursday evening. Several Humvees were parked in rows, and a couple dark colored GMC Yukon SUVs. Black clad men walked about carrying crates, eventually setting them down in stacks.

So, this was the RTC, the Raton Training Center. No doubt about it. The place explained the blips of light and heat imaged by the NRO's space-based platform. Blips that appeared and then abruptly and unexplainably disappeared. The netting had to be sporting some sort of thermal concealment in addition to camouflage. This was the spot first excavated and then constructed by VA&S Construction Company and their new owners, J.J. Breeds Corporation.

Dave flattened himself against the ground as his ears caught the distinct, unmistakable and muffled humming of…rotors? Apparently, there was also a helipad nearby. He looked down at his wrist and uncovered the watch face. It was after midnight and yet this training center was alive and buzzing? Why? He eased himself backward from the edge and the camouflage netting, turned around and crawled back, following his scratchy marks in the ground.

Dave stood and slowly crept across the flat ground to the spot where he'd seen the sleeping sentry. He bent low as he spotted the man now sitting upright on the ground ahead. No longer asleep and no longer snoring, the man appeared to be drinking something from a can. Maybe a soda? A beer? The man was facing downhill, his back to McClure and the flat ground of the mesa.

Dave reached down for his SOG knife. A good pummeling on the head with the metal handle should do it. No, that could possibly cause problems, especially if he badly hurt the man or maybe even killed him. Instead, his hand searched for the grip to the Taser. He pulled it out. This thing will come in handy after all. Pete Novak did indeed think of everything. Dave took one cautious, soundless step after another as he approached the man from behind. He smelled the sweet aroma of…beer. The sentry had been sleeping, snoring, and now he was sipping a brew? *Jeez, takes all kinds*, Dave thought to himself.

He drew close to within two feet of the man's back. With the steady convection of breezes rustling uphill through the foliage and across the mesa, it was impossible for the man to notice a scent or even a slight sound of something upwind, behind him. Dave's right arm reached out, Taser in hand, slowly advancing toward the target–the back of the man's neck. He mused that, afterward, chances were slim the man would be able to explain the time gap even to himself.

The dart-like tips of the Taser touched the skin on the back of the man's neck. Dave forced his hand forward and fired, sending 50,000 volts of electric pulses through the man's body. The resulting jolt was fierce. The man shuddered violently as muscle spasms assailed him. Ferocious streams of excruciating pain ran downward along his spine and upward into his head. The low amperage of the Taser caused a rapid, near instantaneous immobilizing of the man, but stopped short of killing him. His eyes rolled back as he slumped sideways, thumping unconscious onto the rocky surface.

Dave reached down to the man's neck. There was a pulse. Good. He holstered the taser, stepped over and past him, his eyes scanning left and right. Without the presence of another imminent threat, he began a quick descent down the slope. He was well out of hearing range of the two sentries positioned half a football field back on the two-track.

Briskly stepping through the clearing with abundant, fragrant blooms of flowers, he reached Lake Maloya's perimeter road in what seemed just minutes. He began trotting around the lake back toward the entrance gate and raised his cell phone,

"Kevin, Dave here. I'm ready for a pick-up. I'll be at the gate in no time."

"On my way."

Kevin fired the stealth Subaru's engine. It lurched from the shoulder and back onto the road. In just under two minutes, the Subaru rolled through a U-turn at the gate, easing across the pebbly gravel to a soft stop. Dave hopped in.

"You okay, no wounds, Kemo sabe?" Kevin looked him over.

"I'm fine, Tonto. Let's beat feet and get the hell outta here."

Kevin pressed the gas pedal hard, accelerating the Subaru as it zipped west along Route 576. He swerved right into the turn onto Route 72. Once again opening the center console, Kevin's fingers deftly flicked off the stealth options one-by-one. The vehicle, now appearing like a normal Subaru Forester, sprinted down the road toward Raton.

CHAPTER 33

Langley Center
McLean, Virginia

It was a few minutes before six o'clock in the morning in McLean. Hardly anyone had yet arrived at Langley. Secretaries and administrative staff usually trudged in at about seven-thirty. Jack Barrett swiveled in his office chair when he heard the door creak open. It was Novak.

"Pete, what the hell are you doing here at this hour and sticking your nose in my doorway? I haven't had enough caffeine yet to look at your puss," he chuckled.

"Come back later?"

"No, no, come on in. Good morning. Want some coffee?"

"Please."

"Black, right?"

"Correct."

Jack rose and fetched another mug of coffee for Pete. Instead of returning to the fortress of mahogany he called a desk, Jack gestured over to the sitting area with easy chairs and a sofa. Jack plopped into the sofa and Pete settled into the soft, leather-covered cushions of an easy chair. A coffee table separated them. Jack took a sip of coffee and set the mug on the table.

"Pete, what do you have?"

"I got a call late last night, Jack, but I didn't want to bother you at that hour. Not for this."

"Thank you for that."

"It's about the three men at the McClure house that Tony Robertson's team had quickly dispatched."

"Yes?"

"All three had Army ranger backgrounds. All of them single, and all had previous tours in Iraq and Afghanistan. They're from three different states…New Hampshire, Wisconsin, and North Carolina. I suspect they were probably vetted and recruited while they were running around somewhere in Southwest Asia."

"Seems reasonable. You know that we do that ourselves. Have you heard anything from Brent Atwood in New York City?"

"No. I'm thinking it might be they found something that made them want to take a little extra time, look deeper."

"Could be. And McClure?"

"I haven't heard from Dave or Kevin yet. If I recall, they were planning to go operational last night, probably at a late hour that would be even two hours later here. Timewise, it's only four o'clock in the morning there right now. I am anxious to hear what transpired if Dave did go in last night."

"They're probably still asleep, catching some bag time. You know how it is after a late-night op. It can be exhausting. I'm sure you'll hear from them today."

"Hope so. That's it, Jack. I'll get hold of you as soon as I hear something. I'm really hoping today, and soon."

"Thanks again, Pete. You know, I've been thinking about this. We've got operations that are active, ongoing throughout the world, and a couple of them appear to be on a razor's edge, and yet this damn RTC, STARDUST thing is beating the crap out of me. I can't get my hands around the pieces yet. It's…haunting me."

"I know. Me too."

"What the hell, did these guys, whoever they were, really kill cops? If so, why, and who else do they feel authorized to exercise sanction authority on, eh? Just what the hell is going on?"

"Right. Jack, we'll stay on it and as close as we can. Sooner or later, I'm sure it'll become clear as to just what this damn thing is."

"I hope so. Take care, Pete."

"You too. Catch you later," Novak turned and left Barrett's office, quietly closing the door behind him.

Dave McClure and Kevin O'Brien stepped out of Denny's on Clayton Road near the interstate. Breakfast had been pancakes and eggs with a couple cups of coffee. It was filling and that in itself felt good.

"Are you going to call Novak? He's probably waiting to be briefed," Kevin said.

"Yeah, I'll give…" Dave's cell phone rang. They stopped near the Subaru's doors as he pulled the phone out of its holster.

"Hello?" Dave said.

"Barry? Barry O'Keefe, ICE?"

"Yes. How can I…is this Darrell Chilton?"

"Captain Chilton, yes. I'm glad I got hold of you. Are you still in the Raton area?"

"Yes."

"We need to meet. It's fairly urgent. I've got to get this off my chest. Something's well, not right."

"Okay. And?"

"Could you possibly make it a half hour from now, about nine-thirty? I have to go into town for a couple electrical things anyway, so my absence is expected."

"Sure. Just tell me where, Darrell."

"Great. Thank you so much. We can meet on Clayton Road, just west of the interstate, between Price and Emerson streets. There's a motel there on the right, the north side, the Casa Lemus Inn. A storage building is behind the motel and a dirt and gravel lot surrounds it. We can meet there. What will you be driving?"

" A Subaru Forester. There'll be another ICE agent with me who'll be driving, but he'll stay in the vehicle."

"That sounds good. See you then. And again, Barry, thank you very much," Chilton said. They clicked off.

Dave turned to Kevin. "That was the Army logistics officer from the truck convoy, the guy I spoke with last Thursday night. He must have called the number on the business card I gave him, but like you said, it was routed to my new burner cell. He says it's pretty urgent. He wants to meet a half hour from now behind the Casa Lemus Inn. We passed it coming out here to Denny's. It's a motel just down the street from where we are now."

"Dave, I think we should be cautious. It could be a set-up. Maybe we should arm up now, just in case."

"I agree."

They climbed into the Subaru and reached into the nylon bags on the floor in the back, pulling out their pistols and holsters. Slipping on his shoulder holster, Dave turned to Kevin.

"Kevin, you stay in the car. I don't want to spook this guy just in case he really has something."

"Sure, that's fine. I'll cover your back from the car."

Kevin pulled the Subaru out of the Denny's parking lot and onto Clayton road, heading east for the Casa Lemus Inn. He reached down with his right hand to check his belt holster and the Smith & Wesson pistol seated in it. It felt good to do that.

CHAPTER 34

Dave and Kevin watched from the Subaru as the black Yukon pulled into the dirt parking lot behind the Casa Lemus Inn. Dave recognized Darrell Chilton at the wheel. Other than him, the Yukon appeared empty.

As the Yukon pulled to a halt about twenty feet away, Dave opened the passenger door and climbed out. As he shut the door behind him, he saw Chilton drop down from his seat onto the Yukon's step rail and then nearly tumble to the ground. He recovered himself at the last minute.

Chilton's sudden, quirky movement alerted Kevin. He put his hand on the grip of his pistol, his eyes quickly scanning the parking lot and the streets on both sides.

"You okay, Darrell?" Dave asked, pausing in place.

"Yeah, just really nervous. I'm a little shaky," Darrell walked slowly toward him, eyeing Kevin in the Subaru.

"It's okay, take it easy. You're safe."

"Thanks," Dave reached out and they shook hands. The two men stood face to face.

"I don't know where to begin. But I know I have to talk with someone before I go nuts. I'm worried about all this... what I've seen, what I'm hearing."

"No rush. Collect your thoughts."

"Barry, I know that what I'm going to tell you has nothing

to do with the work you do as an ICE agent, but I have no one else in the federal government to talk to about it. You're the only one."

"Darrell, all right. You be honest with me and I'll be honest with you. I'm undercover and working under another identity. I'm not really Barry O'Keefe. I'm Special Agent Dave McClure, FBI. And, I do believe your concern must be genuine or you wouldn't have asked for such an urgent meeting. I am interested in what you have to say…just ease up a bit and let yourself chill out. Would you rather sit in our Subaru and talk?"

"You're FBI. Dave McClure."

"Yes."

"Wow. Thanks for revealing that, for trusting me. Yes, that's a good idea. Let's sit in your vehicle."

Both men climbed into separate doors of the Subaru's back seat. Kevin opened his door and rose from the front seat. Before shutting the door, he leaned back in.

"Guys, I'm going to walk over and see if there's a soda machine in the motel. Would either of you care for a soda, a Pepsi or Coke?"

"No, but thanks," Darrell said. McClure also declined.

Kevin sauntered away across the lot, heading for the side drive by the Casa Lemus Inn.

"Better in here?"

"Yes, thanks."

"Good. Now, what's bothering you that makes you want to talk to someone, especially someone who's with the federal government?"

"Barry, I mean, Dave, remember when we spoke that night by the trucks at Super Save Discount Foods? I mentioned to you that I was going to be travelling back east to visit the three distribution centers. I said I was going to inspect them to ensure they were ready for some kind of impending deployment. Remember?" Darrell asked.

"I do, yes."

"Good. First, all of the operations teams are deploying with full gear and weaponry from the airport at Taos on late Monday night, September 4th. We're in late August–so that's less than a week from now. And, that night falls on a federal holiday, Labor Day. They're flying on chartered airlines. I'm wondering why that is? I don't know which charter airlines were contracted to airlift them to the three locations at BWI, Dulles and Richmond International. It could be any of them–World Airlines, National Airlines, North American Airlines, or Evergreen Aviation."

"Well, I agree that's a bit strange, but there must be some reason, some imperative for it, Darrell."

"Yes, I agree. But even more strange than that is the departure is not until 11:00 p.m. that night. That puts them on the East Coast in the wee hours of the morning…three o'clock in the morning on the day following Labor Day. In the blackest hours of the morning. Why the hell is that?"

"I understand your reasoning. Go ahead."

"Okay. General Blanton's been at the RTC for two weeks now. He's overseeing all final preparations. George Stiles, Director of FEMA, is here with him. On the night of the deployment, September 4th, Blanton and Stiles will be flying into Dulles, but they're not departing until about one-thirty the following morning. That puts them at Dulles just before six o'clock. Why aren't they flying out with the teams? I don't see the sense of it."

"I'm with you. Go on," Dave said.

"Then, there's what I saw at the centers themselves."

"What was that?"

"Dave, each of the three centers is located either right on the airport grounds in empty hangers that are vacant, not being used or in warehouse-type buildings right near the airports. In each one, I saw at least fifty Humvees. They're the newer ones. Those Humvees can do fifty-five to seventy mph on a highway."

"I'm missing something here, Darrell. Humvees are troop movers. So, I have to ask you, why do you think that's unusual for an exercise of some sort?"

"It was how they've been set up, Dave. They're armed for bear. There are M134 miniguns mounted on lots of them and Browning .50 Cal heavy machine guns on others. I also saw Mk 19 grenade launchers. I even spotted a few with Avenger surface-to-air missile systems with Stinger missiles mounted on them. The Avenger Air Defense System is a very lethal short-range missile that can take down helicopters, drones, aircraft, and even cruise missiles."

"I see. You have my attention. Please, continue."

"I had to ask myself, how in hell could that composition of weaponry be intended for any exercise involving anti-gang operations?"

"And, your answer to that is?"

"Dave, those are battle configurations, weaponry alignments that we configure for wartime action. Who the hell are we anticipating battle against? What are we going to do, roll down the streets of Baltimore, Richmond, and southeast Washington, D.C., machine-gunning and blowing up buildings? Jeez. I can't get it out of my head. There's one other thing."

"What?"

"I'm told that this is a live-fire exercise. That means all

the ammo, grenades, and even short-range missiles are being airlifted with them. A live fire exercise in those heavily populated areas? No, something is very wrong in this."

"I've got it. I understand what you're saying. You were right to raise your concern to someone outside the RTC. Now that you've told me how you feel about all this, are you going back to the RTC today?"

"I have to. I'm the logistics guru. General Blanton wants me to meticulously oversee everything that involves the supplies they need to load."

"I don't like it, but I understand. I really think you should come with us. We can protect you. Plus, you understand all the details and can explain it. I very much appreciate your courage in bringing this to me."

"Thanks, Dave. No, I need to be going. I don't want to show up late. It might look suspicious."

"You're sure now?"

"Yes."

"Well, good luck and check your six."

"Thanks again."

The two men shook hands. Darrell left the Subaru. Walking back from the motel with a Pepsi in his hand, Kevin saw Chilton's black Yukon peel out from the parking lot. Back in the Subaru's driver seat, Kevin first took a sip of his Pepsi and then turned to Dave.

"What do you think? Was his meeting with you really as urgent as he thought it was? Anything we should be concerned about?" Kevin asked.

"Unbelievable, actually. Kevin, the craziest damn thoughts are going through my mind right now. They're things that should be impossible to even consider."

"What?" Kevin was perplexed.

"The bottom-line is that we need to get back to the facility pronto, Tonto. I have to brief Pete Novak on what I saw last night, and especially what I just heard from Chilton. Combined, I think this is going to need detailed, expert analysis to figure out what the hell is actually happening–what's going to occur."

"Hey, I like that...*pronto, Tonto.* So then, we're off to the *tee-pee, Kemo sabe.*" Kevin smiled as he fired up the Subaru's engine.

"You're a sick puppy," Dave said in a mild chuckle.

"Dave, the reality is that as crazy as you may think this stuff seems, we should really force ourselves to keep it in perspective. You were very successful last night in Sugarite Canyon. Your ingress and egress went without any incident at all. Except when you zapped that sentry. And, you gathered even more information just now. We're still in control, Dave."

"Yeah, I suppose so. Thanks, Kevin."

They drove west on Clayton to 2nd Street and turned north.

CHAPTER 35

Langley Center
McLean, Virginia

Pete Novak set his food tray down on the table next to Jack Barrett's. The cafeteria in the new headquarters CIA building, even though several decades old now, was much better than the old one. And that cafeteria was excellent.

"So, the big wig aristocrats come down to the cafeteria to eat lunch too? I'm impressed," Pete said, grinning.

Barrett rolled his eyes. "Sure, once in a while. It's a good feeling to come down now and then and mingle with Company's proletariat, the more lowly workers like you," Jack replied.

"Ouch. Well, I have heard that some of our worker comrades here are beginning to refer to your office up on the penthouse floor as the Holy of Holies," Pete chortled.

"I'm Presbyterian, not Jewish. That's still blasphemous."

"I'm Lutheran. Come on, no, it isn't. A bit irreverent perhaps, but that's all."

"Touché then," Barrett laughed. "The roast beef, gravy, and mashed potatoes actually look pretty damn good. I see you chose the same thing. Hear anything yet? Anything at all?"

"I got a short call from Kevin O'Brien. He was on his cell and in the Subaru with McClure." Pete paused, looking down at this wristwatch.

"We set up a conference call for two-thirty our time this afternoon. He said it was substantial, so, if at all possible, it should be in your office. It's eleven-fifteen now. Will that work, Jack?"

"Yes. We'll make it work. Good. I bet that was a relief, right, hearing from them?"

"Yeah. I'll come up about two o'clock if it's okay. The Navy, NCIS counterintelligence, wants us to look at some operation they're considering engaging in along the Pacific Rim. They want our blessing."

"Come up at two. Now, if you don't mind, I'd like to dig into this yummy-looking roast beef," Jack said, smiling.

The two men stuck their forks in their plates and began devouring lunch. They occasionally looked up from their food to see who might be passing through. Afterward, they took the elevators up to their separate floors. At one-thirty in the afternoon, Barrett picked up his buzzing phone. It was Novak.

"Jack, I just had a call routed to me from National Resources Division. It's Brent Atwood in New York City. He says we both should probably hear what they've found out about the stuff we sent them. Can I tell them to reroute it to your office? I'll come up."

"Yes. We'll put it on speaker."

Minutes passed as the call was rerouted. Pete raced up a floor. He took the stairs. They were always much faster than the elevator, just energy draining. After shutting the door to the office behind him, he dropped into a chair across from Jack's desk.

"Okay, go ahead and put the call through," Jack said. They

heard several clanging sounds and then a ring. Jack pressed the speaker button.

"Hi Brent, this is Jack Barrett. Pete Novak is seated in front of me. We're on speaker–he can hear you."

"Great. Jack, this one you guys sent me turned out to be a doozie, at least in my estimation. Of course, you'll get to decide for yourself."

"Thanks for the support, Brent. Shoot!"

"First, J.J. Breeds Corporation. They don't exist, not anymore. The phone numbers reflected on the two business cards have been disconnected. Email addresses don't work."

"Okay," Jack said.

"It gets better. The office address for the company, Suite 1406 in the building at 27B West 24th Street…it doesn't exist either. However, 27B West 24th Street is indeed a ten-story tall commercial building filled with lots of small businesses. The kicker is that any suite numbered after 10XX is just a mailbox on the ground floor. There is no suite, no office. Upon receipt, any mail addressed to them is forwarded to some other address that's been specified in the lease contract. Leasing a mailbox in a commercial building is actually a fairly common practice for small businesses that don't have the resources to rent an office in a big city."

"I see."

"It's common practice in Washington, D.C. too. Companies are allowed to use the term 'Suite' instead of 'P.O Box.' It makes them appear as a more substantial company to their customers," Brent said.

"Brent, I know I didn't make you aware of this part, but considering the amount of money, and I mean millions of dollars, that J.J. Breeds Corporation paid to buy out VA&S Construction Company, J.J. Breeds was no small business,"

Novak chimed in.

"Hi, Pete. I gathered as much. A couple of my folks went to the location and spoke with the building manager about that particular Suite 1406, the mailbox. He was reluctant to speak with them, that is, until they advised him about the possibility of a charge of criminal obstruction and the potential for his required appearance in federal court."

"Good on them," Pete said.

"Yeah, the fellow became real cooperative after that. The names he had for contacts regarding the mailbox lease were the same ones shown on the business cards you sent us for George Mazur and Eric Baranek. The phone numbers and email addresses were also the same. We've since discovered that the phone numbers listed on the cards were actually cell phones. As I said, those numbers have been disconnected."

"Brent, do you know when the mailbox lease was terminated?" Jack broke in.

"Yes, the 8th of March, 2019."

"March? That's only a month after the contract was signed for J.J. Breeds Corporation's buy-out of VA&S Construction! Why would a company with that kind of monetary resources end up closing one month later?" Jack said.

"Right. Jack, we considered that as well. So, that made me decide that I wanted to look a little further. In doing so, I hope I didn't screw this up for you and go too far. However, it's a good thing you sent it to us with the business cards."

"What? What else was sent…you mean the photo?" Novak said.

"That's correct, the photo. The one that was taken at the signing of the contract at Armano's residence. It showed Armano himself, Gianotta, Armano's attorney, both on the right, and Mazur and Baranek on the left."

"Okay?" Pete said.

"With that photo in hand and on a wild-ass guess, I sent our guys over to the Bureau, the FBI's New York Field Office, their Foreign Counterintelligence Division, the FCI agents. We work with their various desk officers occasionally. The NYO's been good in cooperating with us and they've shared information freely with us when we needed it. They're located at the Federal Plaza on Broadway Avenue and Worth Street."

"No, that's a good move, Brent. I don't have any problem with that. Did that bear any fruit?" Jack said.

"Yes, indeed. In spades. The Bureau's tech staff did a digital analysis of the facial features for both Mazur and Baranek. They said it was terrific that it was such a clear photo. They ran it through their data bank's photo watch list."

"Yes?" Jack asked.

"Positive hits for both of them. The tech personnel told me that there's no question about it. George Mazur is actually Nikolai Pavlukhin. He's a 3rd Consular Trade Secretary with the Russian Trade Representation, the Trade Mission, at 353 Lexington Avenue here in New York City."

"Crap. And, Baranek?" Jack said.

"Similar result. Eric Baranek is Dimitri Nikulichev. He's also a 3rd Consular Trade Secretary with the Russian Trade Representation. Jack, the NYO's FCI Russian Desk shared some stuff with us. It rocked my boat and I think it will heighten your interest."

"Yes?" Jack said.

"Both of those positions, the 3rd Consular Trade Secretary positions, have historically been filled with Russian SVR intelligence officers. A check on our own Agency records show that Pavlukhin was previously assigned to the Russian Embassy in Paris. And, Nikulichev to their Embassy in Luxembourg.

As usual, they were assigned at those locations under different identities. They were operational, Jack, active in both locations."

"Dammit. This is unreal," Pete said, staring at Jack Barrett.

"Jack, Pete, please know that I was dumbfounded when I received this information. I knew I had to get it to you both and as quick as I could."

"What the hell…!" Jack Barrett shouted as he stood up behind his desk.

Novak blanched, his face turning white as a sheet. Jack glanced to the window and back, fuming.

Brent continued. "Jack, of course, I have no idea just how it fits into what you might be investigating, what it all might mean. But I did expedite investigating it and informing you."

"Brent, seriously, you did just super. I just…oh, by any chance, do you have residential addresses for these two characters?"

"Yes, we checked that too. Both of them live in Brooklyn. Pavlukhin is down in Brighton Beach. Everybody in the city calls that area *Little Odessa* because of its large and extremely tight-knit Russian and Eastern European population. Nikulichev lives in Sheepshead Bay. That's a stone's throw from Brighton Beach. It has the same dominant Russian and Ukrainian immigrant population. The NYO's FCI agents keep a steady eye on those neighborhoods, who goes in, who goes out, and where to."

"Brent, while I have to admit I'm more than a bit shaken by this, but truth is, I couldn't have asked for better support. Your analysis, your investigative efforts on our behalf have been stellar. Thank you so very much. I owe you. Name the bottle of single-malt Scotch you'd like the next time you're down here in the Magic Kingdom at Langley."

"Well, Jack, your headquarters personnel have helped us immeasurably in the past and on so many occasions."

"I still owe you. Don't contradict the Director in his intentions for generosity," Barrett managed a short laugh.

"Okay. Then, I thank you, sir!" Brent chuckled. "Best to you both. Atwood out."

Barrett literally fell into his chair, managing a furtive glance over at Pete.

"Pete, tell me this isn't happening. I don't get it. Why the fuck would the Russians underwrite some...?"

Jack's eyes opened wide. He reached to his left, yanked open a side drawer in his desk, and pulled out a manila folder. He laid it open and flattened the contents in front of him. His fingers rapidly flipped through the pages.

"What's that, Jack?"

"Blanton's personnel file that I asked for some time back. It's got his entire assignment history. I haven't had a chance yet to review it, but now, as you might guess, I'm suddenly very curious."

He paused on a page. His head drew closer as his finger traced down the printed lines outlining the career history of U.S. Army four-star General George S. Blanton.

"Shit! How the hell did we miss that?" Jack exclaimed.

"What do you see?"

"The sonofabitch wasn't even officially debriefed after that assignment, and that's a standard security requirement."

"What is it?"

"It seems that almost nine years ago to the day, our own General Blanton was assigned as Assistant Army Attaché in Moscow. The record indicates here that he's R3/S3 in Russian. That's probably a requirement for the position...fluency in Russian. Dammit!"

"You're thinking that Blanton may have picked up some Russian friends during his time over there?"

"With what's happening now, I don't see how we can afford to discount that possibility. Can we?"

"Of course not."

"So, it looks as though the Russians used a paper front company, a shell company, J.J. Breeds Corporation, to buy out VA&S Construction. They then went on to bankroll excavation and construction for the RTC. And, after that, expand the STARDUST program," Jack said.

"Right."

"Okay, but expand it for what? And, why? I consider it a given that Blanton's an asshole, a way over-the-top publicly outspoken critic of the president's foreign policies. But...Pete, I don't like what I'm thinking."

"You really suspect it's possible that a West Point graduate who's now a four star general, even though a narcissist like Blanton, could, over such a long distinguished career, actually have committed espionage? Is that what you're thinking?"

"No. I'm thinking worse than that, Pete. Far worse."

CHAPTER 36

Thursday, August 31st
Raton Training Center
New Mexico

Darrell Chilton bent over to examine the contents of a crate being loaded onto one of the large trucks destined to depart for the Taos airport. It was from there that all the crates would be airlifted to the East Coast. The anxiety he'd felt this morning while meeting with special agent Dave McClure had pretty much dissipated. He'd finally gotten his concerns off his chest, and that felt good. He believed he could now look forward to moving on.

In midafternoon as it was, the RTC was humming with activity. They had all been briefed that after the impending deployment set for two days from now, the center would be shutting down to just minimal staffing, security personnel, a few shooters.

Darrell knew that he would also be moving on. The orders he'd received a day ago stated that his next assignment would be to Headquarters III Corps at Fort Hood in Killeen, Texas, halfway between Austin and Waco. He was pleased with the notice and sensed it would definitely offer a change of pace for him and his family. Being at Headquarters III Corps was also an excellent place to be for his upcoming consideration for promotion to major. He saw it as an excellent move for his next assignment. If he was lucky, General Blanton, his four stars displayed prominently as his listed rater, would slip a glowing letter of evaluation into his personnel folder that the promotion board would see.

Darrell looked into the truck's bed. It was full. He wiped his brow, glanced upward to the camouflage netting, and moved forward to the next truck in line. Lieutenant Matt Stearns, Darrell's number two logistics manager, jogged up to him.

"Darrell."

"Yes, Matt?"

"General Blanton wants to see you. He said to come to his tent as soon as you can find the time."

"Okay," Darrell said. As Matt stepped away to attend to his own duties, Darrell made a mental note of where he was in his inspection, turned and walked toward Blanton's tent. Standing outside the tent flaps, he looked down and dusted off his clothing. He announced himself.

"General Blanton, sir, Captain Chilton. You wanted to see me."

"Yes. Come on in, Captain."

The flaps were opened by a black-clad ops team member. Darrell didn't recognize him, but then there were so many of them at the RTC. He approached the folding table behind which sat General Blanton. Darrell looked to the general's right and saw George Stiles, FEMA Director, who glanced at him. The ops team member who had let him in was still in the tent as well, standing back again by the opening.

"Darrell, just a minute, please. I have this huge package

of paperwork that I need to sign and get off to the Pentagon today," Blanton said. The general shuffled some papers and scribbled his signature on several. He looked up.

"What's your assessment, Darrell? Are we ready to deploy? One hundred percent ready?" Blanton asked.

"Yes, sir. Everything's in order. I've scrutinized it all. What needs to be moving is now moving exactly as it should be."

"Great. The timing of all this has to be precise."

"It will be, sir. No question."

"That's superb to hear. Thank you. Now, if I can just get all this paperwork out by the end of today," Blanton said.

"Sir, may I ask what it is? Is there any way that I can help you with it?"

"If you didn't already know, the Army is really murder on training deaths. I've got to get this package of paperwork off, and then also get the body off for an official autopsy. And then, get it released to the man's parents."

"My goodness. What happened, General?"

"On the firing range this morning. Somehow, there was a stray bullet, maybe off a rock downrange. I don't know. In any case, it struck him in his head. The doctor on our medical staff said he was killed instantly. We have to work fast to expedite the arrangements. His body and coffin are supposed to be sent back and released to his parents in Indiana within five days."

"I'm sorry to hear it, sir. An accidental death in training. Don't you think Headquarters will understand? Training deaths happen, perhaps rarely, but they must happen. I'm sorry you have to struggle with that mess of paperwork."

"Thanks, Darrell."

"General, you said the man's parents were in Indiana. That's where the body will be returned. That's my home state too. Sir, may I ask who the man was who was killed in the accident?"

"Sure, you can. Actually, it was you," Blanton replied.

Darrell's eyes bulged and locked with General Blanton's. Blanton glared back at him in anger.

The ops team member standing behind Chilton raised his arm, pistol in hand...a sound suppressor affixed to the end of the barrel.

CHAPTER 37

Friday, 10:00 A.M. EST
September 1st
Fairfax, Virginia

After two rings, Karen reached into a jeans pocket and pulled out her burner cell phone. She slumped into an easy chair in their family room and, seeing the number, began smiling with anticipation.

"Dave?"

"Hello, baby."

"I knew it had to be you. Oh, it's so good to hear your voice, Dave. You're the only one with access to this phone, the only one that I know of anyway."

"Where are you, Karen?"

"I'm at home. Sitting in an easy chair and feeling very lonely for my husband."

"Sweetheart, are you okay to be back at the house already?"

"Yes. And, Dave, everything is so sparkly clean, it's awesome. You would never know that anything at all happened downstairs...everything, even the window, was replaced."

"How about you? Are you pretty much over it or still a little bit shaky?"

"I'm fine now. Yeah, I have my pistol loaded and up in our bedroom at night, but it's just a precaution. I'm fine. The Company has a car with shooters at both intersections of Pumphrey Drive with Commonwealth, and there's one out in front at the curb. Pete said they'd be there 24-7 for several weeks or so, and then a frequent drive-by after that. That certainly has helped to know. He also said for me to take a break for a couple weeks. He wants me to stay out of National Resources operations for a while. I don't know, I don't feel good about that."

"Novak's only thinking of you, honey, that's all. Kevin and I have a conference call set up for this afternoon with Jack Barrett and Pete. I'll have to remember to thank Pete for all he's done for you. I love you, baby."

"Baby? That's the second time you called me that."

"What, you don't like it?"

"No, I do, it's just…Dave, I love you so much. I want you back here with me. And I guarantee that you being here will totally relax me! Are you still out west? How much longer do you think it will be?"

"Yeah, I'm still out here in the Wild West. No telling how long, really. I think I'll have a better handle on that after the conference call this afternoon."

"Well, whatever you do, bring yourself back home safe to me. You know Pete doesn't want any more hospital bills for you!" Karen laughed.

"I'll do my best. Hey, I remember George C. Scott playing General Patton in the movie and saying, '*No dumb bastard ever won a war by going out and dying for his country. He won it by making some other dumb bastard die for his country.*' Well, I've sort of taken that advice to heart, Karen, so no need for worrying," Dave chuckled.

"I remember that too. Good. I want my hubby back and completely well. We have to make up for lost time," Karen grinned.

"Oh, I like the sound of that, hmmm. Sweetheart, I have to get on the phone again soon for our call to Langley. I promise that I'll call you again and as soon as I can. Stay safe. I love you."

"Love you bunches, Dave. Bye."

"Good-bye for now," Dave and Karen clicked off.

The phone rang in Barrett's office at two-thirty on the dot. Novak sat in a chair in front of the desk. Barrett picked up the line.

"Barrett."

"Sir, you have an incoming secure call from Kevin O'Brien and Dave McClure. Shall I route it through?"

"Yes, and thanks," Jack said. There were several clicks.

"You there, Kevin, Dave? Jack Barrett here."

"Yes, sir. Are we secure?" Dave asked.

"Yes. Pete Novak's sitting here right in front of me. We're on speaker, so go ahead."

"I guess I'll start with searching for and going into the RTC last night."

Dave went on to relate how he and Kevin drove into Sugarite Canyon, his meandering around the lake and entering the forest to search for the location of the RTC. He mentioned finding the carcass of Lester Hadley's dog, Baxter, which had been shot in its hindquarters. That confirmed Lester had been killed in that immediate area and not out west on Route 555 where his body was discovered.

"Intentionally shooting and killing a civilian who's not an

armed street gang member? Outside the charter. That is bad. Okay. What else?"

"There's a fairly well concealed two-track path at the far end of Lake Maloya that Loretta Hadley told me about. It ascends to near Horse Mesa. I spotted two armed sentries up just off the two track path. They couldn't see me in the camo suit. That was a nice break. I backed off, moved slowly down to Lake Maloya's perimeter road, walked around it, and then went up into the forest at another point about fifty yards away. I began another ascent up through the woods from there."

Dave told Barrett and Novak about the sleeping sentry. The one he'd hit in the back of the neck with his Taser later when he was leaving, after surveilling the RTC. He continued informing them about what he'd seen–how buzzing with activity the place seemed to be even though it was at midnight, the Humvees, trucks, and Yukon SUVs. He also mentioned hearing the sound-suppressed rotor hums of a helicopter coming or leaving the center, so there must be a helipad. Finally, he recounted his observance of some kind of camouflage netting that probably had a capability to contain thermal emissions.

"Good work, Dave. Such netting would explain the disappearing blips the NRO's imagery platforms saw. Ah, you didn't kill that sentry, did you?"

"No sir. I checked him for a pulse and he had one. Since he never actually saw me, I don't think he'll even figure out for himself how to explain the time he lost. He was drinking a beer before I zapped him."

"The guy was sleeping and then drinking a beer on sentry duty? Good on what you did. Thanks."

"Ah, Mr. Barrett, Mr. Novak, I think that what I now have to tell you will heighten your interest in all this. Darrell

Chilton, an Army captain detailed to the RTC, a logistics guy I met after sitting in that grocery store parking lot, watching the convoy of trucks being loaded. He called me and said he needed to talk and that it was fairly urgent. We met this morning."

"Go ahead," Jack said.

Dave went on to tell Barrett and Novak what Chilton said about all the ops teams deploying late, near 11:00 p.m. on the evening of Labor Day, September 4th…all on some chartered airlines like World Airlines, National Airlines, North American Airlines, or Evergreen Aviation. Pete Novak asked him to slow down a bit as he was taking notes. Dave mentioned Blanton and George Stiles were to be departing later, after the teams, at one o'clock in the early morning hours. Everyone would be arriving on the East Coast very early in the morning."

"Dave, you said, the night of September 4th? Labor Day?" Barrett asked.

"Yes. Mr. Barrett, Chilton also said he'd seen no less than fifty Humvees lined up at each location at the east coast distribution centers, the newer ones that can do fifty-five to seventy mph on paved surfaces. But what really bothered him was how they were configured, armed up. That's what really alarmed him. He saw M134 miniguns mounted on some of the Humvees and Browning .50 Cal heavy machine guns on others as well as Mk 19 grenade launchers. He also said that a few of the Humvees even had Avenger surface-to-air missile systems mounted on them with Stinger missiles. Further, Darrell said they'd all been told it was intended to be a live-fire exercise so all the ammo, grenades and missiles were being shipped out with the ops teams."

"What?"

"Yes, sir. Chilton emphasized to me that those are battle configurations, weaponry alignments employed for wartime action. He said he couldn't see how those configurations could in any way be intended for an exercise involving anti-street gang operations."

Barrett's eyes widened. Not focused, he stared ahead beyond Novak towards the door. His brow wrinkled. The look on his face startled Novak.

"Mr. Barrett? Mr. Novak?" Dave asked in the pause.

Barrett blinked. "Dave, you were right. But I'll say that 'heighten my interest' is not quite how I would put it. My Lord."

"Sir? What should Kevin and I do now?" Dave said.

"Okay, here it is. I want both of you to stay put where you are. Pete will be contacting you in a few hours and let you know exactly how we'll be responding to this information. All I can really say right now is that you and Kevin have just performed superbly in the service of the Agency and your country as well. Truly, guys, I mean it. It's no less than that."

"Mr. Barrett?"

"Dave, Kevin, what I would like now is for you both to sit tight and wait for our call. At this moment, I do suspect that quite a large number of our special activities, ground division forces, will be joining you down there, and in pretty short order. Stay alert. Okay?"

"Yes, sir. Thank you."

"You two take care. Barrett out."

"Jack...?" Novak began.

"Pete, first thing, I want you to block your calendar. Block it completely for the next three days. Cancel all your meetings. I'm going to need you to work closely with me on this. Have Barb tell anyone who asks her that you're up in New

England and not to be disturbed. I'm going to put the same caveat on anybody asking for me."

"How will…?

"Please, Pete. Second, go talk to your folks in Special Activities. I want at least ten to fifteen teams down in Raton, New Mexico, and fully armed up no later than the morning of the day after tomorrow. We're going to seize this RTC site and all the personnel who'll be left there."

"That's almost a hundred men. Almost the whole force."

"That's right and I think this is a situation that merits it. From what I understand, the facility that Dave and Kevin are in now will support that number. I want overwhelming firepower. If we have that, then the chances of any gunfight occurring will be slim to none. If by chance there's a compromise of any kind, I don't want those STARDUST teams deploying to the east coast to have any place to come back to. We are going to seize and control the RTC."

"Understand. All right, done."

"Good. Have Research and Analysis get you the names and home phone numbers of the two generals who command both the Virginia Army National Guard and the Maryland Army National Guard. To respond to this fast and as quietly as possible, we need to ensure that we keep this out of federal and Defense Department waters, so advise everyone you talk with to keep the lid closed tight on this and our intended actions. No leaks. None. I will personally crucify anyone who does."

"Got it."

"Then please call Lance Hellman at the U.S. Marshal Service. Tell Lance to keep this close-hold and that this is a national level crisis. I need two to three prison buses with a total of thirty to forty U.S. marshals at the Richmond International

Airport, the Dulles Airport and BWI Airport by seven o'clock in the evening the day after tomorrow. Tell Lance that his marshals will receive further orders when they arrive at the airport.

"U.S. marshals?"

"That's right. And, please also ask Lance to coordinate for me with the low security, Federal Correctional Institution, FCI Petersburg, down at Hopewell, Virginia. Advise the institution to prepare for perhaps one hundred to one hundred fifty prisoners in the morning hours of September 5th. If they find they have to double up in their confinement quarters, then double up. I expect that those we send there will be only for a short duration. Also tell Lance that this is a national security crisis in direct support of the president. And, tell him that I know I owe him."

"But...?"

"Stay with me on this, Pete. I'm thinking as I'm talking."

"Sorry."

"Don't be. Finally, have somebody on your staff get me the secure number for Site R. I'll need that by tomorrow night, along with the home phone numbers for the Vice President and each member of the Joint Chiefs of Staff."

"Site R? The underground Raven Rock Mountain Complex, the one out in Liberty Township, Pennsylvania? That Site R?"

"Bingo. Yes, that Site R–the underground complex. I'm going to activate it, stand it up, and then I'm going to get the Vice President, the Joint Chiefs, and their immediate families flown out there on the direct orders of the President. We'll get the President and his family evacuated from the White House and fly them out by helicopter as well."

"You said the President is ordering this?"

"He will be...or I will order it, acting on his behalf."

"Jack…you're scaring the shit out of me. What…?"

"Pete, the President of the United States is scheduled to give a Labor Day speech to a joint session of Congress on Capitol Hill early Tuesday morning, the 5th of September. The Vice President and the Joint Chiefs of Staff will be present. All the major news media will be there as well. Shit, I can't believe this myself!"

"Are you thinking that…?" Novak's eyebrows rose.

"Pete, pardon me for interrupting, but you and I are no longer 'thinking' about anything.

No, we're stopping something. What I believe now is that somewhere along the way, General Blanton, in his twisted mind, imagines he has found another, grander mission for the STARDUST program. And, like Captain Chilton, Blanton probably has more than just a few other active duty military people loyal to him, and as such, he's installed a military infrastructure into the program that he feels will make his new mission work. So, no, you and I are not thinking or acting–we're going to stop it. To coin a phrase, we're going to go 'shock and awe' and stop this dead in its tracks. And, the Lord God help us."

Chapter 38

Friday, 6:00 P.M. EST
Langley Center

Pete Novak gave the operations desk officer the secure number, raised his coffee mug for a sip and waited. It took under a minute and three rings.

"Hello?"

"Novak here. Is this Kevin?"

"Yes, sir."

"Is Dave close by?"

"Yes, we were about to head out for dinner."

"I'm curious, where to and for what?"

"It's called the Historic Ice House. We went there last night and it was so good we thought that barbecue ribs and mashed potatoes and gravy would once again be our menu choice of the evening."

"Sounds good, Kevin. I had no idea I had a couple of vegetarians in the operations directorate!" Novak chuckled.

"Well, we *are* having dinner salads for starters, sir."

"Good, that'll give you green roughage. Kevin, hand Dave another set of earphones, please," Pete said. A few seconds of silence passed.

"I'm on, sir," Dave said, with Kevin now in the listening mode.

"I would like both of you to listen well because here's what's going to be happening. Remember Tony Robertson?"

"I do. And my most sincere thanks to you and Tony for taking care of Karen and ensuring she was safe," Dave said. "Tony's a good guy."

"Dave, you're welcome. That's what we do for our own. Now, Tony's had a promotion and he'll be leading the whole group that's coming to your location. It will be right around one hundred men...our Spec Ops teams and pilot operators for the BATS. They'll arrive sometime around noon tomorrow in two or three charter buses or so."

"Wow. One hundred men? That's a lot of firepower. A small army," Kevin said.

"Indeed, it is and that's what Jack Barrett wants–a large force with overwhelming firepower. That may very well limit the possibility that whoever's left at the RTC after the deployment, some security personnel, some shooters, would want to engage in a gunfight."

"Right. And the BATS, the drones?" Dave asked.

"I'm sending twelve of them and their pilot operators. Their mission is to take down, incapacitate any sentries like those you saw. The drone pilots will be busy...they're going to have to program the BATS for your altitude out there. I think they told me it was 6,680 feet. There's also a possibility that after transport they may have to tweak the optical camera and infrared sensors as well as the EMP and 9mm guns before the op initiates."

"I'm actually anxious to see what they look like," Dave said.

"Believe me, they're impressive. So, tomorrow night,

Dave, you'll guide the group over to Sugarite Canyon to be in place by a little after midnight. I want you to lead them to the two-track pathway you told me about at the far end of Lake Maloya. Then, Dave, both you and Kevin can back off. Tony will take command and his teams will begin the ascent through the forest up to the mesa to seize the RTC. I don't want you or Kevin to be out in front."

"I understand."

"Now, from what Darrell Chilton told you, I think there's a distinct possibility that General Blanton and George Stiles will still be at the site. If that's the case, tell Tony to try to take them alive. They will most likely have a protection detail with them, but probably not large in numbers. I also told Tony not to put themselves at risk. If either of those two or any protection detail members draw weapons, tell Tony he has authority to shoot to kill."

"Got it. Anything else, Pete?"

"If there are any wounded on either side, they'll be transported down in Humvees and then medevac'd up to Evans Army Hospital at Fort Carson in Colorado Springs. It's the closest."

"Humvees? Where are those coming from?"

"We're borrowing five of them from Fort Carson. The leadership there seemed pleased for the opportunity to loan them to us for exercise purposes. That's about it. Questions from either of you?"

"No. It all sounds good," Dave said.

"Ditto," Kevin replied.

"Good. Best of luck and good hunting. Novak out."

CHAPTER 39

Friday, 8:00 P.M. EST
Langley Center

Two hours later and one floor up from his office at Langley, Pete Novak was again sitting in an easy chair across from Barrett's desk. Jack was being connected by the operations desk to the home phone for Major General Cory Anderson, Commander of the Virginia Army National Guard. The general's residence was an upscale river rock stone home on the James River on the outskirts of Richmond. It took five rings before being picked up.

"Hello?" Anderson said.

"General Anderson, this is Jack Barrett, DCI. Good evening."

"Jack Barrett, DCI…at CIA? Is this some kind of joke? How'd you get this number? It's unlisted."

"No, general, it's me, Jack. I'm calling from my office at Langley. Do you see the area code and number?"

"Yes. Please excuse my skepticism…it's not every day that I get a call from the DCI himself. I do have to admit your voice does sound familiar. A year ago, you and I met at an intelligence conference in Washington, D.C. Remember?"

"I do. It was at the Defense Intelligence Agency on Bolling Air Force Base. You're a tall, elderly fellow about six feet four inches, with brown hair turning gray and thinning."

"Elderly? Well, hell, you haven't changed a bit, Jack." He laughed. "What's up? It must be urgent to call me at home."

"It is. More urgent than you could ever imagine, Cory. Ready to hear it."

"Shoot. I don't mean that literally. I know you and your NRO buddies can probably hit me with a space-based laser right where I stand in my study," Anderson said with a chuckle.

"Ah, no comment on that capability, general. Cory, what I'm about to tell you is exceedingly close-hold, burn after reading, okay?"

"I understand, Jack."

"Super. A national crisis is imminent. I'm working in direct support of the President. I have to ask you, what forces can you provide and deploy to Richmond International Airport and Dulles Airport within twenty-four hours?"

"Twenty-four hours? Jeez! That's a helluva tasking, Jack. I suppose it's is doable, but I'll have to inform Governor Wallace."

"General, remember what I said about the extreme sensitivity. You can't take this to the governor."

"Jack, I have to do that. I have to. Please, understand, I need to inform Governor Joe Wallace and obtain his approval. It can be done, but the cost of this will be immense. And Jack, it's the governor who appoints the commander of the state's Army National Guard. If I don't do that, I may lose my job."

"General, if you do that, you may lose your country."

A pregnant pause interrupted. Total silence. Seconds seemed like minutes.

"This is really that serious? It's a national crisis and it will involve armed military forces?"

"I couldn't have described it any plainer myself. No federal forces, no defense department forces are involved. Just your own Virginia Army National Guard. That keeps it tight and as close to our chests as possible. Oh, and I might add, Cory, that after you and I talk, I'm calling Brigadier General Randy Tennyson in Maryland. Same task, different location, BWI Airport."

"Hell. Okay, well, I suppose this comes down to why some decades ago, I put this uniform on in the first place. Damn. All right, Jack, here's what I can give you. I have four companies of the 2nd Battalion, 224th Aviation Regiment, one company of the 135th Aviation Regiment, and one company of the 151st Aviation Regiment. Those are mostly all Black Hawks, but there's a couple of Bell UH-1 Iroquois, you know, Hueys, as well. They're armament is a mix of M-60 machine guns and .50 caliber CAU-19/A heavy machine guns. And, there's hellfire missiles on all of them. On top of that, I have more than 500 combat vehicles positioned at Fort Pickett, southeast of Petersburg that include M1 Abrams tanks and Bradley Fighting Vehicles."

"Cory, tell me about your M1 Abrams tanks."

"The M1 is heavily armored, but what's really special about it is that it's got a 120 mm L/44 cannon. It's one of the heaviest main battle tanks we have. I wouldn't try to put anything on the ground up against those tanks. We can split all these forces up evenly between Richmond International and the Dulles Airport."

"The requirement is to also have two flights of Black Hawks patrolling in the immediate vicinity of the White House. Is that possible?"

"You bet, consider it done. Two flights. So, whaddya think?"

"General Anderson, that actually sounds like a huge Christmas present. Let's do it. The field commanders of your two separate forces will receive further instructions when they arrive at the airports. I just need to have you get them out there. And, general, I would be most grateful if you would stand-by so you, yourself, can monitor the order of battle, that is, if there is one, and I expect there will be."

"Spoken like a true strategist! Will do. The forces will arrive at those two locations by six o'clock tomorrow evening, ready for battle. The budget be damned! Deal?"

"Deal! And Cory, take this from the heart… I, the president, and a grateful nation thank you."

"Bring it on. Anderson out."

Jack eased back into his chair, a broad smile creasing his face. He looked over at Pete, who was also grinning.

"Pete, I think the Lord is watching over us, and He's hovering at a bearing of twelve o'clock high."

"Indeed."

Barrett reached for his phone and gave the operations desk Brigadier General Randall G. Tennyson's home phone number. Tennyson lived in a spacious two-story, red brick colonial home off Route 50, between Annapolis and Bowie, Maryland.

"Hello?" Tennyson asked.

"General Tennyson, this is Jack Barrett, DCI. Good evening"

"DCI? Director of Central Intelligence?"

"General, that's me, CIA. I apologize for interrupting your evening, however, it is of the utmost importance that we talk. Check your phone's display and you can see the area code and number. If you'd like to call me back..."

"No, that's okay. Mr. Barrett, what is of the utmost importance for you to call me at home?"

"General, I'm calling you and requesting your assistance and support on behalf of the president. We're entering a period of imminent national crisis. By the way, I just got off the phone with your counterpart in Virginia, Major General Cory Anderson. He's agreed to provide the support I'm asking for. You can call him to verify that."

"That won't be necessary. A national crisis. Is the Defense Department involved?"

"No, general. What I'm about to tell you is extremely close hold. No DoD forces. No governor involvement. Is that okay?"

"The governor can't be informed? Was General Anderson okay with that?"

"He was. As I mentioned, you can call him. General, I really can't emphasize the urgency of this enough."

"I see. All right, Mr. Barrett. Sir, what are you requesting?"

"As I said, General Tennyson, a national crisis is imminent. I have to ask you–what forces can you provide and deploy to the Baltimore-Washington International Airport within 24 hours?"

"My goodness. Mr. Barrett..."

"Call me 'Jack', please."

"Thank you. I'm not sure I have the budget to back up the deployment, but I certainly can order it."

"Thank you so much. Is it 'Randy'?"

"It is. All right then, hell, I guess if Cory's in, so am I. I can offer you a detachment and company of the 20th Special Forces Group. Also, elements of the Combat Aviation Brigades of the 29th and 42nd Infantry Divisions. Then..."

"Excuse me, Randy, the helicopters...are they Black Hawks."

"Yes, every one of them and fully armed."

"Superb. And, you were about to say?"

"We've reactivated the 115th Armor Regiment, and we have quite a number of Bradley Fighting Vehicles."

"Randy, the armor regiment...are they M1 Abrams?"

"Yes."

"Our requirement is for at least one tank company to be positioned directly at the White House. How many tanks is that, Randy?"

"One company? Twelve, could be up to fourteen, three armor platoons of four tanks each. Position them where?"

"Please split them up evenly to be positioned in front of The White House directly on Pennsylvania Avenue and also behind, on the Ellipse."

"I can do that. It won't be difficult. I assume you'll want to move them into place after darkness, say around 1900 hours, excuse me, seven o'clock p.m."

"That would be optimal and will also limit traffic involvement. I will ensure that we have ground forces re-routing traffic to support your movement."

"That would be ideal. Thanks in advance for that."

"General, please execute the necessary deployment orders. The field commander of your force will receive further instructions upon his or her arrival at the BWI airport. I just need to have you move it to that location on time in order to be effective."

"They'll be there, Jack, armed and ready. You have my word. May I assume then that General Anderson is deploying to Richmond International and Dulles International?"

"You've assumed correctly. He is indeed. Randy, and as

General Anderson has also already agreed, I would be grateful if you would stand-by and monitor the order of battle, if there is one, and I expect there will be."

"I would be honored to do so. Thank you for asking."

"And when this is all over, I suspect there's another star in this for you, General Tennyson."

"That's not why I've signed up to your request along with General Anderson. Jack, you said this a national crisis. Therefore, this is about preserving the republic. How could I ever deny a request from you in behalf of the president to do just that? And, that's despite whatever the hell the result to my career ends up being."

"Randy, I don't have the words. Thank you so very much. After this, I'd like to invite you up to Langley."

"Spook City? That's something I'm not too sure I can risk." Tennyson chuckled. "No, actually I would love to see Langley. Take care and check your six, Jack. From the high level urgency of this situation, I suspect you may need to do just that."

"Very best, general. Barrett out."

Barrett set the phone down ever so softly. He glanced over to Novak whose face was filled with anticipation.

"You know, Pete, we've just spoken with two dyed-in-the-wool patriots. I wasn't in any way confident about how requesting this support would turn out. Now, well, I really do think we may have angels watching over our shoulders."

"If we do, no doubt we'll need it. When do we have to begin the evacuation and flights to Site R?"

"Tomorrow afternoon. The White House will be last. I'll give advance notice to Blair Townsend over at the Secret Service. You and I will go there early tomorrow evening and explain it to the President."

"Jeez, what you and I are planning to do? It makes my hair stand on end. Gives me gooseflesh."

"Well, what is it that we always seek? The truth. Well, now we know the truth. And, we discovered the truth almost too late. But as God is my witness, we will prevail in this. There is no other option."

"You know, Jack, I've always been fond of the Navy. There's a quote from Fleet Admiral William F. "Bull" Halsey, Jr. that I've always admired. It goes like this, '*There are no great men. There are only great challenges which ordinary men, by force of circumstance, must rise to meet.*' I've always loved that quote."

"That is indeed one terrific quote. And, this is indeed one heck of a challenge we're facing. In fact, I have one expression of my own that's not nearly as eloquent, but it does seem appropriate at this point."

"And that is?"

"Whaddya say that you, me, Tony Robertson, Dave McClure, and two generals...go kick some ass?"

"Indeed, sir. This evening?"

"No, just perhaps predicting our immediate future. It's best you and I go home, have dinner and get some sleep. Tomorrow may be a long one."

"Should I come by your office first thing in the morning?" Pete asked.

"Yes. We'll know if any changes to our response are required. Then, later tomorrow when we enter onto the playing field, the other players, the black hats, will be there also. Unfortunately for them though, they won't expect our presence. And that, my friend...will cost their asses the ball game."

"I certainly hope so, pray so. Have a good evening, Jack."

"You as well."

CHAPTER 40

Monday, 5:00 P.M. EST
The White House
Washington, D.C.

Jack Barrett's armored black limo turned off Pennsylvania Avenue a few minutes after six o'clock on Monday evening. It was subsequently passed through the front gate of The White House. The skies over Washington had gone cloudy and mild breezes had picked up. The limo pulled up along the side entrance and eased to a stop. Novak reached down and struggled with his seatbelt. About to exit, Barrett turned to him.

"Jitters, Pete?"

"Nah…well, yeah, a little. What we're about to do is immense," Pete's seatbelt finally unbuckled.

"It is, yes. But, so is the threat. I admit that all this appears just unreal. Unbelievable. Impossible. Only several days ago, I myself thought that no, this can't be happening, that we must be misreading events. Such a thing was not conceivable. Not here in the United States. But dammit, the truth is now in front of us. We can't look away. No, we're going to stop that bastard from pulling this off," Barrett paused.

"Pete, believe me when I say you're not alone. Hell, I couldn't even eat breakfast this morning. I'm running purely on caffeine. And, I'm supposed to be the unshakable Director of Central Intelligence. Russia, China, North Korea, ISIS, Al Qaeda and yet, I've never faced anything as daunting as this. But the fact remains that we, you and I, have been chosen somehow to be the vanguard in this. Let's chill," Jack's face was frozen with determination.

"Right. Thanks for confiding. Let's do it," Pete said, managing a weak smile.

Barrett glanced to the men in the front seat. "Gerry, Bob, stay here and wait for us, please. We shouldn't be long."

"Good luck, sir. God be with you," Bob said.

"Thanks," Barrett replied.

Barrett and Novak climbed out of the limo's back seat and traipsed up the stairs into the west entrance of The White House as two Secret Service agents joined them, trailing behind. A steward in a black tuxedo met them at the door.

"Good evening, Mr. Barrett, Mr. Novak, please follow me. The President is waiting for you," the steward said.

The two agents continued to follow. Jack and Pete looked left and right as they strode down the wide, red-carpeted hallway. The walls were adorned with gorgeous artwork and brass lamps.

Minutes later, the steward opened the door allowing Barrett and Novak to enter the Oval Office. The two Secret Service agents halted and remained outside in the hallway. The President looked up from his desk, set his pen down and rose from his chair. He wore a dark navy pinstripe suit, crisp white shirt, and red necktie.

"Jack, good to see you again. Come on over and sit down. And this is… I know I've seen this man before, right?" The

President's eyes gestured to Pete.

"Mr. President, this is Pete Novak. Pete's my deputy for operations and my right-hand man. I couldn't do this job without him."

"Ah, the DepOps. The man responsible for underwriting our covert operations around the world. Pete, I'm very pleased to meet you, but it does seem to me that we've met before? Your face is familiar."

"We have, Mr. President. Only briefly, though."

"I thought so. Then it's good to see you again," The President grinned and looked back at Barrett. "Anyway, Jack, have you seen the crime statistics that were just published for some twenty cities this morning? Down forty-seven percent! The program is working!"

"No, I haven't. Mr. President, please, we have to talk," Jack replied.

"What's the urgency of this all about? Oh, and do you mind if Regis Ballard here, my Chief of Staff, stays and listens to what you have to tell me?" The President nodded in the direction of Ballard, who stood to his right near a sofa.

Barrett took a deep breath. "No, Mr. President, that's fine. It might actually be helpful down the road. Sir, the bottom-line is that we need to evacuate you and your family to Site R within the hour. Not long after that, a company of Abrams M1 tanks will be arriving and positioning themselves in front of The White House on Pennsylvania Avenue and to the rear on the Ellipse."

"What the hell? A military exercise? Fly us out to Raven Rock? Is that why I just saw my helicopter landing on the grass back there? Jack, why wasn't I informed before about this? Look, cancel the damn thing!" The President raised his voice to a near shout. Novak blinked. Barrett rose from his seat.

"Mr. President, this is no exercise. The Vice President and the Joint Chiefs of Staff with their families have already been evacuated and at this moment are in route to Site R. The Raven Rock complex has been activated. Again, this is no exercise, sir," Jack said.

The President eased himself back down into his chair. "No exercise? What are you saying...please, enlighten me?"

"Sir, time is of the essence. You'll receive a full briefing on your way to Site R. The Secret Service is already upstairs and helping your family pack some things to last for two days or so."

"I asked you to enlighten me. Please do so. And Jack, have a seat."

"Yes, sir. Mr. President, I'll say this as succinctly as I can. We have gathered substantial evidence to believe with a very high degree of confidence that there is an imminent plot to seize the military district of Washington, the National Capital Region, and take over the government."

Barrett's eyes and the President's intersected. The look on the President's face suddenly changed from one of irritation to one of disbelief. He glanced down to his desk and back up. He looked over to Pete. Then his eyes locked again with Barrett's.

"Jack...what, I don't see how...this is hard to accept." His tone was soft but firm. "I'm supposed to speak to a joint session of Congress tomorrow morning. The Vice President and the Joint Chiefs of Staff are scheduled to be there."

"Mr. President, it would happen like this–tomorrow morning, after you have been arrested and charged with treasonous acts against the United States, General George S. Blanton intends to make that speech to both houses of Congress and to the nation. Blanton will use the national media networks that will be present to explain to the nation why his action was necessary to preserve the republic, our democracy, and to protect America from foreign aggression and halt the impending prospects of another world war. The Joint Chiefs will be forced to order their respective military services to stand down and be advised that they have a new Commander-in-Chief. There won't be any option for those generals or they'll be charged as well. Just as important, Russia has been involved in funding Blanton's resources for this coup," Jack took a deep breath.

"Police?"

"The police are no match for the firepower that's coming, Mr. President. They'll be warned, cautioned to back off. And, I feel certain they'll do just that," Barrett said.

"Blanton! That traitor wants to establish a military dictatorship! And, with Russia as a partner? He's more of an idiot than I ever thought him to be! He thinks he can trust the Russians! So, that's what he's up to. Jack, this is bullshit!" He paused. "I guess the more important thing to ask you is, can it be stopped?"

"Yes, sir, and that's why we're here, Mr. President. We have coordinated with the combined air and ground forces of the Virginia and Maryland National Guard. Generals Cory Anderson and Randy Tennyson are organizing their respective forces," Jack replied.

"Continue, please."

Barrett nodded over to Novak. Pete stood.

"Mr. President, we're now certain that General Blanton has planned a three-pronged assault on the National Capital Region that is scheduled to occur tomorrow in the early morning hours. Their force of at least 150 fully armed Humvees and other combatant vehicles will, in the cloak of darkness, rapidly approach and establish control points on the major highways entering into the District from the BWI Airport and I-95 to the north, from Richmond International and I-95 to the south, and from the Dulles Airport and both I-66 and the Dulles Toll Road Parkway to the west," Pete said.

"This is unbelievable," the president muttered.

"I agree, Mr. President, but it is happening. We're confident that it will play out something like this–initially, with the control points formed on those highways just outside the District, they will monitor traffic flow until just before 9:00 a.m. At that time, they'll close down the highways, halting and preventing traffic from entering the District. Another portion of his force will have been dispersed around Capitol Hill, The White House and the Pentagon. After your arrival to speak at the joint session of Congress, those forces will seize Capitol Hill and the Congress. That's pretty much it in a nutshell," Pete continued.

"I see. I'm telling you both now, we're going to have an old fashioned hanging for that traitor, right on Pennsylvania Avenue! All right, gentlemen, what else do I need to know right now, at this very moment?"

"You'll be fully briefed on your flight to Site R, Mr. President. We have arranged that Regis Ballard will postpone your speech to Congress at the last minute tomorrow morning. We've planned for a counterstrike with overwhelming military force so by that time, all hostile forces will have been contained. Connectivity from Site R with the major news media will have been established and you will be able to make your speech to the nation from Raven Rock," Jack said.

"How will I explain the change of venue?"

"Mr. President, you can resolve that by clarifying that an exercise in the Military District of Washington unexpectedly intervened, and that situation has been corrected. That will work. Sir, we need to move now, get you and your family on the helicopter and off to Site R. The pilot has been instructed not to use running lights until you've cleared the air space of the National Capital Region. That should lower your profile after departing. At that time, you'll be joined by an escort of armed Black Hawk helicopters all the way to Site R."

"Okay, let's go. I understand. Regis, stay safe. I'll see you soon."

"Yes, Mr. President. God speed," Ballard said.

The President stood in place. "Thanks, Regis. And by the way, before we get all caught up in this…Jack, Pete, I want you both to know that I'm damn glad that you two warriors are on my side! And, on the side of the Republic. Damn glad!"

The President walked around his desk, firmly taking both Barrett's and Novak's hands and gripping them in his own.

CHAPTER 41

Monday, 3:30 P.M. MST
Raton, New Mexico

Hearing a rumble, Kevin walked over to a back window and peered out. Three steel-gray charter buses were turning the corner of the building and entering the rear parking lot. He gulped down the last drops from the bottle of Pepsi he was holding. Both he and Dave had a quick lunch an hour ago with sandwiches from the Subway shop on Clayton Road.

"Dave, it looks like Tony Robertson and his guys are here!" Kevin shouted out.

Both men rushed out the back door toward the lead bus. They smiled as they watched Tony Robertson come down the steps and hop off the last step onto the ground.

"Hey Tony!" Dave said in a loud voice.

"Hi Dave. Hi Kevin. Good to see you guys again!"

Robertson appeared robust and ready for anything in his black jumpsuit and pistol belt. He walked over to them and shook their hands.

"Same here, Tony. Hey, I have to tell you thank you so very much for taking care of Karen. That was huge. Thanks," Dave said.

"You're welcome. It was a good thing she thought to call Novak, Dave. But she did, and we responded. So, what's the set-up here?" Tony asked.

Streams of men clad in black jump suits and boots began piling off the buses. In addition to the pistols strapped on their belts, most carried Mk 46 light machine guns slung over their shoulders and some had Colt M4 assault carbines. A tremendous amount of firepower. All were hauling large black duffel bags.

"Beds are set up for everybody. They're portable beds, much better than cots. Tell your guys to go ahead inside and pick out the ones they want. There are ample bathrooms and showers. There's a big open area with tables and chairs that you can use for cleaning weapons and other stuff," Kevin said.

"Good, actually, I think we'll use that space for tweaking the drones. Do those two large garage doors over there open up? We could bring the drones in that way. They're hefty buggers. We also have two doctors, general surgeons, with two RNs who can set up there as well."

"Yes, they do. We've tried the doors. Good thinking on bringing some medical staff. Are the drones on the buses?"

"No, they're coming in on an 18-wheeler. The trailer's been specially configured for transporting them. It's got upper and lower floor beds with tie-downs. Six drones on top, six on the bottom. We'll have the buses moved to the far end of the building right away so the truck can maneuver when it arrives. Let me introduce you to the man who's leading the team of drone pilots." Tony spun around.

"You guys all go inside and pick out the beds you want. Settle in and chill," Tony said in a loud voice. "Hey, Terry Cohen, where are you?"

"Right here, Tony," A man stepped out from the crowd of men moving inside the facility.

"Come on over here, Terry. I want you to meet Dave McClure and Kevin O'Brien."

Terry Cohen walked toward the three men. He wasn't carrying a rifle, but he was wearing a pistol strung on his belt. Terry looked to be maybe mid-thirties and about 5 feet ten inches. Dave noted that Terry had a slight paunch around his middle, but not overly so.

"Dave, Kevin, meet Terry. He's leading the AWLs tonight."

"AWLs?" Dave asked.

"Yeah, Assholes with Laptops! Pilots...come on!" Tony laughed.

"You know, Tony, I was with your momma all last night. She said to say 'hi' to her peckerwood son!" Terry answered. All of them laughed.

"Jeez, I can just feel the love between you two!" Dave chuckled. "Terry, I'd really like to get a close look at the drones. When you're ready, show me one?"

"Sure, be glad to. I have three favorites myself...they're named Washington, Jefferson, and Hamilton. Those three have a little extra power–turbos, sort of like afterburners. I installed them myself. All the drones have nicknames. We find that easier than giving them voice orders by their serial numbers. They should be here in a bit. The driver, John Stewart, drives at a little more moderate speed so the drones don't bounce around too much. Not like Mario Andretti here, our Formula One speed demon. He's racked up three company vehicles so far," Terry said, glancing at Tony and grinning.

"All in the line of duty, Terry. So, any idea about what we can do for dinner, Kevin?" Tony asked.

"I'll phone a place here called the Historic Ice House.

We've been there twice. I think they deliver. They have salads, barbecue ribs, and mashed potatoes. In fact, I ought to call that in soon so they can start putting a large order like that together. I figure that we can have it delivered about six o'clock," Kevin said.

"Wow! That sounds great. Please do. All of these guys know better than to eat too heavy before an op. Six o'clock is fine. So, what're you gonna tell them about why such a large order for nearly a hundred people?"

"Right. I'll tell them it's a men's church retreat. So, when they come to deliver the food, you need to look religious."

"What?" Tony asked.

Kevin broke into a laugh. Tony and Dave joined in, shaking their heads.

Dave, still chuckling, glanced to Tony, "Tony, what time do you want to go in tonight?"

"Good question. Well, it's a little after 3:30 P.M. here, and it's 5:30 P.M. on the east coast. So, I would like to be stepping off onto that Lake Maloya perimeter road and moving up into the forest about a half hour after midnight. The buses will move out of the way and make room for the 18-wheeler. The Humvees can follow us to where we ingress–that's just in case of any injuries. If we have to, we can evacuate any wounded right from the edge of the woods."

"You've studied the map. Great. I don't know about the Humvees though. There's a pretty substantial lift gate installed there at the beginning of the lake area?" Dave said.

"I've seen the imagery. We'll take care of the lift gate. Not to worry. We'll launch the drones from outside the gate. They'll go in first at treetop level using their infrared sensors...see if anything, anybody, at the RTC's perimeter needs neutralizing."

"Okay. Let's go in and chill a bit," Dave said. He looked at Kevin, who nodded.

The 18-wheeler with the drones arrived about twenty minutes later. The long trailer was also steel gray in color. Some of the men ran out to assist in unloading and lugging them into the facility. Men inside moved tables, dragging them to the edge of the cavernous room, so the drones could be set on the floor. The drone pilots immediately began tinkering with the electronics on them, ensuring they were synchronized to the laptops.

"Hey, Dave, come over here and I'll show you my babies," Cohen said. As Dave approached, Cohen unsnapped a metal flap on one, exposing switches and buttons.

"This one's Washington," He pointed over to another drone. "That's Jefferson, and that one just to the left is Hamilton."

The drones beeped.

"Whoa. What was that? Can they understand you?" Dave asked.

McClure leaned down and ran his hand along the roof of Washington's short fuselage. It beeped again, which brought a smile from Dave. He walked to both Jefferson and Hamilton, kneeled over and gently rubbed both their roofs. More beeps in response. He chuckled.

"To a degree, yes. They actually have a significant artificial intelligence vocabulary. Their mission can be controlled either by the laptops that their pilots work from or by having topographical mapping and targeting data loaded so they can fly a mission independently. They can even loiter and wait for a specific target to reappear. They have an EMP gun that's good for about five bursts and a 9mm gun as well. Also, an optical camera and an infrared sensor, which we'll be using tonight."

"The EMP guns–can they kill or do you need the 9mm for that?"

"Oh, they can kill, but we haven't yet used them that way. A direct EMP burst to the skin of the target and the pulse interferes with neural activity, eyesight, and speech. With two or more simultaneous shots, it can stop blood flow between the heart's atrium and the ventricle. The heart fails and the target dies in seconds. We normally use just one pulse, one burst to temporarily blind, disorient, and incapacitate a target."

"Damn. Pete Novak did say they were impressive. I think that's an understatement. And an AI voice-driven vocabulary? You ever wonder how far AI takes them?"

"Well, the truth is that I've had cause to wonder about it on several occasions. It can be a little spooky and it has made me wonder. You being so close and having spoken by them, they've probably already mapped and stored your own voice characteristics as a friendly entity. Anyway, these are the BATS."

"Really? Thanks, Terry. Catch you later," Dave said, and walked back toward Kevin who was stretched out on his bed.

Lou Kelly, a drone pilot, walked up to Terry. "I overheard you talking with Dave McClure. Sounds like a nice guy. I heard Robertson say that McClure has a mind of his own and often winds up out in front and in confrontations."

"Yeah, Tony told me that too. He said Novak told him he doesn't want to risk having anything serious happen to McClure. That could be a problem when we reach the RTC, that is, if McClure suddenly breaks off on his own for some reason," Terry said.

"That's why I'm asking. Do you want me to put a protection app for him on Washington, Jefferson, and Hamilton? Like you said, they've probably already data mapped his voice."

"Yeah, go ahead and do that. It can't hurt. Thanks for asking, Lou."

The afternoon went fast. The men were all grins after dinner. It was quite a feed. Dave was happy to please such a large group of ass-kickers like Tony Robertson's men.

By eleven-thirty, the drones had been loaded and strapped down in the truck. The men stepped up into the buses. Dave glanced upward at a quarter moon hovering in the sky as though glancing downward, observing them. Tony, Dave and Kevin climbed into the lead bus. The Humvees would trail the small convoy until reaching the lake's gate.

"All right, game time! Load 'em and lock 'em, you badasses!" Tony blurted out into his microphone as the buses lurched from the rear parking lot. Ninety men glanced in his direction with broad grins.

CHAPTER 42

Tuesday, 12:00 A.M. Midnight MST
Sugarite Canyon State Park
Raton

The steel-gray buses pulled into the open space of the intersection near Lake Maloya's lift gate. It was midnight, and a black night to boot. No lighting around the lake's perimeter. Two men jumped from their bus and walked to the small gate shack. Pulling tools from their pockets, they worked at the lock on the door. It sprang open. They were inside only minutes before the lift gate grumbled, rising abruptly into the air.

"Okay, out of the buses. Drivers, move the empty buses back down the road so the diesel truck can turn around here. Men from the last bus will assist in unloading the drones. After that, night vision goggles on," Tony spoke into the mic on his headset.

Fifteen minutes later, the drones lay on the road, ready for launching. Their miniature GE turbofan engines were buzzing. The teams stood grouped by the gate watching and waiting.

"Launch, Tony?"

"Affirmative. Launch the BATS, Terry."

The men sitting on the ground with their laptops raised their fists in acknowledgement. The engines on the drone's five-foot long wings tilted, and the thrusts propelled the drones vertically into the air. They rose to a height of about sixty feet, then slowly flew ahead in tandem across the lake toward the forest. Dave smiled. It was exciting to see the flight of twelve BATS glide across the lake so quietly.

"Goggles up. It's twenty after twelve o'clock. We'll line up and wait on the road at the edge of the woods. Terry, do you read me?" Tony said.

"Loud and clear."

"Tell me what the drones see on their flight to the top."

"Will do. Good luck."

"Thanks. All teams, move out."

The group of nearly ninety bulky, black shapes began walking forward slowly and silently on the road's surface. Tony, Dave and Kevin sauntered in front.

"Dave, Kevin and I will take three teams, Alpha, Bravo, and Charlie to the entrance of the two-track pathway at the far end of the lake. We'll go up on the road. All other teams will space out and line up along the border of the woods. On my command, we'll begin an ascent through the woods. No hesitation, right to the top. Let's do it."

The drones, their engines muffled, flew a gradual ascent at treetop level over the forest, examining any sign of thermal images. By five minutes into their flights, the ops teams were aligned along the edge of the road and brink of the forest. They squatted, almost invisible in their black jumpsuits in the gloomy darkness of the night. Tony's teams with Dave and Kevin had reached the entrance to the two-track. Tony reached up to his earphones. It was Terry Cohen.

"Tony, Lincoln's got a target. I'm looking at it now. One

man on a rock crest, facing away from the woods. He's smoking a cigarette. No rifle, but he's wearing a pistol. Orders?"

"Have Lincoln take him down. One EMP shot. Terry, tell me when all the drones are on top…and, if there's any additional targets. Have them hover in place and wait for us."

Standing on top of the rise near the forest's border with the mesa, the man heard a slight hissing sound above and behind him. He turned, his right hand gripping the pistol in the belt holster. The drone fired an EMP burst, striking the man on the skin of his right temple. The cigarette instantly slipped from his lips, tumbling down to his chest, then to the ground. His legs buckled and he suddenly toppled over, eyes unfocused, thumping to the dirt.

"Target's down. All drones are now on top," Terry said into his mic.

"Thanks. We're coming up, then over and in. The Humvees have arrived and are parked behind us on the road here."

Tony rose. He backed up a step, took off a black glove and sliced his right arm forward through the air. Along the perimeter road, just under a hundred black shapes rose, abruptly lifting their weapons to their shoulders. Crouched over, appearing like a giant horde of black panthers, the teams slipped inside the tree line and scaled up through dark and murky woods.

There was a slight rustle of low foliage being brushed quietly aside as the force worked its way up through the forest. Tony paused now and then to listen. Nothing. They moved forward closing the distance to the crest.

"What the…something stinks like hell over here. It's gross," a whisper from Neil Haight, a team leader. Dave heard the transmission. He glanced to Tony standing next to him.

"It's a dead dog, a lab. He was shot. Just move around it," Dave said.

"Thanks," Neil replied.

In minutes, the large force exited the woods and stood together looking at the open, flat plateau in front of them. They saw seepage of bright light near the ground ahead.

"That's it, Tony. You're seeing the top of it, the roof... there's camouflage netting that has some sort of thermal barrier in it. The main entrance is to our left. I think there's one at the south end too. I'm fairly certain there's a helipad at the far eastern end."

"Okay, spread out guys...skirmish line, goggles off, weapons up and safeties off. Enter the lit area anyway you can. You might have to crawl under the camo netting. Dave, Kevin, and I with Alpha, Bravo, Charlie teams, are going in the left-side entrance. Search closely and take your time, no rush. Disarm and cuff any prisoners. Anybody fires at you, you have authority to take him down. Let's move."

Tony turned to Dave and Kevin. "I know you're both as eager as I am, but Mr. Novak doesn't want you two out front. Please, drop back behind me and Alpha team," Tony said. Dave and Kevin nodded.

The teams moved silently. One by one the special activities group penetrated the RTC, their weapons raised and at the ready. In groups, they wound around stacks of empty crates. Near the center, they passed by several Humvees and Yukon SUVs. The drones entered the netting enclosed area through the open entrance ways at both ends of the RTC. They hovered near the ceiling, then moved along above the teams.

The men dropped to their knees as several shots echoed through the night air. A staccato of machine gun rounds followed, then silence.

"Tony, two men. They were walking around down here at the south end, saw us, then pulled their weapons and opened fire," Burt Sellman, Foxtrot Team, exclaimed.

"Status, Burt?" Tony replied.

"They're toast. No team injuries," Burt said.

"Good. All teams, be aware. This place ain't empty and you should assume they're all armed," Tony said.

Dave had tracked somewhat left to the north end. He saw rows of large tents filling that area of the RTC. He tapped Tony's shoulder and pointed.

"We have tents to the north, big ones and lots of them. Those of you that are close enough, merge to the north. Use flash bangs on the tents…flush 'em out," Tony exclaimed.

Men began moving to the north end of the RTC. Explosions echoed throughout the center. They cupped their ears. Tony and his three teams moved rapidly ahead and to their left. There was gunfire…it sounded like pistols. Again, blistering rounds of machine-gun fire followed.

"Tony, three bad guys over here." It was Frank Miller, India Team.

"Status, Frank."

"All three dead. Emilio was hit in the left thigh. He's down. The round went out the back of his leg. They showed no hesitation in opening fire on us. And, one of the dead guys was wearing a black shirt over a tan uniform. There's a brass badge on his shirt. I'm looking at it now. His nameplate says 'Carruthers'."

"Tony, Frank, that's Deputy Sheriff Rich Carruthers. Frank, did he pull his weapon and open fire on you too?" Dave said.

"Yes, he did."

"Shit. Apparently, Carruthers has been on their payroll, covering for the RTC. He was in a vehicle that chased me at high speed up I-25. We'll need to inform the Colfax County

Sheriff's office later," Dave broke in.

"Dave, thanks for the background. Frank, have two of your men start taking Emilio down to the Humvees. Get him back to the facility where the docs can take care of him," Tony said.

"Will do. Miller out."

"Got it," Frank said.

Trailing behind Tony, Kevin, and most of the team members, something behind and to Dave's left caught his attention. He paused. A large green tent with a cloth sign bearing four silver-colored stars. Had to be Blanton. Dave broke off to his left.

As he approached the tent flaps, he drew his Beretta, clicked off the safety and with one round already in the breech, cocked the hammer. He pushed aside the flap and rushed inside. One black-clad man stood to his right. He'd heard the gunfire outside. He abruptly reached for his pistol and Dave leveled the barrel of the Beretta at the man's head.

"I wouldn't do that," Dave said as the man's hands froze.

"Okay, don't shoot! I surrender!" The man cried out, his arms rising above his head.

A blur of sudden movement flashed in his peripheral vision. It came from behind the table in the center of the tent. Dave changed his focus. It was George Stiles. Stiles was drawing his pistol…it had already cleared his holster.

"You're not putting me in prison, asshole!" Stiles shouted out, his face contorted in anger.

Dave swiveled his arm, then instead dove for the ground to his right. Four blasts erupted from Stile's pistol. One round blasted into McClure's left leg just above the ankle, slamming between the two lower leg bones, tibia and fibula. The bullet burst out the back of his leg with a spurt of blood.

"Ahh, my God!" McClure shrieked.

Stiles darted around the large table and sprinted toward McClure. In midair, Dave twisted his body, thudding to the dirt on his right side, his arm with the Beretta thrust outward. He fired and kept firing. Three rounds hammered into Stiles' chest, one to his right shoulder. One round pierced the front of his neck, smashing through his esophagus and bursting out the back with sprays of blood.

Four more other rounds whizzed over the top of Stiles' head. Abruptly halting in step, George Stiles' eyes bulged in sudden horror. He fell forward, his face crunching into the ground not fifteen feet from McClure. The pistol slipped from his hand.

Dave swung his pistol toward the man with the raised arms. A look of shock splashed across the man's face as he watched George Stiles plunge to the ground.

"Where's General Blanton?" Dave asked. Two of Tony Robertson's men rushed suddenly into the tent behind him. Seeing the blood pooling near his ankle, they helped him to his feet.

"He's headed for the helipad," the black clad man answered.

"Where's that?" Dave shouted, hearing more gunfire and wincing at the pain running up his calf.

"Over there. It's a narrow corridor that they cut through rock. The helipad's at the end of it, at the mesa's edge," The man said, his left arm pointing to the tent's sidewall.

"Cuff this man and take him outside!" Dave barked.

"Are you going to be okay, sir?" The men asked as they approached and jerked the man's arms behind his back, slapping on handcuffs.

"Yeah, I'll be okay. Thanks," Dave replied.

As the two men hauled the prisoner from the tent, Dave trailed behind them and then turned left, jogging as fast he could but limping badly. The wounded leg dragged along the ground. The sandstone entranceway to the corridor was only some twenty-five yards away.

Dave entered the narrow canyon, dropping out one magazine along the way and ramming in another. He tried with all his strength to ignore the searing pain in his ankle that was now coursing up along his calf muscle. Leaping over small rocks strewn about along the stony path, McClure saw the shadow of a stocky man coming into view just ahead.

"Halt! Halt General Blanton or I'll shoot! You're under arrest! Halt!" Dave yelled out.

The general stopped abruptly. He spun about, his Colt .45 already in his hand and rising. All two hundred-forty pounds of him reversed direction, strutting back toward McClure.

"So, I finally get to meet the asshole who's been poking his head into a classified operation that was approved by the president himself. You think I'm afraid of you, you piece of shit? Do you?" Blanton shouted.

"Doesn't matter, Blanton! The only place you're going to tonight is either prison or hell! Your choice, General! What'll it be?" Dave yelled back.

Blanton fired first. The .45 caliber bullet went high, plowing a crease along the left side of Dave's skull. Blood streamed out and down the side of his face.

His vision suddenly blurry and his consciousness slipping, Dave continued to march directly toward the general, limping as he went. He raised the Beretta, firing repeatedly, several rounds striking Blanton's chest and abdomen. Dave raised the barrel towards Blanton's forehead to finish him. His right leg stumbled sideways, his foot banging into a rock on the stone floor. He staggered, toppling forward to the ground.

Blanton, his face contorted with pain, blood spilling down his chest, gripped his abdomen. He wobbled forward, but zigzagged like a drunk to the right, then left.

"You bastard! Well now, Agent McClure, asshole, it appears that you're not going to arrest anyone after all," Blanton laughed, coughing. Trickles of blood oozed from a corner of his mouth. One of Dave's rounds had punctured one of Blanton's lungs, now filling with blood. He raised his arm, aiming for Dave.

The general was startled by the sudden sound of three loud, metallic beeps echoing along the tapered canyon's walls. He glanced up to see Washington, Jefferson, and Hamilton hovering fifteen feet over McClure's body. Blanton's eyes widened in curiosity at the sight of the drones, then he again leveled his weapon down at McClure.

"You're toast!" Blanton shrieked, his voice cracking from pain.

All three drones fired simultaneously. Three 9-millimeter rounds punched perfectly round holes an inch apart across General George S. Blanton's forehead. The general's eyes, shocked in surprise, rolled up into his head. He fell sideways, his head cracking on rocks laying on the canyon's floor.

Dave pushed himself up on his elbows. He stared ahead to the opening at the end of the canyon and the helipad. Witnessing the entire confrontation, the helicopter pilot turned his attention back to his cockpit's instrument panel. The chopper slowly lifted. Dave glanced upward to the three drones still looming above him and pointed to the ascending helicopter.

"The helicopter!" He shouted.

The drones beeped loudly in acknowledgement. Their

turbo engines erupted with a blast like afterburners of a jet fighter. They surged ahead, roaring down and then out the end of the corridor. Washington shot instantly upward, ramming through the windshield glass and impaling the pilot against his seatback, his eyes swelling out from his head.

Jefferson smashed into the rotor assembly, shattering it to pieces. Large shards of rotor blades made whooshing and whistling sounds as they spun wildly about through the air. The gas tank sitting just under the rotor ignited, detonating into an expanding surge of red and yellow flames.

Simultaneously, Hamilton hurtled into the tail, shearing it in two, the tail rotor spinning erratically away and plunging to the ground. The explosion of light and sound burst into a monstrous fireball, its scorching heat filling the air outside the rock corridor, spewing black smoke.

Rocks, dust, and smoke blew across the entrance and then into the corridor. Covering his eyes from the fiery blast, and with blood coursing down the side of his face, Dave's eyelids began involuntarily to close. The Beretta slid from his right hand. His head collapsed onto his forearms as he lost consciousness, blood pooling under his jaw.

CHAPTER 43

Tuesday, 3:00 A.M. EST
Dulles International Airport
Herndon, Virginia

With the aircraft now in its descent and entering the traffic pattern, the pilot checked his display for the Dulles airport. It appeared that at this early morning hour the only active runway was 19L. It made sense…they had departed Taos, New Mexico nearly an hour earlier than originally scheduled and may have mixed things up a bit. He glanced over at the co-pilot, shrugged his shoulders, and spoke into his microphone.

"Dulles Tower, this is World Airlines Flight 153. Request a straight-in approach on Runway 19L. Repeat, request a straight-in approach on Runway 19L."

Ted McElroy, assistant deputy to Pete Novak and the go-to man for Novak's immediate senior staff, stood next to an air controller inside the Dulles Tower. Colonel Dan Richter of the Virginia Army National Guard stood next to McElroy. It was fifteen minutes after three o'clock in the morning.

McElroy sipped from a mug of now lukewarm coffee and stared out the window into the early morning blackness.

He perked as a transmission from World Airlines Flight 153 burst into their headsets. McElroy turned, nodding to the air controller.

"Flight 153, you are cleared for landing on Runway 19L. You may proceed," The air controller said.

Minutes later, its gear fully extended, Flight 153's wheels touched down on the cement surface. All runway lights around it were brightly lit. The air controller nodded to McElroy as they watched the aircraft rapidly slow its speed to make the turn to the taxiway. McElroy took control and spoke into his microphone.

"World Airlines Flight 153, this is Dulles Tower. You are ordered to stop at the end of the runway. Shut down all engines. Repeat, stop at the end of the runway and shut down all engines! Do not proceed to the taxiway or the tarmac! Acknowledge!" McElroy barked.

The pilot looked to his copilot, his brow wrinkling, and activated his microphone. "Order acknowledged, Dulles Tower. Aircraft stopped." The airliner began shutting its engines down and awaiting further instructions."

The wondering faces of the black-clad passengers were glued to the airliner's windows. Their eyes widened at the sight. A row of M1 Abrams tanks lined the brink of the runway on both its sides. Tank turrets and 120 mm cannon barrels swiveled, following the aircraft as it came to a full stop.

Bradley Fighting Vehicles drew abruptly alongside the tanks near the edge of the macadam. Two flights of Black Hawk helicopters rushed forward from the darkness to hover over each row of tanks, their floodlights shining brilliantly.

McElroy advised the pilot of Flight 153 that a stairway ramp was on its way. He dictated further instructions to the pilot for repeating to the passengers. In turn, the pilot turned on the cabin speakers.

"Your attention, please, this is the pilot. A stairway ramp will soon be at our door. I have been ordered by federal authorities, including U.S. marshals, to advise you that you are to leave your weapons, all rifles, pistols, knives and such, on your seat cushions before you disembark. Upon reaching the runway surface, you are to move away from the aircraft and lie face down on the runway, your hands behind your heads. At that time, you will receive further instructions."

Colonel Paul Brennan, STARDUST Group One Force Commander, rose from his seat, walked forward and stood by the aircraft's doorway. He glared out its window. His deputy, Lt. Colonel Bill Jordan, approached him.

"Colonel, what's your assessment?" Jordan asked.

Brennan turned his head. "Bill, my assessment is we're fucked. We're not going anywhere."

"But Washington?"

"Bill, we're not even going to get to the vehicles, much less travel north to Washington." Brennan lifted the flight attendants' gray-colored handset from the wall behind him.

"All operations personnel, Colonel Brennan speaking. We will do exactly as the pilot has just instructed us, that is, unless any of you have some burning desire to go meet Jesus. The runway has been blocked in front of us and behind us. M1 tanks, Bradley Fighting Vehicles and Black Hawk gunships are lined up out there waiting for us. We are out-gunned and outmanned. Just follow me and leave your weapons behind. There is no other option. Colonel Brennan out," Brennan barked. He stepped aside as the pilot emerged from the cockpit.

"The stairway ramp has rolled up. You are free to disembark," The pilot said.

The pilot then yanked open the doorway. Brennan spun

about, walked to his seat and slipped off his pistol belt. He strode to the cabin door, stepped out, and began plodding down the stairway. He covered his eyes, blinking at the bright floodlights overhead gleaming across at the fuselage. Seventy passengers followed him in single file, stepping down off the stairs and moving away from the airliner to lie face down on the runway.

Personnel from the 20th Special Forces Group emerged from between the tanks, carrying assault rifles. In a slow, deliberate march, they approached the men on the ground. Three white buses emblazoned with the words *U.S. Marshals Service* along their sides drove out onto the runway and stopped. The bus doors opened, allowing groups of uniformed marshals to step down and walk toward the men sprawled on the ground.

Ted McElroy drove up in an airport baggage vehicle and stopped under the tail of the aircraft. Colonel Richter sat next to him. Both hopped off. McElroy abruptly raised a bullhorn he was carrying.

"Gentlemen, you will remain in place on the ground until you are ordered to move. If you run, you will be shot as an escaping felon. Repeat, if you run, you will be shot. You are under arrest. Each of you will be advised of your rights by the U. S. Marshals Service as you are transported from here to the correctional facility near Hopewell, Virginia. I urge all of you to cooperate fully. In doing so, your cooperation will be duly noted and used to mitigate the charges against you. At this time, you may rise from the ground, where upon you will be handcuffed and led to waiting buses. Thank you."

"Whew," McElroy exhaled as he let the bullhorn fall to his side. He slowly wiped beads of sweat from his forehead.

"Well done, Ted. Not one shot was fired...damn well done," Richter smiled. Colonel Richter leaned over and patted him on the back.

CHAPTER 44

Tuesday, 4:15 A.M. EST
1600 Pennsylvania Avenue

A blue and white helicopter bearing the words *Paradigm Modeling, LLC* emblazoned along its sides softly settled on the lawn in front of The White House. Jack Barrett and Pete Novak climbed out. The pilot shut down the engine, the chopper's rotor blades whispering to a stop.

The two men walked up to join Generals Cory Anderson and Randy Tennyson. The two generals stood together not far from the steel barrier fence at Pennsylvania Avenue. General Anderson had his hands cupped over his ears. All smiled.

"Any reports yet from the airports, Cory?" Barrett asked.

"Excuse me, Jack, but I'm listening to Colonel Richter at Dulles at this moment," General Anderson said. A few seconds went by. Anderson looked at the other three men and broke out in a toothy grin.

"Colonel Richter says Dulles is secure. They have taken seventy-one prisoners who are now in the process of boarding the buses for transport to Petersburg FCI. No shots were fired, no injuries."

"Excellent!" Jack exclaimed.

Anderson nodded and stepped away from the group, again cupping his ears. He smiled broadly, his hands falling to his sides, and he rejoined the other three.

"Good news again. BWI is also secure. U. S. Marshals are directing the prisoners. No shots fired. At Richmond, the airliner has just halted at the end of the runway and shut down its engines. The tower is talking to the pilot now. I feel certain Richmond will go the same way as the other two." Anderson's hands clinched into fists of victory. He slapped right hands with Barret.

"Outstanding!" Barrett blurted out.

"What?" His eyes widened in alarm, Anderson suddenly swerved away from the group, his hands back up once again and cupping his ears.

"What is it, Cory?" Jack asked.

The general stuck his arm out, palm facing toward them. He listened intensely. Barrett, Novak, and General Tennyson inched forward, concern washing across their faces.

"What? Dammit! How the hell...where'd they come from? Shit!" Anderson exclaimed, grimacing.

"All right! I've got it. We'll take it from here! Thanks," Anderson's arms dropped. He spun about to face the other three.

"That was one of the Black Hawk pilots. There's a column of thirty-some heavily armed Humvees approaching rapidly from the west. They've just turned onto Pennsylvania Avenue." He jogged away from them and up to the steel black-painted fence to peer down the avenue.

"No, can't be! How is that possible?" General Tennyson asked.

Anderson turned about. "Apparently, they crossed over the Francis Scott Key Bridge from Rosslyn about four, five minutes ago. The pilot said they emerged from some underground parking lot on Wilson Boulevard, not far from the Hyatt."

"What the…? Novak exclaimed.

"Right, dammit. Well, Jack, Pete, we weren't set up for this. Nobody expected a threat to originate from within the district or capital region itself."

"No, we didn't. Where are they, Cory?" Jack said.

"This might be the group that was intended to seize Capitol Hill and position themselves to take control of Congress just before Blanton arrived. They'll be here in minutes. They're rolling fast!" he paused.

Anderson pulled his mike down to his lips. "Hold on! All tankers, listen up!"

The tank commanders' heads suddenly swiveled around in his direction.

"Tankers, start your engines and arm up, including cannons! Move out from the sidewalk and curb and line them up across Pennsylvania Avenue! Position yourselves as tight together as you can and proceed forward thirty yards! We've got company coming and I don't think it's friendly," Anderson paused. He looked over at General Tennyson.

"Randy, call in your Black Hawks! Have them line up along the avenue on both sides," Anderson said.

The night suddenly erupted with the screeching roar of M1 Abrams' engines. Their large metal treads rolled down off the curb, swiveled about and grouped together in a straight line spanning the width of Pennsylvania Avenue. Overhead, a droning hum of helicopter rotors joined in the boisterous cacophony as two flights of Black Hawks appeared on both sides of the line of Abrams. They descended, hovering about one hundred feet off the ground and facing slightly west.

The four men on the lawn walked forward, climbed up and leaned forward on the fence. They saw the column of Humvees approaching. The column abruptly began to maneuver apart, now forming three separate columns instead of one.

"What's that all about?" Jack asked.

"They're realigning to maximize their firepower up front," Randy Tennyson replied. Cory Anderson nodded in agreement.

"Damn. Lexington and Concord revisited. And, we're are at ground zero," Pete muttered.

"Nah, Pete, I don't think…" Tennyson paused.

Without warning, the three Humvees up front opened fire with .50 caliber heavy machine guns and grenade launchers on the opposing line of Abrams tanks. The four men inside the fence immediately leaped off the fence and fell face-down on the grass. The area around the tanks was peppered with ear-splitting explosions from the Humvees' grenade launchers. The .50 caliber rounds from the heavy machine guns ricocheted off the thick armor of the tanks in all directions.

Anderson shouted into his mike. "Return fire! Now! Tank commanders on the Ellipse, proceed up 15th and 17th Streets to Pennsylvania Avenue! Join your armored company on Pennsylvania!"

Tremors exploded through the ground beneath the four men like a 5.0 magnitude earthquake. Deafening, concussive blasts erupted from the line of Abrams tanks. All three leading Humvees erupted immediately into blazing fireballs, bursting apart in molten metal debris, flames, and smoke. The vehicles tore apart as their hulks were lifted fifteen feet into the air, thundering back down to the avenue's surface in burning hulks of red hot metal.

The second row of three Humvees instantly launched Stinger missiles from their mounted Avenger platforms. One Black Hawk just west of The White House abruptly jigged sideways in a countermove. The missile rocketed past it, smashing into the fourth-floor corner of the Executive Office Building. Window glass exploded from the building as chunks of concrete the size of garbage pails rumbled down to pound into the sidewalk below.

On the opposite side of the avenue, another Black Hawk hovering near the western edge of Lafayette Square jigged right and rose up. Too late. The Stinger missile slammed into its tail section and exploded. The tail rotor whirled down and away forcing the chopper into a vertical spin as it rapidly lost altitude and rolled sideways. The Black Hawk crashed into the concrete sidewalk, but there was no explosion. Crew members leaped from the smoldering metal carcass and ran to the roadway, where they fell to the ground.

The flights of Black Hawks on both sides of the avenue immediately launched Hellfire missiles that blasted into the Humvees, cratering the surface of Pennsylvania Avenue. The four men lying on the grass lifted their heads in time to see what had been three Humvees reduced to exploding fragments of burning metal, plastic and body parts.

In the melee, Tennyson, Barrett and Novak failed to notice General Cory Anderson leap to his feet. He rushed ahead and scaled the steel fence. The general drew up to alongside an M1 Abrams, a bullhorn raised to his lips.

"Cease fire! Cease fire!" Anderson shouted into his headset. The general then marched forward to the front of the line of tanks where he could be seen by all.

"Attention! All personnel in the Humvees, attention! This is Major General Cory Anderson of the Virginia Army

National Guard. Exit your vehicles now, lie face down on the road surface and you will not be harmed!" Anderson took a deep breath.

He continued. "You have thirty seconds to comply! I repeat, exit your vehicles now, lie face down on the road surface and you will not be harmed! If you do not climb out of your vehicles within the next thirty seconds beginning now, you will be destroyed where you sit! Last notice...exit now or die on this avenue! Now! General Anderson out!" Anderson's arms dropped.

A short, surreal silence hung over Pennsylvania avenue as all present on both sides watched smoke and steam billowing upward from the destroyed vehicles. Twisted metal parts and bodies were strewn across Pennsylvania Avenue. The nightmare before their eyes was reminiscent of a wartime battle scene.

Barrett, Novak and Tennyson stood inside the fence and quietly observed as men slowly began to climb from their Humvees to lie face down on the street. It grew even more silent as the engines of M1 Abrams tanks were shut down and their crew members climbed out, pistols drawn.

The tankers ambled down the cratered roadway of Pennsylvania Avenue, approaching the men lying on its surface. General Anderson turned about and once again lifted himself up and over the fence. He hopped onto the grassy lawn of The White House.

"I would never have guessed that desk-ridden, two-star generals could climb a fence like that, Cory! And then, do it twice!" Jack exclaimed, chuckling.

Anderson drew near them. "Well, you can tell your spook friends, Mr. Barrett, that you saw it here!" Anderson grinned, glancing up at the eastern sky, now lightening to a faint gray.

Barrett turned to Novak. "Pete, you know, I don't think

there could ever be another Lexington and Concord as long as we continue to have generals like these two," Jack said.

"I agree. You're absolutely right," Pete replied.

"Thanks, Jack, Pete. Randy and I do indeed appreciate that," Anderson said. Tennyson nodded and smiled.

"However, if I may say so, from what we all just witnessed, surreal as it seemed, I believe we have a rock solid need to design and implement a contingency plan to ensure this can never, ever happen again. I have trouble believing what I'm seeing here. On Pennsylvania Avenue...right in front of The White House and in view of Capitol Hill!" Anderson shook his head, frowning.

"Cory, I think we all would agree with that," Jack said.

They turned their faces back to the street.

"Pete, have you heard yet from Raton?" Jack asked.

"Yes, Tony Robertson called on Kevin's satellite phone about a half hour ago. Kevin chimed in several times. All hell broke loose here. I didn't have a sliver of a chance to tell you."

"Shoot."

"Jack, both George Stiles and General Blanton are dead. Each of them was shot to death by Dave McClure in two separate confrontations–they had both opened fire first on him. He killed them both."

"Jeez! McClure! Both Stiles and Blanton are dead? What about Dave? Two gun battles...is he okay?"

"Tony said his medical team gave Dave the attention that they could with what they had available. They said it didn't look good. Dave was unconscious. His leg and a bad head wound. He's being transported to a hospital. I don't have a status on him yet."

"No, not again," Barrett frowned.

"Yeah, I know," Pete replied.

CHAPTER 45

Walter Reed National Military Medical Center Bethesda, Maryland

Three days passed. It was a remarkable achievement-what the city's road crews did working around the clock, day and night, in repairing the extreme damage to Pennsylvania Avenue. Traffic was again travelling in both directions. The President and his family had been transported back from Site R yesterday afternoon.

The news media continued to stick to what The White House Press Secretary had given them...television and radio news stations as well as newspapers across the nations billed the turmoil as a military exercise gone very wrong. Both the Senate and the House Armed Services Committees expressed their anger and promised hearings on the issue. However, other than a blackened, crumbled corner of the Executive Office Building, the capital district appeared as though nothing catastrophic had occurred.

Jack Barrett and Pete Novak strolled down a corridor on the sixth floor of the Walter Reed Medical Center, glancing left and right as gatherings of doctors and nurses chattered loudly.

"You know, Pete, a lot of people still call this place the National Naval Medical Center–NNMC. I can remember George Bush, Sr. having spine surgery here when he was the DCI, before he campaigned for the presidency."

"Wow. George Bush the senior? Jack, I had no idea you were that old."

"Pete, keep that up and I'll assign your ass as the next station chief in Caracas! So, where is he?" Barrett grinned.

"Room 612, just ahead on the left," Novak chuckled at Barrett's threat.

They turned into the doorway of McClure's room and paused just inside. Dave was sitting on the edge of the bed, buttoning his shirt. Karen had kneeled to slip a cordovan loafer on his right foot. A plastic cast was on his other leg just above the ankle. Dave turned his head, revealing a long strip of bandaged area on the left side above his ear. Karen glanced up.

"Dave, Karen, how are you two?" Jack stepped forward to shake their hands. Pete followed suit. Karen rose to her feet.

"Surprisingly, Dave's pretty much a hundred percent now. He had a nasty concussion," Karen said.

"It looks to me as though another half inch in that bullet's trajectory would've resulted in a different story, a sad one. It's a blessing to see you up and moving around," Pete said.

"Thanks. I know. It was a close one, but that didn't happen, Mr. Novak. I'm getting dressed. They're discharging me," Dave replied.

"How's the leg, Dave?" Jack asked.

"It hurt like hell that night, but the doctors said the bullet passed directly through the gap between the, ah, tibia and fibula. Other than stitching things up, they say the cast will probably be on for only a week, maybe two."

"Excellent. Dave, I've been told that you shot and killed both Stiles and Blanton? They opened fire at you first, correct?" Jack asked.

"Yes, I was dodging their rounds and returning fire as I did so. I got Stiles cold. I stitched Blanton up his middle with at least four rounds, but he kept walking toward me, his Colt .45 raised up. And then...I looked up and saw the three drones, those BATS, hovering just above me. All three fired simultaneously and shot Blanton in the head before he could pull the trigger to finish me. It was...unreal."

"Sounds so. Then?" Jack continued with his questions.

"Blanton's helicopter was lifting off. I pointed toward it, shouted a voice command, and the drones took off at amazing speed and smashed into the helicopter. It erupted into a huge fireball and crashed into the helipad. Truth is, while I'm convinced Blanton would have died from the wounds to his chest and abdomen, the drones nailed him before he could shoot me again. The drones...it was sort of surreal, as though they were protecting me."

"That's an amazing story, Dave. The record will reflect that you took both Blanton and Stiles down in self-defense. In fact, you killed the man who started this whole damn mess of an attempted coup," Pete said.

"The drones though, Pete. That represents a hefty loss of nine and a half million dollars each," Barrett said. He turned to Novak. "I'm thinking of garnishing Dave's wages," Jack said, a smile creasing his face.

"That would zero me out for a millennium, Mr. Barrett," Dave's eyebrows wrinkled.

"Well, I also admit that things are mitigated by the fact that you ended up in a military hospital with no direct charges being billed to the Agency. Not in a civilian hospital. In any case, you're three for three now, Dave. Three big ops followed by three hospital visits that we had to make along with a great deal of concern on our part. So, as I told you before up in Maine at the medical center in Bangor, we are once again giving some serious consideration to having a medical staff travel with you on all future ops," Pete couldn't hold back. He began laughing. Jack, Karen and finally, Dave, joined in.

"I'll be more careful. I promise."

"You said that last time. And, the time before that," Pete said.

"Have you heard anything at all from Germany?" Dave's eyes revolved from Jack to Pete.

"Wiesbaden, yes. Dead end. We missed him or her," Pete said.

"Crap."

"It's only a matter of time. It's always that way. It's inevitable now that you delivered the information that will ultimately lead us to him or her. We'll just keep turning over rocks until we find the snake," Jack rang in.

"Hope so," David said.

"By the way, do you remember that receptionist gal, Sheryl Kosko, at the Best Western? You said that you thought she was a bit overly inquisitive?"

"Yes."

"I had the FBI pick her up on a hunch and take her in for questioning. After they advised her that the RTC no longer existed and that Blanton, Stiles and Carruthers were dead, she spilled everything. She said Deputy Carruthers was paying her for monitoring comings and goings at the hotel. She didn't know much, very low level. The Bureau probably gave her a stern admonishment and then let her go. However, it did confirm your gut assessment," Pete said.

"Wow. Thanks for that, Pete," Dave replied.

"One final note." Novak's face turned somber.

"What is it?" Dave asked.

"The helicopter, the one taking off from the RTC's helipad."

"Yes?"

"Dave, Forensics found a body bag in the wreckage. There was a corpse in it, male, badly burned. There was a set of dog tags with him. Identification on the tags read 'Darrell Chilton, Captain, U.S. Army.' They found two bullet holes in the back of his cranium."

"Oh no, shit!"

"He was your source in Raton, right?" Barrett asked.

"Yes. It was because of Chilton that we ramped all this up. Blanton must have discovered that and had him killed. Dammit."

"Dave, seriously, there's nothing you can do about that now. Chilton served his country in providing a valuable service. We'll see that it's acknowledged," Barrett answered.

"Thanks for that, Mr. Barrett. Jeez, that's too bad."

"Okay, look, since you're being discharged, we'd like you and Karen to come with us. We'll bring you home later," Jack said.

"My car?" Karen asked.

"Well, just give me the keys, tell me what you're driving and where it's parked, Karen. I'll have someone drive it over to your house," Jack said.

"Wow, thanks. White Camry, third floor of indoor parking." She took the keys out of her purse and handed them to Jack's outstretched hand.

"Well, let's go then. You think you're okay to walk, Dave?" Jack asked.

"I think so, just not real fast."

"Where are we going?" Karen asked.

"You'll see," Jack replied.

The black, armored Yukon Denali was waiting outside the hospital's entrance doors. Karen stepped up and in onto the soft leather back seats. Pete helped Dave climb in, then slid in next to him. Jack sat in the front passenger seat.

"Take it a little easy, Phil. We have a wounded combatant in the back seat."

"Yes, sir, will do," They all chuckled.

The black Yukon exited the hospital's drive, turning left, south onto Wisconsin Avenue. As the streets rolled by, Dave and Karen gazed out at all the storefronts whizzing past. Going south, Bethesda transitioned to Chevy Chase and then to the District itself. Phil turned the Yukon left onto M Street. The Yukon cruised along the length of M Street and passed over Rock Creek where the SUV veered to the right and merged onto Pennsylvania Avenue.

"Pete, where are we going?" Dave leaned over and asked. Barrett overheard him.

"Go ahead, Pete. We're only a couple minutes away now anyway."

"We have an appointment with the President," Pete said.

"Oh…Mr. Barrett, I'm not dressed right for this," Dave exclaimed.

"Neither am I," Karen echoed, her eyebrows raised.

"Don't worry about that. You two are coming from the hospital, so you're dressed just fine," Jack said.

"They turned right into The White House drive and were waved through. Phil pulled the Yukon up by the entrance. Karen took Dave's hand. Hers was trembling. She glanced over at him, anxiety written across her face.

"It's okay," Dave squeezed her hand.

With a little help from everyone, Dave managed to walk down the red-carpeted hallway, all of them trailing a steward. No Secret Service followers trailed along this time.

The President glanced up as the four were ushered through the door and into the Oval Office. He rose from behind his desk and walked over to greet them.

"Jack, Pete, good to see you again," the President said, looking curiously at Dave and Karen.

"Mr. President, this is Dave McClure and his wife, Karen. Dave is the man who, in two separate confrontations where he was under fire and in self-defense, dispatched both George Stiles and General Blanton in Raton, New Mexico. Dave was also responsible for gathering the intelligence that allowed us to respond to the assault on the Capital. Karen's assigned as an agent in our National Resources Division," Pete explained.

"Karen, I'm very pleased to meet you. Dave, you saved me having to preside over a hanging!" The President exclaimed. They shook hands.

"Dave McClure? Didn't I award you the National Intelligence Cross barely even a year ago? It was for something that occurred up in Maine...Spetsnaz and subs, if I recall."

"Yes, Mr. President, you did," Dave replied.

"That's the highest award I can give this man. What the hell can I present him with now? We don't have anything higher!" The President said, bursting into a laugh. They all broke out laughing.

"So, I ask you, Agent McClure, may I assume you like your martinis shaken, not stirred? And, who shall we send you after next?" The President asked. Everyone continued to laugh.

"Oh no, sir. Mr. President, you see, both Mr. Barrett and

Mr. Novak are so concerned with my wounds that I no longer have double-0 status and no longer have sanction authority," Dave replied.

"Well, what authority do you have now?"

"Sir, I only have authority to use harsh language."

The room broke into howls of laughter. Barrett and Novak shook their heads as they chortled.

"I like this guy!" The President declared.

"Karen, what do you think? Should we keep him?" The President asked.

"Yes, sir. I love this man, Dave McClure, so much, more than anything else in the world," She wrapped both her arms around Dave's left arm.

"Well, that being the case, Dave, I guess you'll remain on the payroll. Let's all have a seat, shall we? Iced tea will be here in a few moments," The President walked back around his desk as the four guests slipped into easy chairs.

"Mr. President, I have two executive orders for you to sign," Jack stood.

"Really? What are they?"

"The first one immediately terminates Annex K, the authority for Special Means, to the FEMA charter. We need to have it rewritten to ensure safeguards are in place, sir."

"I completely agree with that, Jack. And the other one?"

"The second one is a substantial budget transfer from Homeland Security to the FBI to enable the Bureau to establish a robust gang program of its own, hire additional special agents, weapons, vehicles, things like that."

"I agree with that one too. All right, it was my mistake buying into Jim Owen's solution embedded in FEMA's charter. I know that very well now. Putting this securely back in the hands of law enforcement is the right way to curb gang violence. Give them to me and I'll have the staff tweak and polish them for signature."

"Thank you, Mr. President. This has been an outrageous, heinous event–a nearly catastrophic national crisis. A travesty. We need to ensure it can't happen again," Jack said.

"Well, I'm personally glad that everyone up on the Hill, as well as the media, are going along with the broken military exercise explanation. Frankly, I don't believe the nation could handle the truth in this. Not now anyway. And the investigation...have either of you heard anything?"

"My sources tell me that the joint investigation by the Senate Select Committee on Intelligence and the Senate Committee on the Judiciary is going nowhere and fast. The interest is dwindling, fading out. I don't think anything more will come from it," Jack said.

"That's good to hear. This attempted coup was something that none of us believed could ever happen. Not here, not in this country. But, you and I, all of us here, we can't avoid facing the truth of it."

"A travesty," Jack repeated.

"Travesty? Jack, I think it was really about where we are as a nation right now, how we've forgotten who we are, what we stand for...more than it was a travesty. The world is in turmoil, including our closest allies. Uncertainty is rampant, and uncertainty breeds fear. Fear can be dangerous. Many think we've lost our rudder–our morality, our ethics, and perhaps soon our freedoms. I myself don't think our rudder is lost. I think we just need to re-attach it and steer this ship called the USA into clearer, calmer waters. That's what all of us will work toward, beginning today."

"That's certainly the bigger picture, Mr. President. Please know that we're with you," Jack said.

"Thanks," the President said. They all shook hands.

Ten minutes later, once again seated in the Yukon, they all watched with curiosity as Phil turned right onto Pennsylvania Avenue.

"Where we headed now, boss?" Pete asked.

"Why, to lunch of course."

"Lunch? May I ask where?" Pete asked again.

"At the Willard."

"Jack, you need reservations for that, even for lunch at the Willard," Pete said.

"And, I have one. Not to worry. And Karen, if you don't mind putting up with three other spooks, we'd love to have you join us. In fact, that's director's orders," Jack said.

"Actually, I'm honored, sir. Dining at the Willard with the Director of Central Intelligence, his Deputy for Operations, and my own double-0…how could I refuse?" They all chuckled.

It was a short ride of just a few minutes. The Willard Intercontinental was just down the street at 1401 Pennsylvania Avenue. They soon found themselves seated in the dining room at a window with tied-back curtains. Chandeliers tracked down the middle of the spacious room. Multi-light lamp fixtures hung from the walls. *Elegant* would be an understatement.

Barrett nodded to the waiter. In less than a minute, a sterling silver bucket filled with ice and its own stand were delivered to the table. In it sat a bottle of Dom Pérignon. Their eyes opened wide as crystal champagne glasses were set in front of them, the cork popped and champagne was poured into each. The waiter departed.

"Dom Pérignon? Wow! Now this is a treat! Thanks, Jack!" Pete gushed in appreciation.

"Yes, sir, thank you," Dave exclaimed as Karen's eyes grew wide.

"No, it's I who must thank each of you, both for your service to the Agency and your loyalty to the nation. Now, who has the first toast?" Jack glanced around the table.

"Well, given the reason why we're all here, I would like to repeat what I think is an appropriate quote from Thomas Hobbes in his most famous work, *Leviathan*," Pete said.

"And that is?" Jack asked.

"The quote is, 'Hell…is truth seen too late.'"

"That's excellent. So then, I raise a toast…to truth," Jack said. All lifted their glasses.

"John 8:32," Pete said.

"And you shall know the truth…" Dave replied in turn and glanced to Karen.

"And, the truth will set you free," Karen said, smiling and finishing the verse.

"Then, to truth," Jack said.

Grinning, they all extended their arms over the center of the table and gently tapped their glasses together. Each took a sip.

The clinking of the crystal glasses drew the attention of patrons seated nearby. They turned their heads. With beams of sunlight streaming through the windows and filling the dining room with a warm light, everyone smiled.

The End

ACKNOWLEDGEMENTS

Foremost in my mind is a sincere desire to thank Joyce Ragle, my developmental editor, for her meticulous, skilled work in transforming this story into the best thriller novel it could be. Thanks also to my first-draft manuscript readers and editors, Tom Inks and John Fraser. Both provided insightful editorial suggestions that assisted in enhancing plot flow. I owe sincere thanks to former Detective Sergeant Steven Spenard, a previous chief of the Denver Police Department Gang Squad. Detective Spenard provided me with great insight to the level and organization of gang activity in Denver. On this same note, I would also like to thank the Raton Police Department and the Colfax County Sheriff's Office for the information they provided to me while I scoped out the area around Raton, New Mexico as a setting for this story. I am once again genuinely grateful for the top-notch support and encouragement offered by the staff of Outskirts Press in the publication process. They are a great bunch of professionals who know their business exceedingly well and made this novel the absolute best it could be. Finally, thanks to the light in the storm, my wife, Trudi, for her support to my writing.

CPSIA information can be obtained
at www.ICGtesting.com
Printed in the USA
JSHW030136210420
5190JS00001B/19

9 781977 225764